THE GOPHER KING

A Dark Comedy

GOJAN NIKOLICH

Black Rose Writing | Texas

ISBN: 978-1-68433-573-2
PUBLISHED BY BLACK ROSE WRITING
www.blackrosewriting.com

Printed in the United States of America
Suggested Retail Price (SRP) $20.95

The Gopher King is printed in Garamond

*As a planet-friendly publisher, Black Rose Writing does its best to eliminate unnecessary waste to reduce paper usage and energy costs, while never compromising the reading experience. As a result, the final word count vs. page count may not meet common expectations.

For Leslie, Lauren and Olive

Praise for *The Gopher King*

"Nikolich's story shimmers with intersecting layers of identity
and fantastical complexities."
–Authors Reading

"A must-read novel for mystery enthusiasts!"
–Readers' Favorite Reviews

"Nikolich mixes fantasy and reality in a way that's weirdly
reminiscent of both Tim O'Brien's Going After Cacciato and
the 1980's film Caddyshack."
–Joe Barrett, bestselling author of *Managed Care*

"…a quirky story enhanced by acerbic wit
and unexpected creativity."
–Indies Today

THE GOPHER KING

"There are some feelings time cannot benumb
Nor torture shake, or mine would now be cold and dumb."
— Lord Byron
Childe Harold's Pilgrimage, Canto IV

"He had, of course, dreamed of battles all his life — of vague and bloody
conflicts that had thrilled him with their sweep and fire. In visions he had seen
himself in many struggles. He had imagined peoples secure
in the shadow of his eagle-eyed prowess."
— Stephen Crane
The Red Badge of Courage

PROLOGUE
Bull River Falls, Colorado

The old woman and the horse faced into the wind and together they watched the smoke rise and hang in gauzy white sheets above the valley.

The county sheriff had told her not to use the logging trail. She ignored the order, which came in a letter in a fancy government envelope folded under the windshield wiper of her truck back at the ranch house. But her family had been using the old BLM track for fifty years and this was the only way to get up Bellyache Mountain, most of it private ranch property, anyway.

The horse got skittish. She turned the animal with her knees and reined it away from the edge of the mesa. The valley stretched away toward the stony folds of distant foothills, the rubble of darker mountains beyond that. The smoke had lifted into a black anvil above the highest of those hills as the wildfire moved toward the town.

She leaned and spit. The hot wind blew her long white hair and bore with it gritty bits of ash and sand.

"If bad looks like that, I've not seen worse," the woman said to the horse.

The lowest hills were bathed in reefs of lavender twilight and streaked with muted shadows in the late afternoon sun.

For Dora McCoy, the pleasant scenery did not match her gloomy mood.

Something about that fire was not right.

She said to the horse, a weary catch in her voice: "I wish you could see all this the way I see it. How it looks when that old sun goes down. Like the colors are dripping wet."

She took the cell phone from her shirt pocket and in the dusky light squinted at the tiny buttons. She'd promised her husband to carry the gadget while she rode her fences; she being so old, he claimed, and liable to tip from her horse and break a leg God knows where on the 5,000-acre Last Chance Ranch.

She called the house and on the third ring his voice answered, halting nervously at first.

He said: "You've reached the McCoys and we're not home right now. Wait for the little sound and say what you need. We'll get back to you soon enough. Good-by, now."

The 'good-by, now' was her favorite part. He sounded so bashful. She dialed again and waited.

"Good-by, now..."

"Oh, my," she sighed, and turned the horse. She wiped her eye.

Dora McCoy hooked the impossibly small telephone on a rawhide loop hung from the saddle pommel. She spurred the blue roan into a gallop down from the mesa to a berm Hector and she had backfilled long ago to keep blowing dirt from the stock tubs that stood in the middle of her highest pasture.

She sat the horse and let it blow. She leaned into the worn Tapadero stirrups and looked at where her few remaining cattle stood bunched far below where the fire burned, black specks on a rolling sea of brown summer grass. Dust lifted and twisted like spindrift on an ocean.

The horse snorted and danced sideways. She sawed it around.

Dora watched the small low shape move through a field of hay stubble along a fence line that ran down from the lake. In the bunchgrass the creature hid behind some high skunk cabbage, which shook to mark the spot.

She steadied the horse and let it walk.

"So there you are, mister."

She notched her husband's rifle under one arm and sighted. She pulled the safety against the trigger guard, the way Hector had shown her. Smelling the wood of the Springfield Garand 30-06 beneath her cheek, a pleasant stink of hickory and sweat, she took aim at the animal's head and fired, the sound echoing off the hills like a clapping hand. Two wild doves lifted and squawked off a cottonwood tree.

The horse looked away at a sage stump as if in deep thought and tossed its head and snorted as if disagreeing with the woman's choice of target.

Horses, Dora McCoy thought, could understand the tone and weight of sentences. She had always talked to her horses. She combed her fingers through the roan's black mane.

She whispered: "I told you yesterday something crazy was going on around here," she said. "First that fire. Now these critters acting so strange."

The old woman figured she had shared deeper thoughts with the horse than she had with most people, except for her dead husband, whose voicemail recording she could not bring herself to erase. It was the very last of him, alive inside that plastic toy wobbling from the saddle.

The horse bowed its head and stomped one foreleg.

"You," she said, slapping the roan's mouth with her gloved hand. "Don't give me trouble today. You've seen this business before. Now behave."

Dora McCoy eased ahead into a lazy canter, the rifle held loosely in one hand at her side.

The coyote was dog-sized with a white collie blaze on its head. It yelped when it was shot and had lifted puppet-like as if yanked from above by a string. The animal nipped at itself wildly and tried to crawl away, pulling with its forepaws through the short grass.

Dora reined the horse, steadied herself with her knees and fired again, the shot so poor it severed cabbage stalk and raised dirt a yard behind the wounded animal. The roan huffed and crow-hopped into a canter as if cutting an imaginary calf. Dora swung her leg, dismounted, dropped the reins, and walked to where the animal lay. The roan spiked its ears and stood and watched and snorted.

For no reason she could understand Dora McCoy dropped to one knee, took off her gloves, and touched the trembling coyote gently as if it was a sick pet.

She could feel its heart beat beneath the warm hide. Gray eyes followed her hand as the rancher reached to where the bullet had torn away the coyote's hip, the bright red wound deep and meaty as if a spoon had scooped away fur and flesh. The animal made no sound.

She had seen it earlier that day as it loped in a circle around a grazing cow and her calf at the underground spring hole. She'd never seen such a decrepit creature so far from its pack running open-mouthed in bright daylight, tongue hanging and fearless.

Dora had followed on horseback for a while, tracking spoor, catching sight of watery black scat where the coyote had ignored a cyanide trap she kept baited outside a fenced wallow that the herd used during calving season. The old woman had lost three calves that week, each neck-gnawed and left bleeding. The coyote had eaten nothing, and so she figured it had killed for sport.

She squatted. She pressed her hand against the coyote and looked at the horse as if expecting advice. She spoke to the horse. The roan's eyes opened wide as it snapped back its head and whinnied. It turned on the pivot of the dropped reins and shot out one hind leg as if defending itself from an invisible enemy.

"Nag, you got another opinion on this?" Dora said.

The horse pointed its ears and glared at the coyote.

The painless bite came like a nuzzling coolness, as if a dog's wet nose had touched her. Dora looked down and was surprised to see the wound between her thumb and forefinger, a pink oval, as if the sharp edge of a coin had pressed a frown into her skin. The arc of teeth marks looked perfect and pencil-drawn, the blood dewy and pink. A hot numbness tickled up Dora's arm.

"Oh, my," she said, shaking her hand. "Ain't I one stupid old rancid shit."

She looked up at the roan. "You ever see me do a dumbass thing like that before?"

The horse stomped. It pawed. Dora McCoy studied the coyote's watery eyes, the normally black outline of its thin lips now red and puffy, flecks of white saliva spattered on the tan fur of its wrinkled muzzle like it had taken sloppy sips of milk.

"Don't give me that goddamn look," Dora said, turning to the roan. "You saw what he was fixin' to do. Why didn't you warn me?" The horse pawed again and stepped back, dragging its reins. It jerked up its head.

She lifted the rifle to finish things when the coyote calmly lowered its jaw and breathed deeply and regarded Dora with a sideways gaze. With a soft growl it closed its eyes.

"Varmint," Dora said as she stepped away and lifted herself into the saddle.

Bracing herself against the stirrups, she stood and shouted at the dead coyote.

"Didn't you have it coming? Killing my cows that way, you sorry sonofabitch. Shame on you."

The roan had not liked the blood smell. But that puzzled Dora McCoy because the old horse had dragged away a hundred carcasses in its time.

"Don't you spook on me," she said.

The roan's withers bunched and trembled as if preparing to bolt.

She pouched the rifle. The horse kept studying the coyote as if it might come to life. She dallied her rope, swung a loop, and took the animal by one foreleg and dragged it from the fence and into the sagebrush so her cows wouldn't see it.

"We'll burn it later," she said. "Don't want anything to get what it had."

The ranch house was two miles away, a difficult ride down the steep logging road, so Dora figured she would instead wash the wound at the old family homestead cabin, which she could now barely see at the edge of an aspen grove near the river. She had not been there for many years.

She turned the horse and pulled off her belt and looped a tourniquet. She pulled it tight above her elbow until the brass buckle bit into her skin. The blood moved in her arm the way the coyote's heart had fluttered, like a clock ticking beneath a pillow. She felt dizzy, sick.

When she came up on the cabin it immediately stirred old memories. She tugged the roan into a walk, and the horse kept twisting back its head, still upset by the shooting.

Her grandfather had come to these mountains when it was wild frontier filled with lonely 160-acre homesteads. Not like now, Dora thought, with the new supermarket and the shopping center they were building near the Interstate. And the fancy houses spreading from town like weeds. And there was the big ski resort they wanted to build next to the ranch itself. The god awful ski resort. She slapped her heels into the horse. The thought of the resort made her angry.

She was light-headed. She imagined harmonica music drifting from the log ruins of the cabin. The music seemed so clear. She tried to remember the illusive melody, a plaintive diddy her father had played in Dora's childhood. The memory came in flickers, like a jittery movie. For a moment she thought she shouldn't visit this place.

She tied the horse and stepped onto the creaking porch. The iron hand pump, bearded with tangled honeysuckle her mother may have planted so long ago, primed up perfectly. She drew water and let it pool in the grass and watched the roan drink and lift its dripping mouth. She peeled off her denim shirt and slapped the cold water up her arm and onto the aching shoulder. She'd seen dogs taken with rabies many times and was sure the coyote had been afflicted. Poisoned mutts would run blind off cliffs, they got so crazy. Chew their paws off and bite their rumps bloody, spinning like tops until they dropped dead.

Dora McCoy knew the coyote had killed not for food but because it needed to answer a darker hunger.

Oddly, she felt sorry for the animal and wondered if she should have let it die on God's time. Nature had a cleaner way of handling things.

She sat. The old woman was all tight skin and muscle. Her husband had joked that she was long and bony and that he had married a tomboy. Her neck was ropy, tanned. Her square hands looked like they had been whittled by someone who didn't know how to whittle. Her fingers were stubby, the nails worn into buttons from a lifetime of twisting leather and cinching rope. She wore her long white hair gathered up behind a lady's Stetson that was pinched into a worn beak. There was the occasional backache when she stooped to lift a bale of Timothy hay and she occasionally got winded late in the workday, but Dora McCoy could still ride a horse hard and string a mile of wire fence without complaint. On a one-woman ranch like the failing and nearly bankrupt Last Chance, there was no choice.

"Never could shoot straight," she told the horse. "Lucky I was never in a war. Wouldn't have come back alive."

The roan stretched its neck at the grass that stuck up between the cabin porch boards and started to chew.

"Go ahead, don't listen," she said. "You're sure not much to talk to lately."

Dora McCoy wished now for a good poultice for the bite, the kind her Hector would have made from one of his Indian remedies.

He'd been gone now for three years. But in her memory he was forever handsome and young and strong, that voice always with a little gravel in it, like it sounded on the voicemail. She remembered how he'd kiss that hollow on the back of her neck and how she'd purr like a cat when he did. She recalled how they'd sat embracing on the floor of this same ancient cabin, even then abandoned and filled with ghosts, their hungry hands all over each other. It had been their private courting place so many years ago, after he'd come back from his war. Dora McCoy remembered how they each slid from their clothes. They would sit afterwards on the steps and she would curl into his arms.

I don't want to remember this, she thought. I don't want to remember this at all.

The damp, pail-water smell of the abandoned cabin reminded her of how quickly the years had drifted by.

One of Hector's poultices would be the perfect thing now, she thought. Going to the doctor was not what Dora planned to do. But she was worried about the coyote's bite.

The cabin, fragile and teetered like you could kick it down, made her unexpectedly nostalgic. She was surprised by the sudden heat of her feelings, which seemed girlish and not what a woman her age should allow. Dora tried to forget the coyote and the way those rheumy eyes looked at her when it died, as if it had been grateful to be murdered.

She squinted and imagined her mother and daddy sitting by the old woodstove, yellow light from a kerosene lamp licking across the wallpapered ceiling, her father's boot tapping the puncheon floorboards in time to the music whose name she could not remember.

Dora's throbbing shoulder seemed to pulse like the heart of the coyote. On the porch the sound of the horse pulling grass seemed thunderous.

She thought sweetly of her mother, smiling then as if there had never been a happier moment, nodding across the room as Dora sat on folded legs by the bed, chin in her hands, evening smells breezing through window curtains that lifted and fell like the hem of a dress.

Dora had wondered those many years ago if other little girls felt the same happiness, and she guessed they did because God surely could not be so thoughtless as to plan it any other way. She remembered believing that the cabin and this ranch and the town of Bull River Falls and these mountains were the center of a perfect world.

Shirtless, she stepped inside.

Sky showed through the broken ceiling. There were floor scars where the woodstove once sat on iron stumps. Stripes of pale twilight came through the cracked wall chinking. Over there, from a wall peg, there once hung her mother's splint broom. A stubby iron pike mortared into the fireplace wall was where the dutch oven once stood braced in its tripod. Stove embers had long ago stained parts of the floor black. Scrapes from a vanished trundle bed mapped where Dora had slept as a girl beneath sheets that smelled of lye soap and what the family had suppered on that night. The grouse flavor was minty, like sage.

Drying herself with her denim shirt, she stretched and twisted the arm to see if the ache would fix itself. She sniffed imaginary smoke drifting from the stove that was no longer there. It was as if her mother had just stoked her cooking fire. She could hear her daddy play his tune, the melody lifting through the splintered roof where the evening's first star now twinkled.

Overwhelmed, her thoughts were a parade of faces of everyone she had ever loved. Hector as a young soldier. Herself as a bride. Her husband dead and so small beneath the white hospital bedsheets. The doctor's departing footsteps in the empty hallway. Medical contraptions wheezing from the wall.

Looking up at the star, Dora McCoy let out a sob and when she saw the roan raise its head she was embarrassed.

"You're lucky you can't think, you gelded sonofabitch."

She wiped her tears with the shirt. "Just you keep eating and mind your own damn business. Maybe I'll just send you to France. They eat horse sandwiches there, you know. See how you like it."

The roan stared blankly at Dora as if they had just met, and kept eating.

She looked across the valley toward where they were building the resort. She could see the half-framed roof poking from the trees. There was an American flag drooping from a pole atop the enormous lodge building. She could see the town lights from here, the mountains dark and blue in back of that. The dim red glow of the distant burning wildfire. And enough stars in the sky to make her cry all over again.

The thought of such a perversity — the hotel and the golf course and the condominiums coming up to the very edge of the ranch — it angered her all over again. She thought about the new folks in town driving around in fancy cars she didn't recognize, everybody with a ski rack on the roof. Talking on their cell phones. More Golden Retriever dogs than one town could possible need. Fools in white gym shoes jogging around in those tight circus pants.

She sat on her boot heels in the wrecked cabin doorway and dropped her head into her good hand. She looked up and stared at the crippled fence posts leaning in silhouetted rows away from the cabin, the day's last red light like a curtain behind them.

There was a sharp ache now under her arm, where a pebbly swelling had begun. Her heart raced. The bite had turned dark, the skin around it hammy and swollen as if there was now a life apart from her own growing inside the wound. Her head felt icy, heavy. Briefly, like a beery intoxication had overcome her, she did not know where she was.

For one of the few times in her life, Dora McCoy was frightened.

How she wished she could remember the name of that harmonica tune her father had played.

The evening breeze carried the roan's smell into the cabin. Her mother sang softly from somewhere in the dark. She recalled the press of Hector's rough hand on her naked back. She stepped over to the horse and angrily pulled the rifle from its pouch.

In the valley she could see the top floors of the partly built lodge. A row of maintenance buildings were lined up along the river, along with parked construction equipment. Her numb arm throbbed as she lifted the rifle to her cheek and fired at the building as if to kill it. She kept shooting until the empty eight-round military clip ejected past her ear with a metallic pinging sound.

She thought she heard the rounds smack home, deciding instead that it might be another gunshot clapping up from the river. Hunters, maybe, though there was no season she knew of.

Another shot was fired from somewhere and the startled horse stomped its foreleg, but Dora McCoy wasn't sure of what she'd been hearing.

She wasn't sure of anything anymore.

She unsaddled the horse and took the blanket pad and lay it on the cabin porch. With fallen roof shingles she made a fire and used the saddle for a pillow and curled up her arms. Through the flames she watched the moonless night gather around her.

She tried to think about all that had happened up to this exact point in her long life, but she could not.

Coyotes cried unseen out beyond the fire's glow as if they were scolding her. She took the cell phone and once more dialed up her dear Hector's voice. She spoke to him and hoped he would answer, but he did not. She pulled down her hat and brought her shoulders together against the cold night and closed her eyes and wept.

She should not have shot at the lodge, she thought. Crazy old lady.

Somebody could get hurt.

CHAPTER 1

The war was on TV again. Separating the edited Baghdad battle scenes were commercials for breakfast cereal, reflux medicine, new SUVs, pet care supplies and erection pills.

I turned off the sound and stared at the screen in my tiny kitchen in the double-wide trailer that serves as the world-wide headquarters of the weekly *Bull River Falls Beacon-News* newspaper. I am its owner, publisher, editor and star reporter. I also clean up after closing time.

I listened to the sudden chatter on the office police scanner.

They'd found something at the river.

There was space to fill in the newspaper that week. I decided to drive my truck across town, a five-minute trip.

Randomly parked fire trucks and state trooper cruisers sat with their lights blinking at the national forest trailhead. I made my way up a dirt switchback to where a sheriff's car blocked the road.

My nightmares were starting to come back, successive versions of a familiar sadness in which faceless people shouted my name. The dead soldier had appeared again, annoyingly chatty as he made long bullshit speeches about baseball, this time with a flurry of Wrigley Field statistics: 400 feet to the ivy-covered center field wall, box seats at $2.50 in 1959, the year I watched the team pitch 11 shutouts and hit 163 home runs. It was Ernie Banks' MVP year, and still the miserable Cubs finished in the middle of the pack.

All that night I also suffered the soldier's thoughts on politics: LBJ, the Kennedys, Nixon, and his theory about J. Edgar Hoover and the killing of Martin Luther King. Dr. Nguyen, my shrink at the VA hospital in Denver, appeared briefly, his pipesmoke filling the room.

In the dream I reached for the soldier's face and it crumbled in my hand like cake. Dr. Nguyen stood behind his desk and smiled and peeled away a bandage from his scrawny neck, from which swallow-size creatures flew from a dark wound like bats from a cave. They circled and escaped through the open bedroom window.

That's when I thought I heard the gunshots.

I woke up tangled in my sheets and shuffled outside and sat on the porch, where I slept wrapped in a blanket and waited for the sunrise to rescue me.

Now I drove a little faster than I should have. My coffee cup danced off the dashboard. Pea gravel sprayed up from the road shoulder, which on this side of town dropped sharply into the river.

The tires skittered and the truck nosed off the road and tipped briefly onto two wheels as it came to rest at the very edge of the drop-off. Water churned over white boulders in the river below.

With one press of my foot it could be over, I thought. Like you'd turn off a room light. They'd think it was just an accident. Heavily medicated old fart falls asleep at the wheel. Happens every day.

At the police checkpoint I fished out my press pass. The sheriff's deputy watched me yawn.

"No reporters."

"Call Tom Cherry," I said. "He's the police chief."

The young officer unclipped his pocket walkie and stepped away. He looked back over his shoulder.

"Yeah, I know who he is."

I took out my small hunting binoculars.

The body lay at the edge of the river, resting against a mound of wet brush and burned tree limbs that had washed down from the upstream wildfire. The woman lay face-down, her soaked hair pasted across one arm. One leg was cocked at the knee, her other arm snagged beneath a submerged rock, where it wagged back and forth in the current as if she was half-heartedly trying to swim away.

In the warming morning chill a gray mist lifted from the river. Blue police lights flickered. Yellow crime scene tape fluttered like an announcement to a happy festivity.

I wished desperately for more coffee. I could work nights with the owls and the hunting coyotes, I thought. Perhaps the nightmares wouldn't come if I slept during the day.

She was dressed in baggy bib overalls. The current had forced the hood of her zippered sweatshirt against the back of her head so that it framed her face like the soaked vestment of a sleeping church madonna. A shoe lay nearby on the gravel beach. Her arm had now come out from beneath the rock and it was paddling faster as if the corpse was trying to get away from the police.

The bullet had formed a deep pucker in the center of her forehead, as smoothly symmetrical as if you had poked a finger into bread dough. The back of her head, where the fabric of the hoodie seemed to be getting sucked in and out by the flowing water, was hollow.

I called to one of the deputies. "Who found her?"

The officer pointed over his shoulder. "The dude up there."

I saw the man sitting handcuffed on the hillside behind me and he was being questioned by an officer.

The place was swarming with uniforms. There were Bureau of Land Management people and feds from the Forest Service. Two Colorado Parks and Wildlife rangers were taking photos of a fence that marked the boundary of the campground trailhead. A county squad car blocked the logging road that marked the entrance to the Gold Gulch Resort and Golf Club. I saw Bull River Falls Police Chief Tom Cherry's beige Crown Victoria parked on the road shoulder, lights flashing, the driver's door open, a 12-gauge tactical shotgun clipped upright against the dashboard.

"Said he was fixing a fence when he found her," the deputy said. "He works for the resort."

I took out my notebook. The officer folded his arms. "You can't quote me unless I give you permission, can you?"

"If you don't tell me first, then yes."

"That's not fair."

I looked down at the dead girl. "You're right, it's not fair."

I ducked under another row of police tape.

A cop in rubber hip boots waded into the river. He stooped and carefully moved the girl's wet hair to one side as if he was afraid to awaken her. Her one eye was open, the other lid shut. Her lips were parted in a snarl. She wasn't wearing socks. Something was not right about the socks and the lone, unlaced hiking boot that lay a few feet away.

I watched another county deputy who was wearing civies, his investigator's badge clipped to his belt, join two uniformed Colorado State Troopers as they lifted the corpse and carried it to shore like solemn pallbearers.

One trooper took a pen and probed the girl's ears. He wiped her teeth with a swab and removed a bracelet from her right hand and placed it into a ziplock bag. He put a plastic baggie over each of her hands. The county coroner stood nearby and spoke into a tiny voice recorder. Unsmiling, she looked at me and raised her hand and waved.

They tried to straighten the girl's legs but they would not get straight. I knew the body had been there for a long time. I looked up at where a cattle guard with a No Trespassing sign marked the property line of the Last Chance Ranch. Across the river a fleet of pickups and trailers were parked in the Gold Gulch Resort equipment yard. A few workers stood watching outside the crew shack, their arms folded.

A sudden breeze brought the smell of burning woodsmoke down from the mountain. A TV crew from Denver arrived in a helicopter, stirring up a blizzard of flying police hats and dust. The crime scene tape fluttered.

A hand touched my shoulder.

Police Chief Tom Cherry nodded toward the hill where they were questioning the suspect. He started talking like we'd already been in the middle of a conversation. His face was flushed and he was breathing heavily.

"The shooter tried twice. Missed once. Big weapon, I think," he said. "Left a bore as big as my thumb in the tree behind her."

Cherry looked me up and down.

"You know you're not supposed to be here."

"Police boy let me in."

"Not that anybody knows who's jurisdiction this is right now," Cherry said.

"Any tracks?" I said.

Cherry took off his cap and smoothed the top of his head. He looked at his hand.

"Not any that make sense," he said. "It hasn't rained for months, so that doesn't help. Our genius up there walked all over the crime scene. We're waiting for a warrant to search those maintenance shacks."

I pointed up the hill. "You already made the arrest?"

Cherry said. "It won't stick, I'm afraid. Company lawyer is on his way and promised that the guy would show up later for questioning. His name is Jergen. Billy Jergen. Drives a truck for Gold Gulch. So far, I'm not sure it's the town's jurisdiction. Bureau land, federal forest, a little state park dirt here and there. Private ranch property place starts a hundred yards from here. There was a report of gunfire not far from here last night. Somebody also got cited for firing a weapon up at the new subdivision late yesterday. Suppose I'll visit with Dora, but I doubt she'll say much except to bitch about the resort. Who the hell knows? Somebody had to make a decision. So I arrested him."

"You must have a good reason," I said.

Cherry winked. "We know a few things."

"And you're not talking."

"You're fairly bright for a newspaper man."

Again Cherry lifted his hat and touched the top of his head and studied his open palm.

He said: "Haven't seen you in town lately."

"Busy," I said. "Been under the weather. I'm way behind on everything."

"Paper has had a few mistakes lately, if you don't mind me saying. People were joking at the cafe. Those prairie dogs you write about in your column. I gotta say, my wife thinks you are totally crazy."

I yawned. "I'm shorthanded, Tom. Paper has a lot of space to fill."

Cherry sighed and tore a sheet from his notepad. He presented it like he was issuing me another speeding ticket.

We both watched them carry the girl's body to a waiting van. Her bare foot poked out from beneath the gray rubber sheet.

"I'm sure you know her," Cherry said. "She wasn't hard to ID. We haven't found any slugs. I'm guessing where she was and the angle of the shots, they hit the river. Best we can hope for is to find the shell casings and to see what our suspect tells us."

A TV crew started setting up their equipment near where they found the body. Two more state police squad cars arrived with their lights flashing.

Cherry tucked in his shirt. I read the note.

"A shame," Cherry said. "She was the prettiest girl in town."

I crumpled up the piece of paper and tossed it into the river and watched it float away.

The police held a meeting and Chief Cherry, standing in a circle with a half dozen other uniforms, seemed pleased after it was agreed the victim had indeed met her grim death within the municipal limits of Bull River Falls.

I took a picture of the coroner's van as it drove away. I took another photo of the girl's lonely boot lying on the gravel beach before a trooper came and bagged it. I sat in my pickup truck and waited for the police traffic to clear up. I nodded off and woke up startled when the TV helicopter lifted and hovered above the river, a camera man leaning out against his safety straps like an army door gunner heading for combat.

CHAPTER 2

It hardly snowed that winter and never rained in spring. By July it was dry everywhere. Hot and dry and without a cloud. Hay fields turned to red dirt, like it was summer on Mars.

Cottonwood seeds hung suspended over Main Street like flying white fairies. The place looked like it wanted to blow away. The Bull River Falls Town Council had to cancel its annual Independence Day fireworks, it was so dry.

The wildfire started on Bellyache Mountain and burned across the high Aspen slopes outside of town in smoky finger shapes that glowed at night like coals. Or cowboy cookfires from the old days, depending how you imagined things.

Strange, sick looking coyotes with singed fur began wandering through town like stray dogs. Some were shot for sport, because everybody has guns around here, but people got used to them like they got accustomed to the elk that were chased by the fire into the post office parking lot.

And how those coyotes howled at night. They sang for hours, stopping spookily on cue as if directed to do so by the maestro of all creatures out there in the dark.

There was a sense that nothing knew its place anymore. As if the mountains were home to something that had not been foretold.

The wildfire stopped burning, then started up again. Once more it stopped, then burned. After another pause, it flared up once more until a hotshot firefighting crew from Montana came and got things under control.

I took advantage of the break to visit the VA hospital in Denver. The nightmares were getting ridiculous, and my shrink wanted to run more tests and adjust my meds.

On the second day at the hospital I tried to keep my head occupied while I waited for the nurse to return with my results. Uncle Sam gives me plenty of tests, and I take a lot of pills and have killed much time in hospital waiting rooms. Sometimes I wear medicinal patches. Blue, pink, green patches decorated with corporate pharmaceutical logos. I drink medicine from thimble-sized cups. I take long, deep breaths like my shrink taught me to do when it seems like my brain is getting ready to rev up and sprint away without my permission.

Which it does now every day, so my shrink Dr. Nguyen tells me to always keep my head busy.

When the nurse walked into the neurology department patient waiting area and butchered my name: "Prezoooo…prezeeee," I raised my hand and followed her into the examination room.

"How do you pronounce that?" she asked.

I said my name and she smiled. "I didn't even come close, did I?

She shut the door and I was alone again.

They'd given me a pill that morning so I could relax before my final test, so I shut my eyes and tried not to think of the two-hour drive back home from the city. I worried about the fire in Bull River Falls and hoped the local freelancer I had hired to write that week's front page story would be squared away by the time I got back to work.

Far down the hospital hall a toilet flushed and growled and that's all it took for my thoughts to unspool again.

I breathed deeply and listened as the public restroom latch rattled shut. Footsteps came past the room where I sat in a reclining chair thinking of how as a boy I built a Spanish galleon from a milk carton and plastic drinking straws. With its paper lateen sails my mighty ship and I explored the imaginary and windy blue waters of a back yard puddle in search of pirate treasure. I was courageous and strong. I was Errol Flynn and I would save the fair and lovely Arabella from harm.

Errol Flynn; this tells you how old I am.

The simple sound of a flushing toilet made me think of that.

My mind was starting to rev up and so I did what lately had helped put the brakes on these wild brain riffs I was prone to. I disassembled my M-16 rifle.

First, make sure the weapon is unloaded and cleared. Press the magazine release and watch it fall clear of the magazine well. Hold the charging handle at the rear of the receiver and draw it back. Look into the beautifully funneled, oily light of the smoothly bored chamber to make sure it's clear so you don't fucking accidentally kill somebody. You can smell the vaguely vegetable-scented lubricant when you get this close; like bananas and engine oil. In the correct light the greased curvature of the chamber glints like a ribboned fuel slick on water. Now find the retaining pin; it's above the pistol grip. Push the sonofabitch with the tip of a bullet or something stubby like a bullet because the mechanical, low-bid government genius who designed this thing doesn't allow a mere finger to accomplish such a simple task, except you don't carry around bullets anymore, stupid. But if you did, that's what you would do. The upper receiver will now swing free at this point, connected only by another damn pin.

The nurse walked in with her squeaky shoes and glued wires to my head and wrote on her clipboard. She studied the image of my digitized bright blue brain on a wall-mounted TV screen and gravely explained that my catecholamine levels were too high.

"And your glucocorticoid receptors are going crazy," she said.

"I'll eat more prunes."

"It's not a joke." She pointed with her finger at the blob on the screen that was shaped like a warped map of Jamaica, which itself was nudged against another deformed red gash that looked like the part of Patagonia where it crumbles away like broken teeth into the Straight of Magellan. I've always loved the sea.

"And your hippocampus is too small."

The nurse handed me a prescription for another giant bottle of pills, and in a mildly hopeless voice she rattled off a list of unsuccessful treatments I'd received on the government's dime during these many years: Yoga, Qigong sessions, Reiki healing, animal-facilitated therapy (I was forced to pet a sheepdog), aggressive deep muscle massage, eye movement desensitization, acupuncture, meditation, aromatherapy, botanicals by the gallon...you name it.

During this visit, not long after I tried to erase myself in my kitchen with a half-inch double-braid nylon dock line that should have held three of me, I had sat for two hours in a dimly lit room and wore giant Exposure Reality Treatment goggles so I could safely, as they explained, confront the setting in which I had experienced my initial trauma.

A *setting*, is what they called it.

The hot hospital room with the lumpy linoleum floor, its walls cluttered with military posters and a giant United States map filled with color-coded push-pins, smelled yeasty, like somebody had been baking bread.

The nurse examined the pink welt on my neck and typed into a laptop decorated with smiley face stickers.

"It broke?"

"Strong enough to tow a boat," I said. "But it broke."

She kept typing. "Did you report this to your provider?"

"My new shrink, yeah," I lied. "Doctor whatshisname."

"Doctor Nguyen," the nurse nodded.

I looked at the wild kaleidoscope pattern of my scanned skull on the TV screen and followed the coast of Argentina north, making note of where, far offshore to the East, a pumpkin orange piece of my broken brain formed the Falkland Islands.

I lied again: "We talked. It's being handled."

"Good," the nurse said, obviously relieved as she made a check mark on her clipboard and reached to shake my hand. "We'll see you next month, mister...

I pronounce my name again.

Like she'd been goosed by an invisible hand, she said: "Prezoooo..prezeeee."

"Close enough," I said.

CHAPTER 3

Before I left for the long drive from Denver to Bull River Falls, I picked up a travel brochure in the hospital lobby that showed a bunch of old guys smiling in front of a beautiful rice paddy in Vietnam.

It seemed like a good idea. It could help explain myself to me.

I also had unfinished business over there, so I got caught up at work, scribbled a few long-winded newspaper columns and arranged to turn the *Beacon* over to my two summer interns and a part-time employee and booked my trip.

Later that week I was squinting through a tiny window as the aircraft made its approach toward the airport at Ton Son Nhut, wondering if it had been a mistake to tell anybody about my stunt with the rope.

The city lay blinking in the dark below, a looping oxbow in the river filled with the shapes of anchored ships that had come in from the sea. There were more lights than I remembered.

We taxied down the runway and I saw abandoned quonset huts and cement bunkers flickering past in the shadows like an old 8mm home movie. The windowless corrugated metal buildings were covered in graffiti, half-crumbled on their asphalt slabs and poking out from weedy empty lots and behind them stood a long broken white wall decorated with more spray-painted exclamations. The faded outline of a stenciled American flag on a collapsed air force hanger was now covered in tangled vines and it was then that I began to remember everything.

At the hotel they gave us all a nice embroidered cap, a backpack and a stainless steel water bottle with the flag of the Socialist Republic of Vietnam on it.

During my trip we drove everywhere in a giant air-conditioned bus with its own bathroom. We visited the sites of old battles. A catfish farm. Villagers got dressed up in costumes and danced for us. They let us crawl through those damp tunnels the VC dug at Cu Chi, where a mousy little woman wearing a pith helmet gave a lecture about subterranean ventilation techniques and convection currents while we climbed down a slippery clay stairway.

There was the long drive north to Dak To, where mostly everybody died so we could stand on a few ruined dirt hills for a while. The A Shau Valley was wide and green with square rice paddies arranged in the hazy heat like an emerald checkerboard.

They let us explore the old U.S. Army fox holes and we had a picnic at a shabby village park where kids were playing soccer and where one guy on the tour who'd been with the 4th Infantry in sixty-seven said they used to store bales of concertina wire that was later trucked up to the triple-canopy jungle everybody hated.

We visited a prosthetics factory and an orphanage and on the next day walked for hours through the ruins of a mossy jungle temple in the warm rain and followed a tour guide who held high a pennant flag as if he were leading compliant children on a school outing.

We were just a bunch of old men on a bus.

In that comfortable giant bus we drove past more beautiful green rice paddies where people once tried to murder each other. Famous battlefields all over the world sometimes have such lovely names: Passchendaele and Gallipoli. Flanders. Chicamauga and Shiloh. Pleiku. The syllables tumble off your lips like poems.

One day they brought a group of geezer NVA and Viet Cong veterans to meet us. We stood facing each other in two rows in a parking lot next to the bus while somebody from the tour company took pictures. One guy came and gave me a little hug and started talking non-stop and I smiled and tried to be polite, but I didn't have a clue what he was yapping about. Perhaps it was that fellowship of soldiers thing.

There was a guy in our group named Earl. I never got his last name. He'd been a medic in the Mekong Delta, which meant he probably saw a few things. Earl, who carried a humming oxygen concentrator tucked under his arm, slept a lot on the bus and his wife did most of the talking. She was a small, fussy woman and she wore a beehive hairdo and lots of makeup, which isn't a good idea in all that humidity. Earl was frail and he wore white sneakers fastened with velcro straps. He had a gray pallor to him and always seemed on the edge of losing his breath and he dressed in baggy khaki pants and suspenders and a Detroit Tigers baseball cap that was too big for his head. In the suffering heat he mostly wore a long sleeve shirt with his collar buttoned to the top.

Earl had a nervous fit one day while we were touring a museum where grinning mannequins dressed in GI uniforms were torturing a Viet Cong soldier who was strapped to a chair with bamboo rope. The Americans were holding pliers and stood bent over like they were supposed to be yanking out the VC's fingernails. To me it looked like they were giving him a manicure. The plastic figures were scratched up and chipped like department store dummies.

One entire wall at the museum was filled with a display of captured American rifles and pistols and various caliber bullets and mortar rounds, all carefully labeled in Vietnamese and English and mounted behind the glass like a butterfly collection.

Earl stood in front of the exhibit, leaning with one hand against the glass, and just started wheezing and gibbering until his wife came and took him back to the bus, where she pulled away the plastic oxygen tube from his nose and dabbed his face with a wet tissue.

Almost everybody on the trip suffered from an old age ailment: bad hips, bad heart, a pending knee replacement, and we talked a lot about contraptions like shoulder braces and cortisone shots and how to do the tricky paperwork over at the VA. We spoke of everything but the war.

After the museum they took us to another battlefield where I saw Earl standing in front of a rusted armored personnel carrier that lay tipped sideways into an old mortar crater overgrown with jungle bushes. There was a bronze plaque on a cement obelisk describing what had taken place there and Earl squatted and rocked back and forth with his elbows on his knees, and he started bawling. His wife, her cone of aerated hair starting to deflate and lose its shape in the wicked afternoon heat, came running with her tissue box and grabbed Earl's arm and guided him back to the bus, and she teased him about what happened. Teased him.

Not far into the trip Earl's wife found out I wasn't married anymore and so must have believed she needed to take care of me, too. She'd offer me bottled water or try to share the free snacks the tour guide was always handing out. She'd save a seat for me on the bus and showed me photos of the grandkids. Talked about how expensive this trip was and how many pills she had to keep track of for her husband. One time, she picked lint off my shirt collar, her hand lingering on my shoulder, and I finally told her to knock it off, and she never spoke to me again.

They don't call it by that name anymore, but Saigon was hotter and bigger than I remembered. Everything looked different and re-arranged.

There was a McDonald's with a pagoda roof on Dien Bien Phu Street where I almost got killed by a horde of motor scooters when I tried to walk across the busy roundabout. My knees are shot, so it was a stupid stunt.

They have something called a McPork burger on the menu. I drank strong coffee from a tiny cup with a saucer and it was very sweet and I wondered if they had used condensed milk, which is what people always drank over there. There was bassy, thumping techno music playing in the restaurant that shook the walls and the place was filled with glum teenagers with phone cords plugged into their heads. They all wore sunglasses. Everybody over there wears sunglasses now. I finished my coffee and took my sandwich next door to a quiet cafe and ordered French Larue beer and wondered if it was still brewed over in Da Nang. It didn't taste at all like I remembered it.

Our tour guide was a beautiful girl from Nha Trang who said she had a degree in economics from the University of Wisconsin and she told me, with an expansive wave of her arm and much pride, that there was now a golf resort and luxury spa next to what used to be the Ho Chi Minh trail, up in the central highlands where I spent some time. I told her this was very nice and it was good we were finally winning the war with hamburgers and putters instead of M-16 bullets and napalm, but she was not amused. I asked if there was still that wonderful white sand up in Nha Trang on the China Sea where the navy nurses used to sunbathe topless on the beach, but she just looked confused and surprised by the question and I didn't talk to her much after that.

Like I said, we were a bunch of old men on a bus.

One day on the way back to the hotel our driver took a short cut through town past the old American MACV headquarters near the airport. I asked him to stop and said I would go the rest of the way on foot. We argued for a while and he finally shrugged and pulled over and I stepped off our beautifully air conditioned bus into the muggy ninety-six-degree Saigon heat and started walking, sweating like a horse the whole way, my knees throbbing. Earl's wife watched me from behind the smoked gray bus window and gave me a worried smile. Her husband was in the seat next to her and he was asleep.

The old enlisted barracks was boarded up and there were vines growing on the roof. Sooner or later everything over there gets covered with jungle vines. Nearby, the French cemetery where the VC once buried rifles in fake coffins they could dig up later is now a pleasant grassy park. You can still see the phantom mounds where the graves once were, lined up perfectly like mogul bumps on a ski hill. I found out the locals don't use the park after dark because they believe it's haunted with round-eyed colonial ghosts, even though they shipped the corpses back to France a long time ago.

I got lost in a dark alley on the way back to the hotel and came out on a street in a very poor neighborhood with plywood shacks where people stared at me like I'd just dropped from the sky. I gave coins to an old lady who was begging next to a two-wheeled cart in front of a doorway that smelled of cabbage and fish. There were tangled coils of electrical wire and badly installed power conduit pipes screwed to the outside walls of the shacks where every open window had a little TV in it.

I made my way to the Majestic Hotel on a street with expensive stores. It was the best day of the tour, I thought, just wandering around. I didn't care if I got lost. I was already lost.

Everything old that had memories for me now looked apocalyptic and abandoned, as if some predicted evil in the planet's history had just commenced. Somehow, it gave me hope to think the world might mercifully come to an end.

The whole tour was going to last too long and it had already cost a fortune. I was the only guy on the trip who didn't bring along his wife or carried a cell phone. I decided to cut things short and head back home, pleading that I had a medical emergency that needed swift attention.

I should have known such a trip wouldn't fix anything, although it was nice that they had a bathroom on the bus. The hand towels were cloth, not paper.

On the final night in the city I decided not to go to the fancy dinner they had planned for us over at the Hotel Continental, where Somerset Maugham once spent time getting drunk and writing about the neighborhood during the old colonial days. Some of the guys had been forced by their wives to buy new suits and neckties for this. The hotel is a grim place, anyway. They said American TV reporters would be there to do interviews, so this was a good reason not to go. I was worried Earl might have another one of his fits, but I figured his wife would be there with her tissue box and it was none of my business. I have plenty of problems of my own.

I had stayed in the Continental long ago when I was a kid in the army during a short medical R&R. I used money I'd saved up to eat a meal in a fancy restaurant with the high ceiling fans. I remember feeding soup crackers to the fat carp in the courtyard pond under the old frangipani trees.

It was a very exotic place at the time and the hotel was crawling with news reporters covering the war, each of them wearing khaki vests and looking frantic and very committed, their shirt pockets stuffed with an over-abundance of pens. I'd just gotten out of the hospital and hadn't healed up yet and I wore a black eye patch which, to my delight, made me look sinister and dangerous. With my swollen face and crazy, scabby stitches I looked like a deranged buccaneer sitting on the hotel balcony in my civilian clothes, chain smoking Lucky Strikes and getting drunk in the cruel humid heat and scribbling profound nonsense in this notebook I'd started carrying everywhere.

On the final night in Saigon I made my way over to the old post office the French had built a long time ago. I'd been there too while mending up after my little adventure up in the A-Shau Valley. There were bright yellow flowers standing in tall clay pots along the crowded street, and they made the old cathedral on the Cong Xa Paris look gray and tired in the late afternoon rain. Where I live now in my little town in the mountains we never get much rain. I forgot how wet this part of the world could be.

Pigeons with drooping wings sat bunched on capstones above the arched church windows, and when I walked past the birds lifted and flapped in dark sheets across the city plaza.

I stumbled through traffic to the giant post office building where I found the long wooden bench I remembered. I sat and put my hands in my lap and studied the famous five old wall clocks that told all the world's time.

I daydreamed about my wife and for a while it seemed like she was sitting next to me there on the bench. I do this a lot, lately...think of her sitting next to me, like she was still alive. It's crazy, and the pills I take sure don't help. But I miss her a lot.

Back home, I thought, I'd be trying to get some sleep after a long night listening to the gasbags at Town Hall debate obscure horseshit revisions to the Bull River Falls community building code.

After the war I never spoke to anybody about Vietnam. Avoided the subject completely. Nobody in those days wanted to hear about it, anyway. Seems the older I get the more I remember stuff I want to forget.

When I told Dr. Nguyen about taking this trip he looked at me like I was one crazy sonofabitch and said to make sure I took my blue pills with me and then he tried to discuss the rope.

"Chickenshit," I said.

"You confuse me. I thought we were discussing the rope," Dr. Nguyen said, putting down his little notepad.

"Do you wish my help or not?"

I told him: "It's what they all call me in the dream. 'Chickenshit,' over and over."

At this last appointment I noticed how the doctor's face was creased up like a dirty shirt, a constellation of liver spots fanning across his hollow cheeks.

I said, "Lately, during the day I start thinking I can talk to animals. I look up at a tree and there's a bird up there and soon the two of us are in a deep conversation. Crazy stupid shit. My wife comes and we have long discussions. It's like she's there right next to me. I recognize her perfume. I've told her about the rope, and she gets pissed."

"I'm interested in all of that," Nguyen said.

I yawned. "I'll cover it next time. I'm tired. How many of these appointments do I get?"

"As many as you want. With your service-connected injuries and your past difficulties, as many as you believe are necessary."

"Seems like the young guys should get the attention," I said, but I don't think he heard me.

There was a long lull while the doctor scribbled in his notepad. I liked this guy for not using a computer. I looked around. Nguyen's office seemed transformed, the walls stretched taller, books squeezed onto shelves, some familiar, as if they'd been lifted from my own library. The doctor's enormous desk, on which sat empty in and out boxes, intruded into the room like the prow of a ship.

"The medicine, it's not helping you sleep?"

"I don't know what sleep is anymore. I close my eyes and I just hover a few inches over the mattress."

A copy of *Robinson Crusoe* lay face down on a small reading table. I imagined Alexander Selkirk chasing his goats along a tropical beach.

"You seem reluctant to talk about your experiences. You're afraid I won't understand?"

"You weren't there. You can't possibly understand."

Nguyen smiled like he had a secret to keep, pipe smoke lifting sideways from his parted lips and rising toward one of those 10,000 hour energy saver light bulbs beneath a fake Tiffany lampshade.

"Your thoughts of eliminating yourself," Nguyen said. "In your case it would be indicative of a great many things. Shall we discuss this? Shall we talk about the rope?"

The doctor stood and turned his back and stared out the office window. Then he floated back to his chair.

"Often, people experience what you've described many years after the fact," he said. "The uncomfortable thoughts. For a time life is predictable. And then things are awakened."

"Things," I said.

"Men your age are prone to it. In youth there are diversions, an anticipated life to live. Hope. A family. Career. Love."

There was a pause, during which Nguyen flipped a few pages in his notebook.

"Tell me about the soldier in your dream. And please continue the medication during your little journey. It's not wise to stop suddenly."

"You seem to avoid speaking about your military record. The awards, for example."

"The medals."

"It's not ordinary, you must admit. So many of them."

"I don't talk about it."

"To anyone?"

"If they don't ask."

"You are humble, then."

"I'm a first class bullshitter, actually."

Then my time ran out on the doctor's shapeless clock made from cheese that appeared to be melting in stringy yellow tubes down the office wall.

Chickenshit, said the voice in my head and when I closed my eyes I saw a horde of gophers armed with little rifles charging into battle across a rice paddy. This brief, wobbling vision appeared within a flashing aura that radiated from the corner of my eye, a half-moon of dazzling light whose contents seemed as real as if I'd glanced at something sideways while walking down a street.

I knew if I told Dr. Nguyen about this eyeball thing he'd give me bullshit about retinal detachment symptoms or say such weirdness indicated a coming headache. I'd heard this all before. Often, what I imagined was more real than what could indeed be seen.

CHAPTER 4

The post office in Saigon was built by the same guy who dreamed up the famous iron tower in Paris. It had marble walls and a glass atrium roof suspended from metal struts and it was very hot inside. You'd think those communists, as comfort to the proletariat, could pump AC into the place. The faded inscribed outlines of former French street names marked where the government had long ago torn away exit signs above a row of revolving brass doors.

Their black shapes reflecting in the ceiling glass, school children in blue uniforms stood and pointed up at the portrait of Ho Chi Minh, the giant banner flooded in a honey light that seemed to drip from tulip-shaped wall lamps. Two bare-shouldered monks draped in red robes walked past, absorbed in their folded hands, their dusty feet in rope sandals. I watched until I could no longer see their shaved round heads among the crowd of people.

Young men dressed in summer weight sports jackets, sockless in fashionable shoes and creased white linen pants, walked past staring seriously at their cell phones. Their speech was not quite British, but I couldn't tell. One of them cocked his head when his phone rang and looked for the longest time at the ceiling before answering the call.

Everybody has cell phones over there now. You would see an old papasan in torn shorts and flip flops riding a crummy bicycle piled high with bamboo cages filled with chickens and he's talking on a cell phone. A wrinkled granny washing clothes by a river, just like they've been doing for a thousand years, and she's chattering on a cell phone, wagging her hands around and yapping while she bangs away at a pile of underwear with a big rock.

It was raining, a persistent tropical drizzle that felt like warm steam, so I ducked into the old French cathedral across the street.

It was packed with people and at the altar a priest was preaching; a tall man with a sharp, hawkish face. He was yelling and pacing back and forth like a caffeinated Pentecostal snake pastor. I didn't know Catholics did such things.

It was hot, everyone fanning themselves with hymnal books. The pews were full, so I stood in the back of the church. The priest was very animated behind his pulpit, his long limbs wagging loosely as if powered by bolts of irregular electrical current. His gleaming hair stood as high as fancy pastry, sunshine flooding gloriously from behind him through tall stained glass windows.

Neck wattles shaking behind a black clerical collar, the pastor raised his stiff fists so high his shoe heels lifted and he began to shiver like he'd just been dipped in the holy river Jordan. He seemed to levitate as he commenced with a sideways pop star moonwalk, cufflinks shining like tiny fires on his wrists. He shivered violently as if in a deep fever, eye-whites rolling. He walked back and forth in front of the altar in short, nervous steps, pausing with each pass at the oak podium to consult his bookmarked Bible.

"Peter five-eight!" he screamed. "I'll say more about this later but for now I want you to hold these words close to your heart! *Be sober minded, be watchful. For the devil prowls around like a roaring lion, seeking someone to devour.*'"

The worn marble church floor was bright white, the walls paneled in blond wood. A carved wooden Jesus slumped from a mounted cross, his five wounds bleeding, and with his face tilted he stared down at me. The pastor, now in his groove, seemed to grow taller as he leaned over his Bible and pushed up his bifocals with one finger. He looked out at the congregation.

He licked his lips quickly: "I tell you, brothers and sisters...I beg you to be watchful. In *Corinthians* we are told Satan disguises himself as an angel of holy light."

Like I said, I didn't know Catholics could put on a show like this.

There were gasps from the congregation and a pained moan swept through the cathedral. The people began to sway. They smiled in rapture. The noise of scuffling shoes made it sound as if an unseen crowd had just entered the church, though everyone remained seated.

"Salvation is not a single event!" the priest screamed, lifting his book high above his head. "And if your right hand causes you to sin, cut it off and throw it away. For it is better that you loose one of your members rather than your whole body go into hell."

And now everyone took this as a reason to sway again. I started swaying, too. You just couldn't help it.

The pastor lifted his arm higher toward the ceiling. "And this is what Mathew tells us very clearly right here in this book!"

Gravely, lowering the Bible slowly as if the words might spill from its pages, the preacher said: "You'll do well to heed the signs that come your way. Be ready. Or redemption will avoid you!"

Speaking in staccato bursts, he began a wild-eyed discourse about Gideon and the fleece and his dealings with the men of Ephraim. He transitioned with a wind-milling motion of his long right arm to the story of Samson and how his strength was used to "...afflict the Philistines," and then, his baritone voice descending with a weary slowness, its tone woeful, the priest who-was-not-a-priest described Samson's capture and terrible suffering.

He gulped back his tears and licked his lips. It was hot. I was so thirsty. I wondered what they were eating back at the hotel banquet. Probably the prime rib. Cold beers. The nice air conditioning.

"And what does that prove, my brothers and sisters?" the preacher asked, closing his book and stroking it...stroking it. "When the Philistines took him? When they put out his eyes and brought him down to Gaza to bind him with bronze fetters? Would he ever be able to find redemption?"

The church turned silent and I sensed the people were trying not to breathe too loudly. The only sound came from the row of old bamboo ceiling fans spinning and clacking high above our heads, useless in such suffocating and hellish heat.

"Sin!" the pastor hissed. This drawn-out wheeze, mind you, lasted several seconds and sounded like hot steam leaking from a busted radiator.

"Ssssssiin...will always take you farther than you want to go and cost more than you ever intended to pay."

He slammed down the closed Bible with such force that a cloud of dust lifted from the podium and hung suspended in the dead air like a holy corona above the priest's head.

He screamed about Samson lighting the tails of three hundred foxes on fire and then setting them loose into a cornfield.

"Now just you think of that!"

I very much tried to think about that, but it didn't work. I thought about the fire back in Bull River Falls. I thought about the dead girl by the river. I thought about my brain up there on the hospital TV screen.

I stood near a table stacked with magazines and a glossy brochure showing a groomed and athletic Scandinavian Jesus posed barefoot on a fluffy cloud, his feet so tan, his hands grasping a gleaming drop-shadowed cross. The headline, written in English, proclaimed that summer's group church visit to Jerusalem: "Tiberius and Sea of Galilee Brunch and Boat Tour!"

I now watched heads bob in agreement as the preacher aimed his sermon home with a convulsive jiggle as if God, eager to get on with the show, had poked him with an invisible finger. Some of the people looked puzzled. Many wiped away tears. Most sat there smiling, enchanted.

The preacher jerked across the stage. He paced back and forth, shaking his head and smiling with his eyes closed as if a profundity had just been whispered to him.

I was struck by the pastor's words: *"...or redemption will avoid you,"* as if such a fate was swift and fleet-footed, like an NFL running back in heaven dodging his salvation.

A Vietnamese lady in the back pew turned and smiled and slid aside to make room for me. I shook my head and gave a polite wave. It was very nice of her.

The congregation began to sway violently, like passengers on a ship on a stormy sea. The people lifted their arms heavenward into a tangle of bent elbows and flashing hand and wrist jewelry and they broke into joyous spontaneous song as the pastor lead his flock in a rousing rendition of *Praise Thee, Though I Am Not Alone in Sin Against Thine Name.*

A woman lowered her head into her hands and began to sob. A man stood and raised his clenched fist and shouted "hallelujah!"

The sweating pastor twitched up his long limbs and howled off-key in a scratchy, forced tenor: *"...not alone in sin against thine name!"* Everybody then joined in song, standing to raise their own hands higher in fierce jubilation.

I got dizzy and, just as the preacher began a story about Daniel and his capture and exile by Nebuchadnezzar, I quickly made for the door.

I faced the church nave the way I'd been taught as a child to depart a church. I made the sign of the cross and shuffled backwards onto the noisy wet street.

CHAPTER 5

I stood in the drizzle on the cathedral steps, wishing for an umbrella and wondering if I should head back and eat dinner with the rest of the tour group. I could cheer up old Earl.

But I knew there was something important to do.

I hailed a taxi, and when I took my seat and handed over the address the suddenly chatty driver immediately explained in great detail how his brother lived in Baton Rouge, Louisiana, America... and that he himself had been in the war and had not lost his legs or his arms and for that he was grateful.

I had not asked for this information, though I could understand why this guy's brother had moved to Baton Rouge. It gets crazy hot there, too.

I was thinking about what the priest had said concerning salvation when the taxi driver explained he had been a grammar school teacher of French language studies before the war, and for that crime had spent four years cleaning latrines in a communist re-education camp. He then described the art of proper toilet maintenance in disturbing detail and with a gleeful energy that I found endearing. I had never heard such excited talk about how to dig a shitter in the jungle.

He laughed and drew his breath quickly. "I lived on ten kilograms of rice each month," he said in perfect English.

"Food now is very mystical to me. I scarcely want to swallow because I'm afraid I'll never experience such a wonderful thing again."

He slapped his belly with one hand. "Which is why I am so fat!"

He named the camp and the province and I said it was up along the Laos border near Quang Tri where I'd also once been, hoping the uninvited conversation would end. I started to think about the long flight home and the pile of work waiting for me at the newspaper.

The man looked up into the rear-view mirror and asked if I was in the American war but I never answered.

The taxi windshield was cracked, the battered side mirror fastened with twisted hanger wire, and when the vehicle turned down a street toward the river the steering wheel wobbled in the driver's hands and I could see that all the dashboard instruments had broken long ago. With the rain spattering outside, inside the taxi there seemed to be a ceaseless trickle coming from somewhere beneath the torn seat cushion.

The driver wiped the windshield and the heel of his hand left a watery comet's tail on the foggy glass. I'd forgotten how humid this place was. The rain always seemed wetter here.

On the glove box of the taxi was taped a small photo of a young man dressed in faded khaki and a pith helmet and embroidered red military collar stars of a style not seen in that country for half a century.

I asked if it was him in the photograph.

The driver shook his face quickly into the mirror and shivered as if I'd just put ice down the back of his shirt. He spoke with a heavy, enunciated slur. Something was not right with the way he jerked his body and I wondered if he was drunk. Just my luck, I thought. I come back after all these years and get killed by a boozed up cab driver. I noticed his queerly sheared hair that clung to the back of his head like a lopsided monk's cap. The skin on his deformed neck was mottled like dirty wax.

"It was taken many years ago," the old man said. He reached and gently touched the photo with his fingertip and let out a sigh.

He explained how his father was later killed by the French in the valley of Dien Bien Phu. An unnecessary and prolonged slaughter, he added. He said he too had been wounded, but by American fire in the north not far from his village. In the same year I got hurt.

He apologized for speaking so forwardly and blamed this on his old age. He said he no longer had opinions about war. He said the names of the old, blundering men who command such battles are rescued for history by the bravery of those who had no choice but to fight and die unremembered and that it was beyond his abilities to explain wars or governments, and so he would not try.

There was a funeral procession crossing the street, hunched mourners dressed in white walking slowly in slippered feet from a dark alley. While the taxi sat in traffic the driver said with another weary sigh that of all things whose truth is absolute it is impermanence, and if we cling to all else we welcome disappointment.

Such a mouthful to hear from a stranger, I thought. All this when I'd just wanted to be somewhere quiet. I wished he would stop speaking.

I fished through my wallet to make sure I had Vietnamese money for the taxi fare. I found the store receipt for the damn rope instead and crumpled it up and shoved it into my pocket.

I told the driver how I believed this too. Impermanence, and the stuff you think will last usually turns to bullshit.

The man laughed. "Booolsheet, yes!"

I saw part of his big blue jaw turn and smile into the colored neon street glare of the taxi's mirror.

"I like Americans," the driver said, turning to point at tourists who were taking pictures of the funeral with their cell phones, his shapeless open hand, like the back of his neck, oddly pale and colorless.

"Look at them. So innocently rude, like large happy children."

He laughed: "The Russians want things for free. The British are gloomy and always look disappointed. The French these days are seldom seen. The Americans are my best customers. Did you know there is now a golf course next to what the round eyes once called the Ho Chi Minh Trail?"

"So I've heard," I said and asked the driver to follow So Loi Street to the old wharf and the driver said he knew the area well and that the neighborhood had always been very poor.

He looked into the mirror and I noticed the old man's face seemed not to reflect in the glass.

The taxi stopped. The vehicle seemed to contract in spasm as if its metal innards had come undone. The wounded vehicle moaned, one complaining gear grinding loudly as the driver's knuckles gripped his shaking wheel. The old man drew his breath and quietly laughed. I looked at those doughy hands with half the fingers missing, a long puckered white scar running the length of his bare arm as if something had been poured there and left to dry.

Outside in the rain the dripping black awnings of the noodle sellers stood in angled silhouettes beneath bright vapor lamps along the wharf. The stark yellow lights seemed theatrical, like a grand entertainment was imminent. People walked past the parked taxi and were followed by their own shadows.

"They will soon tear these old houses down," the driver said with a tired wave of his cupped hand. "To make way for the new. Always to make way for something new."

He lifted his wrecked arm over the ripped seat and turned. His face was terribly scarred.

Again the taxi driver apologized for talking so much, but I had been his fifth customer and he was now happy he would not end the evening with an unlucky number.

"We are born of our parents but formed by others seen and unseen in this life," he said, nodding in surprise as he took my payment and the big tip, folded the bills carefully with his crippled hands, and placed the money into a leather pouch on the front seat.

The driver stepped outside, walked around the vehicle with a Charlie Chaplin waddle, and opened my door with a clumsy flourish. He had a bad limp, one bony shortened limb as thin as a child's leg beneath his trouser. The foot was wrongly canted below the rolled up cuff, its snubbed shoe wider than the other. He waited politely like an attending butler as I stepped from the street onto the curb. He stretched his ruined face into that goofy smile, took his seat and drove away, the taxi rattling down the rainwatered street, one tail light missing, yellow sparks glittering from the dragging muffler.

I walked. I swallowed one of my pills. I looked at my folded city map and returned it to my shirt pocket. After all these years, you would think I'd have the address memorized.

I kept walking.

CHAPTER 6

Cilexa, Effexor. Especially Valium. That's what the medical geniuses gave us when I got out of the army. Later, it was Restorel, Xanax, Adderall, Haldal, Risperdal. I swallowed them hopefully, without questions.

For a while it was Neonoprin, Wellbutron, Atavan. I took comfort in the iambic rhythm of their names.

I loved each pill dearly, their personalities distinct, though none worked better than the pretty blue one I was taking now, if you didn't count the side effects.

When I was discharged they gave everybody Thorazine; something to make you calm. Then it was Prazosin for blood pressure, which was actually an accidental medical miracle. It did the trick for my mood, though it gave me violent shits for two years. When my asshole wore out it was back to Thorazine and I lived for a while cacooned in a state of chronic peaceful anxiety, something always bubbling menacingly deep inside my head. I was satisfied with being unhappily calm. Smiling with absolutely nothing to smile about.

I walked.

I took the street map from my pocket and studied it, getting my bearings. In this older, cluttered part of Saigon hardly any of the buildings showed an address. Sometimes there would be a numbered metal badge nailed above a midget doorway. Other signs would be hand-painted with Vietnamese circles and alphabet darts. The newer apartment buildings, cloned low-rise boxes, confused me further by showing the latinized district name and then the street and whether it was a lane or a road. I didn't even know if the place I was looking for would still be there.

Now my mind wouldn't slow down. I shouldn't have come on this trip. I should have known geography never changes anything. There's no future in the past.

I tried to remember my mother's favorite German Hummel figurine, a smiling freckled boy in leather shorts peeing into a Bavarian pond. I tried to recall how much a Claymore mine weighed. I ran a few artillery scales and trajectory tables in my head, just to keep things busy up there. If there's anything I've learned, it's to keep things busy up there.

Then I tried to imagine something else to give the blue pill time to work.

Like disassembling my M-16 rifle.

This forced brain riff gave me temporary comfort:

...*the upper receiver will now swing free at this point, connected only by another damn pin. The M-16 is a glorified, over-engineered .22 pea shooter. The AK-47, the international weapon of choice for the Taliban, FARC, Boko Haram fighters wearing sweaty doo rags and ripped Disneyland tee shirts, ISIS and Hezbollah...isn't at all this pin-happy.*

Now take off the charging handle and bolt-carrier. Push the forward retaining pin free. Another damn pin. Lay the top and lower receivers and the charging handle aside. Make sure you put them aside in reverse order. Take out the bolt cotter-pin which secures that square-headed sonofabitch inconveniently tucked in the dent below the gas tube vent. Take out the bolt and firing pin.

Now do everything you just did, but do it backwards. At night. And quickly this time. While it's raining during monsoon season, with your soaked poplin field shirt collar cowled up along the back of your sunburned neck. With water sluicing down your stinking poncho liner. While somebody is shooting at you, the green tracers flashing by in the wet night like tubes of jittery neon.

I took a deep breath.

My head became ticklishly lighter, like stuff had been sucked out with a syringe.

I'd wept that morning in my hotel room as if every sadness of my life had tipped and spilled through a door at the bottom of my heart. At breakfast Earl's wife asked if I was okay and I nodded and studied my scrambled eggs. She just wouldn't give up.

I hadn't had those repeating nightmares for a long time but in the hotel they came back with a vengeance. It was like experiencing high definition TV after years of watching on an old vacuum tube Zenith with a glass screen, the dreams were so real.

I walked past a crucified red paper kite suspended from a dripping electric power line.

This sent my brain reeling, and off it went...

And then I thought of how, so many years before, I once saw something hanging from a tree in the jungle.

It swung from the limb of a palm like a seed pod, not five feet above my head, pale and fresh and fleshy. We were standing on a dirt path that wandered ahead through the forbidding jungle, not a place anyone wanted to walk so late in the day. From the distance we heard gunfire, like the cackling of eerie birds, and then the deep pop-pop of a larger caliber weapon.

At the base of the tree and on the underside of its leaves and broken branches there were signs that told you somebody had gotten hurt here. On the ground lay pulverized bottle glass, bits of broken weaponry and sheets of stringy green cloth, a charred wooden pistol stock, and a meter-wide wet blotch into which the insects had already begun to crawl.

I had to strain my neck to look up at it. There's no blood, the flaccid piece so cleanly cut you can see the incised hole where the obvious missing part had been, magenta-red and obscenely butchered, like this happened only moments ago. Like it had been carefully sculpted as improbable art from colored clay.

Our platoon that afternoon had been sent to police an ambush site, the Hueys patrolling overhead as they secured the area before the medevac choppers could arrive for a second lift. One aircraft, its damaged rear tail skid dangling, comes so low I can see the gunner behind his chin turret, aiming a 40 mm grenade launcher at the treetops through the open bay doors. He is hatless, grinning from behind a drooping mustache and sunglasses, his long non-regulation hair blowing.

The place had the usual assemblage of battle scrap, like somebody had overturned a trash dumpster: crumpled paper caught in the broken foliage, here and there an orphaned boot, unopened food ration cans and clumps of bloodied first-aid gauze, lost boonie hats, empty ammo clips and torn rucksack webbing. The dropped rifles and discarded trench shovels. Deeply gouged earth where the mortars had landed. The scattered mess was a cryptic annal of the battle's ferocity. The altered jungle had been clipped of its recognizable contours and carved down to gummy wet red clay as if everything had been plowed by a drunken excavator. You could tell it had been a significant fight the way the smaller perimeter trees were mowed down. The jungle birds were gone, every natural living thing absent in a place normally filled with screeches and howls and maddening insect noise.

Now it was windless, quiet. The world indifferent. You could push aside the dewy humid air with your hand.

Out there in the twisted mess in a small clearing lay four neat rows of multiple body shapes within their zippered black rubber bags where two boys from another platoon now stood guard. They seemed nervous and kept looking around, sucking nervously on their cigarettes.

I was still light-headed and feeling pukey because of what I think was spoiled C-ration lasagna and cold canned Vienna sausages wolfed down when I was ordered to report to the helo pad for a 4 a.m. lift-off.

Looking up now at the tree, I wonder if they belonged to an American. Nobody seems to know for sure, though theories abound. A few more soldiers come along and soon there are five heavily armed teenagers studying what's above, tipping back their dirty bush hats and helmets and removing sunglasses to get a better look, side-stepping the puddle of gore that's starting to congeal like Jell-O at the base of the tree.

From somewhere, a single bird squawks and every head turns because we're grateful for any normal sound. The chatter of wildlife is encouraging, as if the world might surely one day return to what it had been.

A landing Huey bends over the tops of the remaining trees. Loose branches fly. I can smell foliage freshly cut by rifle fire and a few of us agree the ambush had come from three sides, considering the manner in which the lower bushes and saplings had been swept aside.

There's the reek of manure from a rice paddy where a chewing ox stands up to its hocks in brown water. I remember wiping the sweat from my eyes. The soldiers with me are mute; somebody spits loudly, a heavy hocker that lands with a distinct splash, and another guy lights a smoke, and PFC Harmon Gillespie from Conyers, Georgia squats and gazes up in bewildered solemnity, his mouth open as if what's in the tree has profound artistic value and seeing this is so unique it invites speechless awe.

"Never seen that before," he says softly, not intending for anyone else to hear.

This is a group of hard-boiled short-timers, a month left on their tours, who can joke about taking off somebody's head with a Browning automatic rifle or discuss with clinical calm the fried eggs sizzle white phosphorous makes when it strikes human flesh.

But this is different.

"I think they cut it off on purpose and just tossed it," says Gillespie in a louder voice, and then takes out a sugar packet from his bulging shirt pocket and casually empties the contents into his canteen.

"I have also not seen such a thing," says Anders, the veteran platoon medic, who HAS seen it all and is nearing the end of his second combat tour, as he takes a wooden tongue depressor and scoops Rexall surgical powder from a screw-cap tin. He pats the stuff on the back of his sunburned neck. Holding open his shirt collar, he squirts insect repellent from the plastic bottle he's kept under a giant rubber band on his helmet liner and works the bug juice into a beige paste and starts rubbing that into his skin. Anders has a wild rash the color of pie crust worming up the side of his neck, the cracked parts seeping a pale red liquid. He's wearing a knotted para-cord necklace with three tracheotomy tube corks hanging from it. On his bush hat is a peace sign drawn in chalk.

Anders drawls, with carefully constipated southern pauses — he always spoke with great, syrupy effort through paralyzed lips: "Is...it...one of OURS or one of...THEIRS? That's the question, gentlemen."

He said *gentlemen*: the oldest in our squad of PFCs, Spec 4s and two buck sergeants is twenty-two.

Another soldier, smoking lung-numbing French Gitanes he claims he found in a hooch at the division's unofficially sanctioned brothel in Pleiku, flicking off ashes with each drag...HE thinks it's from a Claymore mine and the rest of whoever owned those things blew into a thousand pieces and if they can't find the rest of him it's what's left that must be shipped home.

Everybody agrees the theory is shit.

"In a little box," the soldier says, not giving up and holding his hands apart. "About this size. With a little flag."

"To Fort Dix, New Jersey," somebody else says.

Anders the medic takes out a Sanka packet and starts to make coffee. He moves as slow as he speaks.

In this terrible heat he's making coffee.

He pours water into his dented field cup and stirs it methodically with a dirty finger like he's making the last coffee he'll ever drink and then takes out a heat tab. He ignites the tab carefully as if he's lighting a votive candle in church and settles in like he's got all day. The tab sputters and dies and then rises into a thin blue flame.

"Army has to have a rule for that. Don't you think?" the Gitanes smoker says. He looks up at the tree limb. "Even if it's parts, you can't just leave human parts behind."

You can't just leave it behind...

As I've done a thousand times, I tried to shake off these old thoughts that keep coming back in an endless loop of remembrance.

I continued walking.

At the pier I walked past the empty decorated flower boats, past food stalls where from a rocking barge shirtless men lifted heavy baskets piled high with silver fish.

From the river came the smell of oily cargo ships anchored beyond where I could see. And from the far shore, the faint rumble of traffic lifting from the city. A muffled horn sounded from behind the foggy buoy lights.

I had dreamed of an enormous fire the night before, great roaring curtains of it chasing me and a crowd of strangers, and hoped it foretold good luck when I got home, though in the dream the nameless people turned and stood before the red flames while they cried out, their dead faces frosty and white. Their arms reached at me, those eyes ardent and pleading, and when I stepped forward they were gone. I awoke at night at the hotel with an aching urge to cry, but I could not. I was plugged up.

From the old pier where they'd already lined up construction equipment to tear this neighborhood down, I watched shreds of lightning flicker behind storm clouds that hung above the dark river. Thunder muttered softly.

The wet ghost footprints of running children showed on the wood pier boards and when a young couple holding hands walked past I smelled the woman's lingering perfume in the muggy air and it reminded me of what I no longer had.

In the soft rain I walked, rows of wet paper lanterns blinking along the gray planks. There was the church bell afterclang of heavy buoy chains. Out across the water, the shore lights seemed tethered to their smeared reflections. Someone wearing a restaurant apron and carrying a stack of white dishes passed, and a man beneath a canvas awning raised his arm and with a flourish poured coffee from a pot and sweetened it with condensed milk. There was laughing from people unseen on the river. The shoreline streets were hung with illuminated banners with yellow stars on a red background, and they did not move in the warm and windless night.

Two boys dressed in ragged shorts fished for bait from the pier, their tossed nets splashing softly with a hiss on the water like scattered stones.

Beneath a ratty canvas tent with only two tables I ordered a drink and took another one of the pretty pills the VA gives me. I love my pretty blue pill.

Watch for any side effects, my shrink told me. Don't believe everything you see.

The pier was peopled with pale mutants of similar color and shape and in my addled, over-dosed state I was convinced they were walking the world in search of victims; all of this as I drifted in and out of a morphined drowsiness. A man walked past wearing a black plastic grocery bag on his head like a babushka against the rain and I flinched and stepped away as if I'd seen a monster.

Again, my head came unhinged as I fought the familiar inertia and hoped for time to pass like a starving man who has been promised food.

A car sluiced down the wet street and the dull gleam of its headlights reminded me again of rifle fire in the jungle so long ago, where nobody wanted to stop looking up at that damn tree. I remembered the two glass-domed Loaches bristling with guns that appeared above the tree tops as they flew toward the shooting.

There's the rubbery, hollow sound of another mortar tube unloading in the distance and I palm the top of my bush hat and bring my shoulders together. This shell lands close enough to see the flying cakes of red mud. But nobody in our little group moves. We are fascinated.

It could have easily ended for me that day. Our platoon could have been rotated to patrol this very same spot, but another had turned up on a list of units on a clipboard on a desk back at the battalion.

The small and least expected fates seem always to lead to someone's demise, unknown but plotted with certainty like the city map and the address I now carried in my pocket.

So I remembered how the medic Anders, who is the same rank as me, though he's had his stripes twice as long, sips his hot coffee. My God, in this heat, but he's enjoying every last drop of one of the last cups he'll ever drink.

I squat and look up at the tree. A bead of gravity-defying sweat trickles sideways along the inside of my thigh.

The smoking PFC's tossed French cancer rocket lands with a sizzle in the wet elephant grass, which lays flattened into a stunning Ferris wheel shape formed by the medevac choppers that have been landing to take home the dead. Later, the corpses and any retrievable parts will be transferred to official transport bags kept in cardboard boxes stacked on skids unloaded from a cargo Chinook at brigade field headquarters.

Up in the tree there's a yellow flower growing out of the same branch, not six inches away from that thing: perhaps an orchid, its swollen pistil and curvy, bright pink stamen vaguely sexual. A lovely botanical still life.

One soldier who nobody recognizes, his field pants brand new like he just reported for duty from AIT school, says to take the thing down. But nobody moves and nobody takes it down.

I kept staring up at the tree until I was the only one left standing there, and when more Hueys started to gather overhead for the final trip back to base camp I heard my lieutenant yell, "Sarge, get your ass over here!"

The officer pointed at the two soldiers standing guard over the array of occupied body bags, which lay in tidy rows arranged apart from the churned-up mess where the fire fight had been. Away some distance from the tagged bags sat a mounded canvas tarp weighted at the corners by empty metal ammo cans.

"Go see what that's about," the lieutenant said. "I want those remains loaded in twenty minutes."

I strapped my M-16 smartly and walked with difficulty through the mud to where the guards were standing and then came back and told the lieutenant there were body parts under the tarp and nobody knew what to do with them, since they didn't match.

"I know there's parts. It's why I told you to go over there. How would those jokers know they don't match?" the Lieutenant said. "Tell them to get it loaded."

I walked over again and came back. "Nobody wants to pick the stuff up. It's sloppy, sir."

"Everything here is sloppy," the lieutenant said. "Tell those two Einsteins to put everything into a regulation bag."

I again walked over and came back.

"Sir, they said they need to talk to their squad leader and they want to wait until he gets back," I said. "He's up the trail on recon."

"What's he doing on recon?" the officer said. He looked at his wristwatch. "He's on recon. Jesus."

"That's what they told me, sir."

"Jesus."

The lieutenant took a cigarette from the zipped pocket of his shirt sleeve, clothing he must have gotten from a chopper jockey warrant officer because it sure wasn't an infantry issue poplin shirt, and he lit the thing with great ceremony and took a deep drag and angrily tossed the match at his feet and watched it burn for a while.

"Tell those sorry shits if they don't load those remains, and I mean pronto, they don't get on the evac chopper and they can squat out here all night. Tell them they'll be singing campfire songs in the woods with Charlie cong. Tell them I can't make it any clearer."

"Yes, sir." I said. I glanced at the two soldiers. They looked confused and both were smoking hard on their cigarettes. They stared at me and when the lieutenant looked at them they turned away.

One soldier was pumpkin-toothed, a spray of freckles across his sun-burned cheeks, and the other was fat with a flushed pink face and his shirt tail was untucked and they were both privates, probably on their first trip into the field. I tried to be polite. I was a brand new buck sergeant. I wasn't used to people listening to me. They straightened up when I walked over.

"The officer over yonder suggests you gentlemen can't board the returning aircraft unless you gather those particular remains and place everything properly into a regulation United States Army container."

"A bag," the big guy said.

"A bag, yeah."

Now pumpkin tooth spoke: "You see what's in there, sarge?" He lifted the edge of the tarp with the toe of his boot and flies buzzed out.

Under the wet edge of the tarp was the half-moon chunk of somebody's thigh with the trouser fabric burned away, the stained and torn boxer shorts showing, and below that something similar to a green sock and a row of canvas shoelace notches torn from a jungle boot. Heaped on top of that, a human face. Not the head, just what looked like a peeled-away kisser with a little costume wig, like a collapsed Halloween mask with a pug nose. The eyelids were closed, wrinkled and pinched together into a look of greatly anticipated concern. Everything else had bled out but for the dried black blood crusted in clumps everywhere and what I thought looked like the crumbled inside of a watermelon that had been chewed and spit out, red and wet and here and there plugs of more hair mixed with dirt and torn scalp and then the watery puddle of the soldier's viscera where everything had pooled in a shallow depression of mud beneath the center of the tarp. The guts were a string of deflated gray cylinders. There was more beneath the tarp, but I didn't want to look. More flies buzzed out.

I tried not to be obvious about covering my mouth so I pretended to wipe my chin with the heel of my hand, like I was thinking things over.

"Who put this here?" I said. "Under the tarp like this."

"Somebody else," pumpkin tooth said. "A guy from Alpha. But he got sick and walked off into the trees and barfed. I ain't seen him since."

The young soldier grinned and took a drag on his cigarette, his smile growing wider behind the white motionless smoke that hung around his face in the humid heat.

"Said they could Article Fifteen him and put him in jail, but he wouldn't do anything more with that stuff. Said what was the point? Said it could be two, three guys all mixed up together. Said there just wasn't a point to it."

I tried to take a quick breath without using my nose and took a few steps away from the tarp. The flies now followed me.

"Look. How's this for a point. Somebody has to move it," I said. "Use a shovel. You can't just leave this stuff here. It has to go back."

"Does it look like something you can just pick it up?" the fat kid said, looking over at his partner "Maybe in a bucket, but no way you can just pick it up."

"No way," pumpkin tooth said.

"Then get a goddamn bucket and pour the motherfucker in the bucket and then put the bucket in a regulation bag. It's got to be in a regulation bag, understand?" I said.

Pumpkin tooth crushed his smoke against a tree. "Is this a kind of order, sarge?"

"Yeah, it's an order, dickwad. My lieutenant has a stick up his ass today, and he's on the hunt for a captain's bars, so you have six minutes to put what's left of this poor soldier inside a proper bag and get him ready for the ride home with every other dead sonofabitch."

The two soldiers grinned at each other.

I said: "You guys know what an After Report is?"

"Yes, sir," Pumpkin Tooth said.

"You in the British navy?"

The two looked at each other.

"Then don't call me sir. I'm not a fuckin' officer," I said and held up my palm and made like I was writing something down with an invisible pen.

"There's the little checkbox on the After Report — and yeah, I'm the guy who has to write the report for this whole mindless mess we got here — and the report asks if I have any comments which might enlighten our glorious leaders back at headquarters. You know what I'm gonna' say?"

Pumpkin Tooth took a deep breath and looked up at the sky.

"I'm gonna' write down the names of two shithead grunts I met who didn't want to follow a simple order and thereby jeopardized the safe and timely evacuation of KIA from the battlefield. You'll be on permanent bush duty and the latrine shift for the rest of your tour in this stinkin' country."

I turned and walked off and heard the tarp rustle behind me, the two soldiers coughing and groaning, and when I was some distance away I could still smell it. The flies had mysteriously multiplied and I swatted them away. I gave the lieutenant a crisp salute and looked down at my muddy boots and didn't say a word and walked on. I took my place in line behind the others on the LZ they had cleared for the evac Hueys still circling above the tree tops.

On the far side of the clearing stood a row of grass huts and crooked livestock fences made from woven sticks and there were villagers gathered into small groups guarded by riflemen, one of whom stepped away and took out his Zippo lighter and walked casually up to the low-hanging thatched roof of one hut and set it on fire, waving the flame back and forth like an anointing priest at a religious ceremony. The women started wailing and flapping their arms and pointed at the smoking hut. The shack quickly burst into flames, a black cloud rising, and from one of the animal pens pigs squealed and a tiny old lady came stumbling out from the smoke pulling an ox by a rope.

I watched the lieutenant walk to where they were questioning a boy who had been dragged from one of the hooches.

The boy was squatting, his hands tied behind his back with bamboo twine. An old Master Sergeant, a grizzled lifer who I recognized from brigade, was yelling at him. Each time the sergeant shouted the Vietnamese ARVN translator spoke and walked up and slapped the boy and stepped back and waited for the sergeant to say something else. It continued like this, and the boy's nose was bleeding, his one eye swollen into a puffy slit, and he began to cry while the lieutenant watched calmly and wrote in a small notebook he'd pulled from his fancy aviator shirt pocket.

35

The boy's skinny legs were shaking and the front of his filthy torn pants were wet where he'd peed himself, and then the sergeant, apparently unsatisfied with the answer to one of his questions, kicked the boy. The lieutenant shouted something. Everybody stepped back and held a meeting, which was puzzling because the lieutenant had seemed to be in such a hurry to get out of there. They talked for a while, everybody nodding and shrugging, the old sergeant glaring over at the boy the whole time.

A stripe of blood flowed darkly across the boy's chin, and he was still crying. He swung his head around and looked at us and then at the three men who were still engaged in their little chat; the ARVN translator, the sergeant and the officer, who after a time seemed to agree on something and so each nodded and looked over once more at the boy, who had gathered himself together and wobbled to his feet unsteadily. The boy then screamed at the three men in a high pitched voice that was obviously some manner of terrible insult, because the translator hesitated before he carefully relayed to the sergeant what had been said.

The women who were squatting and watching their burning village shouted and shook their heads.

The boy turned and staggered toward the trees, stumbling back and forth because his hands were still bound, all the while shouting blood oaths over his shoulder.

The sergeant fired first, a short automatic burst with his M-16, and he missed. The lieutenant slowly withdrew his .45 from a holster rakishly slanted against his pistol belt, gunslinger-style, the handle forward-faced, and he fired and also missed, the round throwing up a chunk of spinning mud near the boy's running feet. The next shot hit home and the boy's head exploded into a dark plume that faded into a pink mist while his small body tumbled away loosely, as if all the bones were gone, and he came to rest against a pile of broken supply crates.

While we stood in line and watched the lieutenant shoot the boy we continued to talk about the PX at Da Nang and whether it was the best place to buy a stereo, the new model with four channels, and those big fancy speaker cabinets. We debated weight limits of what the army would ship home for free after your tour was finished.

The lieutenant holstered his pistol and motioned to take the boy's body away and we continued our conversation about wise retail shopping habits and how much a bag of weed cost at the old river wharf in Saigon and I agreed, yes...Bangkok and the Windsor Hotel with the strip bar in the basement was the best place to take your R&R. All the married guys, which meant officers, traveled to Hawaii. Sydney was too expensive and uppity, especially if you hung out at the King's Cross district.

Where the tagged bodies lay pumpkin tooth was picking something up with a long stick and sliding it carefully into a black bag, a tee shirt knotted around his mouth and nose.

Inside the chopper nobody spoke until I shouted a half hour later when we were about to land, my voice lost in the rotor vacuum of the Huey's open doors: "It was shitty to leave that thing hanging in the tree back there."

The medic Anders was counting out a package of ammonia inhalants and writing notes in his inventory book. One of his front shirt pockets was stuffed with rolls of camo gauze. His other bulging pocket overflowed with compresses and tubes of Petroline ointment. The Gitanes addict lit another one, the smoke blowing sideways from his face out the sliding bay doors of the chopper as he slowly replaced the cheek pockets of his gas mask with a clean set of white filters.

Nobody ever said another word about the stuff hanging in the tree or the boy or the burning village, though we did wonder out loud where the lieutenant had gotten his fancy aviator shirt.

I can recall every detail of those events instantly.

The next day Anders, Gillespie, the kid with the ridiculously new green fatigue pants, the lieutenant and the others in my squad would all be dead.

I had this same memory a dozen times during my trip over there. I tried to disassemble an M-16 in my head, imagining green tracer bullets flying a few inches past my face. The memory of tracer bullets lets me forget things for a while.

...make sure the weapon is unloaded and cleared. Call your doctor if you shoot yourself.

I finished my drink at the crummy little tent cafe and I kept walking.

CHAPTER 7

During my last visit with Dr. Nguyen I noticed the copy of *Huckleberry Finn* tucked into a row of thick medical reference books which stood between two carved jade tigers. The office smelled like pipe smoke.

"After your injury," he said, turning a page in his notebook. "You were discharged from the hospital in Japan."

"The crazy hospital."

"Actually, to treat your eye," he said, consulting his notes. "And the hepatitis."

"They tied me to the bed. They tie up crazy people."

"And this was after your first tour?"

"No, my second. I went nuts after my second tour."

Nguyen chewed hard on his pipe and wrote in his notebook. He looked at a loose page he'd pulled from a file folder.

He pointed at the sheet with his pipe. "You were there for three months. In Japan. Yokohama."

"No, I was in Busan, Korea for three months. I got hurt and got hepatitis from a bad blood transfusion. But that was in Busan. Not Japan. After they fixed my liver that's when I started acting goofy and they sent me to Kishini."

"I see," he said.

"No, I don't think you do," I said. "I've explained this to you people a dozen times and everybody asks me the same question. There's a lot going on with the scribbling notes and still it's the same questions. And I know what you're going to ask me now."

"And what is that?"

"Why did you volunteer for a second tour…is what you're going to ask me next. Am I right, doc?"

I pointed toward Nguyen's desk. "Forty years and you're using the same fucking folder. The same paper folder. Somebody around here could spend fifty cents and buy a new goddamn folder, what do you think?"

The doctor stared at me and said, "Well..."

I kept walking down Nguyen Hue Street where there were more yellow potted flowers left over from the Tet holiday. I watched two sunburned tourists stoop before a brightly lit shop window beneath the balcony of another old French building, its colorless stones so muted they seemed to fade into the evening sky. The woman wore a stretchy purple skirt. The man wore a floppy souvenir cap and he was thin and shorter than she, his tiny camera swinging like a purse from a delicate plastic shoulder strap.

Dr. Nguyen, the third shrink assigned to me in the last two years, during this last visit got annoyed when I used the phrase "cracked up" to describe my condition so I explained "cracked" was once a true middle English word signifying "crazy," and so I was within my rights. I reminded Dr. Shrinkenstein that I had every reason in the world to invent things — indeed entire worlds, in order to keep my brain busy so as to harmlessly negotiate each day. Kiss my ass, I thought. Children do this all the time.

I said to Nguyen: "I don't know how my wife put up with me for all those years. In the end, I guess I just wore her out."

I walked.

A lovely young girl dressed in a white Ao Dai sat on a stool beneath an umbrella and played a bamboo flute while people in fancy evening clothes stepped carefully into a lacquered black boat moored at the end of the pier.

From a man behind a wheeled trundle cart that smelled sweetly of apricots I bought ban trang, spring rolls in rice paper. I walked to where the pier ended and leaned over my elbows to study the moonless water while I thought again about the past few weeks.

Just a bunch of old men riding in a bus.

I walked and thought about the kitchen back home in Bull River Falls.

I'd taken the twenty-foot length of rope from its package. I closed the drape on the window. I studied the ceiling light fixture, staring up from where I'd dragged the chair to the middle of the room. How much weight would it hold? Would there be enough space for the arc of my swing? A bowline knot might not slip and tighten. I fastened a clove hitch to the brace behind the light and put my weight on the nylon boat rope and swung, my feet lifting off the linoleum floor as I carefully rehearsed my own oblivion. I stared at the hanging rope and tied two half hitches before I changed my mind and tripled a slip knot into a noose. I was surprised how easy it was to decide to finally make the noose. I sat in the chair and proudly nodded at my feet. I drank a beer and put the rope around my neck. A half-inch, double-braid nylon dock line.

I remember swinging for the longest time, my face icy and numb like it didn't belong to me anymore. And then my head was pounding like I'd been whacked from behind and I was flat on my back staring up at the plastic fluorescent ceiling fixture, the noose biting into my throat. The broken rope swung from the ceiling.

I looked down at my chest. The frayed end of the rope was as wet as if it had been dipped in spit.

In Saigon, I kept walking.

The pill wasn't working fast enough. I felt the familiar smothering cloak embrace my shoulders, a sense of helpless and immobile futility. I wanted to flick a switch and vanish. Erase myself. Nothing dramatic, no letters left behind, no noise or mess somebody had to clean up. Nothing that could invite a discussion afterwards. Of course there's always a mess, always a discussion. If I did it here they'd have to ship me home, which would be a lot of trouble. But it would be so easy to do, and I'd been thinking about it from the moment I stepped off the plane.

I walked back into the city in the warm rain until I could no longer smell the river. I looked at the map.

I was now in a crummy neighborhood on a street lined with corrugated metal roofs patched with plywood and weighted with stones. Scrawny chickens cackled from wired cages. Twisting alleyways cluttered with trash and so pinched and narrow you'd have to walk sideways to get anywhere. There was construction equipment parked behind flashing barricades and orange work cones that announced the future of another building they were ready to tear down. The entire street was prepared for demolition. Most of the old homes were attached in long rows, only a few of them occupied. An illuminated billboard explained in English the coming of a grand hotel and stylish shops that would, as the taxi driver had explained, soon replace the old wharf.

From my wallet I unfolded the envelope and looked at the photo wrapped in tissue paper that I'd kept all these years. I studied the address and ducked under an enormous beveled wooden beam that might have once held an entry gate and found myself in an empty courtyard where walls were lined with identical window shutters, each with its address inscribed onto a clay tile.

My number was up there, on the far right.

The broken structure was from another age, with its ornate pagoda roof decorated with terra cotta figurines of birds and snarling tigers. Flourishes of writing covered one plaster wall beneath dragon drawings and images of robed warriors with chin whiskers holding broadswords and old powder muskets as they fought in an ancient battle. The frescoed chronicle was gouged in places like a museum artifact, whole heads and shoulders missing from its characters, another wall collapsed into rubble someone had already tried to sweep into a neat pile. It all had the odor of sweat and woodsmoke and nesting animals.

I stepped inside. Blistered varnished walls glowed in the pale light. A tipped round-cornered refrigerator lay on the floor, something rotten and clotted spilling from its blackened open door. A dirty porcelain sink spidered with cracks. The warped roof was splintered and tipped as if a heavy beast had sat on this house whose former occupant had led me here.

Bowed rib bones the size of drinking straws stood half-buried in the dirt floor; a bird perhaps, the wet feathers pressed into the mud. Scattered kitchen tools lay rusted next to perfectly white and unbroken dinner plates that seemed incandescent in their shadows.

How much absolute sorrow had soaked into these walls over all these years? Everything I saw was the remnant of a hastily abandoned life.

I took out the small photo, a black and white with the scalloped edges of an old fashion snapshot taken with forethought, the two subjects stiffly posed and uneasy as if they'd just seen their first camera. The woman was tiny, an elf in sandals and a shapeless skirt; the infant in her arms staring blankly with enormous dark eyes at something off to the side.

I had killed her husband long ago under a moon so bright I could count the buttons on his baggy black shirt.

I returned the photo I had kept all these years into the envelope and leaned it on an empty shelf where it might have sat in an ordinary and better time. It was the best I could do. After all this time, it was all I could do. Soon this house and the accumulated memories of those who had lived and died here would be scraped away and forgotten.

In another tiny room a toilet broken in half lay in a pool of water, the cracked commode walls blotched with a startling fan of bright green mold rising from a gaping floor pipe. Filthy seepage everywhere. A foot-high dike of petrified sewage blocked the doorway.

I covered my mouth and turned and stepped outside. There was nothing more to see. This ridiculously sentimental notion — to go to this house and return the photo as a final, clumsy call for forgiveness — it had led me nowhere.

I walked.

In another alley a man knelt before a tiny alcove where candles flickered, casting his giant stooped shadow against a broken cement wall which should have fallen down long ago in this abandoned world filled with abandoned things.

The man heard me approach and looked up briefly without surprise and returned to his task at the small altar where burning incense sticks stood in a bowl of sand, a shrine of some sort. The delicate and beautiful flowers in their fluted porcelain cups were yellow, the color of the Buddha. The man took one upright stick between his pressed hands and bowed twice, once as a blessing for the dead and once for those who were not. Who was he trying to say farewell to?

I walked on with my aching knees and wondered how it would be nice to have two lives to live, one for practice and the next to finally get things right. Seems we'd all do a lot less damage to each other if it were so.

CHAPTER 8

During the flight home, years after I quite smoking, I decided to have a cigarette in the airplane restroom.

High above the Pacific, after the pilot encouraged us to look out the window as the aircraft took a right turn above Tokyo, I stood balanced on one leg on a stainless steel toilet seat with my face inches from the ceiling and tried to carefully direct the exhaled smoke toward a ventilation fan. After a few practice puffs I got cocky and exhaled a ring that *please, please no...* suddenly floated too far beyond the vent, where the foggy wisp broke apart and curled itself around a tiny red ceiling smoke detector.

The lights blinked. The alarm shrieked like a police siren and a flight attendant started pounding on the door.

After being told I'd committed a federal crime I was escorted to my seat and told to stay there until we landed in Hawaii for the connecting flight. Hours later I tried to apologize to one of the crew on the way out, but she gave me an icy look and then smiled warmly at the passenger behind me.

I hardly got any work done when I came home to Bull River Falls. Another returned letter I had addressed to the house on So Loi Street sat on top of a waiting pile of mail.

Even with those snacks they fed us on the bus and the giant hotel buffets, I still lost weight.

I was cleaning things up and sorting through paperwork when I found the photo album.

I picked it up carefully like it was a hot pan. How the album had migrated to the closet is still a mystery, though I remember packing it away after I sold the house and moved things to the trailer here in town.

My old uniform hung in the closet on a nail behind a row of military field shirts and a green laundry bag stuffed with orphaned Army things I'd never unpacked. The brass buttons on the green Class-A jacket were sticky; my combat infantry badge, dulled and bent like a cheap fork, dangled loose on a single pin and behind it a faded yellow rope braid hung from a torn shoulder lapel. Below that my name on a plastic pocket badge, the letters crowded together: *Przewalski*

Three rows of skewed ribbons had slid halfway into the unbuttoned left breast pocket like they'd had a mind to hide themselves from view. I didn't remember what any of the gaudy yellow and red and striped green and blue rectangles signified anymore. I'm sure some awful manner of pointless, grim death was involved.

The last time I'd worn the jacket was on the chartered TWA flight home from Vietnam. It was 2 a.m. when we landed in Seattle. The protesters were leaning against the passenger lounge window, their signs bobbing up and down as we approached the gate. Me and two guys from the same battalion were walking into the terminal when one of the demonstrators runs up and starts shouting about how does it feel to kill babies and women?

It didn't take much in those days to flick my switch so I snatched the sign and tore it in half and tossed it back at this pimpled kid with spaghetti arms, thinking he must be nuts to want to mess with somebody like me. The tops of my ears got hot and I was getting ready to take things to the next level when my two buddies grabbed the back of my shirt and dragged me away. The three of us headed to the men's room and changed into our civies.

I swallowed my pill and looked at the album.

The pictures were mostly poorly exposed Polaroids and scratched snapshots taken with a Pentax I'd bought at the Tan San Nhut PX. One photo showed me dressed in this very same green jacket wearing an idiot's grin, an empty champagne glass in my hand as I stood in a room lit by fancy table lamps and filled with people dressed in dark suits and cocktail dresses.

I'd already been out of the hospital for a few weeks when they flew me back to Saigon with orders to show up at the Rex Hotel, where the army brass used to get drunk up on the snobby rooftop bar they had. That night they read the citation in the lobby at a reception attended by Vietnamese government bureaucrats, embassy people and MACV brass. People kept coming up to slap my back, saying "let's see, let's see..." A *Stars and Stripes* reporter took my picture.

"What's this with the 'let's see' thing?" I asked a second lieutenant from the division Public Information Office who'd been assigned to be my chaperon.

"What do they want to see?"

"They want to see you, sarge" he said, smiling as he grabbed food from a passing hors d'oeuvre tray. A few people gathered around and grinned like I was a child who had just uttered something precious.

"Liet sy," the lieutenant said, pronouncing the phrase slowly. "The Vietnamese word for hero. You're the hero of the night. The hero of the night. Enjoy it."

The photo album's drab canvas cover was decorated with a stenciled collage of battalion and brigade insignia encircling the division's four-leaf clover logo. In the badly focused photo on the first page I wore a tan flak vest, which looked flimsy and useless, nothing like the fancy Kevlar body armor soldiers wear now. Nobody ever wore a flak jacket out in the field. When I see such luxurious stuff now on a soldier on TV I get jealous.

My helmet was cocked rakishly, a pack of smokes and a squirt bottle of M-16 lubricant tucked into the dirty camo cover. A feathery mustache showed like a shadow on my lip. An M-60 hung at my side, its bulk tugging down my shoulder. I must have been playing dress-up day because nobody ever stood around at base camp wearing all that gear.

Behind me in the photo stood a Quonset wall dented by mortar shrapnel, the unit's skewed logo painted above a canvas doorway flap. The squat, corrugated structure was encircled by sandbag corner pillars that leaned crookedly like parapets on a child's sand castle.

In the photo other soldiers loitered nearby, each frozen in a moment of youthful clowning. I remembered some by their nicknames, which is what you called each other then: Bozo, Cool Hand Luke, Froggy, Maggot, Hooch Humper, Mexican Joe, Snoopy and Super Kraut. Polack and Dago Dave and on and on. Pappy, the Greek kid whose real name was Minos Pappas, had his middle finger raised at the photographer, a guy from UPI who had been doing a story on our platoon. Pappas, who wore a thick, brushy mustache and sideburns whose illegal reach below the earlobe always got him in trouble, had two bandoleers of .60 cal. rounds stretched across his chest like a macho Pancho Villa character, even though he was a radio operator and would never rig himself up in such a way. He likely hadn't fired a sixty since infantry school. But we all carried an abundance of improbable and unauthorized weaponry as we monkeyed around for the reporter's camera, hoping one of the shots would turn up in our hometown newspaper.

One shirtless PFC whose name I couldn't remember, dog tags hanging across his bare chest wrapped in black electrical tape, slouched casually against one wall of the sandbag fortress in a rebellious James Dean pose...squinting, detached, his thoughts elsewhere. Cigarette smoke drifted across his face. His floppy field cap was covered with chalk-drawn scribbles.

Enough of this bullshit, I thought. I was chilled, like something had touched me from behind, and so I shoved the album and everything else back into the closet.

I flopped onto the old army cot I kept at the office and felt a sudden rush of unexplained adrenaline. After all these years the nightmares were more real than ever, violent head movies in which the long-dead taunted me. Those little flickers of light were firing off at the corner of my eye again.

I'd lost count of how many pills I'd swallowed, which usually means trouble. I hadn't slept the night before. Or the night before. I couldn't stop thinking of our big air-conditioned bus rocking past those rice paddies, where ghosts rose from the dirt and stood in their torn and bloody uniforms to point their fingers at me.

I was now more than three times older than Pappas was when he died, and that's what I was thinking when the phone rang.

"Budget meeting with the feds was today, did we forget?"

It was Gus Curry, from the Bull River Falls fire department. I was supposed to cover a Bureau of Land Management meeting for a story I was doing on yet another wildfire that had started south of town not far from the new resort.

There was also the matter of the body they'd found by the river. My intern had faxed the details to me at the hotel in Vietnam and I had already roughed out my front page story during the flight home.

I'd known Curry since we worked as young summer smoke jumpers in Idaho, not long after I got out of the army. It was Curry who told me years before about the weekly newspaper in the mountains that was up for auction in bankruptcy court. A lost cattle town in the high Rockies, he said, located in the Sawatch Range, where they were starting to build ski areas and where he had landed a full-time job as a firefighter. The prettiest place you ever saw, he told me at the time, where a man could figure things out on his own and put the past behind him.

"I did not," I said. "I worked a twelve-hour stretch yesterday at the paper. Things got backed up while I was gone. Taking that trip wasn't a smart thing to do."

"Yeah, nice timing," Curry said with some annoyance in his voice. "The paper looked like shit while you were away. Just so you know. Anyway, I took notes for you. I'll drop off the meeting minutes on my way to the airport. Thing is getting bigger. They're positive a pyro started the fire. They brought in two more jump crews yesterday. You sure you don't want to join the party? The Feds are looking for experienced contractors. You could run one of the crews. I'm short-handed."

"My knees are shot, Gus," I said. "I couldn't keep up with those kids."

"You could work at the command center. My boys could use an old geezer's guiding hand. Think about it."

"I just did," I said. "I'm not sticking pins into a wall map all day. Sorry."

"Just keep it in mind," Curry said.

"Hey, you know what I was thinking today?"

"Are we changing the subject?"

"The feather and heels dancer from Vegas you married."

"My ex," Curry said. "You were thinking about my ex?"

"Yeah, those leopard leotards she wore to the Chamber of Commerce banquet."

"Why would you remember that?"

"Must have seen spots somewhere, I don't know," I said. "You're not insulted, are you?"

"What?"

"Me thinking about your ex."

"Haven't seen the woman in ten years," Curry said. "Why would I give a shit?"

"Good. Anyway, I thought I'd tell you."

"You're very thoughtful. A weird-ass dick, but thoughtful. Why would you dredge up stuff like that?" Curry said.

"Can't control what you remember," I said.

There was a long silence and Curry laughed and rattled off containment statistics for the fire. The blaze had started as a suspected dry lightning strike just north of the McCoy ranch near town and then grown inexplicably to several hundred acres. The fire crews had determined it had flashed up simultaneously in three locations, all within a 24-hour period, a sign that things weren't quite right.

"No worries, just remember my offer. The BLM pays top dollar. Besides, I got a bad feeling about this thing. If I'm right, we'll need all the experienced help we can get," Curry said.

Curry's voice faded away while he had a brief side conversation with somebody at the fire station and then he shouted instructions about getting another slurry aircraft scheduled for a suppressant drop that afternoon.

"Stan, I've got a little shit storm over here. It's flared up again south of town. I'll drop the BLM report off at your place. Give me your two cents after you read it. I'm not getting a warm and fuzzy sensation at all. Lots of unexplained bullshit, if you ask me. Think about what I told you. I could use the extra hand."

Curry laughed. "Welcome back, Stan. You're the only asshole I know who flies nine thousand miles to visit a place for only three days."

CHAPTER 9

I met the gopher while driving home at night from Ben Archer's ranch up on McGregor Gulch.

I was covering a story about a dead cow Ben had found in his barn. The cow's throat had been slit.

Ben said Martians had done it, and could I come over quick before he burned the carcass? I still had a big front page news hole to fill and my only part-time summer employee, a teenager named Tuesday, had called in sick.

The dead heifer lay on its side. There was a long red wound where the animal's tongue and windpipe had been removed, along with a strip of hide that ran from jaw to shoulder, all without spilling a drop of blood. Ben jabbered about spacemen and the coming wrath of God and reminded me how there also wasn't the trace of a human footstep on the muddy ground inside that barn.

I ran a picture of the victim on the front page of the newspaper with the headline:

RANCHER CLAIMS COW BUTCHERS
CAME FROM THE RED PLANET

Driving back to the office in the rain that night I saw prairie dogs running back and forth across the old state highway. These things never look both ways before they cross a street.

One of the rats leaped up from the side of the dark road. I swerved, but must have nicked the creature with my fender because suddenly this thing that looks like a flying brown sock is twirling through the air and it flips end-over-end and lands on my windshield. The prairie dog's face remained pressed against the glass and when I tried to straighten out the truck I see the little stinker is holding on to the wiper as it goes back and forth, hanging there with its tongue out, gripping for dear life, those tiny toothpick claws embedded into the rubber blade.

I skidded to a stop and removed the rodent and for reasons I'll never understand I took him home and placed him on the kitchen counter and covered him with a towel. The animal was in shock. It kept staring at me and blinking.

And then its mouth started moving like it wanted to speak.

Exhaustion often brought on the very worst of my symptoms, a fever-addled weirdness that allowed me to convince myself all was normal when it certainly was not.

And so, for no special reason, I said: "Hang on Sloopy. You'll be okay," and I poked the prairie dog's tummy with my finger. The rat blinks his raisin eyes again and now he's staring straight up at where the length of busted rope was still hanging from my kitchen ceiling. He had a knowing smile on his face.

And then he spoke.

"Nineteen sixty-five, *The Strangeloves*. Number one song on the charts that year," he said in a helium induced voice. "They beat out the *Dave Clark Five*."

Well.

I allowed myself to go along for the ride.

That's when I first learned that this gopher likes to show off his knowledge of obscure rock and roll facts. And he also likes to speak in rock and roll lyrics. I'd like to say I was shocked when it started talking, but in my sleepless and medicated state nothing surprised me, so I took things as they came. My little blue pill is a big equalizer: nothing is important, yet everything is terribly important.

"I want to hold your hand," the gopher sang, shaking off the towel.

And I answered, "Maybe next time."

I noticed his clothes. The black military beret. His neatly creased camo field pants and the old-school leather paratrooper boots, the kind the 82nd Airborne Division used to wear. He had a vertical weave pistol belt. A tiny field knife and a .45 pistol hung from his hip. Two itty bitty smoke grenades were clipped to his left pocket, above which was neatly stitched the word: Chaz

By now it was very late. I carried the rodent into the darkroom and carefully set him down on a light table used to wax newspaper layout flats. This is the way we do it around here: no computer, no fax machine (I use the one at the library), a rotary dial telephone, an Underwood typewriter and a 3,000-pound Linotype machine built in 1922.

That's when he began to relate his extraordinary story. Was I hearing this? I truly hoped I was.

Chaz told me he had spent the day meticulously organizing his collection of *Peter, Paul & Mary* albums. I told him I once drew a mustache once with a Sharpie on a photo of Mary Travers' face and gave Peter a long ZZ Top beard and Chaz threw a fit and with his tiny pistol he shot me several times, leaving scarlet welts like bee stings on my ankle.

I apologized and Chaz explained breathlessly that he and his clan hold the formerly famous folk music trio in high regard — almost religious regard, much like the Rastafarians who believe the former Ethiopian emperor, Haile Selassie, was divine. I don't know much more about that story except I know the Rastas seem happy and content and wear their hair in long plant-like knots and smoke reefers the size of cigars. Chaz, however, doesn't smoke or drink, but has an addictive fondness for Zinnia seeds and wheat grass. I tried not to ask too many questions because I still wasn't sure this wasn't Dr. Nguyen's goddamn pills talking.

I checked my wall clock, which was melting, and looked through the front door to where I could see the lights on Main Street. I looked at the rodent, his little hairy ass bathed in the fluorescent backlit glow of the light table, which I had turned on because I thought it might give this poor animal some heat.

Chaz kept yapping and said he had also spent part of the day repairing a damaged cassette tape of the *Greatest Byrds Hits*, a personal favorite of his. He also likes *Smashing Pumpkins*, who I'm told is not a famous band anymore, though Chaz has a vast collection of their tee shirts. You won't see too many gophers who wear rock and roll tee shirts that say *Quiet Riot*. Or wear a black military beret. And there's the Uzi machine gun, though he also likes the AK-47, the world's leading weapon of revolt.

Chaz's vast army of loyal soldiers, he explained, are usually dressed in crisp military camo shirts and trousers bloused into shiny paratrooper boots and they drive tanks the size of bread toasters. They look like they just graduated from jump school at Ft. Benning, he said. And they tool around in Hummers the size of shoe boxes. But more about that later, along with an explanation of how those improbable vehicles get that way.

I learned that Chaz himself was once in a rock band whose specialty was five-part harmony. Like the *Byrds*. He played bass guitar and the tenor sax, and when he performed John Coltrane's music he pulled his head fur back into a weenie man bun that made him resemble a celebrity TV chef on one of those cooking shows where people break into tears when their carbonara sauce doesn't turn out just right.

I do believe I saw a cow that had been dissected by skilled surgeons from outer space and that I've had deep conversations with a gopher who owns a semi-automatic weapon.

I do, indeed.

Nobody seems to know how old Chaz is. Gophers — black tailed prairie dogs, live about eight years, but I've talked to other rodents in the Upper Bellyache Mountain coterie that dwells just south of Bull River Falls who say they've heard stories about Chaz from their grandparents, who also heard stories from their grandparents, and on and on.

Chaz could be a hundred years old, though he looks freakishly buff for an ancient rat. He could be like one of those ageless and troubled teenage vampires in the movie where everybody is attractively pale and has unbelievably straight white teeth. It looks very appealing to be a young vampire in love.

If you ask Chaz about his age he gets shy and nervous and does what most gophers do when they are uncomfortable in a clumsy social situation: they shit uncontrollably. The stuff pops out like it's being ejected from a Pez candy dispenser.

On that rainy night, apparently under duress because of my constant questioning, Chaz nervously took a giant poop right in front of me, and while I was sweeping up the pebbly milk duds he apologized and started getting agitated until I told him to calm down before he became incontinent again, and so he climbed up on my desk and washed his face in my cup of cold coffee, which I had hurriedly abandoned earlier to take the phone call from the guy with the surgically molested cow from Mars.

It was getting late and I still had newspaper work to finish. I made more coffee to stay awake and told Chaz to keep his distance, but I have since learned you can't teach these rats anything. They don't have manners. They're more civilized than us in many ways, but you have to always understand they are armed and dangerous. When I'm with Chaz I try to remember the guy who attempted to raise a four-hundred-pound Bengal tiger in his studio apartment in Brooklyn. It ended badly.

A failed hanging. My badly advised return to Vietnam. The Martian cow. A killer loose in town and a raging wildfire. And now a talking gopher, all in the same strange summer.

Well.

CHAPTER 10

When it seemed Chaz had recovered from his face dive into the windshield of my pickup truck, I carried him to a back room of the trailer, where I watch baseball games on TV and live in purposeful squalor. I have enough potato chips, bean dip and beer in my tiny space to live undisturbed for at least six months. Maybe a year, if I ration the beef jerky and peanuts.

There's nothing fancy there, just a small bed and a crippled faux leather recliner that I bought at the Lions Club annual yard sale. I like to drape a mosquito net over the bed, not because there are many mosquitoes here at 6,500 ft. above sea level, but because it seems to calm me down. The thing somehow evokes an imaginary tropical, bathroom dampness I find comforting.

I eat out an awful lot, mostly at the Grill & Griddle Cafe on Main Street. This is where I remind you again that I'm not married anymore, though I've had a few dinners with the county coroner, Carmen Ruiz. This brief social fire thankfully never ignited and we are now just good friends and operate under a sort of romantic truce. I don't know what I was thinking, and apparently neither did she.

Human companionship is the last thing on my mind these days.

I put the rat down on the folding ping pong table where I once built a scale model of the battle of Dien Bien Phu, which at this time of the month was also where I stacked my laundry. I shoved aside a pile of boxer shorts. Chaz casually made himself at home and sat on a box of detergent, draped a white tube sock over his lap, and let out a long sigh and said, in a plummy British accent: "It's been a hard day's night."

Chaz studied the little toy lead soldiers: the painted figurine of General Vo Nguyen Giap directing his troops from the top of a twelve-inch-high mountain made of paper mâché and hobby moss, pointing across the table at his French rival, Henri Navarre. There were carefully affixed labels for all of this, the battlefield built to scale, the three Vietnamese divisions positioned on cardboard hills surrounding a valley exactly eleven miles long and three miles wide. An undershirt lay draped over a row of artillery bunkers and a bottle of fabric softener sat blocking any approaching aircraft that might want to land on the four-foot-long airfield.

Chaz, apparently unimpressed by my exhibit, blinked and explained how his whole clan was being chased up into the mountains because of all the real estate development around town, namely the evil golf and ski resort they were building. He spoke gravely of how his people lived in caves at the old gold mining camp south of here, where there had long been a ghost town filled with crumbling shacks and dangerous mine shafts. He confirmed, with a smile, how he'd been responsible for the damage done recently at the new golf course. Gophers, of course, hate golf courses and believe they are Satan's work. He described how he and a few dozen of his little rodent commandos had also been responsible for the mayhem done at the Town Hall recently, where the police discovered chewed up computers and a big hole in the wall where the animals had broken through and destroyed thousands of official government files, one of which I hoped was one of my speeding tickets from Tom Cherry.

"I suppose you can read?" I asked.

Chaz looked at me with the expression of a two-year-old toddler who has been asked to explain the contribution of Niels Bohr to the world of quantum mechanics and its relationship to Einstein's theory of...you know, the E and the square M thing that floats across the screen during Twilight Zone reruns.

"Of course not," he said, genuinely shocked. "But I'm trying."

Now I had him: "Then how did you learn to talk?"

"TV," Chaz said.

I pointed to the nickel plated .45 cal. weapon holstered to his belt. It sagged heavily, like a power drill strapped to a child.

"And I suppose you purchased this in a gopher gun store?"

"Sort of," he said. "But we could have. Money is not a problem for us. And we like to shop."

"So you're rich," I said. "You're a talking, violent and wealthy tee-shirt wearing gopher who enjoys rock music and has his own army."

He let out that long sigh again, which sounded like a squeaky bicycle wheel. He seemed annoyed with me.

"Well, we live up at the old gold mine and we do know how to dig, so what do you think?

I waved my hand and told him to continue. I had nothing else to do. It was late and I sometimes don't go to bed on Wednesday deadline night at the newspaper, and I figured even if I was dreaming or swaddled in a drug stupor I might as well enjoy the ride.

For all I knew, my prescription head pills from the VA were acting up again. But that's another story. There's much I must talk about later because I just can't remember anything in a straight line anymore.

When I woke in the morning I could smell somebody making coffee. Next to me lay the kitchen towel with which I had comforted Chaz, still wet, one corner stained with a bloody tuft of apricot colored fur. The little jackass had left me a gift on the floor.

Tuesday was already at work and she called through the door and asked if everything was all right.

"I'll be out in a minute," I said in a fake-cheery voice that wouldn't fool anybody. I looked around for a broom. The place smelled like pet food.

"The old lady from the ranch kept coming by while you were gone," Tuesday said. "I told her you were on vacation. She got all mad and said there was too much important stuff happening here for you be on vacation. Said she had a story for the paper."

"Old Dora is mad at the whole world these days. She always has a story for the paper. I'll give her a call."

"She looked crazy," Tuesday said. "Her arm was messed up. She smelled bad."

I opened the window. Smoke from the wildfire was drifting down Main Street and from the direction of the airport I heard sirens wailing. Two older Huey helicopters, relics still used for training at the Air National Guard Center, made a low rumbling pass over the town, their rotor noise once again awakening unwanted memories.

CHAPTER 11

Around lunch, though I should have been catching up on work, I fell asleep at my desk while reading a book about the explorer Meriwether Lewis, who killed himself at the age of 35. When he heard of his friend's death at a remote Tennessee roadhouse in 1809, Thomas Jefferson said, "I fear the weight of his mind has overcome him."

"Having understood that the village of those small dogs was at a short distance from our camp, Captain Lewis and Captain Clarke with all the party, except the guard, went to it; and took with them all the kettles and other vessels for holding water; in order to drive the animals out of their holes by pouring in water; but though they worked at the business till night they only caught one of them."

SERGEANT PATRICK GASS
Lewis & Clark Expedition, Journal entry
September 7, 1804, in present-day Boyd County, Nebraska

Gass, who lived long enough to vote for 18 presidents, from Washington to Grant, was forcibly removed from an army recruiting station when he tried to re-enlist to fight in the Civil War when he was 91 years old. He died in 1870, age 98, the last surviving member of the Lewis & Clark Expedition.

It was Gass, a carpenter, who built the box used to ship the prairie dog captured that day in Nebraska to Jefferson, who kept the animal as a pet.

With the edge of the open book creasing my face, I woke up angry from a dream in which there was a gopher who was dressed like a doorman at a fancy hotel. The rat handed me an engraved wedding invitation that was expensively letterpress-printed on a heavy prehistoric Kluge press with lead type, the machine I had in the shop. And then everything fell Alice-ass-first into the rodent hole.

In this dream, which was sprinkled with flickering images of poor Meriwether Lewis romping across the prairie in his buckskins, a furry Shriner with a tail wore a turban, knee britches and carried a curved sword in a gold scabbard.

The catered wedding luncheon was wonderful. The Chaz in the dream wore a beret and black yoga pants. He winked creepily at me and spoke French, which I understood perfectly. During the meal the gopher guests tapped gold spoons against their Baccarat crystal champagne glasses, hoping to spur kisses between the bride and the groom. The love rats obliged again and again by clicking their big yellow teeth together. The bride was dressed in a black bra and a garter rigged with blinking LED Christmas lights, her plunging neckline revealing one of six raisin nipples.

The wedding had a Las Vegas Mario Puzo theme.

On a big buffet table there was a whole Venice cityscape carved from ice, canals and gondolas, and a miniature replica of the Plaza San Marco made from spun sugar. Somebody released a flock of white doves and the local birds of prey began dive-bombing the gophers, which prompted the armed Shriner bodyguard to start shooting.

The father of the gopher bride was dressed like Don Corleone, his hair lacquered. Gopher musicians in tuxedos played Duke Ellington music while a particularly tall rodent crooner in a bow tie who looked like Vic Damone sang Italian love songs.

When the gopher bride danced with her father everybody tossed yellow flower petals, while outside on a driveway crowded with expensive cars I watched grim FBI agents take photos of license plates. Important looking Gophers in fedoras and pin-striped, shoulder-padded zoot suits stood guard to keep out the reporters, while helicopters filled with gopher TV camera crews tried to buzz the wedding but the security force brought them down with shoulder mounted Stinger missiles and a thunderous barrage of coordinated mortar fire.

Everybody clanked their champagne glasses while the newlyweds clicked together their enormous buck teeth and licked each other's faces like a pair of kissing brown socks.

The father gopher presented the bride and groom with matching Hummers, a briefcase filled with cash and nice household Ikea furnishings.

When the minister or vicar or priest or gopher shaman…anyway, somebody in a tie dyed *Grateful Dead* tee shirt, commenced to join the love rodents in holy ratrimony there arose a sudden clatter as the guests jumped from their seats, knocking over two Elvis impersonators who'd been taking samples of frosting from the wedding cake with their thumbs.

The shovel of a backhoe appeared through a tear in the white canvas wedding tent, lifting with it a dozen gophers who hung on for dear life as the vehicle plowed through the frightened crowd. There was screaming. The bride tripped on her gown and stumbled backwards into a crystal punch bowl shaped like the Roman coliseum.

Something hit my head, and I blacked out. I think I was struck by a little missile.

After the gopher wedding they took me to the doctor and gave me an oversized version of the pretty blue pills I've been getting from the VA. When I brought them to my mouth they turned into enormous communion wafers as big as my palm, like holy tortillas. And then they sent me for an x-ray. But the machine at the clinic was broken, so they drove me to the veterinarian's office on Main Street.

There I sat between a Doberman pinscher with prostate problems and a Sharpei who had the flu and whose face wrinkles looked like isobars on a weather map. The Sharpei kept coughing on me. The Doberman was reading a fashion magazine.

The vet walked in carrying his clipboard and called my name, and I stood.

"Sit!" he said like he was, of course, talking to a dog.

And I obediently sat and looked up. I explained I was there for an x-ray. The vet took out the thermometer from his shirt pocket and he shook it.

"Lets take your temperature."

I opened my mouth, but the vet gave a sly smile.

"That's not the way we do things around here."

I turned and bent over.

That's when I woke up with the book in my face.

I heard the sound of the garbage truck doing its weekly pickup from my newsprint recycling bins outside the back of the trailer. I heard loud music and a pounding bass riff that sounded a lot like Geddy Lee from *Rush* doing a funky bass groove on the song about Tom Sawyer.

When I reached across the rolltop desk for my coffee cup Chaz was sitting there, a wise-ass smile on his furry face, his clawed feet tapping in time to the music. He winked at me and started singing.

"No, his mind is not for rent..."

"Enough." I said.

"To any god or government..."

"Okay, stop. I just woke up," I said.

Chaz spoke the final lyrics to the song slowly, like a melancholy balladeer, which I also found annoying.

He said: "Always hopeful, yet discontent."

"How did you get in here?" I said.

The Gopher King shrugged and picked up one foot and rubbed his calf. He was dressed in full military field gear — the bloused paratrooper boots, vertical weave pistol belt with two Ruger pistols and a smoke grenade clipped to one strap of his rucksack webbing.

"Thanks for saving my ass last night," he said. "I'd like to return the favor."

CHAPTER 12

In the bathroom I affixed a medicated happy patch to my bare chest, another anxiety drug from the VA clinic.

The police scanner chattered as a dispatcher announced the wildfire was burning at yet another location up at the old ghost town. Somebody explained that another blaze was headed toward the new ski resort, which had been shut down by the feds because of Native American burial relics discovered at the construction site.

It was my last patch from a box of expired sales samples. I ticked off the inventory of remaining pills lined up on the sink counter: low dosage Valium, Xanax. B-12 capsules. A large bottle of those blue-and-orchid oval tablets that were almost too lovely to swallow. My chest thumped, like my heart had dropped too low behind my ribs; as if it were walking around on its own feet. My head pounded.

I thought about Meriwether Lewis, the 10-inch barrel of a U.S. Army flintlock action pistol pressed against his chest, his thumb clumsily hooked forward through the beautifully designed round trigger guard as he turned the weapon toward himself. There would have been the dull click of the cock lever and a brief, blinding powder flash that sent the .54 caliber lead ball through his young heart.

The weight of his mind, Jefferson had said.

I stepped outside. Black asphalt on Main Street shimmered brightly in the heat.

I saw my dead parents.

They were walking hand in hand, much younger than I ever remembered them. My mother turned, her dark hair lifting in a soft breeze as she smiled sweetly over her shoulder and raised her hand in a lazy wave, as if this were just another day. They both strolled on, unhurried. My father never turned. My heart ached as I realized I couldn't remember what their voices had sounded like.

The rodent poked his head out of a hole near the front steps of the trailer. Like I've said, this is also the home of the *Bull River Falls Beacon-News*, which I believe was founded in the 1800s by gold miners or drunkards, I'm not sure which. It's not much of a newspaper, 32 pages each issue if I'm lucky. I get by.

Chaz was wearing ear buds connected to an iPod fastened to his arm with Velcro. He had on a *Jefferson Starship* tee shirt that was torn precisely across Grace Slick's open mouth so the singer looked like she was screaming at me. He wore his black beret with the People's Gopher Army logo on it. At the edge of his burrow, one of hundreds he maintains around town for security purposes, he sat crossed-legged and started cleaning his M-16 rifle, looking at me with that buck-toothed smile.

My head was swimming and I was hearing familiar voices, one of which again screamed "chickenshit!"

The rodent spoke: "We're attacking the fourth tee at the golf course today."

Chaz said this in a very casual manner as he stood, shouldered the rifle, and walked to where a tiny Chinook cargo helicopter sat, it's drooping rotors turning slowly.

Minutes later the Gopher King waddled from the aircraft dressed in the most outlandish collection of military gear I'd ever seen. He could hardly walk. His flak jacket had a dozen zippered pockets positioned at various angles, each bursting with every imaginable 21st century battle accoutrement. His rifle looked like a large upside-down vacuum cleaner. I believe it was an AWC G2 sniper rifle, the kind with a rotating bolt that fires a 7.62 x 51 NATO round. But I'm not sure. It must be a sonofabitch to clean, I thought.

Three extra 20-round ammo magazines were clipped to his belt. He wore a helmet, leather gloves and those paratrooper boots.

I told him I had important newspaper business to do and that his late night belly flop onto my truck windshield had screwed my whole schedule up. Besides, I hadn't slept and my meds were giving me trouble today.

I admitted to Chaz that I unfortunately believed he indeed existed.

"In fact," I said, looking up and down Main Street. A few tumbleweeds bounced along the sidewalk, made a sharp right turn, and came to rest in the doorway of Amanda Vanderclaussen's aromatherapy shop.

"Do me a favor and don't ever come here again. People see me talking to an eight-inch tall rat and I'm finished in this town. Finished."

Chaz wobbled away with that arthritic hipless gait rodents have when they walk on their hind legs. He turned and kneeled into a battle crouch and took aim at a bright blue plaster garden gnome somebody long ago had placed under a bird bath next to the trailer. He fired a short burst and the bearded figurine with the Tyrolean hat exploded into a cloud of white dust.

Again, with the wise ass grin, Chaz said. "I'll come by tomorrow when you're in a better mood. I've got another surprise for you."

I swallowed a fossilized glazed donut that had sat for a while in my desk drawer and washed it down with a flat ginger ale. When my head was sufficiently sugared up I forced myself to get work done.

I had an update on the Martian cow story to finish and then an interview to do.

I drove to the new subdivision at the golf course, part of the ski resort complex that had most of the town in a civic uproar. I had gotten a phone call from a woman who said her husband had been ticketed by the police for firing a weapon within the town limits. He had shot at some prairie dogs, which is not unusual around here.

The 1,200 homesites of Bull River Ranch Estates were encircled by a split rail fence broken by an elaborate ironwork entry gate that sported a giant version of the Gold Gulch corporate logo rendered in a fancy serif font that belonged on Hopalong Cassidy's wedding napkins. Artfully placed pioneer wagon wheels, refurbished with fancy brass hub bands and varnished spokes, surrounded a raised bed of groomed wildflowers where a billboard proclaimed: "Howdy folks! Our Model Homes Are Now Open!"

I remembered when this was a quiet cow pasture, part of the old Voorhorst ranch. Except for a few strategic cottonwood trees and pinion groves preserved for aesthetic purposes, the land had been bulldozed flat and all I saw now were concrete driveways and cul de sacs and parked trucks unloading rolls of green sod grass and roof shingles.

In the distance, on a hillside overlooking the partially built ski lodge, the BLM had fenced off where workers had recently discovered what was described by the sheriff's office as native American body remains. The feds were doing an archaeological survey of the site and had called for a pause in all construction at the lodge, citing the Native American Graves Protection and Repatriation Act.

I waved at a uniformed guard at the security gate who was dressed like a mall cop. Chalky construction dust hung in the air and through the haze you could see the golf course taking shape in the distance, shallow swales marking where artificial ponds would be bounded by fairways and bunkers and the landscaped site of the future Bull River Falls Country Club, where they already had a chef hired from Denver. They'd raised the rough stone walls of the new movie theater and workers were busy on the gables of an ornate roof that would cover the town's community recreation center and convention complex. In the distance stood the enormous ski lodge itself, its half-finished shake roof towering over everything like the centerpiece of a giant party cake.

I parked my pickup in front of a big faux bungalow with a dismantled child's swing set in the driveway. A backhoe was busy carving out the new bike path behind the home. I unfolded the phone message from my shirt pocket and checked the address.

A blonde woman shrink-wrapped in a tee shirt and wearing an impossibly short denim skirt emerged from the house. She lifted her coffee cup and gave me a hithering smile.

Amanda Lewandowski nervously walked over and flitted her hands as she spoke between coffee sips. She waved me inside and began a frantic monologue, explaining how her husband had been recently hired by the Gold Gulch Company. These days, she said breathlessly, good jobs were hard to come by. She cuddled the giant cup to her chin as if yearning for its heat and said wasn't it a pleasure to have no shortage of honest work available for everyone these days.

She refilled the cup in the kitchen. I noticed her sky blue fingernails. A white, pug nosed dog the size of a hamster appeared out of nowhere and starting snorting at my leg.

"Ed said it was okay to talk to you," Amanda Lewandowski said as I followed her into the living room.

Stacks of unpacked boxes sat on the white Berber carpet and on the fireplace mantle stood photos of the Lewandowskis in various outdoor vacation settings: biking in the desert, skiing, whitewater rafting, and the two of them dressed in beachwear, lugging scuba tanks across a boat pier. An exercise bike draped with laundry stood in the corner of the room.

"He thinks the town over-reacted," she said. "Ed figured you'd be putting something in the paper anyway — the police blotter you run every week, and he wanted to tell his side. It's why I called. We just moved here and didn't want to get off on a bad foot. I appreciate you coming. I read your paper every week, you know."

She called the dog and combed it's curly white fur with her blue nails.

"I thought, with the problems we've been having lately with these gophers, people might be interested in our story." She eyed me warily over the rim of the two-quart coffee cup and squirmed against the plush cushions of her white sofa.

"Ed was driving the new mini tractor he got for his birthday," she began. "He did that lately when he came home from work, just tooled around to let off a little steam."

She bent and kissed the dog. She straightened up and pushed back her long hair and again sought the comfort of her cup, her shoulders narrowing as she sipped.

"Then I saw him...like, sink,"

"I don't understand," I said.

She swiped downward with one hand, her eyes widening.

"Sink. Like he got sucked into the ground," she said. "I ran outside. He was pinned under the mower. Thank God he didn't have those blades moving. I thought he was hurt. Well, Ed jumped up like a crazy man and said, oh boy, was he gonna' kill himself some gophers today."

The tiny dog sniffed my leg, licking the bare spot where my sock had rolled down. I shook the runt away.

"Ed screams, 'get my gun!' So I, like... get his rifle," Amanda said. "The big one he hunts with. Ed starts shooting, hollering how he was going to...like, slaughter every gopher in the, excuse me, goddamn county.

"You have to understand," she said, almost whispering, "...we've had trouble with animals. I'm just not used to wildlife like you have here. We moved from out east. A coyote took our spaniel last month. Those little rats ruined the patch of yams I just planted!"

She called the little white dog. She leaned forward and scratched its ear.

"I'd hate to lose my precious darling."

The dog jumped into her lap. Amanda gave it a long kiss and squeezed its apple-sized head between her palms and then smothered the entire animal between her freakishly large breasts.

"Then those terrible elk came," she said. "Like, wrecked the garden. And now, like, here were these gophers. He just lost it.

"Ed showed the burrows to the policeman. They were caved in under the tractor, like an escape route at a prison. I never saw anything like it. We'd paid three thousand dollars for that lawn and now with this drought the town won't let us lay a new one. And now Ed gets this silly ticket. Almost two hundred dollars! Last time I looked, gophers, you know, weren't an endangered species. What's all the fuss for?"

"I think the problem might have been firing a weapon in the town limits," I said.

"Now you can't defend yourself on your own property?"

"Not with a gun. Not outside in a neighborhood. Not unless the gophers march into your house and physically threaten you."

Amanda giggled. "That would be something."

"Yeah, it would be something," I said.

The dog jumped off her lap and started barking at me.

"There's a fella who vacuums up the gophers, but that costs real money. We tried to hire an exterminator. Well, the town got on Ed's case about using poisons. Said it could seep into the water table. You're not writing down everything I say, are you?"

I looked at my notebook. "Well, yes I am."

"Just so you get Ed's side of the story."

"I promise I won't interview any gophers," I lied.

She sipped her coffee and re-crossed her legs. She smoothed her hand over one knee. Amanda Lewandowski wore a tattoo of a stylized green cloverleaf behind the sandal strap on her left ankle. I stared at it.

The yappy little dog jumped into my lap. I set it down carefully like I was lifting fragile glass, and it snarled and thankfully walked away.

"You might want to keep your little dog inside," I said.

"Oh, don't worry, we're building a very tall fence," Amanda said.

I closed my notebook and looked at the muted 72-inch TV screen where a Denver weatherman was silently forecasting another week of no rain for the mountains.

"An eagle can lift eight pounds," I said. "A fence won't help."

I looked around the yard and took pictures. The house was close enough to the river to hear water rushing over the falls. From behind the home I could see the entire valley, narrow and brown with dark pines flowing toward the mesa like the broken green stroke of a paint brush.

The back yard had been completely excavated. This was Chaz's handiwork. I didn't know those crazy prairie dogs ate yams.

CHAPTER 13

I once asked Chaz how gophers, lacking opposable thumbs, managed to manufacture their military hardware. Surely there wasn't a factory where three-pound rats with welding masks assembled little helicopters?

Chaz smiled: "We don't make stuff. We obtain it. We find it and make it small. Is that a dirty word, 'opposable?' It sounds dirty."

"Who teaches you to fly helicopters?"

"YouTube," Chaz said.

"And to fix them when they break?"

"YouTube."

I wondered if I'd taken my proper medication that day. Sometimes I mix up the pills.

In my repeating nightmare, the PFC in my photo album appears with a half-exploded face and hovers over my bed and says "chickenshit, chickenshit...chickenshit." He's dressed in combat fatigues and a field hat and he always carries a weapon: M-16, M-60, you name it, like an arms merchant come to peddle his wares in the dark of night. I know what he's referring to, of course. The part about calling me a chickenshit.

I closed my eyes and allowed my brain to gallop away…

Now we were outside behind the trailer. Chaz casually reached over and touched the side of the garbage dumpster we'd been standing next to. He squinted and wrinkled his nose. He clenched his forepaws. The dumpster shuttered and shrunk to the size of a shoe box.

"I can small you, too," he said.

"You're no bottle of perfume yourself," I said.

"No," Chaz said. "Not smell. *Small*...like in *shrink* you. Then you can understand us. Then you can help us. I can have you over to the house for dinner."

He explained how they obtained all their things: weapons, vehicles, amusements like giant TVs and motorcycles, as well as the underground shopping center with the Cineplex movie theater located in caves south of town where much of their clan lived, apparently funding their civilization by digging up gold nuggets at the mine at the old ghost town on Bellyache Mountain.

Only Chaz and certain members of his immediate family could do this shrinking of stuff. He said it didn't hurt, and it wouldn't last long. And when I said I was game he told me to close my eyes and hold my breath.

What the hell? It would be something to talk to Dr. Nguyen about. I'd been running out of things to say.

And so he touched me tenderly with a single claw. A hissing corona of blue vapor encircled my head like a diaphanous fairy veil. It felt briefly like the flu, then like something icy deep within my sinus cavity; like I had a fever and was about to get sicker. After Chaz's paw touched my foot I gave a little shiver, feeling bloated and gassy like I'd eaten something bad.

When I opened my eyes the little potentilla bush I'd been standing next to a few moments before looked like an oak tree. The newspaper building — my crummy double-wide trailer with the tar paper roof, towered above my head like an enormous warehouse. All my clothes fit, my cheap shoes looked the same, and when I took out my wallet to make sure everything was still there it was the size of a postage stamp, my library card smaller.

I was the same size as a plastic Ken doll ready for a wild date with Barbie.

"Speak," Chaz said. "Let me hear you talk. Sometimes the voice part doesn't work."

"What the hell did you do to me?" I said, pinching my face and touching myself up and down. A U.S. Forest Service slurry bomber made its approach toward the airport and came low over the town and I ran and hid behind an eighteen-inch high bag of trash next to the dumpster.

Chaz smiled proudly.

"I once smalled a herd of Angus cows, just for practice. When they mooed they sounded like cats," he said. "I was afraid you'd squeak when you talked, but you're okay."

Chaz hooked one claw under the bill of my baseball cap as if inspecting my hair. We were now eye-to-eye and he patted me on the shoulder. The Gopher King's breath smelled grassy, like he'd eaten a salad.

"Follow me," he said.

We boarded the waiting Apache attack helicopter, it's four-blade rotor turning slowly in a gusting wind that had begun to blow down from Bellyache Mountain, where I'd heard that morning on the police scanner that yet another wildfire had been sparked by what was officially being reported as dry lightning. I had my doubts.

The chopper sat next to my pickup truck in the alley parking space, the top of the aircraft barely reaching past the middle of the front tire. When it took off, the aircraft sounded like a low decibel weed whacker.

We were airborne quickly and as we gained altitude we passed a flying crow that wheeled and looked like it was going to attack us. The gopher pilot, who wore wrap-around sunglasses and a big pinkie ring on his throttle hand, flicked a dashboard toggle switch. The Apache's 19-tube rocket launcher lurched back on its hydraulic slider and spit out a missile that struck the approaching bird and turned it into a ball of spinning black feathers.

"We've had trouble with birds lately. They're not used to us flying around like this," Chaz said. "Got chased for ten miles last week by a hawk. Those guys are very fast."

I asked Chaz what he and his gophers were going to attack.

"You'll see," he said. "I've designed the plan according to T.E. Lawrence's battle at Aquaba in 1917. Except without the camels, of course."

Chaz is a student of history. He can quote Aristophanes, the Jerry Seinfeld of ancient Greece, and knows in great detail the strategies of Wellington at Waterloo and he has the annoying habit of reciting long, punctuation-free passages from *Infinite Jest*, the novel by David Foster Wallace. He absorbs his information during marathon weekends of watching PBS documentaries. The Gopher King also loves audio books.

Chaz destroyed something in town each week, usually related to the Gold Gulch Golf Course and Resort, which occupies land on which there once was a vast settlement of gophers who now must live in a prairie dog diaspora in the hills surrounding town.

Chaz removed his flak jacket and scratched at his tee shirt, one paw claw tugging at the silk screened image of Bob Marley — or a shadowy version of the man with a musical halo floating above a dreadlocked head. Where he gets these shirts I can't tell you. But every day it's something different. He's very big on rock groups of the 1960s: the *Stones*, the *Who*, *Led Zeppelin* and the *Kinks*, *Pink Floyd*.

Chaz's four body guards, each armed with a machine gun, eyed me suspiciously.

Chaz told me. "I didn't appreciate you making fun of us in the newspaper last week. It was a low blow calling us prairie rats."

"You destroyed the high school baseball field," I said. "They have to replace the sprinkler system. Who's 'gonna pay for that?"

Chaz knew better than to press his luck with me, for he understood I was the only human friend he had in the world. He nodded to one of the guards, who took out a notepad and started writing.

"Still, you were rude," he said.

"Live with it."

Chaz stretched his back. He looked like he was in pain. Carrying such stupid weaponry couldn't be good for him.

"I sprained myself yesterday when we were training. I better go to the doctor."

"You have doctors?"

"We have hospitals. We have orderlies and nurses and the hospitals have cafeterias in them. We have Chiropractors. We have health plans with high deductibles."

As we gained altitude — oh, two hundred feet, the Apache was quickly joined by a whole squadron of other aircraft: Warthog attack planes, two cargo Chinooks filled with armed troops, and a pair of World War Two Grumman F6 Hellcats, which I now remembered had been reported missing following a vintage air show at the airport last spring.

Chaz swiveled his night vision goggles down across his furry face and pointed at the open bay doors of the chopper.

It looked like we were headed toward the golf course.

CHAPTER 14

Changing geography doesn't make things better.

After Vietnam I carried a portable Olivetti typewriter across Europe in a backpack. I brought a notebook filled with cryptic doodles and poems copied from the *Oxford Book of English Verse*, which I read openly in cafes, hoping it might attract women.

During one aimless trip I composed a letter on the Olivetti for a cousin in Zvornik, Yugoslavia, back when it was still Tito's Yugoslavia and filled with reluctant socialists. I sat drinking slivovitsa brandy beneath a plum tree at a table covered with a checkered oilcloth while my relatives watched me type, entranced as I wrote a letter to the American embassy in Belgrade, vouching for my cousin's fine character and career prospects if they would only issue him a visa to study business administration in Chicago.

It was quite a show, a bottle of 180 proof hooch at my elbow, the entire clan marveling at the compact beauty of the modern Olivetti. Everyone smooched me on both cheeks as if it were a joyful family wedding. I could hear sheep bleating on the hillside above the clay roof tiles of my father's childhood home. Down the rutted dirt street came a wooden cart mounted on car tires and pulled by a skinny horse and I raised my hand and the old driver lifted two fingers and touched his cap and snapped his reins, but the miserable animal hardly changed its half-dead gait.

The cousin was killed years later in his orchard while gathering Bosnian brandy plums. My father's home was burned during that war, the family graveyard tilled, headstones crushed into gravel.

In Paris I ordered unpronounceable liqueurs at the cafe Vendome, where Hemingway once drank. I sat on the steps of Gertrude Stein's house on the rue de Fleurs, where I scribbled nonsense in my silly notebook.

Like a pilgrim I visited where the Hemingways lived in their shabby alley flat off the Notre Dame de Champs and from there walked to the train station where

Hadley lost her husband's manuscripts in 1922; the beginning of the end for them. The station was a sooty version of the old French post office building in Saigon, a dark cavern filled with iron luggage buggies and pigeons cooing from oily skylights.

Hemingway drove a Red Cross ambulance in his war. Wounded while chauffeuring chocolates to the real Italian troops, he came home and limped around his Oak Park neighborhood in a cape. Hemingway hadn't killed anyone during his brief fling with danger, though he wrote with a literary boner for violence. And that bullshit about grace under fire; there was no such thing. Nothing resembled grace on any battlefield I had ever seen. Gallantry and mindless violence were abstract strangers. Bravery was what you did when nobody was watching. If they were watching it became spoiled and untrue.

Witnessed honor is a deception.

You alone could keep score if it was to count for something. They could award boxes of shiny medals and it still would not matter. Cowards captured women with poetry books.

I met my wife in Paris as the rain fell on those slanted canvas bookstall canopies along the river, my face reflecting in the street lamp glow of the wet train window as it rolled slowly from the Gare de Lyon.

A stunning girl across the aisle was sleeping against one folded arm, long dark hair splashed across her bare shoulders, and I studied her while smoking a cigarette in the days when you could smoke almost anywhere. She was pale and beautiful in the starved sad way of someone in a confusing black and white French film. I watched her, hypnotized, and fanned away the blue cigarette fumes with my hand so as not to wake her. She wore a thin scarf and the fabric lifted and fell against her skin as she breathed. The closed hooded eyes, her modestly updrawn legs and the way her shadowed face lay against her arm gave her a mysterious aspect that made me catch my breath.

When she stirred and re-curled herself with a soft moan, nesting against the train seat like a snuggling cat, I snuffed my smoke in the armrest ash tray and grabbed my bag to stand and leave.

I was within steps of where my life would have changed forever. A moment longer and this certain time and place would have slipped away and she and I would have never been.

Instead, she woke and stretched her arms and looked at me sleepily through the strands of her parted hair and softly said, "Hello."

She had the bluest eyes.

CHAPTER 15

My dangerously unoccupied head was threatening to wander and I needed to give it a task, so I thought about my little friend.

At the golf course the gopher commandos of Chaz's aerial assault team assembled themselves into three perfect squares, each platoon of two dozen rats aligned in a classic infantry defensive formation made famous by Lord Wellington when he faced Napoleon at the battle of Waterloo in 1815.

It looked ridiculous, of course. I imagined these rodents as they assembled before battle, dressed in tiny red regimental uniforms, crisply saluting officers wearing plumed hats and yoga pants.

I was not accustomed to being so small. I stumbled as I ran, falling over six-inch high clumps of grass as if they were grown bushes. I stepped on a worm the size of a python and dodged a resting black cricket as big as my foot. I heard a deep growl and saw two slobbering golden retrievers the size of school buses galloping toward me. The dogs were employed by the golf course to chase away Canada geese, feathered shitting machines that routinely fouled the manicured putting greens at the golf course. I'd done a story on the pooches once for the newspaper and they were named Bobo and Bernice. They now had me in their sights: a chihuahua-sized man in khaki shorts and a Chicago Cubs baseball cap running for dear life across an open field. What a treat.

I crouched behind the wheel of a stainless steel beverage cart and watched as a Chinook helicopter unloaded another horde of armed gophers onto the shake roof of the Gold Gulch Golf Course clubhouse.

The charging gophers were not noticed by the golfers who had gathered for tee time. The day was sunny and dry, hardly any wind. Chaz's aircraft, a custom Tiger EC 665 attack helicopter which he'd stolen from a crew of visiting French military pilots who'd been training at the Air National Guard Center, had landed atop a two-seat portable outhouse hidden in the trees.

With complex arm signals Chaz the Gopher King directed his troops.

I have to admit, the little rat looked dashing. The tasseled white silk ascot was an especially nice touch. Chaz wore his black beret with the red star on it, two .45 cal. Ruger P90 pistols at his side. On his furry face sat a pair of $200 Maui Jim sunglasses he'd stolen from the cockpit seat of a parked Lear Jet at the airport. His paratrooper boots were spit shined. He fired off a purple smoke grenade and the battle commenced.

Five hundred screaming, charging gophers sound like peas rattling in a paper sack, so nobody — the humans, especially, heard anything. One infantry platoon carried shiny cavalry swords and wore feathered hats and tight white britches. They looked like a gang of angry, over-dressed ballet dancers. They carried a giant flag. It proclaimed: "Imperium Subterraneis." I don't know what that means.

Bobo and Bernice deftly scooped up two of the costumed gophers and trotted happily away, their tails wagging.

The Gold Gulch golfers on the course didn't notice a thing. Except one old guy, his beltless lime green pants hiked over his ribs, saw the swarm of charging rats and dropped his putter and started running in that hip-splayed, wobbly way all of us old men have. Two shoebox sized Apache attack helicopters appeared from behind the tree tops, tipped forward, and you could see the red muzzle flashes as they strafed the old man mercilessly with their M-60 machine guns. The tiny rounds, the size of lima beans, of course, had no effect. The geezer golfer swatted at his head and looked at the sky at what he probably thought were swarming crows. I clearly saw the gunner in the door of one chopper. He wore a black headscarf adorned with a white peace symbol. He looked very disappointed.

Across the field another armed gopher squadron was chasing two women in a golf cart, hardly gaining on them as they puttered slowly along an asphalt path behind the Third Hole. The women stopped, stepped out. A leaping gopher who lay in ambush latched onto one lady's foot and as she ran screaming I could see a tiny helmet and a pair of boots bouncing in the grass behind her. The gopher dropped his M-16, his pistol, and then his little camo military trousers ripped away. The woman turned and drop-kicked the rodent twenty feet and then sat on the grass and massaged her bare foot while two Wart Hog A-10s sprayed her with 30mm cannon fire. She picked a few of the harmless rounds out of her hair and examined them like they were bird shit. She stood, brushed off her monogrammed white sweater, and limped away.

The battle continued for another embarrassing hour.

More paratroopers landed on the clubhouse restaurant roof and rappelled onto the patio and got tangled on the control knobs of an eight burner stainless steel barbecue grill. Another crew with bulldozers managed to dig trenches in the putting green, but then their vehicles slid into a pond filled with twenty-pound Japanese Koi fish who hungrily attacked the drowning and helpless gophers.

Bobo and Bernice, now in Golden Retriever Paradise, were having a hell of a time over by the duck pond, swatting away the attacking Blackhawk helicopters and terrorizing twenty gopher Airborne commandos who'd been stranded on an island of giant water lilies. Gophers do not know how to swim.

Chaz the Gopher King stood watching it all from the roof of a Porta-a-Potty. He did not look happy.

CHAPTER 16

I couldn't sleep and I knew the pills would soon stop working like they always did and they would have to show me more hospital TV pictures of my brain.

This thing with the gophers had left me suspended between two perplexing worlds.

Meanwhile, Chaz and his gang burrowed into backyards and chewed up more telephone company cables. They dug another trench under home plate at the high school ball field and gnawed to pieces a whole pallet of boxes at the Gold Gulch Country Club that were filled with those stubby Number Two score card pencils. Gophers are fascinated with pencils.

A mountain lion, the same one that had torn apart the Castle Peak State Bank's ATM machine, strolled into town one day and ate the county fair champion sow. I put the photo of the mauled pig on the front page of the *Beacon-News*. Kneeling next to the victim was its sad owner, a teenager from the 4-H Club. In the photo the boy pointed down at the cat's pug tracks and forced a smile for the camera.

The caption said, "Hungry visitor kills boy's blue ribbon dream. Colorado wildlife officials warn of a prowling lion who is apparently fearless. County Fair boss vows to catch cat at all costs."

A state wildlife officer and a volunteer citizen posse found the bacon murderer, a toothless old male who could no longer hunt, and they shot the senior citizen cat while it was napping in an abandoned cabin at the old ghost town south of town — not far from the caves where I knew Chaz and his militant rats had taken up residence.

The newspaper photo caption read: "Murdering cat caught asleep. Mayor proclaims Fairgrounds safe."

In my opinion they should have left the killer alone. The world has enough pigs and too few mountain lions.

The fire raged and more Montana smoke jumpers came to town.

This did not go unnoticed by Chaz and his commandos, who believed the wildfire had a good chance of destroying the golf course and the resort, which was their aim all along.

They chewed through a six-inch PVC pipe and drained a portable 500-gallon water cistern that was being used to fight the fire, flooding the Bureau of Land Management Command Center office. Gus Curry told me everybody at the fire department was certain the blaze, which had been re-igniting itself in several locations, was the work of a crazy pyro.

The newspaper had too many typos after I returned from my Vietnam trip, which might have been a sign I was loosing my grip on things. One week the front page banner was printed upside down and nobody noticed. I was digging into my backup supply of sample medications from the VA, so I mostly didn't care.

Another week I used the entire editorial page to apologize for the paper's poor grammar and syntax, as in this mention of a local used apparel fund raiser:

"...the ladies of the church have cast off clothing of every kind and they may be seen in the church basement on Friday."

And this inspirational quote from the weekly Community Worship Corner: *"Don't Let Worry Kill You. Let the Church Help."*

Once the police announced that the wildfire was an arson case and the perpetrator's motive might be to destroy the ski resort, the TV crews arrived. Whole caravans of white satellite trucks, like there was a circus coming to town.

I rented a corner of the newspaper office to a guy from USA Today for a hundred bucks a day and charged an NBC crew from New York a couple hundred more to park their trailer next to my alley garbage dumpster. A helicopter from Fox News landed in the Town Park, where the mayor was having lunch with BLM officials at a picnic bench. The chopper's rotor wash blew the mayor's fake hairpiece into a tree. I took a picture of the hanging toupee and captioned it: "Magic mayoral carpet flies high and turns heads at Town Park."

Things were getting interesting around here.

CHAPTER 17

With a touch of his claw Chaz reduced me to the size of a cereal box.

He wrapped a towel around my face and took me to his house. I still wasn't trusted completely.

It was a bumpy ride in the back seat of a military Hummer. At the end of the journey two furry hands directed me gently by the elbows into what seemed like a severely slanted tunnel, in which I felt clumps of vegetation bump my head. It was like stumbling through a damp, cold Halloween spook house. The ground underfoot was rocky. I splashed through shallow pools of water. There was the occasional chattering of unseen gophers running past me, more politely insistent hands guided me, and then I heard a door open and the same two clawed paws deposited me onto an overstuffed sofa, where the blindfold was finally removed.

The lavishly appointed underground lair was dazzling. These rats were filthy rich. On the walls hung an eclectic collection of priceless art, and since Chaz lives not far from COSTCO there were three side-by-side 72-inch LCD televisions mounted on one wall. Dozens of enormous bags of Cheezos were stacked in a kitchen with a large commercial Jenn-Air dual-fuel range oven with a pair of hefty 20,000 BTU stacked burners. The griddle was chrome. People should see this, I thought.

On the wall next to the fancy oak fireplace mantel, one particular painting showed a naked woman with bright blue breasts and four cheekbones. Her head, like an origami creature from a Monty Python cartoon, was twisted toward her shoulder like she was ready to do a backflip. Both of her browless eyes were on one side of her face, and they stared at me suspiciously. Her arms were jointless, without elbows, each of a different length and stretched out like taffy. Like French baguettes on swivels. I was fascinated by this alluring woman with chubby Nutty-Putty toes that pointed backwards. She looked very uncomfortable.

"Picasso," Chaz said proudly with a casual wave of his hand, explaining that the painting showed how reality can be disassembled. The artist, he said in the smug nasal tone of a lecturing professor, was taking apart the accoutrements of reality, which adhere to no order.

"Reality knows no alphabet," he said rather sadly. "In this work the artist exposes the stark truth of life's vicissitudes, distilling our temporal passions into..."

"I saw people turn blue in the army lots of times," I said, interrupting. "I still have dreams, you know."

Chaz stared at me, confused. He shook his head, annoyed that I had interrupted his recitation of what I was certain was a memorized You Tube video.

"You're mocking me."

Then he pointed to the wall. "A wonderful Degas. There's my Surat, and my Monet. I have a Van Gogh locked in a temperature controlled vault downstairs."

"Isn't everything here downstairs? " I said. " You live underground. How can there be a downstairs when you're already downstairs? Even upstairs would be downstairs, don't you think?"

But he continued: "The great Italian masters are here as well — Tintorelli, Boccaccio, Bellini."

"I own a 1935 *Bride of Frankenstein* poster," I said. "It's a copy, of course. Boris Karloff has bolts in his forehead."

We had a long conversation, during which Chaz's wife, Tinka, brought me a tray of salty snacks and then rolled her eyes when her husband pointed to a large painting of himself that he had commissioned following his consolidation of all the prairie dog clans on Bellyache Mountain. All great despots do this. The famous painting of Napoleon being coronated is thirty-three feet wide. In Chaz's portrait he was outfitted in full dress uniform, gold braid encircling intricately woven shoulder epaulets. He looked like a South American dictator.

After I drank a cognac from a crystal snifter the size of a goldfish bowl, I learned from Chaz how gophers are not at all impressed by computers but they are entranced with the magic of pencils and how such enchanted wooden yellow sticks can be used to make cipher marks on paper which somebody else can understand.

I told him pencils and paper were old fashioned and are hardly used these days, except by children and golfers.

"You have been deceived,"the Gopher King said.

Chaz explained that he does not comprehend the concept of cooking, though he is fascinated by the Food Network Channel in the way we humans are mesmerized by horror movies. Chaz said when he first witnessed someone grilling burgers he wondered if the meat experienced any pain. He seemed very concerned about this.

Chaz has varied interests when it comes to his audio books. He likes novels by R. Pilcher and chick lit fiction whose introspective and unemployed women characters live in sensitive emotional denial and/or wrenching turmoil in well furnished, apparently mortgage-free homes on Cape Cod.

He asked if I had ever met Huckleberry Finn. I told him yes, and that we had once fished together in Missouri. He promised to show me his library of audio books. Chaz also enjoys looking at pictures in hardware catalogs.

Chaz's wife brought out pizzas and beers. Chaz ate nothing, but he studied me as I tore into my dinner.

I gulped a foaming glass of stout and asked: "What's it like being a supernatural gopher?"

Chaz brought one black claw thoughtfully to his lip and contemplated the vaulted ceiling of his giant living room. In the kitchen Tinka was wearing her iPod ear buds and humming the soundtrack of *West Side Story*, the solo part where Maria sings *"...I'm so pretty and witty and bright."*

"It's like you're drunk," the Gopher King said. "But you never slur your words or lose your balance, no matter how much you drink."

CHAPTER 18

At the cemetery, the rows of gravestones with their chiseled psalms and declarations of grief began near the tree where I once took her picture.

The dates of her first and last day were carved into the black marble. I placed the flowers below her name and smoothed the dirt around the clay pot with my hand.

At night, lately, she came and sat at the edge of my bed.

Today it was hot and cloudless, nothing in the sky but the black smoke rising from the fire. Gus had asked me again to help with his young crew, but I told him I would be a useless teacher.

I keep the photo in the rolltop desk at the trailer. In it one shoe dangles from her toe as she smiles, her palm outstretched to blow a kiss at the camera.

Go ahead and groom the dirt with your hand and sit and press your cheek against the cold stone. Kiss her name through your parted fingers and touch the stone words and sit as if you weighed a thousand pounds.

I stayed for a while and tried to recall the long path of life that had led me here to this place on this day, but I could not.

I whispered, "All those years. I just wore you out, didn't I."

I walked away and sat beneath the cottonwood tree where I had taken her photo. The creek here made a bend next to the gravel road that stretched away lonesome and empty toward the town.

A giant among trolls, the ancient cottonwood had grown as if it had changed its mind many times during its long life, sprouting such a profusion of branches in every direction that they trailed the ground like jungle vines.

Many of its limbs had meandered until the tree had begun to grow up its own trunk so it could search for sunlight all over again. This tree, I thought, had been recycling itself, a trick the younger cottonwoods nearby apparently had not learned. Many of them remained hopelessly stunted beneath this larger cousin, as if they'd abandoned the hunt for sunshine years ago.

Someone long ago had abandoned a truck axle and its attached steering wheel shaft near the base of the tree. Over the years the cottonwood had embraced the rusted steel as if the wood and bark had melted over it. The axle now seemed to grow from the tree like blackened iron fruit. It looked like it was meant to be, the improbable swallowing of steel by the patient and indestructible tree. I ran my hand across the rough bark, knowing that within its deep elephant wrinkles lay a map of all this indestructible giant had ever seen.

I tried to imagine how the tree would look on the groomed golf course they would soon build here. Most of the gopher holes nearby would soon be buried and gone, forcing their inhabitants to move higher up the mountain. Their world was disappearing, as each known world must.

Without battles left to fight, the old cottonwood might also finally give up and die.

I drove to the Colorado Air National Guard station west of town. The parking lot was filled with leased yellow school buses lined up to shuttle the out-of-state smoke jumpers to the fire.

I'd seen a strange arc of bright light high on the mountain that morning, but thought it might be the crazy sparklers going off again in my head.

I signed in at the Bureau of Land Management shack and squeezed behind a catering truck dispensing free hot coffee and snacks. I grabbed a package of chips and a candy bar, shouldered my gear and watched one of the fire crews assemble next to a helipad where a trio of Black Hawk helicopters circled overhead.

I sat in the grass and untied my boots, which were gummy with dried red fire retardant I'd sloshed through the last time I was here taking pictures for the newspaper. I yanked off one sock and rubbed my foot.

The scars on my shin were colored pepper red where the skin had sloughed off long ago after a bad case of jungle rot. Anders, our medic, had called it a tropical ulcer, the biggest he'd ever seen, which at the time sounded oddly exotic and something you could write home about in a letter. Which I did, many times. It was how you worked through stuff in those days; talked about getting hurt. Or how it felt waiting to get hurt, which was always worse. The fungus had eaten to the bone, and my calf tingled with a permanent electrical numbness. The nails on the foot were gone, the toes shapeless.

I scratched the swelling beneath my chin. The inflamed knot below my ear itched like crazy. Earl's nosy wife had noticed it one day on my trip and said she had magic old lady cream that would take care of any rash. She said Earl had eczema, too. I told her I didn't have eczema. To hide the wound I wore a goofy speckled bandanna around my neck until somebody on the tour asked if I was headed to a square dance.

My surplus military boots had cotton-canvas uppers. They were rubber-soled and they were non-reg, with ridiculously long and double looped laces. I have this thing about long laces. You're not supposed to wear them because they can snag or catch fire. In the old days a BLM safety officer got on my ass for this. But the shoes never caught fire. Not in all these years did I ever catch fire.

So I looped my old army canvas rucksack over my shoulder. I drew the straps down my back. I tightened them evenly. I put on the yellow safety helmet and then took it off and tried again. With one hand I reached to make sure my prescription head pills were in the compass pouch that hung on my left side on the top web-keeper strap of the padded part of the worn suspenders. I snapped shut the brass buckle on the vertical weave pistol belt, lingering with my thumb at the worn notch where I had once carried a weapon holster. I swung around the butt pack, also flammable Army issue canvas, and lay it in my lap and smoothed it with one hand. Three small metal snaps on the pack that had broken long ago once held my extra grenades, their lever releases taped flat so they wouldn't catch on a tree while I moved through the jungle.

I took out my canteen. I swallowed a pill. *Side effects may occur. Call your doctor if you experience dizziness.*

Call your doctor if you experience nausea or spontaneous bowel movements, numbness, headaches, giant boils, lethargy, fever, unexplained backwards walking, crusty rashes, loss of sexual appetite, disinterest in sports, blurred vision, seizures, a crookedness of the toes, itchy scalp, blindness, joint pain.

An insistent weight pressed on my shoulders again, those bright flickers of light flashing behind my closed eyelids as if to announce what was about to happen. It was so much more than simple, explainable sorrow.

I waited for the joyless poison to settle in as I stared past the yellow Nomax fabric of my shirt sleeve at my disfigured naked foot, hoping nobody would stop and try to talk to me. I knew this would pass.

But lately it was different, as if something sinister had been awakened since I'd tried my stunt with the rope in the kitchen. Like I'd stepped over a forbidden line.

I tried to think about my little gophers, but it did not work. I tried to think about my wife, but that did not work. I thought about the photo of the suspected arsonist I had picked up from the sheriff's office, but this too did not work.

Call your doctor if you see melting timepieces, witness ghoulish apparitions, have dreams of sinking into quicksand, thumb numbness, change in fingernail coloring and shape, a love of broken glass, the eating of dirt, a sudden urge to crumple telephone book paper or pop plastic blister wrap, the pleasure in the scent of the funneled extruded metal part on which a garage door slides — the lubricated rail thing. Fainting.

I listened to the familiar avalanche of strangers' voices in my head, some shouting, others laughing, a man with a deep baritone cussing in the background like some liquored-up whiskey-righteous drunk...HEY CHICKENSHIT! YOU FUCKING CHICKENSHIT, YOU!

Oh, I knew what he meant.

My heart pounded. Maintain the airways, I'd always been told. Stop the bleeding, administer IV fluids, keep vascular volumes steady and watch blood pressure.

If somebody tries to stop and talk to me right now, I swear...I'll kill him.

You can relax yourself by blowing something up in your head.

Concentrate and pretend you are still in the jungle:

...just wire together two live 155 mm artillery shells. Cover them with Centex and put a butane canister on top. Strap the fucker tight with electrical tape. When the temp of the blast briefly reaches seven thousand degrees, twice the heat it takes to melt rock, the force hits you at one thousand times the pressure of the atmosphere. But the kicker — oh, God, the sweet spot is when the secondary wind arrives, that angry displaced ball of gusting air moving wildly back into the low pressure space once occupied by the initial explosion. This hungry vacuum is what gives you a headache. Shit, that's what melted bronze temple Buddhas at Hiroshima. Call your doctor if you experience headaches. But I just didn't have any spare artillery shells laying around the house these days.

Now I'll just wait, I thought. Until the medicine kicks in I'll give my head an assignment. I can always take another pill. The sonofabitch medicine that makes you feel like you're packed in cotton. The pretty China blue one, the one labeled with such a delicate numerical font that I'd sat on the floor once and stared at the lovely thing for hours. And this will trick it, because the gray jelly beneath my bone helmet is under my command. So I'm the boss, I thought. In the end, I'm the boss. The commanding general of my private neuron army.

But I'm running out of tricks, because my head is a quick learner and I always have to be on my game. I squeezed my palms against my ears and wished only that I could evaporate and happily be gone. I ached for my rope swinging from the kitchen ceiling.

Behind my closed eyelids, the voices now reduced to a whisper as if people were passing by as they spoke, like the muted cries of cicadas. I saw the swinging rope again. How could it break so easily?

Something had bitten it.

I heard boot steps thunder through the dry grass. The turbine growl of another lifting helicopter. Jesus, I hope no one tries to speak to me. Not now when I'm crazy. Not until Dr. Nguyen's lovely blue pill kicks in.

People have been staring at me, the younger men eyeballing my antique backpack and old boots like I was a homeless vagrant who had infiltrated the fire zone. Who is this guy? The look was one of annoyance and pity. I thought: now I lay me down to sleep and hope I die before I wake. Another timeless day is not what I want.

If my wife were here she'd know what to do.

I tried to think about the Gopher King.

CHAPTER 19

When the Bureau of Land management scheduled a media update on the wildfire, I was compelled to attend. There are not too many news conferences in Bull River Falls, Pop. 875, give or take.

More TV people arrived in a procession of logoed white satellite trucks. Bull River's only hotel hung out a NO VACANCY sign for the first time in its history. The Lions Club served donuts and coffee from a picnic table in the middle of Main Street, which had been blocked off with abundant, fluttering yellow police tape.

A brunette in high heels and a little black dress stood next to the network TV satellite truck, interviewing the mayor. The news lady was attractive in an anorexic way: pale green eyes, the I-just-woke-up hair, pouty mouth. I wanted to take her to the Grill & Griddle Cafe on Main Street and buy her a few calories.

Nearby, a reporter for *USA Today* scratched at his notepad, distilling things into Haiku paragraphs and good declarative sentences. Next to him, a *New York Times* correspondent typed wildly on his laptop like a mad pianist. A cigarette with an inch-long ash dangled from his mouth and his Yankees baseball cap was turned backwards.

Waiting for the news conference to begin, I nodded off into a hovering half-sleep where the world mingled seamlessly with the one that did not exist.

The gophers arrived before the news conference began.

I had not seen Chaz for a while, during which he and his commandos, armed with chainsaws, had brought down two cell phone towers, something which police wrongly blamed on the same lightning strikes they once said had caused the wildfires. Everybody knew the fire had been sparked by a crazy pyro who the police said was hiding out somewhere in the hills, but I knew Chaz would be annoyed I had not credited him in the newspaper for the sabotage.

The lady news reporter was the only one to spot the charging gophers.

She peeled off her spike heels and began chasing after the heavily armed prairie dogs, her sound man following behind with sixty feet of spooled coaxial audio cable.

The attack was vicious.

The gophers swarmed the white media tent, one squad climbing with rope ladders up the side of a satellite truck. Soldiers the size of large oven mittens leaped on a fleeing TV news reporter, clawing their way up his leg. The reporter's hair was poofed up like a gray soufflé and one soldier took out a machete and began hacking off his locks. The reporter screamed when another gopher jammed a smoke grenade into the man's high hair and set it afire.

Just then an NBC network truck backed up, *beep-beep-beep*, and a dozen gopher bodies flew up like a cloud of brown socks.

Wounded rats lay everywhere, some carried off on stretchers by combat medics with chalk-drawn peace symbols on their helmets. The gophers' lingering cries sounded like squeaky Tupperware lids being rapidly opened and closed.

Another squad of commandos, their faces smeared with green camo paint, leaped from a lilac bush and angrily charged the truck. Two Blackhawks the size of Barbie Doll cars, followed by a diving Warthog attack aircraft, strafed the vehicle with a hail of bullets the size of Rice Krispies. The commandos, some wearing black ninja bandannas, clambered into the window of the truck. The driver opened the door and jumped out as the vehicle wobbled into a ditch.

And then the gophers vanished.

The TV people walked around aimlessly, holding bitten electrical cords, complaining about chewed seat cushions; all except for the barefoot news lady, who was now crawling on all fours up the side of a hill, a sagebrush branch tangled into her long hair.

On top of the hill, softly silhouetted against a halo of brilliant sunlight, stood Chaz the Gopher King, his hands on his rodent hips. He was wearing a sleeveless *Paul Revere and the Raiders* hoodie sweatshirt and this time I noticed the image of Diana Ross and *The Supremes* tattooed on his right forearm. He looked like a Benedictine Monk in combat boots.

The news lady continued her desperate crawl up the hill toward Chaz, holding out her microphone, obviously wanting an interview. Her cameraman was close behind and the lady was starting to re-arrange her hair and set things up to start filming when Chaz calmly crapped out a few prairie dog Milk Duds, smiled and saluted and vanished down his burrow hole.

A guy from *The Worldwide Globe Tattler Newspaper* came to me and pointed at the hill.

"Can you tell me who that was?"

"A rat," I said. "He's a rat."

"Doesn't matter. I'd like to talk to him."

"You the one who wrote the story in this week's issue of *The Globe*? The one with the picture of Joseph Stalin embracing a naked spaceman?"

He nodded.

"I admire your work," I said. "I'll see what I can do."

CHAPTER 20

The front door of the newspaper office swung open on a broken hinge, and when I reached inside for the light switch the wall was sticky with dripping film developer.

At the world-wide media headquarters of the Bull River Falls *Beacon-News* we still turn Kodak camera film into pictures in a darkroom lit by red safelights.

Papers and file folders lay scattered everywhere. I sniffed the scent of melted Linotype lead. File cabinets, dented clunkers arranged against the wall, had been opened. The top drawer of the roll top desk had been yanked out, spilling more papers and a bag of Snickers bars left over from Halloween. My 1926 Underwood typewriter, the space bar worn smooth by thousands of thumb strikes, lay on the floor.

I'd been tempted to remodel the old double-wide trailer that was referred fancifully in the newspaper each week as the *Beacon-News* "building." The trailer had been assembled with mis-matched pieces cobbled together over the years and still rests on the original river rock foundation of the miner's shack where the newspaper was founded in 1898.

I enjoy the vinegar odor of darkroom chemicals and the way the furnace fan rattles. I adore the old Linotype; love its noisy sprockets and heavy flywheels and the greasy, clattering iron cams that resemble parts from a steam locomotive. I enjoy outwitting the machine's habit of spitting hot lead onto your forearms if you run it improperly.

I am also the proud owner of one of two functioning rotary dial telephones in Bull River Falls.

The Town Board has long been pushing me to fix the place up, and recently sent a certified letter warning the *Beacon* was the only Main Street business that hadn't adhered to its new "architectural improvement" ordinance. They ordered me to replace a 175-watt front porch mercury vapor lamp, claiming it spilled unwanted light on the neighbors at night ("light pollution" was their term).

So I took a single green red Christmas bulb and hung it from the porch roof with an extension chord. I published a photo of the dangling light in the newspaper with the caption: "After Pressure From Mayor, Newspaper Adheres to Dim-Witted Watt Ordinance."

Police Chief Tom Cherry's beige Crown Victoria pulled up in front of the trailer with its lights flashing. Tom crept up the front steps with his pistol drawn. He stepped inside and lowered the weapon quickly when he saw me.

"You can put that thing away," I said. "Somebody broke in, is all."

Tom looked around warily and holstered the .45.

"Somebody called and said they heard a ruckus over here," he said. "I came as quick as I could."

"Wouldn't matter how quick you came," I said, looking at where the intruder had drop-kicked a wastepaper basket across the room.

I picked up the cracked bottle of Kodak film developer. There was a brown blotch on the ceiling. This person had been very angry.

Tom surveyed the scene and took out his notebook. "Any money missing?"

I took my wooden Arturo Fuente cigar box from the counter and pulled out a few wrinkled bills.

"Nothing missing."

Tom stroked the pry mark on the door jam. He scribbled another note.

"I haven't locked this place in years, Tom. Window doesn't even have a latch on it. Whoever did this could have crawled right through and saved a lot of effort."

"Town's changed," Tom said somberly. He looked warily at the Linotype machine, not sure of what to make of the strange iron beast.

"What's that?"

"It's like a computer," I said.

"You should surrender to technology," Tom said.

"I'd like it the other way around, actually."

A hot wind pushed through the open doorway and puffed up the police chief's baggy pants. Tom is a small man, and his face looked lost beneath his big hat. There seems to be no dress code at our three-person police department. Tom Cherry likes uniforms that resemble something heisted from a theatrical wardrobe room: fancy blue pants, epaulets, silver rank insignia on his collar. Sometimes he wears black leather knee boots, like he's a highway motorcycle trooper. Mostly, Tom Cherry favors the straight khaki look: desert-tan shirts, the classic Smokey the Bear patrol hat, his belt loaded with everything from cuffs and a pair of pepper spray cans and two sheathed flashlights next to a nickel-plated pistol that sags halfway down his leg.

"A lot of monkey business around town lately," Tom said.

"Those gophers trying to eat up the Town Hall. Somebody said they spotted a cougar near the playground. Now we got this fire. I suppose you'll print the suspect's picture in the paper?"

"Of course," I said. "He's an ugly sonofabitch".

"Yes, he is," Tom said. "The Feds are all over it. The FBI special agent out of Denver called yesterday. State fire marshal is sending investigators. It's a lot of paperwork for me. But he can't hide for long. Not with the mountains crawling with firefighters."

The policeman studied the room. His fuss seemed abundant, but I figured he hadn't had this much excitement since they found a body floating in the recreation district swimming pool on Christmas Eve, wearing nothing but a Santa Claus hat and a pair of red knee socks.

"I need to get work done, Tom," I said impatiently.

The policeman kept writing. He looked around the room like he'd misplaced something.

"There's no such thing as a small crime," he said, poking out his tongue as he scribbled into the notebook.

He buttoned his plaited shirt pocket and smoothed it with his palm. He straightened his big hat and hitched up the heavy gun holster. He handed me a three part form to sign. He nodded toward the door.

"Whoever banged off the latch must have been pissed."

"I feel neglected if I don't get somebody pickled at me at least once a week," I said.

"A few folks around here are mad at you because you don't take a stand on that resort they're building," Cherry said.

"And your question is?"

"People have strong opinions. It means jobs. For others it's the beginning of the end for this town."

"It's not my job to take a stand on anything," I said. "If people are mad because I'm not on their side, tough shit. I start taking sides, then half the people won't ever believe anything I report."

"Just saying, it might make somebody mad enough to do this," Cherry said. "Not to mention your theory about the fire being arson before anything was official. It doesn't help our investigation when you speculate in the newspaper."

Tom Cherry knelt and studied the linoleum floor, which for reasons I could never explain, has a pattern of cowboys and Indians on it. Everybody has the same cloned, smiling face, except the Indians have pigtails and the cowboys are wearing white hats. They're shooting at each other, but they seem very joyous about it.

"Gypsum dust," Cherry said, wiping the floor with his finger.

"Have to go out of town a ways to get this on your feet. It had time to dry, too. Is this your foot?"

He pointed to a muddy boot mark on the floor.

"Could have been anybody."

"I suppose a customer could have made it during the day," Tom said.

"No shortage of dirty boots in this town. Or people mad at the newspaper. Or gypsum dust."

"Looks like a hiker's boot," Tom said.

"If you say so."

"Or a construction worker's shoe."

"Or Cinderella's slipper," I said. "Look, Tom...I have thirty-two pages of crucial world-wide news to assemble painstakingly by hand and without the help of a computer...all before tomorrow morning."

I handed him my signed forms.

"Now I'd like to get to work."

Police Chief Tom Cherry studied the floor again and I could tell he was puzzled by the image of the happy cowboys and Indians who were trying to massacre each other.

"I hear old Dora refused another offer from the golf course people to buy her ranch."

"They want the water rights," I said. "They don't give a shit about Dora's ranch."

"Millions, I hear," Tom Cherry said as he studied the forms. "The old lady should just take the money and run."

"She won't run anywhere, believe me," I said.

Cherry gave me an accusing stare: "By the way, the story you did on the poor girl they found by the river— Melinda Barstow? Thanks for holding back on our conversation about that Jergen fellow. We had to release him, anyway. The company posted bail and I got heat from the DA. In my book he's still a suspect."

There wasn't much to say, so I just nodded. "I expect I'll be talking to her dad soon about the obituary. Not looking forward to it. He works for Gus Curry at the fire department. Haven't been able to find him."

"You can visit him in the town jail," Cherry said as her turned and made for the door. "He attacked Jergen while we were questioning him outside the station. Took three deputies to hold him down. Almost took the boy's head off with one of those shovels the firemen carry. I thought you would have heard about it on your scanner."

Cherry smiled at ne.

"He buried the shovel in a deputy's windshield. I figured you knew. I was expecting you to put the picture in the paper."

Cherry shrugged and I followed him outside. "Watch your back, Stan," he said. "Somebody around here hates your guts. In my experience people don't dislike you only once. He'll be back."

CHAPTER 21

I switched on the bedside device they gave me at the VA to help me sleep. It's shaped like a tiny farm silo with a speaker on top and it can play hundreds of sounds that are supposed to fix my insomnia. I can make it rain. I can summon the cries of seagulls on a seashore, or crickets and cicadas.

I pressed a button and there came a whooshing rush of white noise, like the cocooning hiss of the inside of a jet airplane. I placed the speaker on the nightstand and closed my eyes and tried to give my brain something to do.

I thought about the gophers.

Among these rodents, as far as I can tell, the women do most of the work. When they're not committing municipal sabotage, the male prairie dogs of the Bellyache Mountain clan are swaggering braggarts who spend a lot of time watching sports on large TVs while snacking on giant bowls of wheatgrass. While the men make a ferocious, full-footed show of excavating holes — the dirt spraying high like mortar blasts, it's the ladies of Chaz's kingdom who truly can dig a better burrow.

Young gophers start dating at the age of two, and according to my math there might be up to 22 teenagers in Chaz's house at any given time. And mom is in charge of them all.

Thankfully, gophers don't have cell phones. Or bathrooms with mirrors.

Tinka is Chaz's fifteenth and favorite wife. I'm told she is lovely, gopher-wise, and has a natural elegance that serves her well during her husband's frequent public appearances, which include ribbon cutting, school dedications, and occasional exhibits of feats of strength during the colony's annual Glutten Free Sauerkraut & Lederhosen Pow-Wow & Indian Dance & Log Rolling Jamboree.

Tinka is famous for her flamenco dancing and, despite her clawed paws, can play the castanets while laying on her back. She is a talented singer, too, and does a killer rendition of "Valjean's Death" from the play *Les Miserables*. She once forced Chaz to attend *Phantom of the Opera*, where His Royal Highness fell asleep by Act

Two. When Tinka jabbed him angrily in the ribs Chaz woke up and shouted "Go Cubs!"

Tinka once sang the theme song from the Broadway show about cats and brought a crowd of gophers to tears. I cannot describe how heartbreaking it sounds to be in a room filled with crying prairie dogs.

No slouch when it comes to military matters, Tinka can break down and re-assemble a Kalashnikov AK-47 rifle in three minutes flat. With green tracer rounds flying over her head at the gopher training center over at McKenzie Gulch.

Chaz, like most male gophers, gets — well, squirrelly — in winter, when there are a lot of underground saloon fights and testosterone-driven territorial disputes. During one cold January Chaz decided to get two nipple rings made from a pair of hand grenade firing pins. He also declared to his wife during a family gathering that he wanted a tattoo of a serpent on his neck and would shortly be bringing home a brand new armor plated pickup truck fabricated with twin M-60 machine gun turrets. There would be a silhouette profile of himself emblazoned on the hood.

According to witnesses, Tinka, always on the lookout for her husband's excessive ego and hyperbolic charms, smiled calmly and curled her claw and motioned for Chaz to step aside so she could speak to him privately. The suddenly subdued Gopher King was silent for the rest of the evening. What she told him I'll never know.

Gophers live in constant fear of fumigants, detonated propane burrow bombs, and poison-laced food dropped into their living rooms. Giant vacuums sometimes suck them from their beds while they're watching M.A.S.H reruns.

Tinka is also the colony's chief safety officer and trains toddler gophers how to detect the trickery of zinc phosphate-soaked oat pellets. She is the founder of the "If You Don't Know, Don't Go" safety program, which teaches senior citizen gophers how to cross a busy street.

More on Chaz's family and his colleagues later on, including the history of how the Gopher King first obtained his supernatural powers.

Here's a hint: Plutonium-239

Which leads me to the day when a diesel fuel storage tank at the Gold Gulch Resort exploded. Chaz wanted to see this up close, so I stuffed him in my backpack, showed my press pass at the BLM's wildfire command center and hitched a ride on a fire department pumper truck headed up the mountain.

Chaz kept poking his head out so I tied him with a bungee cord and asked him to behave. I could tell he was getting excited and agitated.

"Control yourself in there," I warned.

Chaz occupied himself at the bottom of the backpack, his hair spiked with hair gel, practicing his Christopher Walken impersonation, which sounded surprisingly good.

Gophers are easily bored, so during the long ride he started squeaking, and I told the firefighter next to me that it was my cell phone ring tone. I don't own a cell phone. The firefighter looked away just as Chaz's pointy head appeared from beneath the backpack flap.

The firefighter, his forearms the size of smoked hams, curled his nose and sniffed.

I took the blame. "Pardon me," I said.

I heard a faint giggle from inside the backpack.

The driver took us to the top of Bellyache Mountain. I released the Gopher King and opened the backpack so it could air-out for a while.

We both watched the fire. In the pale light the smoke had grown as the blaze burned a slow, zig-zag path toward the town.

Chaz stood and looked across the valley. "We don't have much time," he said.

I told Chaz the sunset looked lovely.

"Yeah, Shakespeare. I see it," Chaz said. "But I have more important things on my mind."

The gopher king then reached above his head with both paws and gave a long, chattering bark.

There now came a chorus of answering whistles and brief puppy howls as head after brown head appeared on the grassy plain below us. Where the fire had begun to burn and grow, a thousand prairie dogs were standing at their mounded holes as the early evening breeze urged the thick smoke toward them.

I pointed admiringly to where the fire had gained strength in the tinder dry lodgepole pines further up the mountain. We both watched the toppling snags of burning branches which exploded brightly, tossing up sparks that blew like little stars across the darkening sky.

"Wow," I said.

"You always talk this way?" Chaz said. "I don't see nothin' pretty. The only thing I see is that bunch down there getting trapped. We have to get them out."

"I assume there's an airlift involved?"

"Does a gopher shit when you lock him in a backpack?"

The gopher king whistled again, this time a long shrill note I hadn't heard before. The mass of standing rodents below performed a wave, like the surging crescendo of hands and arms you see at a ballpark, little paws rising and falling far into the distance. I had never seen so many gophers in my life.

Chaz pulled out a walkie talkie the size of a matchbook and mumbled something, then rattled off what sounded like artillery coordinates. He put on his black beret. It wasn't long before a row of those familiar helicopters appeared on the horizon: Chaz's entire air force of Blackhawks, Chinooks, Coast Guard MH-65 Dolphin choppers, a few F-15 escort jets...all had been summoned to the rescue.

The fire was getting closer and I could feel its heat.

"I can't make you small right now, so you're on your own," Chaz said. "I hope you understand."

The little rat dropped on all fours and ran down the mountainside.

I hitched a ride to town. On the way back we drove past where a smoke jumper sat cross-legged sewing his parachute behind the mess tent, wrinkled blue nylon puffed up at his feet like the hem of a grotesque prom dress. Two Black Hawks behind him were being prepped and fueled, their four drooping rotors turning in the hot wind that had gusted down from the mountain.

I looked inside my backpack. I shook it empty and out came a scrap of paper on which Chaz had written:

"Be at my place in the morning. Oh-eight-hundred hours."

I didn't know the little sonofabitch had such good penmanship.

CHAPTER 22

I woke in a windstorm, but it was only the sleep therapy sound box whooshing next to my head.

Tuesday called in sick. She only works on Monday and Friday, so I was in a jam.

I drove to the old ghost town at the abandoned gold mine, where a family of tourists had reported being chased by a bear. The state wildlife people came and caught the bear, tagged its ear and let it loose. I took pictures.

After the rangers left I hung around for a while. The national news reporters in town were starting to annoy me and I wasn't eager to get back to the office, where a pile of public notices and classified ads were waiting to get typeset.

There was gray mist in the pine tops, and where the sunlight had burned the fog away the half-collapsed mining shacks looked like they were suspended in clouds. Behind one roofless cabin stood a grove of cedars and from it a creek flowed and broke over a beaver dam. The wind moved something on one of the structures, the metal clanging like pots knocking together. The fog faded and the sun broke in white shafts through the dark trees. The empty town was bathed in light, the dirt street dry and brown and bright, the only sound that of creaking wood and birds and the blowing trees. Somewhere off in the distance the wind slammed a door shut.

I walked toward where I heard the prairie dog whistles and sat down in the heat beneath a tree whose hypnotic, swaying top made me sleepy.

In the distance Chaz and his mate were sitting hip-to-hip on a burrow mound, and when Tinka stood Chaz did too and the two lovebirds touched their teeth together and squirmed in each other's arms like kids on a clumsy first date.

Whether this was a form of gopher intimacy I'm in no position to say, but I turned away and let the rodent Romeo and his Juliet have their privacy. I'm told these creatures only get seriously romantic for a few days each winter, so perhaps this was just practice for showtime in January.

After a while the two gophers looked up and studied the sky. What they were staring at I didn't know, but soon others from the colony emerged, running back and forth between their holes until a gopher crowd assembled as if they were getting ready to watch a parade.

They got an air show instead.

The shadow of the bird cut sharply across the field, its silhouette growing larger as the shocked gophers began to run for cover, their little hind feet kicking up a storm of dust and sticks. The eagle lifted and leveled into a drift toward the beaver pond, where it gracefully tucked and dived. Soon something wriggled in its talons, wings tipping as the bird adjusted its path of flight and swooped past where I was standing with my camera.

Here was my front page picture for the week and its caption: "Bold Bald Eagle Snatches Snack at Gopher Town."

Chaz ran to the spot where the bird had attacked as if this might give him an explanation for the sudden kidnapping. He studied the eagle as it flapped effortlessly across the valley with its flailing cargo, and then the other gophers whistled and scattered, except for Chaz who remained and turned to me and gave a casual shrug.

This seemed to be a cold hearted reaction, I thought.

What everyone had been waiting for were the rescue helicopters, which soon started landing. The packed aircraft were filled with gophers evacuated from the fire, and some were put on stretchers and carried to where the medics were doing triage. Soon the whole field was filled with gasping, sooty gophers encased in all manner of white bandages, some standing crippled with their crutches.

It looked like the scene in *Gone with the Wind* where Atlanta is burning and the high camera shot shows a shocked Scarlett O'Hara in her puffy Tara dress surveying the bloody mayhem of war.

Two of the landing gopher air force choppers were antique Hueys, still armed with 2.75-inch rockets and turreted M-50s. Chaz must have robbed a museum. On each aircraft was the improbable insignia of the 1st Air Cavalry Division, which meant Chaz had been watching the film *Apocalypse Now*, lately his favorite movie.

A tired gopher medic with the smeared face of a chimney sweep walked by. He was dressed in Vietnam era poplin shirt and pants, a pack of Marlboros tucked into his floppy field hat.

I asked Chaz later why he had been so casual about the eagle murdering one of his people.

He looked down at his combat boots somberly. "Bird has to make a living," he said. "It happens."

He explained that many more had been lost in the fire, and the new refugees would soon tax the colony's resources.

"We're running out of room. Out of food. They're onto to us at COSTCO. I need another supply source."

"Can you shrink me again?" I asked. "I have some ideas. But we need to have a meeting. You and your top staff."

Chaz shook his head. "Too dangerous. If I do it too much you might not recover. You'll be small forever."

"I'll risk it."

"I'll think about it."

I drove to town and returned later with whatever I thought gophers might eat: salted sunflower seeds, two dozen bulk boxes of Slim Jims, pork rinds, bean dip...jalapeño shoestring potatoes. Savory Cheese Whiz and crackers. Who doesn't like that stuff?

Miniature deuce-and-a-half Army trucks appeared and started loading the food. A Chinook lifted a pallet of frozen pizzas.

Chaz, who likes to over-accessorize his wardrobe and loves hyperbole, stood dressed in full field gear, wearing a helmet and tanker's goggles, a silver gym whistle in his teeth, screaming and directing traffic with his baton like George Patton at the Battle of the Bulge.

Tinka, his lovely wife, was standing over there at the makeshift dispensary, hair tucked under a white Florence Nightingale nurse's cap. She wiped her brow with one arm and surveyed the hundreds of wounded gophers.

You think you got problems now, I worried. Wait until they eat those bacon flavored onion rings.

CHAPTER 23

In town, the carpenters were hammering together a platform to accommodate the reporters who wanted to do their stand up shots against a background of the burning mountain.

The mayor stood in front of a camera, talking to a newsman in a suit and necktie who looked miserable in the afternoon heat.

I headed to Bellyache Mountain, down main Street and past the county building, where they were unloading portable toilets and blocking off a parking lot with orange cones for the town's upcoming annual Old Gold Days festival.

Chaz was listening to his music when I got past his body guards and the triple coiled, razor-spiked concertina wire that surrounds the Gopher King's compound at the old gold mine.

He was in a sour mood. His claw kept getting stuck under the shuffle button of his iPod. He told me he'd discovered the device was loaded with *Rolling Stones* music. He spoke to me in rock and roll lyrics and memorized album liner notes, including long passages from *A Whiter Shade of Pale* by *Procol Harum*.

When I asked him why he didn't take advantage of his army's natural skills to foil his enemies, Chaz tapped his foot and said: "...'cause I try and I try and I can't get no satisfaction."

"You guys are the best diggers around," I said. "You can chew through electrical conduit, for godsake. They don't even notice when you shoot at them with those tiny guns."

Chaz seemed offended. He clamped on his earphones and began to sing, off key:

"...don't hang around 'cause two is a crowd."

Chaz's wife Tinka was in the living room, watching re runs of a popular PBS series about wealthy British aristocrats where the men wore suits and neckties all day long and hardly ever sat down in chairs. It must have been an especially sad episode, because Tinka tried to restrain a gulping sob and quickly wiped her eyes with a tissue when I walked past. She offered me tea and raspberry scones, which I politely declined.

She shook her little furry head and, without turning away from the massive 72-inch TV screen, said: "Oh, it's so heartbreaking."

This was said with a perfectly posh British cut glass accent.

Chaz's library walls were paneled in oak. A painting of an 18th century English fox hunt hung behind an enormous desk. On the desk was a brass nameplate engraved with the words: IT'S LONELY AT THE TOP.

Endless Ikea shelving, which Chaz said took him three weeks to assemble, was stuffed with audio books: three Judith Krantz titles stood side-by-side like a treasured literary trilogy. All of Proust's *Remembrance* books were there. A few Tom Clancy novels. Then a pile of *National Geographic* magazines, arranged carefully by date. Chaz liked the pictures, he said.

Chaz bobbed his head and began to sing: "I met a gin soaked barroom queen in Memphis..."

"That's enough," I said.

An odd assortment of posters of lady rock and roll legends covered one whole wall, each illuminated carefully with a single LED light: a shockingly svelte Aretha Franklin, thigh exposed, from the 1960s; Joni Mitchell looking fashionably cadaverous; Joan Jett, Patti Smith...on and on. Chaz pointed at each of them reverently, naming their musical hits.

He said he'd tried to UPS himself to an exhibition called "The Women of Rock and Roll" in Cleveland one summer, but sadly couldn't find anyone to accept the package. He said he wanted badly to see the dresses worn by Janis Joplin and Cher. He said his wife was fascinated by Tina Turner's stiletto-heeled shoes.

"If only I'd known you then," he said. "You could have shipped me second day air."

He turned and gazed longingly at a framed portrait of Karen Carpenter that was bathed in the beams of a blacklight.

I tried my best to stop him, but Chaz began to sing: "...Something in the wind has learned my name, and it's tellin' me things are not the same."

I glared at the ceiling and its crystal chandelier and whispered to myself.

Then the gopher king lifted his paw and directed my attention to an enormous oil portrait of folk singers Peter, Paul & Mary that hung in an alcove illuminated by a bank of flickering aromatherapy candles. The room smelled like lavender.

With a wide grin, Chaz loudly sang: "Puff, the magic dragon lived by the sea...And frolicked in the autumn mist in a land called..."

"Enough!" I screamed, and reached over and grabbed the king's earbuds and put them in my pocket.

"You've got work to do. Now let us talk about how you build these tunnels."

At Cu Chi in Vietnam the army used to pour hot tar into the storage tunnels the VC built beneath the streets of Saigon, but it never worked. We'd flush them with gas, toss in grenades and sometimes just flood miles of that subterranean world with water. Whole fire engines would be emptied trying to drown whoever lived down there, but it never worked.

I told Chaz his burrow entrance seemed airy and pleasant, though I'd expected the place to be a bit ripe, since his and hundreds of other holes within the extended prairie dog coterie are interconnected and share a common airflow.

I've shared sand-bagged dirt bunkers in the army, and it's no visit to the fragrance aisle at Macy's, believe me.

Chaz seemed surprised by my compliment, since I often make fun of him and tell short people jokes and tales about seeing rats the size of cocker spaniels emerge from sewers in Saigon.

Gophers hate any comparison between them and other creatures with large buck teeth. They believe they are the smartest, the handsomest, the most emotionally well adjusted and culturally refined rodents on the planet. Nobody else constructs homes the way they do, or has such a complex and interdependent social structure that's geographically stable and long-lived. There is a gopher colony in Texas, he said, that has been in the same place for longer than Rome has been a city.

Chaz walked across his expansive library and pushed his paw into an upturned Harley-Davidson cycle helmet filled with pistachio nuts.

The gopher king tossed a nut at the ceiling, watched it bounce off a lamp sconce, and caught the thing in his mouth.

He said gopher tunnels have separate rooms for sleeping, for raising children, for storing food. They have winter quarters deep within their lairs, their version of February in Florida. They also construct listening platforms at strategic locations beneath their mounded entryways.

If gophers could vote, the physical scheme of their towns would be as easy to politically canvas as a big city ward boss handing out free turkeys on election day.

Chaz proceeded with a dissertation about how burrow openings were dug to induce cross ventilation. Convective air, he explained, when it encounters a gopher burrow, enters through the lower opening and skedaddles through the higher hole, where mounds are often altered to force warm and buoyant air to exit more quickly.

He lifted his paw and stretched apart his long claws. "And we do it all with these," he said.

Chaz said HOA covenants for gopher towns require exactly 33 ft. between burrows. Anything less and you get flagged and labeled as a wrong-thinking anarchist troublemaker who deserves to live alone. This threat of a shunned life without anyone to click teeth with is enough to keep the riffraff surprisingly well behaved.

I was then taken on a brief tour. Shafts of sunlight pooled on the packed dirt floor as we passed beneath the sunlit burrow openings. Dark bores twisted in every direction like perfectly drilled big city subway tunnels. A few times I leaped away as gophers dropped down from above and raced by.

I heard a loud chorus of barks from above and Chaz said somebody in a blue shirt had been sighted for the second day in a row and his sentries were sounding the alarm.

"You can recognize a guy in a blue shirt?"

"It's a punk kid in a blue shirt with a BB gun. He's been here twice this week. Works at the NAPA auto parts store in town. We've had our eye on him."

Chaz smiled. "He'll be walking home. We chewed up his bicycle tires."

"That's what I mean," I said. "Use those big buck teeth. You don't like the new ski lodge they're building?"

"We despise it," Chaz said.

"Then eat it. Chew it up."

"They have guards with guns."

"So do you. Put those claws to work, commando boy. Clint Eastwood dug himself out of Alcatraz with a coffee spoon."

We turned a corner and I squeezed past hanging plant roots. A spider the size of a pony crawled past. I heard a loud racket and deep grunting and saw a blindfolded ferret bound with rope, his arms tied against the curved dirt wall and he was being interrogated by two gophers wearing sunglasses, a glaring bare light bulb swinging from the ceiling.

"Don't worry," Chaz said. "He'll be released after we ask a few questions."

Further along the tunnel we finally emerged and I squinted in the bright sunlight. Chaz motioned for me to lay low as he pointed to a large tank mounted on a parked truck. A long industrial vacuum hose stretched away from the vehicle, its end disappearing a dozen yards away down a gopher hole.

Chaz and he had a smirk on his furry face. He winked.

The driver of the truck pulled a lever and the hose convulsed. Loose dirt rattled, and the hose twisted and jumped like a giant snake. The big air compressor on the truck wheezed as if the vacuum had encountered an obstruction. The man ran up and yanked the kinked hose out of the burrow hole, and with it came a dozen chattering gophers hanging there by their claws, tiny hind feet braced against the ball of sticks and grass they'd used to plug up the hose.

The man shouted and jumped away, his arms flapping as if swatting hornets. He picked up a tree branch and tried to poke at the gophers, but the rats dropped off the hose like a precision Navy Seals assault team exiting that helicopter at Bin Laden's mud house in Abbottabad.

Two attacking gophers clamped their jaws on the man's ankle.

Exterminator Man fell face-down and started howling in a soprano voice. He sounded like a Swiss yodel version of the aria from *Madame Butterfly*. He tried to crawl away, the gophers still gnawing furiously at his leg like they were in a county fair corn cob eating contest.

Then the other team of rodents, each wearing red Willy Nelson bandannas, some dressed in black ninja outfits, hauled around the business end of the vacuum hose and rammed it against the man's rear end.

Then the guy started bellowing as the hose convulsed, wagging back and forth like a hungry sea lamprey fastened onto its unwilling host. The man tried to stand and run, but each time the hungry sucking hose pulled him down. He stood. He stumbled again, clawing the ground desperately.

Chaz ran over and climbed on the vacuum's control lever and shifted the motor into high gear.

The gophers stepped away and watched as the vacuum whined and made a terrible shrieking, slurping noise. The shirt was the first thing to come off. Then the pants. Then the man's heavy work boots and the socks.

The last thing I saw of the exterminator was him galloping away through the little hills of gopher town, barefoot, wearing only polka dotted boxer shorts and a baseball cap, a few of Chaz's amused brethren nipping happily at his heels just for sport.

CHAPTER 24

At the office I finished the classifieds and scribbled a rough draft about the bear and the tourists at the gold mine. Paid a few bills. Souped two rolls of Kodak film in the darkroom. I made dinner on my hotplate, took a pill and poured a drink. I thought about having a cigarette but then popped a piece of nicotine chewing gum in my mouth instead.

I turned on the war on TV. I tapped the mute button.

I cranked back the leather recliner and tried to take a nap. I held the drink close to my chest. I shouldn't be boozing, I thought, though a whiskey sometimes helped me sleep. It also played games with my meds.

My memories lately arrived as if snipped with scissors, without sequence or context, like my mind had sprung a leak. I pinched the bridge of my nose and thought of how the cyclone fence surrounding the construction site at the ski lodge had reminded me of concertina wire, the toothy coils like a giant Slinky toy suspended between bamboo pickets that were wet in the hazy tropical sun. I saw white Mefloquine malaria tablets in my dirty palm.

I woke up the night before nagged by a question about a Claymore mine which I agonized over while shuffling into the bathroom, where I stared at the toilet bowl, certain that my insides weren't working anymore. Did the Claymore weigh three or four pounds? In the morning I left another message for Murial Taponas at the Bull River Falls Library, suggesting I might need the answer soon for a newspaper article I planned to write. Had I already asked her that question? My head is filled with bookmarks.

I sipped with my eyes closed and felt naughty for being on the edge of a buzz. Dr. Nguyen had warned me about this. The ice rang like bells in the whiskey glass and reminded me of wind chimes made from the leg bones of a dead NVA soldier we'd found in a tunnel filled with bags of contraband rice that was crawling with rats.

I drank and thought of the highland jungle in that country, a weirdly dark forest beneath a forbidding dense canopy. From above, the land was laced with bushy black cracks and partly glimpsed brown rivers that twisted past miserably small villages hidden beneath so much green the color no longer had meaning.

I pressed my closed eyes, liquor-fueled sparklers firing behind both lids. I saw a dirt highway with red dust lifting in the sun. Quang Tri was an hour away, the busted road littered with war garbage. An abandoned deuce-and-a-half truck sat nosed into a ditch. A tipped Jeep, its army green paint turned to powder gray, lay in a tangle of incinerated and broken equipment of no known description. Something rusted and crushed with unreadable fire-peeled lettering. The road passed through drab villages with underfed dogs and skinny pigs and skinnier children peeping from doorless huts. No adults to be seen.

I pressed the TV remote against the recliner's leather armrest, savored the sweet bite of another whiskey sip, and listened to the TV news anchor describe thunderous missile strikes as sounding like the footsteps of a giant. No, that's not what it sounds like.

I puzzled over what might have happened to the laminated photograph of a girlfriend I'd carried in my pocket for six months during my first tour. Right next to the salt tablets and chewing gum and jack knife. I'd lost her somewhere east of the Laos border, the thick plastic perhaps still preserved in the jungle dirt. I'd long forgotten the girl's name, though I could now see her face clearly.

My head pounded. I smelled grenade smoke and insecticide and the unmistakable odor of the dead soldier in the cool and wet tunnel, boy-sized within a dissolved quilted vest, black hair tufting from dirty skin stretched over a small skull that lay cradled in a broken pith helmet. A foot bone hemmed by a shredded trouser leg inside a bleached rope sandal. What little flesh remained was not enough for the insects to be interested in. The soldier lay on his back, pretzeled into an agonized death flex, and in his reaching hand bone sat an old Chicom grenade, ribbed and rusted. My First Sergeant, crouched behind me in the tunnel with a flashlight in his hand, hadn't seen one since the Korean War.

"They might win this thing," the sergeant said.

"What?"

He pointed and wobbled the flashlight beam across the body, where it caught the reflection of a red star on the soldier's square metal belt buckle.

"Damn grenade. It's from the fifties, for godsake. When the Frenchies were here. They got nothin' and they don't know they got nothin' and that's all you need to win. These guys can climb a mountain wearin' shitty sandals made from truck tires. They're tough. Tougher than you and me."

I snapped off the soldier's finger and tried to take off the belt buckle, but something crawled out from beneath the body and I stepped away. I put the bone in my pocket and carried it around for two weeks before tossing it in a trash heap behind the mess hall at base camp, feeling weird for thinking such a thing might be a souvenir. More things to be ashamed of.

The old sergeant shined his light down the length of the twisting tunnel, its dripping clay walls gouged with shovel marks, the beam showings matts of grass litter and abandoned tools in pools of rainwater. An empty light socket hanging by a cord tacked with bamboo pegs to the ceiling.

"They're awful good soldiers," he said, studying the dead man. He breathed deeply. "But what makes them dangerous is this: we own all the clocks but they got all the time. We count the days until we go home but these people know it's all for the duration. There's no rotating home. No weekends with hookers in Bangkok. We got calendars on our walls and in our wallets. We make little notches on sticks. Always keeping fuckin' track of time. Time don't mean nothin' to these people."

The sergeant jittered the flashlight beam across the dead man's body. "Little fucker. Tougher than shit. Look at him. What was he, five-foot tall? Shit."

I turned the TV volume up when the chirpy announcer smoothed back his JFK hair and said, "Here, let's listen..." and there came the steady thumping of anti aircraft fire and then somebody being interviewed in the foreground of a landing helicopter. The Black Hawk, bristling with twin M-50 machine guns, came into view within a hurricane of blowing sand.

The news reporter appeared again wearing night vision goggles — brand new, like they'd come from the box. He described in breathless detail how ambient moonlight was converted by the device into amplified electrons and then projected onto a tiny phosphorous screen, allowing a soldier to fight the enemy in near darkness.

Except for the M-16, I didn't recognize any of the weapons the reporter displayed in rows at his feet like booty from a police bust. Something looked suspiciously like a mortar attachment. Another weapon seemed a smaller version of the M-16, and fastened to the barrel of a carbine was something resembling a grenade launcher, except without the fat leaf foresight half way down the barrel. But I just didn't know, and this bothered me, and for some reason I was jealous of the soldiers who could now use such weaponry.

I allowed the ice in the whiskey glass to melt into a cold pool on my cupped tongue. I'd already drank too much. Inside my head I could hear the voices shouting at me again, chuckling as they chanted... *chickenshit, chickenshit.*

I took a deep breath but it felt like I wasn't getting any air at all.

In bed I summoned a steady summer rain from my sleep therapy machine, but this only made me go to the bathroom. I settled instead on crickets and cicadas, to which I added a touch of a cascading 4,000 Hz forest waterfall.

CHAPTER 25

We met at the trailhead. Chaz was dressed in...well, nothing. Today he looked like a normal prairie dog. No *Motorhead* tee shirt. No combat boots.

With him was a distinguished-looking rodent who I hadn't yet met. Chaz introduced us, walked hurriedly up the trail, and said he'd see me later at the gold mine where the colony's wealth lay hidden in a labyrinth of ore-rich gopher tunnels.

Jools is Chaz's second-in-command. He looks like a sleepy professor with an odd left-swooping part in his hair that reveals a bald spot on the right side of his head. His whiskers are missing. He walks with a limp. I'm told he usually wears a neatly creased shirt with a pocket protector filled with an array of Sharpies.

Both hair style flaws are the result of a violent encounter with a 52-inch commercial Honda lawn aerator at the Gold Gulch Golf Course. That was the day Jools tried to steal a box of No. 2 scorecard pencils and a box of shiny tin foil from the clubhouse cafeteria.

A squad of gophers later poured ginger ale into the machine's gas tank, dug up three putting greens and dropped M-80 firecrackers into a men's room toilet, which triggered the outdoor sprinkler system and soaked the mayor of Bull River Falls and a foursome of town council members who were playing on the 8th Hole.

It's not surprising that Jools keeps the books for the Bellyache Mountain gopher colony, though his portfolio suffered a setback several years ago when he was caught investing heavily in bio fuel, financial futures and exchange-traded derivatives.

These days much of the colony's cash reserves are parked in short term bond funds and four-week T-bills. He says he trusts nobody and claims corporate annual reports are written by psychotic liars and thieves. He deeply regrets that he sold several thousand shares of Apple stock when it reached $22 back in the 1980s, thinking the company would never amount to anything.

Jools is also the colony's historian and claims his people arrived in Colorado in the 16th century after following Francisco Coronado from Nueva Galacia, Mexico during the Spanish conquistador's search for gold in the New World. These ancestral gophers later migrated to Alamogordo, New Mexico, where they lived peacefully until the 1940s, when they were again displaced by the World War Two Manhattan Project.

Many gophers died that year in Alamogordo, thanks to the government's large construction project, and the colony was nearly destroyed. Jools believes the unusual powers that Chaz and only a few others of his immediate coterie have is due to exposure to Plutonium-239, the material used to make the first atom bomb.

Jools couldn't tell me Chaz's age, but claims the gopher king stole a pair of sunglasses one day from the pocket of a government scientist in 1944. A few hours later, while he was staring intently through the glasses, wishing they weren't so big... he fainted.

When he woke, the sunglasses had shrunk to gopher-sized Ray Bans. And the rest is history.

Jools led me up the trail to the gold mine entrance, where Chaz waited, a stupid grin on his fuzzy face.

"We bit through the big white PVC pipe at the ski resort. The one they use to get water from the river."

He tugged at those two big yellow front choppers in his mouth.

"My teeth sure hurt," he said, smiling.

A creek tumbled fiercely through the trees and gathered into a pool at which rows of gophers squatted and panned for gold. A row of sluice boxes and large vibrating rock tables were being loaded with pay dirt by yellow bull dozers. Backhoes were scooping piles of round river rock in the distance. A gopher wearing headphones and carrying a metal detector walked past and Chaz gave him a friendly slap on the back. From within the mine entrance came a rumbling explosion, then a belching cloud of dust. We covered our eyes.

"We do deep rock and placer mining up here," Chaz said.

"Anything so we get the shiny stuff. They abandoned this place a hundred years ago, but they just didn't go deep enough. If there's anything we know, it's digging. I could show you nuggets as big as your head."

My head was now three inches wide.

I patted myself with both hands, still not used to being shrunk. I was chilled, like I was getting the flu. I shouldn't be doing this. It can't be healthy. I wiggled my numb toes. My shins tingled.

Chaz put his hands on his gopher hips. He surveyed the scene, looked at the sky.

"We have to work fast before the fire gets here," he said. "And we have to hide those tunnels. That's why it looks so crazy today. I don't want those fire people to see this."

I walked to where smoke lifted from the valley. Far off, a BLM crew was cutting a fire line through the forest. Firefighters in yellow shirts were appearing and disappearing behind the blackened trees. A gang of sawyers slouched along a trail, chainsaws on their shoulders. Yellow flames torched up behind the treetops like somebody had turned a dial on a stove.

Saucer shaped clouds hung above the valley like they had been drawn in chalk against the blue sky. I knew there were hurricane gusts up there which could easily funnel down and stoke the fire. And we were down wind.

I had to tell Chaz and his rats to get home, and pronto.

But the gopher king seemed to be having fun watching his millionaire rodents gather their fortunes. He waved at a convoy of loaded trucks, almost leaping with joy as somebody held high a bucket of shiny nuggets.

Chaz saluted and tipped back his head and gave one of those gopher yips, like he'd just sat on a pile of stinging bees. He did this over and over again, barking and whistling and clawing at the air with those little black paws. He jumped up and down. I'd never seen him so happy.

And then everything turned dark as a hot wind funneled through the trees and swallowed us all in a cloud of soot and smoke. I heard gophers screaming.

The wildfire was heading toward us...and fast.

My impulse was to stuff Chaz in my pocket and make a run for it. But I was his miniaturized kinsman now and as the roaring flames raced up the mountain I tried to figure out what to do next.

A dozen beady black eyes were staring at me. The rest of the gopher gold miners, thanks very much... had run away.

Chickenshits.

Gophers, who rarely stray far from home, are flatlanders to the extreme. They live in a treeless and groomed world of conforming holes and tunnels. And they fear fire like nothing else. Light a match in front of a gopher and he's off to the races.

These rats were now out of their familiar element. And I, unfortunately, was in charge. In a stern voice reserved for misbehaving toddlers, I told my rodents to stay put.

Chaz, of course, tried to take command.

"Look, Napoleon," I said. "You might be the royal emperor of 20,000 well-armed, helicopter flying commandos without peer...but zip your buck-toothed mouth, okay?"

Chaz looked hurt. For the first time, I saw his lip tremble. Insulted, he shrugged and crawled back under the tarp I had hauled over our heads to protect us from the thickening smoke and heat.

I stepped away and walked into the trees and tried to think. I didn't know what to do.

Glowing embers the size of barbecue coals were lifting from the trees below us. I wondered how the blaze could have moved simultaneously from so many directions.

Then I saw him.

He stood alone in a grove of dead cedars, his jacked up and battered Toyota pickup truck parked on the old logging road. I crept closer. I knew he couldn't see me because, of course, I was no bigger than a chihuahua. I saw the rifle, an AK-47, hanging from the window rack above the back seat of the truck.

I hid behind a stalk of skunk cabbage and watched. He was a tall, bony freak with spindly arms, hair lifted into a man bun, his lean and long-nosed Ichabod Crane face covered with a scraggly beard that now blew sideways in the hot wind.

He dropped a row of gray paper tubes the size of cigars that were fitted with brass button taps at each end. He snapped open the blasting canister daisy-chained to the last tube and stepped away and then put a match to a long wick that looked like twisted pillow ticking. He stood and watched, hands on his hips, looking quite pleased with himself.

The kerosine soaked fuse sputtered and caught fire. There came a loud pop. Sparks lifted into a hissing flame. Pale smoke blew sideways and bloomed into something dark and alive as the fire curled up a tree with a crimson tendril, turning blue as it clung to the dry bark.

The man studied his handiwork. He seemed entranced. He watched as the flames crept into the gloom of the forest to where the birds started going crazy in the trees. It was perfect tinder in there, I thought. Filled with beetle-killed pines as dry as wood in a lumber yard. And this guy knew it.

I heard little feet scurry behind me and there stood Chaz and his pals, and we all watched as the man jogged away and quickly hopped into the truck. In the smoky darkness the only thing I saw were two red tail lights receding down the dirt road. The gophers began yipping and barking and running in circles. They stretched their paws and tipped their faces and whistled their alarm at the sky. But there were no other prairie dogs to hear them. We were now all alone.

I knew Chaz wished he was safe in his hole, watching a *Starsky & Hutch* re-run, or listening to his cassette tape collection of the *Greatest Jimi Hendrix Guitar Solos*, which lately has fascinated him.

The confused gophers skittered back and forth and touched their teeth together and turned and looked at me hopefully like I was the adult in this catastrophe.

Chaz put one paw on my shoulder and stepped close. His breath was not pleasant.

"We're in trouble, huh?" he said.

"Oh, we're in deep shit," I said. "Up to our necks."

"Why was he starting a fire?"

"Because he's an insane dipshit," I said.

"I can find out where he lives," Chaz said. "Once we get out of this mess, of course."

A breeze urged the smoke further into the thick timber. The fire gained strength as it moved into the taller lodgepole pines, toppling snags of dead branches which then exploded brightly, setting a whole grove of aspens on fire.

The embers settled into the scrub oak and flared again into a cloud of more sparks. The fire tried to rise, and as the warmer heat of the ground began to lift, the cooler air sank and fed the struggling embers. These coals, begging for oxygen, pulsed and came to life where they lay on the dry ground. The fire repeatedly retreated and flared, each time burning stronger.

I walked to the edge of the cliff. A quarter mile away another fire lifted burning branches and broken chunks of bark. It looked like something inside a flapping red wall was hurling out garbage and cleaning itself as the fire moved toward us.

I heard the sound of a large aircraft overhead, and a thin sheet of fire retardant settled around us like falling red sand. Chaz brushed the stuff off his head with one paw. And then the wind started blowing.

I gathered my rats together and pushed them back under the tarp. All I saw was yellow teeth and glowing eyes. Chaz took out a flashlight and held it under his chin like he was about to tell ghost stories.

We had only moments to make a decision.

I pulled Chaz close. "Make me big again," I said. "Un-shrink me."

"It's too soon. It should happen naturally. In another few hours..."

"There's no time. I have to be full size, or I can't help you," I said.

"You'll get sick. It won't be pleasant," Chaz said.

"A little stomach ache? Some gas. How bad could it be?"

Chaz grinned. His two front teeth were illuminated in the glow of the flashlight.

"Oh, it's worse than gas," he said.

Flying debris rattled against the tarp, which was now almost too hot to touch. We all started coughing.

"Go ahead. Do it," I said.

Chaz closed his eyes and touched my forehead. The Gopher King's black nose got snotty and he shivered like he was having a deep spiritual experience. He twirled one claw in a circle above the top of my head. Then he clenched his mouth and opened his bright black eyes and gave a few little gopher grunts. And that's when all hell broke loose.

CHAPTER 26

Everybody that day believed we should stay away from the old French farm. I didn't listen.

The house had ruined iron porch railings with peeling blue paint and giant black vines that ran like lacework across the broken clay tile roof. A stairway torn from its bolts and decorated with fleur-de-lis scrolls twisted along one inside wall and dangled loose where the plaster had been blown away. The exposed rooms with their bent plumbing and tipped tables and scattered boxes made everything look like a hastily abandoned theatrical set. Exploded clothes closets were filled with hanging rags. Dark, furred clots of mold growing on everything. The place threw off a sour, forbidding reek.

The platoon's new second lieutenant, a wiry Alabama boy with a vowel starved name — *Klepscziwiscialicz*, something like mine — had given the order to prepare a landing zone two kilometers away. We had only a few hours to do this and the recon alone would take half that time, so I decided to take my squad on a shortcut past the French house along an unsecured dirt track not shown on our topo maps. They'd been telling us all week to stay away from open and unsecured trails.

The others — twelve in my crew — were not happy with the plan, and they'd been grousing at me all morning. But I was eager to please the lieutenant, who had stayed behind on a field phone to talk to somebody back at the battalion. So the crooked line of grumpy kids followed me, shuffling along the narrow, overgrown trail in the stifling jungle heat, each of us staring in silence as we passed the spooky house.

There had been a rumor the war would soon end. There was always that rumor every few months. Nobody wanted to press their luck.

We passed through an abandoned village and came out into a meadow encircled by pygmy date palms that marked the edge of a rice paddy. There had been bomb drops the day before and artillery had mowed down the surrounding tall grass, making a groomed and charred spot in the jungle broken by craters. Insects sawed loudly.

To show my confidence in the squad's safety, I decided to walk solo point along the rice paddy much too far ahead of the others. At times I would turn and wouldn't see anybody. This was a stupid thing to do, yet the adrenaline rush was pleasant and impossible to resist. There was plenty of daylight left and in a few hours we'd be safely in our camp.

Glassy sunlight flickered off the brown patty water, the rice shoots reflecting upside down, dreamy and green in the sunshine like a smeared painting. Roosting birds squawked, the trees swaying in the heat. I was sweating. I could smell myself. Everybody was filthy and in a bad mood and short on rations and all we wanted to do was finish our task at the LZ and hunker down for the night.

That morning Anders the medic had spent fifteen minutes digging a fat tick from my nostril. My swollen nose had been bleeding and itching all night and when Anders took a look with his flashlight he saw the chigger hanging there.

He laughed. "Another inch and he's in your sinus."

"Just get it out," I said.

He made a long tweezer from a piece of split bamboo and snubbed off the ends on the toe of his boot to soften the wood and maneuvered the stick carefully up my nose. He slowly pulled out what looked like a bloody black grape and studied it.

"Big fella, what's left of him," he said.

"What do you mean?"

"His head is still in there," Anders said.

"His head."

"His head. You swelled up and the head broke off and now it's stuck. You have to wait for it to fall out. Just hope it don't infect. That's all I can do for you now. Keep your fingers out of there. You'll live."

He handed me a plastic camera film canister filled with ointment. "My special brew," he said. "Maybe they'll give you a Purple Heart."

"You said the head is in there."

"Don't be a fucking pussy, Stan."

My nose itched as I walked the trail and watched for trap signs. They used toe-popper mines in this area, single .50 caliber gun shells filled with powder and scrap metal. It wouldn't kill you but your day would be ruined. Sometimes you could see the exposed wax pressure caps sticking up on a trail if the ground was wet. I stood for a moment and studied a pair of branches hanging above the narrow track and detoured around the disturbed vegetation and walked in a deep rut made by a bicycle tire. I avoided stepping on anything in the shade, and the bars of sunlight filtering down through the trees forced me to stop and study everything. I looked for any odd alignment of rocks and sticks. Fresh animal tracks were relatively safe. Don't over think this, I whispered to myself. Walk slowly. Forget the itching in your nose. Look at your feet and watch where you swing the barrel of your weapon.

I stopped. Two small boys were riding an ox slowly across the rice paddy and one child's bare legs made a slapping sound as he spurred the animal through the shallow water. From behind me came a brief metallic clicking noise. I crouched. I heard the others coming: the dull knocking of somebody's canteen, shuffling boots, the rustle of pack webbing. I was about to trot back and signal them to stop when the boys on the ox both twisted backwards and jumped off and began to run, high-stepping as they splashed through the water, looking back at me as they disappeared into the trees like they'd seen a ghost.

By then it was already too late.

CHAPTER 27

The smoke flowed overhead like an inverted torrent of black water. When magical Chaz, the hairy and buck-toothed Merlin of the underworld, finished unshrinking me I looked like a Mr. Potato Head doll assembled by angry pre schoolers.

The Gopher King and his cohorts, all of whom didn't seem to appreciate that we were about to be sautéed alive, thought this was very funny. Twelve giggling gophers sound like an Alvin & the Chipmunks Christmas song played backwards.

My nose remained small and I looked like I was wearing a pencil eraser on my face. I watched one finger, then two...then the remaining digits swell and pop loudly into their normal size, like those skinny balloon creatures that clowns make at birthday parties.

I took a step and fell on my face.

"Give it a minute," Chaz said.

My left arm was only a foot long. The other was over-sized and rippled with pumped-up muscles I'd never seen before in my life.

Chaz stifled a laugh. "It takes a while to sort itself out," he said and poked my shin with one paw. "You're almost there."

A wall of red flames moved toward us. A baking heat descended from the trees and a hot wind blew away the tarp we had been hiding under. The gophers started running madly in circles.

And then my grotesquely buff right arm twitched itself into a familiar shape. But when I looked at my feet I was wearing giant Mickey Mouse cartoon shoes, which actually felt comfortable.

My button nose tingled and returned to normal size and when I asked Chaz how I looked, he said it was like I'd been in a bar fight with a drunken gorilla.

"There," the Gopher King said, stepping back to admire his sorcery.

"But I don't want to do that again," he said. "No, sir. All the parts don't always come back, if you know what I mean."

"No, I don't," I said.

"If you know what I mean," Chaz said very slowly and grinned.

Dear God.

This was no time to wonder if I looked like Clark Gable or the Hunchback of Notre Dame, because just then three hysterical gophers screamed and crawled up my leg as the grass around us caught fire. Chaz charged ahead toward an opening in the trees, but I scooped him up and told the others to hop aboard. And then I started running. My knees were killing me.

Twelve rats clung to my shirt. Chaz rappelled up the side of my face and sat on my head.

I shaped my shirt into a sack, and this is how I carried the gophers...except for Chaz, who seemed to like his perch atop my skull.

I broke through the burning scrub oak with my bag of rats. I stumbled on my bad knees over burning stump holes that glowed like openings into the netherworld. The dangerous pits were only a few feet apart.

"We have to go slow now," I said. "Step into one of those and we're toast, literally."

I walked carefully. The heat came through the soles of my shoes. Briefly, the smoke cleared and I said we should wait for a minute until we got a sense of the fire's direction.

I walked to a scorched tree and ran my hand along the bald wood and felt the heat inside. It was eerily quiet, a muffled crackling in the dark distance like static from a broken music speaker.

Eleven sooty gopher faces poked out from my shirt.

Where the fire had broken free from the tree I could see a corkscrew shape, like a thick pencil doodle impressed into the wood that marked the exit and direction of the flame. The black gash was leaking pine sap that was now baked into a glassy resin. I sniffed my hand. Kerosene.

"Fucking pyro freak has been all over this place," I said out loud, remembering the guy in the pickup truck.

I smeared away the ash from Chaz's head. I searched my pocket and came out with a half eaten candy bar and started chewing. I offered some to my rodents, and they declined politely.

Something snapped and exploded far away, the crash follow by a long hiss. A breeze, cool and dry as if a vent had sprung open in the sky, stirred the burning trees. There came a low moaning sound. The wind pushed the smoke aside and we were again swallowed by a cloud of sticky soot. I covered my face and tucked my bag of squirming gophers under one arm.

I kicked a burned tree stump. The black wood tossed up a ball of sparks.

"This thing has been burned twice," I said. "Something set it on fire again."

I dug into the base of the stump with my heel. The dirt was hot, the wood much too dark and the ground duff for as far as I could see had long burned to the soil's mineral layer. This told something of the fire's age and strength and of what might be expected further along the trail.

"This thing has been cooking for a long while," I said, knowing we didn't have much chance of getting off the mountain.

I leaned and spat. I heard the expected sizzle. Ahead lay another field of glowing stump holes just waiting for my feet to disturb their slumber.

I had once taken one of my newspaper interns to cover a wildfire. The kid showed up in shorts and a tee shirt, like he was headed for the beach. He stepped into a stump hole and the heat melted the plastic zipper on his shorts. They had to take him back to town on a tool gurney. He called me from the hospital and said it was the most exciting thing he'd done in his life.

Another breeze brought with it the peppery scent of newly ignited smoke, the kind that carries with it the smell of green bark and fresh leaves.

A small herd of elk came stumbling through the trees. They stopped and bunched up, snorting when they saw me, my satchel of chattering rats, and the live gopher hat I was wearing on my head.

I guess they hadn't seen this before.

A big bull, his shoulders streaked with soot, lowered his head and pawed the soil while the other animals back-stepped nervously into the smoke. I knew exactly what had chased them toward us.

"Let's get out of here," I said.

Chaz's tail started thumping against the back of my head and he jumped off and ran to a large outcrop of rock that looked out over the valley. The gopher king stood and tossed up his short paws and started screeching the way gophers do when they're warning others of a coming danger.

Then the others started jerking around and they jumped from my arms and ran over and did the very same thing. There they were, a dozen fur balls, standing and bowing and yelping like a row of excited acolytes in a weird outdoor temple, praying for salvation to the dark and smoking sky.

I let them do their thing for a while before I shouted that we should get going before the barbecue caught up with us again.

That's when I saw the squadron of twin-engine, tandem motor, heavy lift Chinook helicopters heading toward us in perfect military formation.

And they weren't being flown by humans.

The six miniature aircraft hovered while Chaz, ever the commander-in-chief, gestured at the sky with complex hand signals and furious tail bobs. He hopped up and down and stretched his paws as he directed the aircraft to our rescue.

He looked like a drunken Kung Fu master practicing his moves.

The ropes, as flimsy as kite twine, were lowered. Chaz and two gophers remained on the ground while the others were hauled aboard the choppers. From behind, bright flames reached at us from the trees like lit torches.

Chaz bit my leg.

"Now listen. Pay attention," he said sternly. "Are you afraid of heights?"

I explained that my personal best was the top rung of a six-foot ladder. Higher, and I vomit and faint.

"How nice."

"Do what you have to do," I said, still wondering if my best option wasn't to head back to town alone and let the rodents fly to safety. But Chaz would have none of it.

"Not possible," he said, looking back at the approaching fire.

"It's too far, and you're wearing shorts. I've seen you run on those knees."

I watched a pine tree explode into a rising pyre of yellow flames.

Chaz fluttered his forepaws at the choppers and motioned for me to lay down on my back. Two gophers took the dangling ropes and tied my arms and legs. One of them twisted my hips and fashioned a sailor's bowline knot that connected yet another rope which, when pulled, folded me up like a farm sow ready for butchering.

The Chinook engines whined loudly and strained to lift me a few feet off the ground, their rotors trembling with effort.

I hung there in my ridiculous rope diaper.

The gopher king and his two soldiers hitched themselves up and were pulled through the chopper's bay doors. Chaz gave a thumbs up sign. The Chinooks lifted me higher, their turbine engines struggling with my weight.

I looked down and where we had been standing was now covered with burning grass, the flames lapping over the edge of the cliff. Smoke swallowed everything as the helicopters tipped and swung me over the precipice. The canyon bottom was a thousand feet straight down. The ropes tightened around my ankles.

And then I got sick and chucked my lunch like a kid on his first roller coaster ride.

My sudden lurching movement was too much for the overloaded Chinooks. They wobbled off course, one aircraft loosing altitude while the other lifted on a rising thermal wind so I was now stretched sideways with my crossed legs headed in opposite directions.

One chopper tried to compensate, but the ropes got more tangled so I now was positioned with arms held high, legs splayed as I realize we were headed back toward the burning mountain.

The turbines howled as the aircraft, fighting the winds, struggled to keep my hefty flesh aloft. It wasn't looking good. I closed my eyes.

There came a loud grinding sound, and then all three choppers, as if they'd practiced this maneuver, descended in a controlled auto rotation emergency landing that dropped us along the vertical face of the cliff and into the valley below. I twirled and tried to scream, but nothing would come out.

I landed with a hard thump in a mess of tangled rope in a field next to the new ski lodge they were building south of town. The gophers hopped out of their choppers and untied me. I stood and wobbled on unsteady legs.

"I'll call in more helicopters," Chaz said.

I waved him off. I was dizzy. "Please, no more."

There was no danger where we stood, but we were down wind from the fire and I knew there wasn't much time to come up with a Plan B.

The lodge stood in silhouette against a wall of smoke, and off to one side stood a large water cistern propped on twenty-foot high metal legs, like a bucket sitting on a stool. A long hose swung from the tank, its end fastened to a nozzle with a valve. Downhill from the tank the pine trees had already caught fire. I knew by the way the smoke was blowing that the rest of the blaze wasn't far behind.

Our safety was temporary. I kneeled and gathered my rodents in a circle, and I picked up Chaz and pointed him toward the giant water tank.

"Can you chew through the hose?" I said.

Chaz squinted. "I think so. Why?"

"Time to put those big buck teeth to work," I said, and explained how I wanted all of the gophers to climb the tank and chew through the three-inch canvas fire hose.

"And when the water starts to come I want you to get back down real quick. There's no time to explain. You have to just trust me."

"Are you thirsty?" Chaz asked. "I don't understand."

"Please just go do it," I said.

"We don't like water," Chaz said. "We hate water when it moves."

"Do what I say."

Chaz shrugged and turned and all twelve rodents clambered up the metal tank legs like little paratroopers climbing the sheer sand dunes of Omaha Beach. Chaz hung from one paw and swung from rung to rung. He scuttled around the bottom of the tank and grabbed the swinging hose in his teeth. The others joined in, gnawing frantically like senior citizens at an all-you-can-eat buffet.

It didn't take long for the water to start spraying, and when the hose finally split apart a gushing torrent issued forth. The wet gophers screamed hysterically and slid down and assembled at my feet.

I ran and got a large wheel barrow from a tool shed. I scooped up my rodents and tossed them in, grabbed the handles and stood there until the 10,000 gallon tank gave a loud belch and suddenly transformed the place into an instant whitewater rapids.

And then our ark lifted, spun around, and began to float away

"Surf's up!" I yelled as the big wave of muddy water carried us downhill.

The wet gophers huddled together like refugees from a shipwreck. My head snapped back and I held on as the water torrent shot us away like some adventure ride at an amusement park.

We rafted for about a quarter mile, bouncing off trees, the surging water funneling us into a gully as we rushed safely through the heart of the fire. We all screamed. We were covered with wet soot. My frightened gophers looked like...well, drowned rats.

When it was over Chaz and his commandos hopped out and stood there dripping wet, shivering.

And then they started shitting violently. Just scampering around in circles and dropping milk duds everywhere in celebration of their sudden salvation. I stepped out of range. This is what always happens when they get excited. I've told you this before.

Chaz blinked. "You saved our lives," he gasped.

I told him to keep his distance. "Are you boys finished?"

Chaz looked around. "What?"

"That shit dance you always do when you get worked up. Are you finished?"

Chaz blushed and looked at me like I'd just asked him how many cigars General U. S. Grant smoked at the Battle of Vicksburg.

When a gopher blushes, only its nose turns red.

"Let's get out of here," I said, stepping past the piles of wet rat pebbles.

I gathered everybody up. I hoped I wouldn't meet anyone along the trail back to town.

It would difficult to explain why I was carrying a dozen soaking wet rodents on my shoulders.

CHAPTER 28

Miriam the librarian called and reported with amused suspicion that a Claymore mine weighed exactly three pounds.

"You doing a story?"

"Sort of."

"Sort of a column in the paper again about those gophers? The little darlings, I'm sorry for them."

"Well," I said.

The librarian asked, "Stan, are you still using your old typewriter at the newspaper? You know, I could teach you how to use the computer here at the library. You could look this stuff up yourself. Save a lot of time. It's very easy."

I said, "My typewriter is easy, too."

I imagined 700 tiny steel balls spraying 50 yards in a sixty-degree arc, mowing down my platoon. I remembered the medic Anders on the day of the ambush. He was crouched in the grass, struggling to cut away somebody's web gear, a packet of gauze clenched in his teeth. The blue-green tracer bullets sprayed over his head but Anders never ducked as he tended to the unseen wounded soldier. A few times he took his .45 and fired at the trees. A moment later Anders vanished behind a cloud of mortar smoke and I never saw him again.

Two pounds, three pounds, did it matter? I remembered digging up a dud ChiCom booby trap mine with my mess kit spoon, laying on my stomach to disarm it, my cheek inches from what I hoped was a disconnected trip wire. Brushing away the dried mud with my finger, I was close enough to recognize the creosote they'd used to waterproof the pie-shaped metal cover. There were two detonators, a spidery pressure fuse at the top and the detachable o-ring that held the trip wire. The fuse was already bent inward toward the detonator and the wire was as taught as a guitar string. I placed a stick beneath the fuse and stretched the wire loop away from the small tree it had been fastened to until the wire got slack and I could lift up the mine itself. I cut the wire.

The lieutenant had given me a slap on the back for that little trick, though I sensed the others in the platoon thought I might have been just a little dim for such a hot dog move. We could have easily called in the engineers, though it would have meant staying another night in the field because everybody would have missed the chopper flight back to base camp. Still, I gloated, my bravery perceived only by me, the others thinking I was a showboating asshole. For a while they teased me and called me Stan Without a Plan.

My wife had always asked why they reassigned me after I got my embarrassing medal, after which I was put on tour like a champion dog. Another reporter from *Pacific Stars & Stripes* interviewed me in the hospital in Busan. There was the long R&R in Bangkok and then Saigon and a shopping spree in Tokyo, where a full bird colonel met my plane at Yokota and walked me around the HQ and then pulled strings so I could ship my new giant Panasonic stereo speakers and a couple of Nikons home for free.

It would have been cruel to tell her what else I'd done during my second tour.

I'd given her a predictable story; a linear tale with a beginning, a middle and a satisfying end. Nobody with sense would want to hear the rest of it. How do you explain how a tongue is the last part to dry, so that's what the birds go after first. You don't tell people such things.

But I might tell Dr. Nguyen about arms swelled so big in the heat they would burst through the shirtsleeves of the abandoned dead.

I wanted to tell Nguyen how surprised I was to discover that it was easier killing another human being than it was removing a hook from a fish you did not wish to harm. I would, with shame, admit to him how my time over there was the most exciting and absorbing period of my life

I would tell the good doctor I feared dying only because I might be compelled in the afterlife by whoever supervises things up there to meet those I had murdered. These people would be standing in a row like a reception line at a wedding, wearing the clothes they had died in, each in their particular state of decrepitude —armless, faceless, parts and pieces seeking an apology I knew would never be accepted.

I proofed the layout galleys and made changes, leaving open space on the front page. I checked off the display ads on a clipboard that hung above the roll top desk. Twelve hundred paid column inches this week, along with six full pages of public notices, most of which were municipal annexation advisories between the town and the Gold Gulch company, along with a lengthy water rights agreement nobody in their right mind would read that allowed the resort to increase its snow making capacity from the river. I expected Dora McCoy would have something more to say about that.

A pile of file folders, yet more public notices, lay on my chair: county trustee sales, the monthly town budget, county construction bid requests, and an avalanche of bankrupt timeshare legals that had come by courier from a Denver law firm, along with a check for $4,075.53 and instructions to send tearsheets by FedEx on the day following publication. All good and easy money.

Cassie, my summer intern who worked when Tuesday wasn't there on Wednesday, handed over my phone messages and said a production manager from CNN had dropped by to ask if his crew could park a satellite truck overnight in the driveway next to the office.

Cassie turned up the scanner and listened to the police chatter.

"Hope you didn't mind, but I said it would be okay to park. They said they would pay. Can you imagine, CNN here in our little town?"

"I'm very thrilled," I said.

I tossed the film roll into the wicker basket on the front counter, marked ten column inches off on the layout flat with a blue pen, and labeled the empty news hole: MB. The top quarter of the page was set aside for a sidebar on the suspected arsonist.

I flipped through more phone messages, one of them from the county coroner, Carmen Ruiz.

I pointed toward the darkroom "I need the film souped tonight, please."

"A picture of the body?"

"Not the way it's done, you know that."

"I knew Melinda," Cassie said. "We weren't, like, good friends…but she was sweet."

Cassie stepped to the light table. She was a pleasant girl. Chronically perky. She had watery gray eyes. Today she wore a flimsy teen tank top, shorts, flip flops. Her hair was tied back with a rubber band. A delicate tattoo of barbed wire encircled her tanned forearm. She examined the film canister.

Cassie stared at the floor and took a deep breath. She wiped her eye with the heel of her palm and let out a soft moan.

"The last time I saw her she seemed so happy."

"We're just doing the obit and an update this issue," I said. "So keep things to yourself for a while, okay?"

"Mister P…she worked on that archaeological thing with the bones they found at the resort, didn't she?"

"Came back from college in spring, yes," I said.

"She was famous at school. Her scholarship to CU and everything. She was beautiful. Just really pretty and smart. Who would want to hurt her?"

"I left a page one hole," I said. I was in a daze.

"I'll get something for you later tonight. Tom can give you the other cop details. I have to go over to the coroner's office."

"I can write the story. Please, I can," Cassy said.

"You can add the coroner's update," I said. "But I'll handle the obit myself."

I knew I had to talk to Melinda Barstow's father about his daughter's relationship with Jergen. I wasn't looking forward to it.

CHAPTER 29

...when tall coarse grass surrounds, they seem commonly to destroy this within their streets, which are nearly always found paved with a fine species suited to their palates. They must need but little water, if any at all, as their towns are often, indeed generally, found in the midst of the most arid plains — unless we suppose they dig down to subterranean fountains. At least they evidently burrow remarkably deep. Attempts either to dig or drown them out of their holes have generally proved unsuccessful.

Approaching a village, the little dogs may be observed frisking about the streets — passing from dwelling to dwelling apparently on visits — sometimes a few clustered together as though in council — here feeding upon the tender herbage — there cleansing their houses, or brushing the little hillock about the door — yet all quiet.

JOSIAH GREGG (1806-1850) Explorer and
Santa Fe Trail merchant. From a journal entry.

I tried to get work done, but fell asleep in my chair instead.

Something startled me awake. The Cheerios cereal box on the roll top desk was overflowing with pure gold dust.

Chaz was sitting on my typewriter. I don't know how these gophers get into my office.

He was wearing a black eye patch and a sparkly *Van Halen* tee shirt. He was listening to his iPod. His face was scratched, an oval patch of fur singed off the top of his head. He looked like a Benedictine monk pirate.

"All that dough," I said. "Thanks."

"We're grateful for your help. Buy something nice."

"It's not so easy," I said. "You can't just go to the bank and turn a few pounds of gold into dollars. People notice stuff. Uncle Sam notices stuff."

"Chump change," Chaz said, as he shuffled his feet and jived to some unknown headbanger bass line.

"Buy a Ferrari. Fly to Paris for lunch with a lady friend. There's more where that came from."

"Folks here already think I'm nuts. They see me all of a sudden buying stuff, next thing the cops show up. And I don't have a lady friend."

"The Coroner," Chaz said. "She's sweet on you."

"Nobody is sweet on me. The last thing I need is somebody being sweet on me. How do you so much about my private life?"

"I know a lot of things," Chaz said.

"Shit you do," I said.

"Welcome to my world."

I changed the subject. You can't reason with Chaz when he's caught in a paroxysm of rock music. A few months ago he became obsessed with Stevie Ray Vaughan and then declared a whole week of public observances in honor of other rockers who perished in plane crashes. On Buddy Holly Day all gophers were encouraged to wear sunglasses and face east toward the Iowa cornfield where he died. On Rick Nelson Day nothing aired on Gopher TV except *Ozzie & Harriet* re runs.

I pulled off his earbuds. He gave me that hurt gopher look: eyes all squinty, whiskers twitching.

I told Chaz about a phone call I'd gotten from old Dora McCoy, the owner of the Last Chance Ranch, who said gophers were giving her problems.

"You know anything about this?"

Chaz smiled. "Sorry, not my clan. Those rats on her property are a different breed. We don't get along. Watch out, they're dangerous."

The royal rodent explained how a few thousand of his kind were still trapped near the ski resort next to the McCoy property, unable to escape the construction crews digging up their land. They were running out of food, but had declined Chaz's offer to help them escape.

"They're very stubborn," Chaz said. "We tried to evacuate them, even flew in supplies, but they pitched rocks at us."

A Hummer filled with heavily armed commandos came and picked Chaz up at the back door. I didn't want to ask where he was headed. I waved as the tiny vehicle bounced through the grass and swerved away through the alley in a cloud of dust.

And so I headed to the Last Chance Ranch, following a lumpy switchback road to the top of a mesa that overlooked the 5,000-acre property. The old lady had left me a message to say she had a news tip.

The ski resort had been trying to buy Dora's property for years, offering her a quick fortune for the water rights alone, but the old lady always refused to sell.

I parked next to a crippled tractor. The place was a mess. Over there was a broken corral filled with lumber scrap and junked refrigerators and discarded appliances. Piles of chairs. Two chewing cows regarded me dumbly as I walked by, their heads turning as if on ball swivels. The place was badly kept and weedy, frayed at the edges like something about to be abandoned. I stepped over piles of horse plop on a crooked flagstone path that petered out abruptly a few yards shy of a sagging front porch. Dora's tarpaper roof was weighted with river stones, one broken window patched with duct tape. A confused-looking chicken walked back and forth on the porch, pecking at the sun-bleached floorboards. Off to the side a relic pickup truck with a mismatched door sat parked next to a crumbling outhouse.

The old lady stepped out and peered at me from beneath her wrinkled Stetson and hooked one thumb into her belt. The other arm hung in a sling, the fingers swelled like red sausages.

"Dora, you look under the weather," I said.

"Been better," she said. She leaned and hocked a wad of tobacco sauce and spit. Wind chimes made from rusty horseshoes clanged on the porch. A horse whinnied somewhere and a cow answered it, then a dog barked. The landscape everywhere was empty beneath a dome of hazy sky, noiseless, except for the hot wind and the distant growl of firefighting equipment.

"Snagged myself on barbed wire, is all," Dora said, regarding her arm suspiciously. "Was chasing a varmint."

"Looks infected," I said.

"Nothing a poultice won't fix."

"You should see a doctor," I said and offered to drive her to town.

"It'll mend," she said and started to rattle up something in her throat again. She looked around for a place to spit, but changed her mind and swallowed.

"Suit yourself," I said.

"Aim to."

"All right then."

I wanted to spit myself, just to honor this conversation.

The old woman wiggled her wounded fingers, which glistened and were wrapped in something leafy. She steadied herself on the porch rail with her good arm.

"You sure I can't take you to the clinic? It's no trouble at all."

"Been alive awhile without no doctor's help, thank you," Dora growled. "Don't care for those over-priced butchers at all, no sir. But you're a gent for asking. By the way, I've been calling your place for days and you're never there."

"Sorry," I said. "I got your message. Been fairly busy. I was out of town for a while."

Dora's creased face broke into a smile and she reached into her denim shirt pocket and tugged off another plug of tobacco and started chewing. She lifted her hat and ran one hand through her flowing white hair. She raised her good arm and pointed.

"Follow me," she said.

We walked. Inside the dim shed behind the cabin a dusty light lit the leaning walls. It was as cool as a cave. Old blackened ranch tools lay on the floor and the remains of rusty bedsprings stood tipped into the corner. An ancient stovepipe leading nowhere hung from the ceiling. Dora said the place had once been used for storing grain and hay, and before that served as a bunkhouse.

"Be careful," she said. "That wall is set to surprise somebody. There's a foot of river rock in it and it's a heavy thing to have drop on your head. Anyway, there it is."

She shot off another wad of tobacco juice. She brought out a flashlight from her pocket.

"Varmints," she said, pointing. "It's the same everywhere except the cabin. Seems they don't touch what's lived in."

I kneeled. There were claw marks everywhere, as if somebody had dragged a thousand dinner forks across the foundation mortar at the base of the stone wall. A neat trench had been dug around the inside perimeter of the building. Another hole had been excavated, forcing the wall to buckle.

"This isn't the only place, no sir. Had to move the horses from the summer shed," Dora said, chuckling. "Those critters chewed through the support beams and made short work of a whole wall of two-by-fours. Never seen the likes of it. But they don't seem to want to touch the house. It's because I live there, I think. They don't want to hurt nobody. I think they got manners or a sort of animal code."

I tried to look stupid and decided not to ask questions.

"They're at war with us," Dora said. "Have seen the signs for a long while. There's thousands of those little fellas over in my old hay meadow. Seen them there since I was a little girl. And my daddy said they were there before that. We always left them alone. They never bothered us, and we stayed on our side of the street. But now I think they're taking back what belongs to them. All the trouble in town? I seen it in your newspaper. Them gophers are fighting back. They don't like all this ruination. I don't like it, neither. Golf course and all. The fancy resort, especially — but don't get me started. You ask me to take sides and I'll take those gophers over any rich jackass in a golf cart any day, yes sir. Any damn day."

Dora enjoyed another well-aimed spit. She was one phlegm-filled lady. As we walked back to my truck she pointed off toward where you could see the roof of the ski lodge poking up a half-mile away. She gave a long sigh and looked at her boots.

"My father once stood right here and pointed yonder and said when he was a boy he'd seen smoke from an Indian camp. Not far from the golf course that wants to take my water. Utes, they were, and they'd snuck back to hunt on their old land one last time."

The old lady moaned and rubbed her sore arm. Her eyes teared up and she swallowed.

"There's a ghost behind every tree up here, and they're always reminding me of what's happened on this land. It ain't easy being the last of something, let me tell you. It's why I understand what those animals are up to."

I decided not to mention anything about the police report saying someone had heard rifle shots from the direction of the ranch on the day of Melinda Barstow's murder.

I took more pictures and pretended to write in my notebook. She started to walk off and as I began to drive away Dora shouted: "Don't you dare tell nobody, but you might want to take a close look at that ski lodge. See what them rats have on their minds. I suspect you'll be entertained."

And then the old lady studied a fence post about twenty feet away, took a deep breath, and let go with another airborne hocker that easily hit its bullseye.

That woman sure can spit.

CHAPTER 30

I took an involuntary nap at my desk while getting ready to typeset a story Cassie had written about a play they were performing at the high school. I fell asleep with the blue editing pencil in my hand.

And my brain, of course, galloped away…

The Bellyache Mountain Gopher Playhouse holds performances on most weekends in a giant cave somewhere at the far end of the colony. The acoustics are amazing, if you don't mind the flying bats. And the dripping stalactites. The place reeks of wet cement and gopher shit.

The theatre schedule is eclectic. Most of the time it is standard fare, the stuff high school drama classes perform: *Man of La Mancha* and *West Side Story*. Gophers are fascinated with Broadway musicals with titles that have exclamation marks, like *Oklahoma!* and *Oh, Calcutta!*, which was shut down one night by the gopher police because it had naked dancers in it. Most gophers run around in their birthday suits anyway, so I don't understand that.

The idea for a gopher theatre came from Tinka. Chaz's energetic 14th wife coordinates set construction, does the marketing, auditions the actors and supervises costume design. She once tried to persuade Chaz to play the part of the mentally unstable, delusional Willy Loman in *Death of a Salesman*, but the suddenly shy king said he couldn't pretend he was crazy in front of his subjects. They'd get the wrong idea.

These little rats can surprise you. I attended the opening night of *Waiting for Godot*, a dark, unhappy and plotless play written by a famous Irish guy. It's about two depressing geezers who wait next to a tree near a road they seem afraid to travel on. That's it. It is all they do: talk gibberish and nonsense and stand next to a tree, waiting for a guy who never shows up. No chase scenes, no sword fights with men in capes, no confessional soliloquies. Nothing. What kind of play is that?

One of the old men is deaf, the other is mute. I couldn't wait for *Waiting for Godot* to be over. When it was, I wanted to cut my wrists.

But the show brought down the house. There were numerous curtain calls and bouquets of tossed flowers. The chattering gophers absolutely loved it and seemed to see not despair and hopelessness in the play's message of doom, but rather joy and revelation. Chaz was sitting next to me in the theatre and he had tears in his eyes, a big smile on his face...like he'd just had a private chat with God. He couldn't stop clapping.

Puzzled, I asked him what the play was about. He shook his head like I was a dunce.

"If you want to have a headache about the meaning of things, then you have to provide your own aspirin," he said. "You figure it out."

I mention this theatre business only because I noticed gopher trucks loaded with two-by-fours and sheets of plywood making deliveries to the colony. I was told the Gopher Playhouse was staging a production of *Cats*, and the lumber was being used to build the set.

You heard me: singing rodents dressed up like cats. Now, that's entertainment!

***

I woke up drooling on my reporter's notebook. I looked at my wrist and realized I needed to gather another story for the newspaper.

The town police blotter, which I publish each week in the *Beacon-News* because...well, other people's misery sells newspapers, had reported the theft of a load of lumber from the Gold Gulch ski resort construction site. Also stolen were enough Mikita drills and table saws and assorted carpentry tools to fill Home Depot during a Father's Day sale.

And so I drove to the lodge. Because of the wildfire, the sheriff had already closed the road and there was police tape strung around the place to keep people out. I showed my press pass to a deputy and said I was taking pictures for the paper and he let me in. Cops never read what's on a press pass. I could have presented my library card.

The half-framed walls of the building towered over me. The unfinished main floor of the lodge was stacked with enormous cedar beams that would soon support the roof. River rock and sacks of mortar were piled next to a giant hearth that looked like Orson Wells' fireplace in the movie, *Citizen Kane*.

In the center of the room an enormous I-beam soared through the open roof, its top decorated with a fluttering American flag like this was 1812 and we'd just captured the place from the British.

Now I heard a familiar scratching sound.

The gophers were standing in a row, hunched along the perimeter of the building like pigs at a trough. They ignored me as I watched them nibble at the bottom of the wooden support pillars, which looked like they'd already been chewed in half. I clapped my hands and when they turned they looked annoyed and resumed their gnawing.

I yelled: "Hey!"

They seemed angry now, and after much squeaking and fluttering of forepaws they resumed their sabotage with renewed vigor.

When gophers do something with renewed vigor, it's usually a bad sign.

The wind started blowing, bringing with it the scent of the wildfire.

The roof of the lodge groaned and swayed noticeably. I heard more scratching, and over by the unfinished fireplace in the lobby another crew of rats were clawing away like insane gardeners.

"Hey!" I yelled again.

When they turned, I recognized a few of Chaz's people because of the camo military pants they were wearing. And the sunglasses. These rodents love their sunglasses.

But the others looked different; wild and feral, like the gophers I had seen at Dora McCoy's ranch.

Chaz's gophers were handling little bricks of what looked like modeling clay and packing the stuff around the spots they'd chewed. I hollered again and started walking toward them. I waved my arms. They scattered.

I kneeled and picked off a chunk of the C-4 explosive. This material burns but won't explode unless it's detonated in a specific way.

I removed as much as I could reach, but a few feet up the beam I could still see the light gray explosive clinging to the roof joists like little swallow's nests. I didn't know gophers could climb so high.

I hurried away. I needed to see Chaz and give him a piece of my mind. Now he'd gone too far.

CHAPTER 31

These rodents don't have names for each other. Chaz says everyone has their own scent, so there's no need. He's never addressed me by name, though he routinely calls me Chump, Hey You, Big Fella, Newspaper Boy, Dork with Outdated Mustache…as well as many unmentionables. Hang him blindfolded and upside down from a tree, spin him around a few times, and Chaz can detect his nameless third cousin from fifty yards away and tell you what he ate for supper.

For all the Gopher King cares, I could call him Grumpy, Sneezy or Dopey…though he admits the name Chaz has grown on him and comes in handy when he buys stuff he doesn't really need on the QVC Shopping Channel. The credit card he uses bears the name Chaz Von Rodenthaus.

I wanted to confront Chaz about what Dora had told me about the ski lodge. Instead, I came across someone who I'd only met once before: Genghis, the military Chief of Staff of the People's Gopher Army (PGA).

Genghis was smoothing out a topographical map with his forepaws, spreading the sheet on the ground outside the main burrow entrance of the Bellyache Mountain gopher colony. Two uniformed soldiers eyed me warily as I approached, cocking their little AK-47s and taking aim until their boss waved them away.

Genghis, a distant cousin on Chaz's mother's side, is expectedly very rugged-looking. He walks with a limp and his fur is covered with nicks and scrapes and scars that speak to a lifetime of violence and daring military escapades. He is a legend among his kind.

Like Chaz, Genghis refuses to tell me his age, except to say he was at Alamogordo when the first atomic bomb was tested…and then he winks, as if alluding to Plutonium-239, which allegedly first gave these gophers their unusual powers.

At 15 lbs, he looks like an obese marmot. He towers over all the other gophers. Genghis wears a speckled doo rag on his head and has a single dark, expressive eye. The other one is scarred over and puckered, like a dimpled pillow. He lost the eye when he got smacked in the head with a nine-iron during an attempted amphibious assault at the Gold Gulch Country Club ornamental fish pond, during which a Hellfire rocket misfired, killing 475 Japanese koi and forcing Genghis to land his Blackhawk helicopter on an outdoor buffet table.

I have witnessed Genghis hanging from a rope beneath a hovering helicopter while holding an M-60 machine gun in one hand, a loaded bullet bandoleer clenched in his teeth. He is one rough character and is a gopher of few words, though he'll start shouting if you bring up the subject of computers or telephone technology of any kind. He favors the AK-47 over the M-16, which he says is a glorified and unreliable pea shooter, the weeny rifle of the uneducated.

Genghis is in charge of Chaz's personal body guard, a platoon of a dozen creepy looking rodents who sport neck tattoos and wear pinky rings and remind me of deformed Soviet KGB agents. He also accompanies the king on special missions. He collects photos of famous Prussian field marshals, can bench press three times his body weight and has never married, but claims he has twenty-six children, which is not unusual among these gophers. They are not depraved, but rather uncontrollably lovable.

When he's not rappelling down a mountain or tossing grenades at a golfer dressed in pastel-blue walking shorts, Genghis likes to ride his classic liquid cooled, fuel-injected Harley-Davidson V-twin at top speed at midnight through the COSTCO parking lot in Bull River Falls.

Genghis studied his map and looked at me.

"Where's your boss?" I asked sternly.

The fat rat wiped his paws on his black multi-pocketed Ninja trousers and poked his chin toward the mountains.

"Monthly training up at the caves," he said.

"Training to hurt innocent people at the lodge?"

"What's it to you?" Genghis said, putting his paws on his hips...such as they were. Gophers have a hard time with pants, let me tell you. I need to introduce them to suspenders.

I explained that shooting harmless bullets the size of peas was one thing, but making an entire building collapse was dangerous.

"There's other ways to make a statement," I said.

"You should talk. Do you know how many of us get killed crossing the street around here every year?"

"I've tried to show you how to look both ways," I said. "But you won't listen. Don't change the subject. When does your boss get back?"

"Tomorrow," Genghis said. "We have a shipment of night vision goggles coming in."

"And from who, may I ask, did you steal that stuff?"

Genghis pulled out his pistol and took aim at my knee. "How about I end this conversation right now?"

General Genghis, his fur bristling, then raged on about the evils of telephonic discourse and explained how our miserable human world had been robotized and appified and automated to such a vulgar extreme that we were heading for a time when our unused brains would turn to mush and lose all ability for independent thought.

I said we weren't always like this and Genghis said, rather sadly: "Yes, so I've heard. You people were once almost human."

Genghis now explained in a remarkably calm voice, that the shortest path is always the most appealing and we had exchanged our hard-won common sense for speed and utility, and those conceits were only bait disguised as reward and that our end would not be pleasant.

"I could never understand," he said, tucking the 9mm Baretta into his belt. "You creatures live so very long. But you live so badly."

Genghis shook his head and pooped profusely, surrounding me in a deluge of Gopher Milk Duds. And then he disappeared down the nearest burrow hole.

CHAPTER 32

After finishing up in the darkroom and laying out the public notice pages — waxing each full spread by hand and boxing the Trustee sale announcements with black border tape, I poured another drink and killed the lights and sat in the dark.

The melted lead popping in the Linotype machine sounded like gunfire. I watched the soft, molten glow. Red light pulsed across the ceiling.

I thought of how, a lifetime ago, white muzzle smoke drifted across that rice paddy in Vietnam as short rifle bursts sprayed the trail on which I had told my boys to walk. I could hear shouting as I dropped and crawled into the trees.

Their shapes twisted and fell into the high grass. Our M-60 gunner fumbled with his tripod, his shoulder burdened with a 100-round ammo bandoleer, and as he squatted to aim and fire I watched a mortar splash into the rice paddy a few meters behind him. With the delayed burst came a fountain of rising brown water and spinning clots of mud. When the debris settled the soldier's four-quart field canteen lay next to the mangled machine gun, yet he was gone. I fired a few shots with my weapon, but there was nothing to aim at.

There came more rifle noise and three boys who had inexplicably remained standing on the exposed trail had also vanished. Birds lifted in noisy sheets from their roost in the plantation house, a twisting mass of tropical colors, and flew over the heads of the dying soldiers as if scolding us for our rude disturbance on this quiet morning.

A soldier stood holding his helmet with one hand and I watched his head and arm come off while the rest of him staggered upright for a while, his legs uncertain, and then what remained of him fell and lay twitching until the body decided it too should die. From the soldier's rucksack a smoke grenade fuse sputtered and ignited and lifted into a yellow ball that floated toward me like a curtain.

The noise was vulgar, a mindless racket that was very brief but seemed unstoppable and promised to last forever. The flying cakes of mud and branches themselves seemed filled with menacing life. Time felt compressed. The insistent noise was overwhelming, a single organism gathering itself to destroy only me.

More bright muzzle flashes came from the trees. I stood, and because of the sheltering smoke I never got hit. My unforgivable stunt of walking too far ahead of my squad, ignoring what I had been taught, had saved me.

I dropped into a squat, held my rifle at the horizontal, and managed to crab-walk toward higher grass. A few meters away, Pappas the radio telephone operator stood and hopped on one leg, smoke drifting from his shin. Something shook the bushes behind him and the shrapnel spray lifted Pappas in a spray of chunky mud, his arms windmilling in the smoke as if he'd rebounded from a backyard trampoline.

Pappas and his family owned a restaurant on Halstead Street in Chicago and he was short and olive skinned and liked to tell impossibly lame Greek jokes.

In mid-air, one of his legs broke cleanly away from his body and smoke came from where his hip had once been. Bright red arterial blood sprayed from the hole and the spinning limb landed with the unlaced boot still attached.

All these years later, the whiskey glass cool in my hand there in the shabby trailer, and I was still puzzled about how those laces could untie themselves with such precision.

I drank from the glass. I pondered the deadly trajectory of a Claymore mine. It might say something about that poor boy's shoe laces.

I drank again. The only thing worse than getting shot at is thinking about getting shot at.

I should have known better than to send my boys down such a dangerous trail.

Chickenshit.

I crawled and knelt beside Pappas' orphaned leg and touched it. The leg still had heat. It smelled of spilled C-rations, rifle lubricant, insecticide; the sour cologne of a soldier who has been fermenting in his damp clothes for too long.

A twitch heaved beneath where the bone stuck from his skin, disturbingly white and clean against the filthy fabric of the green field pants. His thigh gave a phantom twitch and a few Vietnamese coins and a folding knife fell from a pocket. There was a notepad, too. And a laminated card showing radio frequency codes written in pencil, which was non-reg and could have gotten Pappas in serious trouble. I put the radio codes in my shirt pocket.

Pappas wore an accessories bag attached to the straps holding the radio in place and it was stuffed with antenna components. A spare handset for the PRC-10 radio poked from the pocket flap. He had been carrying a flare, three smoke grenades, his map, a short field machete. I put the map in my pocket and jammed the sheathed machete behind my belt.

Somebody emerged from the smoking grass and came behind me and hollered: "Go! Go! Go!"

The PFC with an Italian name or an Irish name, I don't remember, slapped the top of my head and pointed up the trail. We both ran as another mortar raked through the trees. Rifle rounds snapped past.

When we were further up the trail, I turned. The PFC was chewing gum. The pink wad bounced against his tongue. He brought his face close and cupped his hands and shouted again.

"Sarge, what do you want us to do?" He held one hand to his ear like he was making a phone call.

The PFC pointed back toward what was left of Pappas.

Pappas, who was always talking trash about the old Greek playwrights and Homer and the Trojan War. Pappas, who knew about Elektra and Helen and Agamemnon and Clytemnestra and spoke of them like they were his favorites from a TV soap opera. He quoted once, during a card game in a bunker, rubber-lipped and drunk, jokes from the comedies of Aristophanes that nobody could understand. He referred to any beautiful women he saw as an "Aphrodite." Pappas could quote from the speech Pericles delivered during his funeral oration honoring the Athenian dead on the first anniversary of the Peloponnese War. He was thrilled when they assigned him to Delta Company because delta was the fourth letter in the Greek Alphabet. The fourth company of the 4th U.S. Army Infantry Division — the four-leaf clover its logo. How lucky could you get?

"Cover me," the PFC said.

"What?" I said.

"Cover. Me." The boy said it slowly like he was speaking to an idiot.

"What?"

"Jesus. Shit, sarge. You heard me. Are you hurt?"

"No," I said. "What?"

While I drank on the recliner in my trailer, so many years removed from that trail, I imagined I had been shot. With my eyes closed I touched the wet fabric of my shirt, but only found the overturned whiskey glass on my stomach.

I walked to the back of the trailer and put the empty glass in the sink. I turned on the little TV that hung beneath the kitchen cabinet.

The music, a flourish of military trumpets to announce another CNN report from Iraq, startled me. The spinning TV logo flashed BAGHDAD in fluorescent letters above the head of a reporter in a desert 7,000 miles away. The camera zoomed to a clean shaven soldier working at a laptop computer, casually typing an e-mail to his family back home. He wore a beautifully crisp and clean tan camo uniform, his collar lifting in the breeze of a table fan as his fingers danced effortlessly across the keyboard.

Chickenshit.

CHAPTER 33

It was not a large animal, perhaps a hundred pounds, but when the mountain lion wandered into the town park children's playground one hour before the annual Old Gold Days Festival parade was set to begin, things got touchy.

The cat, licking its singed forepaw, lay on the top rung of the yellow Jungle Gym while two police officers stretched crime scene tape and shooed folks away from the park.

Tom Cherry got waved over by a TV reporter, who positioned the police chief so the camera shot would show the lion sitting clearly in the background during the interview. Smoke gusted down from the mountains in gray sheets while Cherry kept smoothing his hair with one hand as he leaned into the microphone.

"And then I see this little white dog," he said, narrowing his hands together like he'd just caught a disappointing fish.

He smoothed his hair again and wiped his face with the back of the same hand and described how the pet dog had tried to attack the lion, which had apparently been chased into town by the fire.

"Little rascal was half-way up when it just stopped and sat down like it knew it'd made a big mistake," Cherry said. "Cat shot out one paw and sent the dog flying. The lion made a howly noise, the way they do. What made such an itty bitty thing go after a lion I don't know. A wolf instinct, I guess. My cat is bigger than that dog."

They shot a tranquilizer dart into the lion's hip and it went limp and fell off the Jungle Gym. They hauled the cat away in the back of a Colorado Parks and Wildlife pickup truck, the TV people filming the whole thing. Tom Cherry carried the dead white dog away in a white plastic bucket.

"Town is turning into Noah's Ark," Cherry told the TV reporter. He looked at where they were cleaning blood off the Jungle Gym with a garden hose.

"Fire burning everything, critters going insane. Gophers eating up buildings and chewing phone wires. That poor girl killed down by the river. I just don't know what's happening here."

They then interviewed the mayor of Bull River Falls, Anton Kirchenhausen, who insisted the parade and the festival would go on as planned. He said the wildfire was under control and there was no safety issue at all.

"I'm not telling our visitors to go home just because a little smoke might get in their eyes," he said. "The dog should have been on a leash, like the law says."

Thirty-six parade floats were lined up behind the county courthouse. Shriners in red vests and tasseled fez hats were gathered in the parking lot, practicing their famous figure-eight parade maneuvers on tiny motor scooters decorated with red pennants.

When the show got underway the mayor sat in an antique Colorado State Patrol squad car, a beige 1949 Ford sedan with whitewall tires and chrome bumpers. His job was to toss candy from the car for the kids who lined the parade route along Main Street.

Everybody was nervous about the fire. People kept looking at the sky as if they were waiting for a comet to appear. Two national guard helicopters performed a flyover like they did each year, but this time the choppers continued past the town limits and banked toward Gold Gulch, where you knew they were going to fight the wildfire now surrounding the golf course.

The parade featured a fleet of antique John Deere farm tractors that clattered down Main Street behind the Shriners on their scooters. One Shriner, shirtless and wearing a turban and carrying a curved sword, fell off his cycle and was carried away on a stretcher.

A flatbed truck piled with horse turds had a banner on it: "Enter the Manure Pile Tug-O-War on Saturday!" and everybody cheered wildly when the float rolled by.

The mayor, finished with his candy dispensing, rejoined the parade dressed in a Smokey the Bear costume. He strutted in front of a banner carried by two park rangers that warned people to be careful about starting forest fires.

The parade had rope-twirling cowboys dressed in wooly chaps who lassoed onlookers as they walked behind a team of pack mules loaded with sacks of fake gold ore. Two more National Guard helicopters came roaring low over the assembled crowd and the noise and rotor wash spooked the six draft horses pulling the Bull River Falls Fire Department's antique pumper rig. The team had to be coaxed to the library parking lot so the animals could calm down.

A float from the Gold Gulch Resort Company featured two girls in bikinis and fur caps performing skiing tricks on a jump ramp coated with synthetic snow.

A sidewalk vendor was doing great business selling prairie dog hand puppets.

Then the sky turned dark, and a black and red cloud appeared above Bellyache Mountain like the glowing red tongue of a volcano.

The blaze had now aimed itself directly toward the town.

The high school marching band stopped playing, lost its way in the smoke, and headed blindly down an alley. Mayor Kirchenhausen looked up at the burning mountain and angrily lifted off his Smokey the Bear costume head and threw it onto the street.

The eighty-third annual Bull River Old Gold Days celebration was officially over.

I took pictures and walked back to the office.

I opened the back door of the trailer and walked directly to the darkroom where I unloaded my camera and tossed the film into a little wicker basket. With a blue marker I scribbled a note on my empty page two layout sheet: "PLAYGROUND POODLE ATTACKS LION AT TOWN PARK."

I didn't hear the footsteps.

I didn't notice the shadow stretched faintly across the wall behind me, its elongated shape twisting past the ceiling corners.

I turned on another light, then flicked it off just as a cool breeze blew past my ear. I swung wildly at nothing in particular, catching the edge of somebody's chin with my lucky knuckle as I lost my balance and fell down hard on my bad knee.

In the dark I saw a trouser leg, then the blur of somebody's boot shooting past my face. I reached out like a teetering drunk. The leg came up again and when I grabbed it something smacked me from behind and I fell. I tried to stand. I grabbed the intruder's waist and stood, the two of us now jostling like clumsy dance partners, waltzing and banging into what little furniture there was in the small room. A chair tipped over. Empty plastic film developer trays clattered to the floor.

When we separated, the man swung first and I ducked and blindly reached for the sink where my hand splashed into a pan of Kodak film fixer solution. I flicked the pan and watched the chemical spray his face. He screamed and lowered his head and slammed me into the wall. I grabbed him and we started our ballroom tango again, yanking each other's arms and grunting and trying to lift our knees and trip the other guy to the floor. It was like a blundering schoolyard fight, him coughing and spitting and trying to squint through the No. 200 film fixing acid that now covered his face.

We stumbled out of the room. I shoved the man toward the old Linotype machine, where there was a pot of hot lead simmering next to the keyboard. He stumbled into the machine, flapping his burned arm and shouting nonsense as he came toward me again. I tried to push him away, but I tripped and then he was on top of me again, this time with a pair of scissors he'd grabbed from the layout table.

Then he unexpectedly stood up. He started jumping around, flailing both arms like he was electrified. Like he was shaking off a swarm of ants. He shivered and wobbled his head back and forth. In the dimly lit room I couldn't see well at all, but it now looked like he was wearing a long coat.

In this heat? A fur coat?

I turned on the light. It was the pyro, the guy who had started the fire. Mr. big, bony and ugly himself.

He was covered head-to-toe in a pelt of squirming, biting gophers.

They ran up his back. Over his head and across his face. Up his leg and down his arms, each toothy rodent yipping and biting while the guy — perhaps he was in shock, I don't know — just stared straight ahead like a zombie. He couldn't catch his breath. He started gulping, both arms hanging limply at his side.

And then he turned very carefully, like he didn't want any of the gophers to fall off, and started walking stiff-legged toward the back door of the trailer. He gave a long, deep moan. His man bun came undone. He stumbled and fell and stood again, those gophers still clinging and clawing away. The man's shirt was in tatters, his burned arm swinging at his side. He'd lost one shoe. He walked outside and tumbled down the steps. He was halfway up the alley when the horde of gophers finally dropped off and stood there, watching while the man staggered away.

And then a lone AH-64 Apache Longbow attack helicopter piloted by a smiling prairie dog in World War One flying goggles appeared and took aim and unloaded a pair of smoking 70mm Stinger missiles into the guy's ass as he, surprisingly invigorated, hopped the newspaper recycling dumpster and disappeared down the empty Main Street of Bull River Falls.

My little gopher rescue squad stood there clapping their paws and shouting at the hovering chopper.

CHAPTER 34

Chaz said I looked like I'd been smacked with a bag of nickels.

The Gopher King laughed so hard I got a disturbing full frontal glottal view of his yellow nutcracker teeth.

"He won't be back anytime soon," he said.

Chaz's eyes were glazed, his movements sluggish. And there was something just not right about the Gopher King's laugh today.

He slurred his words: "What did you do to make the guy so mad?"

Chaz kept grinning, and the smile broke into a demonic grimace and then he began to wheeze and double-over into a convulsive laughing fit the likes of which I'd never seen before. He shut up and stared at the wall, where the dripping darkroom chemical had formed strange creature shapes that apparently fascinated the Gopher King.

"Are you okay?" I said.

The gopher commandos who had viciously attacked the intruder sat in the corner swapping stories, laughing and slapping their rodent knees. One of them held the guy's baseball cap and started chewing on it. He passed it around and everybody solemnly took a bite. This ritual seemed to have great symbolic meaning for them.

The office was a mess. A broken sink supply pipe was gushing water up the wall. Molten lead had dribbled out of the Linotype machine and formed a tube of hardened shiny metal that now snaked its way across the linoleum floor. This would take a while to clean, and I had twelve hours to get the entire newspaper typeset and ready to deliver to the printer.

I told Chaz I desperately needed photos to fill the newspaper, but he wasn't listening.

He said his stomach hurt.

"I ate too much last night," he said. "The tobacco. It was awful."

Gophers, of course, don't smoke. But they're suckers for leafy foods.

I was curious. "Where did you get tobacco?"

He explained how they'd broken into a new store in town. He described the place. It was decorated with colorful 1960s posters: Jimmy Hendrix at the Fillmore, Janis Joplin at Monterey in 1967, *Iron Butterfly,* even a framed 1963 *Yardbirds* album, which Chaz described excitedly in great detail. And there was the pile of tie dyed tee shirts sitting on the front counter, just beckoning him inside.

"They had all these little envelopes of it with names like Alaska Thunder and Lemon Skunk and Purple Kush."

I tried to speak: "I don't think it was tobacco."

"And Jurassic Haze and Iron Snowflake and Slippery Banana," Chaz continued. His eyes were getting shinier and he seemed rapturous.

"And then we saw the cookies! My God, the cookies!"

Chaz gazed off toward some mystical fog knowable only to his walnut-sized brain and he began to carefully describe the trays heaped with the aforementioned bakery products.

A peacefulness overcame him. Gone were his customary gopher habits: the fidgeting, the pumping of his stubby tail. The flapping paws. Always caffeinated, like people who visit Starbucks too often. Right now His Royal Mellowness didn't have a care in the world.

"Funny thing," he said, trying to stifle another ripping, inappropriate laugh. "The more I ate the hungrier I got. We all just got so hungry. Could NOT stop eating those cookies. Next thing I know its three hours later and I'm staring at a poster of *Country Joe & the Fish* and it's lit by a Lava Lamp and I'm thinking this is the best art I've seen since I bought a Vermeer painting online a few years ago from a guy who said he was Dutch, but I swear he had a Russian accent."

Excited once more, Chaz continued to chatter his nonsense, as if his brain required immediate emptiness. His topics ranged from 18th Century carpentry techniques and stamp collecting to medieval textile preservation, rugby, Chinese cabbage recipes...the batting averages of every player on the 1959 Chicago Cubs team.

The last thing he did was quote five minutes of dialogue from a particular 1974 TV episode of *The Brady Bunch*. It was exhausting. I thought the little rodent's skull would explode.

I tried to interrupt. "I wouldn't go to another...uh, tobacco store again."

"But the cookies..."

"It's not always healthy to be extremely happy," I said. "Trust me. You should lay down. Close your eyes and rest."

But Chaz's demeanor had changed again. He became absurdly contemplative. Hours after his apparent midnight visit to Bull River's newest retail business establishment — the Cloud Nine Cannabis Bakery & Cosmic Smokehouse, the Gopher King was staring wide-eyed at an ant crawling across the linoleum floor.

"That's so beautiful," he said, nearly sobbing.

"Yes," I said. "Very nice."

"So true, man," Chaz said. He walked up to my ankle and gave me a long hug.

He looked up and blinked, his tiny black eyes moist and at the edge of a sob. His expression was of someone who'd just found a winning lottery ticket in a laundry hamper. His joy seemed boundless and unconfined as he tried to convince me to share his new culinary discovery.

Here he'd been eating lowly prairie grasses and insects and the occasional garden tuber and boring Zinnia plant while all along the joys of life — indeed the Fountain of Knowledge and the Path Toward Enlightenment, had been contained in a humble mound of marijuana-infused chocolate chip cookies.

"And they sold hippie tee shirts, too!"

Just as he seemed ready to weep, Chaz said: "You really must try their Gummy Bears."

"I've had plenty of candy in my day," I said and picked up the Gopher King. "Now let me take you home."

I looked over at the other gopher commandos, who were still comparing battle notes and slapping their knees and chewing what remained of the tattered baseball cap.

"You boys over there. Let me just take you all home before you get into real trouble."

And so I picked up the gophers' Blackhawk helicopter and put the aircraft in the back of my pickup truck. The commandos fell asleep in a furry pile on the front seat.

Chaz sat on the dashboard, his favorite spot, and took a poop. He turned and smiled at me and said:

"Hey, I know where you can get a great picture for the front page of the newspaper this week."

CHAPTER 35

My chemically addled gophers were in deep REM sleep by the time I drove up the precarious switchback road to Chaz's underground lair on Bellyache Mountain.

Chaz was snoring and whistling like a teapot when I placed him inside a random burrow and assumed he'd find his way home once he woke up. I hoped no wandering coyote or hungry owl would disturb his ganja-laced dreams.

As instructed earlier by the Gopher King, I headed to town, where county workers were tearing down what was once a general store of sorts — a relic of times past I fondly remembered from the days when Bull River Falls was just another ranching outpost alongside a crummy two-lane mountain highway.

As I drove, the ridge above Brush Creek lay under a thick blanket of smoke that sank lower as I gained altitude.

They'd backfired two miles of timber earlier in the week, finally bringing the north side of the wildfire under control. A long black scar of charred scrub oak marked the path of the blaze. A lone helicopter hovered above the mountain.

When I arrived at the old store one of the workers showed me the teethmarks, perfectly spaced gouges that ran along one side of the building like bullet nicks from an automatic weapon. The gophers had chewed completely through the corner posts of the half rotted structure. The rickety building with the shake shingle roof, long on the verge of collapsing, now sat canted forward like it was bending to listen to something along the road.

A stiff wind could have easily blown the thing down.

I remembered this place well. It had been shuttered for twenty years, locked up in some obscure court battle in which the county had been trying to exercise its right of eminent domain so it could widen the road. The owners and their seven children once worked there. All the kids had the same lips and chin and they wore a similar hangdog look of reluctant acceptance that made you want to stare at them. The family was both enchanting and inexplicably weird.

The whole rumpled bunch looked wild and feral. They all had the same red hair. The girls wore old fashioned calico shifts, the mom a Mother Hubbard bonnet; the boys dressed in identical overalls and dirty ranch boots. I never heard any of them speak a word.

Most families look alike in some small way. This bunch seemed like they'd been machine-stamped from a common die or baked in a single batch on a pan like cookies.

It was spooky watching them all gaze at you when you walked into the store, which itself hearkened from another age. I was always surprised when I looked and realized the store indeed had electricity.

The structure had been built when we didn't have much in the way of zoning and building codes around here. Back then you could have a ratty sofa on your front porch and paint your house any color you wanted. Now they have laws on which direction your outdoors lights should point and how long you could park your car on the street.

In this old general store they displayed pickled eggs on the large wooden front counter in a giant jar sealed with a mason lid. As far as I could tell they never sold a one of them. The mysterious eggs just bobbed in that brine like medical laboratory specimens.

The patriarch of the clan, himself a living fossil, wore high leather field boots laced in a long-vanished style and not of a fashion seen in this country for a century. He wore canvas pants with pocket brads and a rope belt braided into knots and fastened with a giant brass buckle. His hat, an Elmer Fudd maple-syrup-havesting winter cap with ear flaps — was wrinkled and black, and he wore it regardless of the weather. Around his neck hung a filthy red speckled bandanna, also from a vanished era and purchased in a store that never existed. This curious place sold everything and nothing at all, because what was for sale seemed utterly useless.

The family abruptly closed the store one day and abandoned its peculiar inventory. They simply vanished without a trace. They left all the lights on and it took three weeks for someone to report the odor of rotten food wafting from the open front door.

When I arrived, the demolition crew had piled the store's contents outside. One item that caught my eye was sitting on the hood of an abandoned pickup truck. I understood why Chaz and his commandos wanted to destroy the building.

In the old days there was a taxidermy shop housed in a shed in the back yard; the old man's work was displayed up front in the store. A dead wolverine with mangy fur hung mounted above the ice cream freezer box, its yellow teeth barred like it was daring you to reach for a cherry Creamsicle. A stuffed Canada goose swung from a wire above the canned goods aisle with a half-burned cigarette jammed in its beak. A dusty dead rattlesnake lay coiled around a box of Gillette razor blades and cans of obsolete shaving powder. A fox, a cross-eyed tree squirrel, a skinny cougar with a missing ear, a whole family of beavers gnawing a willow branch; you couldn't look anywhere in the store without seeing a stuffed corpse.

The general store had also been the town Greyhound station and served as a refreshment stop each afternoon when the eastbound Denver bus rolled through town. Passengers bought soda pop and chips and beef jerky and then stood outside chewing and looking at the bare gypsum hills and at each other like they'd just been discharged without their permission into a lawless foreign land where loitering out in the open might not be the wisest thing to do.

One time I walked into the store and the bus passengers, snacks in their hands, were gathered around one of the taxidermy displays, posing for photos in front of the very item that now sat on the hood of the pickup truck.

The exhibit, mounted on several levels of plywood covered with shag carpeting, showed a group of six stuffed animals, each creature posed in some aspect of extreme alarm. I was very familiar with the look.

The prairie dogs were gazing off in the same direction, as if they'd just detected a prowling enemy. The taxidermist had captured things perfectly: the defined shoulder muscles tensed and almost quivering, the bright black eyes. Forepaws braced against a pebbly burrow mound that looked like it had just been dug. Each dead, sawdust-filled gopher leaned slightly forward as if about to spring, defiant and wonderfully alert. It was masterful.

A backhoe rumbled up to the broken building and lifted its bucket and dropped the thing onto the roof with a crash. The walls trembled and collapsed simultaneously in four directions. A cloud of chalky dust lifted. Another vehicle came and started scooping things away until nothing remained of the old general store but broken conduit and a busted sewer pipe sticking up at an angle from the asphalt like a clay phallus.

I took my pictures for the newspaper and left.

I was worried about Chaz, so I drove back to where I had deposited him in his hole. Bellyache Mountain is crawling with coyotes. When I got there my rodent was sitting in the dirt, alphabetizing his collection of vintage 1960s rock albums. An expensive outdoor sound system was mounted to a nearby tree. There was music playing — Pavarotti singing Puccini's *Nessun Dorma*. Just as the singer was hitting his famous chills-up-your-spine high C, the Gopher King looked at me and his eyes flooded with tears.

"The music," he gulped. "I don't see how it's possible to make such a wonderful sound. I wish I could sing like that."

"Thanks for the news tip," I said.

Chaz wiped his eye and dusted off a mint condition Dave Clark Five album that was still in its plastic wrapper, the British band members dressed in white like smiling ice cream vendors.

"We hated that store," he said. "It was stinky like pickles."

CHAPTER 36

I swallowed a pill.

I tried to stop remembering about what was in that tree in Vietnam and what happened the rest of the day so long ago and so I started thinking about Chaz the Gopher King and I felt much better.

I wondered what a typical day was like for my rodent friend.

His Royal Rodent Rex. Caesar in Subterraneis.

El Jefe de los Excavadores.

I tried to get the answer from the Furry One himself, but he angrily told me to mind my own business. He then bit my foot.

So I consulted the person who spends more time with the Gopher King than anyone else. Chaz's personal bodyguard is named Axe. He doesn't talk much; he doesn't smile.

Axe, a sourpuss who wears a constant expression of distrust, has three digits missing from his left hind paw, the result of a fight with a golf ball scrubbing machine at the Gold Gulch Country Club. His left eye — which looks like it just might heal one day, is currently scabbed over thanks to a run-in on U.S. Hwy 6 with a $5,000 carbon fiber Vorfritzle Gesundheit bicycle whose tires he tried to flatten with his bayonet. But the tire exploded in his face.

This gopher is taller than any other rodent in the colony, except for freaky Genghis, Chaz's military chief of staff. Axe has a tattoo on his leg of two entwined serpents whose intersecting heads form a cupid heart, inside of which the word MOM appears in scarlet gothic script as if on a Third Reich greeting card.

He once shaved his head so he could show off his other tattoo — a snarling ferret rendered across his face from his left eyebrow to the nape of his neck. Chaz ordered Axe to grow his fur back because the tattoo gave his children nightmares.

But Axe has a gentle side. He likes to knit brightly colored scarves and has a deep interest in all the fiber arts. He is credited with inventing a way for gophers, who have no thumbs, to quilt. His weekly textile appreciation classes are very popular among the colony's gopher women, many of whom believe Axe to be the most eligible bachelor in the land, despite his spookily grotesque eye.

There are not too many athletic, tattooed, macho rodents who are licensed pilots who can cross-stitch while firing a shoulder mounted Stinger missile.

He and Chaz both enjoy watching documentaries on French haute couture and food cooking shows on the Gopher King's surround-sound, 72-inch TV while they clean their deadly weapons.

Axe always carries a Czech SA-25 submachine gun, not the weapon of choice for most gopher soldiers, but he swears the rifle is more reliable. He and Chaz, who favors Uzis for personal use and the clunky but durable AK-47 for commando missions, argue constantly about the aesthetics of small weaponry. I've listened to them and it makes me want to go to sleep, this debate about the effective firing range of every imaginable pistol and rifle: which has a better telescoping bolt, how easy it is to clean. On and on. It's painfully dull.

Axe doesn't much care for me and I believe he doesn't trust anyone on the planet, which is a good personality trait for a royal body guard.

But I did manage to pry the following information regarding the Gopher King's daily habits:

Like a college student, Chaz goes to bed at around 3 a.m. and sleeps until noon. Chaz's wife rises much earlier. They sleep in separate rooms because Chaz, who suffers from sleep apnea, snores like a steam locomotive.

Chaz eats the same breakfast each morning: slightly dampened wheat grass, zinnia seeds, and Cheerios, which he steals by the skid load from COSTCO.

Afterwards, he dedicates an hour to watching instructive You Tube videos, from which he gains much of his knowledge. I once saw him intently viewing a video on how to fillet a striped lake perch, though I don't understand what practical value this has for a gopher who will never catch or eat a fish.

"Everything is worth knowing for at least ten minutes. After that it's best to forget what you learned," Chaz told me when I asked him about his endless quest for useless and impractical knowledge.

Unless there is a pressing military mission, Chaz is served a mid-afternoon snack by his personal chef — usually a Thai green mango salad and a couple of protein power candy bars if he has to lead a commando raid later in the day.

After lunch and a twenty-minute nap he presides over a daily staff meeting where everyone sits around a large and mysterious square black basalt stone in a secret burrow chamber whose location is randomly changed every few weeks.

Chaz opens every meeting with a knock-knock joke. His favorite one is:

"Knock knock!"

"Who's there?"

"Madame"

"Madame who?"

"Madame foot's caught in the door."

Then he says: "Okay, lets get down to business."

After an hour of carefully rehearsed and overly long Power Point presentations, transparent posturing by the usual collection of chatty gas bags, and much meaningless note-taking by the Gopher King's worshipful acolytes, Chaz usually dismisses everyone with a clumsy limerick, rude quip or oddly timed personal insult. But mostly he seems to like the knock-knock jokes. Such as:

"Kock knock!"

"Who's there?"

"Doris"

"Doris who?"

"Doris locked. It's why I'm knocking!"

Chaz manages his vast underground empire by simply wandering around. He wanders unannounced into gopher homes. Surprises children in their classrooms. For example, he'll wander into a meeting of the Bellyache Mountain Burrow Owners Association steering committee wearing a Groucho Marx mask and everyone will stand up, of course, because they've seen this many times before. Chaz will take off the mask, frown, then turn around and leave.

"It gives them something to think about," Chaz says. "It makes them focus when they believe I'm angry about something. Keeping people off balance is the way to influence them."

Lunch is served promptly at 7 p.m., which is dinner time for the rest of his family. It's the biggest meal of the day and Chaz tries to have as many of his children at the kitchen table as possible, which is difficult because the Gopher King has 16 girls and 24 boys, half of them morose and introspective teenagers.

From 8:30 p.m. to 9 p.m. Chaz dictates the next day's work schedule and a few inspirational messages, which his bodyguard Axe dutifully records and then takes to Jools, the colony's comptroller, who copies it for playback over the clan's intricate underground public address system.

Chaz then listens to one of his audio books until 10 p.m. Then he will attend to one of his many hobby collections: first day issue Armenian postage stamps;

backstage rock concert passes, autographed documents signed by President Millard Fillmore. You get the picture.

At 11 he and his wife, Tinka, reflect on the day's events over a cup of herbal wheatgrass tea.

After that it's classic movies until about 2 a.m., followed by an above-ground stroll along the colony's perimeter network of hidden guard stations, during which he chats with his troops and takes pot shots with his M-16 at prowling coyotes and anything else that wanders too close to the slumbering underground community he has sworn to protect.

CHAPTER 37

The Gopher King did not visit me for many days.

Meanwhile, the gopher army attacked everything in town. They dug a warren of tunnels under the high school baseball field. They gnawed up a 500-foot spool of coax cable at the telephone company storage depot.

They broke into the veterinary clinic and shredded a filing cabinet filled with old pet x-rays. Among gophers, it's considered high sorcery to take an x-ray. To even gaze on someone's x-ray dooms you to rodent purgatory where you must live in fleshless misery for eternity.

This was how it was explained to me after I once told Chaz about a visit to the chiropractor, whereupon he covered his ears and started screaming hysterically.

The high school principal called to complain I was getting all the sports scores wrong in the newspaper and that my startling inattention to proper grammar was a disgrace to reporters everywhere. I had to agree. I've never been a good speller.

Learning is fun. Remembering stinks.

I was asked by a customer at the newspaper office about the dozens of small two-toothed puncture marks on my arm and I told her I was attacked by a gang of miniature vampires.

A state biologist from the Division of Wildlife, accompanied by a public relations person, arrived at the Town Hall with great fanfare to help the mayor study the town's gopher problem. I was there to take a picture, of course.

CNN, here to cover the growing fire on Bellyache Mountain and the murder of Melinda Barstow, did a short atmosphere piece on TV about "...the unruly wildlife causing havoc in a small Colorado town."

As always, I needed more pictures for the paper, so I decided to visit the Last Chance Ranch. Old Dora McCoy had phoned again, claiming her old hay barn had mysteriously collapsed. I took my pill and took a drive, hoping my head would clear. The nightmares just wouldn't go away, and now Melinda Barstow's death had filled my skull with more unaccounted misery.

For somebody who could spit twenty feet, cuss and toss a bale of hay like a rodeo cowboy, the inside of the old widow's tidy and girlishly decorated house was well-tended and clean.

Frilly curtains on the open screened windows lifted in the hot breeze. Photos in old fashion oval gilt frames sat on a polished shelf: black and whites of wrinkled old men in Stetson hats, one on horseback with a drooping Zapata mustache in a buttoned white shirt wearing shotgun chaps astride a high pommel Spanish saddle. A prim young woman in a blouse buttoned to the chin, her hair bunned beneath a fancy Cordoba hat. A girl in her First Communion dress, her tiny hands grasping a church candle, and an ancient picture of a lonesome corral standing in a bleak sage field on the 5,000 acre Last Chance Ranch.

And alone on another shelf, illuminated by a flickering candle, sat a photo of Dora's late husband, Hector.

She had the TV on, yet another documentary on the war in Iraq. Dora shook her head and wagged her finger at the screen.

"Look at that fool. They make it look glorious. Well, I'm sure it ain't. My Hector was in Korea in fifty-one. He didn't say much about what he saw, but I know he saw plenty. You soldier boys never talk about things. I don't know how you can bottle it up."

We stepped onto the sagging porch. The old lady rolled her cheek and spit out a hocker and watched it fly.

"Can you ride?" she said and shoved another plug of chaw into her mouth.

"Enough so I don't fall off," I said.

We walked to where Dora's magnificent horse stood tied to a fence, unsaddled. The old lady disappeared and came back leading an ugly thing that looked more pony than horse, but I was fine with it.

"She's a little barn sour and slow, but it should do," she said.

Dora gravely explained how her own horse was a true roan on a black coat, as if ignorance of such a fact would render all future description moot and irrelevant. The mane, tail, head, and legs had remained coal dark into its old age, she said. In the right light his hide had a velvet shimmer, and she spoke those words with a certain reverence. As a colt Dora had thought it might be a blue dun grullo, but old grullos fade and lighten and this one had not, betraying its age only with a grayness like a faint brush stroke along the withers. I didn't know what that all meant, but it was a beautiful animal.

"I can leave him loose anywhere in these mountains and he'll find the way home. You'd think horses do it naturally, but they don't. It's a gift."

Dora McCoy took a brush to the roan's back and picked out a few leaf bits and barn dirt. She brushed in long strokes once more so all the hair lay flat. She placed the saddle blanket on the horse's back, forward over the withers, and then slid it into place and smoothed it with her gloved hand.

She seemed to forget what she had done and so took the blanket off and put it on again. Dora did this three more times, struggling with her bad arm. The horse turned its head and looked back at her and snorted.

"Oh, my," she said and laughed in a way that seemed forced and superficial. "What's wrong with me? I've not been myself lately."

She told me she'd left her truck keys in the refrigerator that morning. She'd been dizzy and plagued by a maddening thirst.

Her swollen arm looked worse than before. Half my reason for visiting was to ask her to see a doctor, but she again refused.

"Give me a hand, will you?" she said.

Keeping the saddle straddled on the fence post, I helped her take the offside stirrup and hooked it over the saddle horn. The cinch was attached so she folded it back over the saddle seat. Confused, she did this once again. I helped her lift the saddle high above the blanket pad and she told me to bring it down gently. Now Dora moved to the offside of the saddle and smoothed the blanket again with her good hand and reached beneath the horse and picked up the free end of the cinch.

She made the horse step forward and waited for it to exhale before she tightened the girth enough to hold the saddle in place. I helped her loop the saddle tabs through the big metal D-ring and tied them. She stood at the horse's head and leaned into the horse and lifted one front leg and stretched it forward to see if the girth loosened. It did not. She gave the animal a kiss.

"There, honey. You're all dressed," she said.

Then off we rode, me atop the droop-headed nag at a slow walk with my feet almost touching the ground.

Dora jabbered non stop the whole way, long white hair blowing from beneath her hat. She said she'd refused another sheriff's order to abandon her house because of the blazing wildfire now burning only a few miles away. Dora told me if she left she was certain they'd never allow her back. The golf course people would then make their move.

"It's all a trick," she said. "They want me off this place so the fat asses at the ski resort can take it. I'm no dummy. I know they're just waiting for me to make a mistake."

The part of her hand sticking from the sling was purple and swelled up like a gruesome balloon toy. I mentioned the doctor again and she told men to shut up and mind my own business.

We came up on a rise, Dora's big roan prancing and crow-hopping nervously. She pointed at where one of her pasture barns once stood. There was only a pile of wood there now, one wall left standing.

"Those gophers have been chawing on that thing for weeks. I haven't used the place in years so they saved me the trouble of tearing it down anyway."

"It looks like it was burned," I said.

"Probably sparks from the fire yonder," she said.

"Of course," I said as we walked closer.

There were scorch marks in the grass everywhere. I imagined I saw scattered metal rocket casings. The spiral windblown circle where a chopper had landed in the grass. By now I was accustomed to the signs of prairie dog terrorism and the stories my head would spin if I didn't keep things under control.

I could easily imagine the flying squadron of helicopters, the launched missiles. Out here where nobody could hear or see. Chaz the Gopher King cheering on the whole training operation with sinister glee.

CHAPTER 38

I couldn't keep my eyes closed, so during my hovering, half sleep state of hazy reality Chaz appeared at my house one morning at 5 a.m., his claws tapping on the bedroom window.

He screamed, "Hey, Stellaaaaaaaaaahhhhh!

I motioned for him to come through the back door.

I'd had the dream again: the dead PFC floating above my bed, a corpse. Those people were jabbering in my head, the loudest a guy with a deep gravely voice; like he had a sore throat, saying, "chickenshit, chickenshit" over and over, the other voices joining in until the whole bunch sounded like a monkish church chorus echoing off the stone walls of a cathedral. The sonofabitch smelled bad in this dream; the farty, vegetal food whiff of soaked canvas jungle tents and stale food ration cans, unwashed socks...the whole mess of odors concentrated in that dead sonofabitch flying over my bed. But still I gasped whenever I saw him, like it was the first time.

So I was happy to see my rat friend.

It was a cold mountain morning, the air knifing through the leaky plastic sheets that covered the windows of the trailer, and the Gopher King was wearing his Elmer Fudd hat, the one with the red polka dot earflaps. And strange faux fur Eskimo mukluks. He wore hockey gloves on his paws. He must have robbed a sporting goods store.

Breathlessly, Chaz explained he was on a mission to colonize former North American gopher habitats, in this case a tract of grassland in Canada.

"We're almost extinct up there," he said. "And so I've decided to announce a Homestead Act. I'm giving away free land!"

"You can't give away land you don't own," I said.

"Abraham Lincoln did it."

"You can't give away land that doesn't belong to you."

And so I spent the day filling four large wooden furniture crates with the following items:

Sixteen live gophers. Three Black Hawk helicopters the size of brief cases. One miniaturized Chinook CH-47 heavy-lift cargo chopper the size of a tenor saxophone.

Seventy-five thousand rounds of NATO 5.56 mm bullets packed into 2,500 30-round clips. Two thousand tactical smoke grenades the size of pencil erasers. Three hundred pounds of potted wheat grass. Fertilizer.

Assorted hardware supplies. Garden mulch.

Two John Deere backhoes the size of Barbie and Ken's matching Corvettes. And one Peter, Paul & Mary CD.

I shipped this by UPS to Edmonton, Alberta. The cost was $1,625.47, which wasn't a problem because I recently opened up a bank account in the name of "The PD Rodenthouse Benevolent Re-settlement Foundation," which was then registered with the state of Colorado as a charitable entity.

Chaz, using the alias of "Dnarg Gninepo" (he said he saw this word once on a real estate sign in the rearview mirror of his Hummer) soon became the proud owner of a hefty checking account made possible by 500 lbs of gopher-mined gold dust converted into transferable Japanese Bitcoins by yours truly, thank you very much.

My fifth grade math teacher would be proud.

"Once the colony is established," Chaz said. "We'll be sending more pioneers. To Texas. To Oklahoma. To Iowa. To the lush grasslands of our holy homeland, Nebraska. It's only the beginning. This is one historic day, my large hairless and mentally unstable and chemically altered friend."

I imagined Henry Fonda, himself a Nebraskan from Grand Island, and the whole wrinkled Joad family fleeing the Dust Bowl down Route 66 in their overloaded junky 1922 Hudson.

"If you say so," I mumbled, folding the UPS tracking slip into my pocket so I could later confirm the arrival of Chaz's ark of ragged prairie dog settlers. I only hoped they could control their unpredictable and easily disturbed 10cc capacity bowels during the long trip north.

Once the hopefully odorless crates arrived at the UPS terminal in Edmonton, the gophers were instructed to promptly claw their way to freedom, load the aircraft and fly happily away, in formation of course, to their bleak Canadian frontier homesteads, where much digging and frantic underground procreation would immediately begin.

"They kicked you out once before. You might run into trouble up there," I told Chaz. "And it's tornado season."

"My middle name is trouble," the Gopher King said.

CHAPTER 39

Against my better judgment, I took Chaz with me to the VA hospital in Denver, where I needed to get my prescription refilled.

I almost didn't get past the security checkpoint, where for some reason they decided to take a closer look at my gym bag.

"Whew!" the guard said, unzipping the bag and fanning his face.

And then he took out the weapons the Gopher King had smuggled with him on our little road trip: a fully armed grenade launcher, two AK-47s, a Mossberg 12-gauge shotgun and an M-240 machine gun — all miniaturized, of course.

"And what have we here?" the guard said in a sing-song voice.

He lifted out a loaded ammo belt of 7.60 cal. machine gun rounds.

"It's for my granddaughter's Barbie Doll," I said.

"You're giving this to a child?" he said, popping out the AK-47s ammo clip and squinting as he held it up at the ceiling lights.

"It looks authentic. Where do you get stuff like this?"

"Amazon," I said.

The guard asked me to lift my arms and he patted me down. He found the bottle of pills in my jacket pocket. He examined the bottle. I showed him my driver's license.

"And you have a prescription for these blue pills?" the guard asked.

"I do," I said and opened my wallet. "I'm here to get more. They're pretty, aren't they?"

"They certainly are," he said and handed back the bottle.

Chaz's claws tickled my stomach as he squirmed toward my belt like he was trying to escape. I faked a violent sneeze and twisted myself around and shoved the little rodent back under my shirt.

The guard then brought the tiny seven-inch-long AK-47 semi-automatic rifle up to his nose and sniffed.

"It's been fired," he said.

"Realistic, huh?" I said.

The guard tried not to make eye contact with me. "You're free to go," he said.

"I was free to go when I came here," I said and took the AK-47 and dropped it into my bag and hurried out the door. I had to get back to Bull River Falls in time to attend an important night session of the Bull River Falls Town Council.

Gophers can spot weld sheet metal. They can connect the neutral and ground wires in a light switch junction box while blindfolded. They know the abstractive difference between theoretical and experimental physics. Most gophers around here, in fact, are aware of Einstein's concern, but apparent disinterest, in the Michaelson-Morley experiment on Earth's drift through luminiferous ether.

Which is why I am never surprised by whatever they do.

Lately, I've been finding my mail neatly stacked on my desk — courtesy of Chaz, who explained that he has figured out a way to jailbreak the mail box locks at the post office. I told the gopher I rather enjoy picking up my own mail, but he keeps doing it. And I keep going to the post office to check my empty mailbox.

By the time I got back to Bull River Falls people were lining up outside the Town Hall, a former pool hall and saloon located just off Main Street next to the Grill & Griddle Cafe.

The audience at the Town Hall sits on gray metal folding chairs. You can still see metal brackets on the wall where a bar top was once attached. On cold nights the over-heated room emits a faint briny odor, gassy phantoms from when they used vinegar to scrub away blood and liquor spills from the puncheon floorboards, which are now covered with a worn brown carpet. The knotty pine paneled walls still wear the half-moon indentations of thrown beer bottles, and the pressed tin ceiling is puckered in places with bullet holes. This is a room with a proud history of violence and spilled body fluids.

There was nowhere to stand so I took out my notebook and leaned against a wall. I listened to somebody in the very last row of chairs reminisce loudly:

"I remember when old Kip Hoffman from over at the feed and seed store got his nose chewed off here in a fight. Blood all over the wall. They wrapped his head in a bed quilt. He was never right after that and his wife left him because of his looks. Went insane, jumped on a train boxcar upvalley in a snowstorm and they found him froze dead wearing nothing but a Timex wrist watch and his cowboy hat."

Dora McCoy arrived at the meeting carrying a burlap sack stuffed with something heavy. I figured she'd brought paperwork to help her plead her case against the Gold Gulch development. Someone stood and politely gave her his chair and the old lady sat down, stared at the old tin ceiling for a moment, and carefully put the bag on the floor behind her feet.

The mayor, taking his place on the raised dais alongside the six council members, called the meeting to order and loudly announced the first item on the agenda — a proposed 250-acre expansion of the Gold Gulch Ski Resort.

Guy Winkler from the Bull River Preservation Society stood and pointed at two large paper flip charts that showed the resort's currently approved perimeter and the proposed expansion, which I noticed included the destruction of a good chunk of the prairie dog colony that remained next to the Last Chance Ranch.

He spoke carefully and gestured purposefully at the row of seated council members.

"Tonight I want to make just one point, Mister Mayor," he said. "And one point only. This proposal would destroy the best wetlands we have in the county, natural wetlands that have been proven to be primordial and native to our valley. The real estate developer will say these wetlands are the artificial result of many years of ranch irrigation in this area. I'm here with proof that this is just not true. What we have here is an irreplaceable natural resource whose loss might very well invite a possible lawsuit from the federal government if this expansion is allowed."

The Mayor took off his reading glasses and interrupted.

"Mr. Winkler. We know the background, and our lawyers happen to disagree with you about the feds getting pissy about this deal. They have better things to do."

Winkler looked at the wall clock and handed out copies of his report and thanked the council members for their time. The mayor cleared his throat and squinted out across the room.

"Tonight we have time for only two rebuttal commentaries on the Gold Gulch request. Mrs. McCoy, who I'm sure we are all acquainted with, will be next, but first let me say a few words."

The mayor peered over his reading glasses. "Following the general discussion there will be comments taken from citizens. I urge you to be concise and brief, and try not to repeat what your neighbor has just said. I want to be out of here by midnight. We've had too many of these meetings, as far as I'm concerned, and the longer they take the less we seem to accomplish.

"At issue this evening are the wetlands the Gold Gulch company wants to use as a mitigated buffer between the main ski village and the condominiums that line the adjacent golf course. The company has already submitted the proper wildlife management plan and it has met with the approval of the board, which discussed the subject during a working session this morning with our planning and zoning commission. I'm not saying anything here which hasn't already been expressed publicly in the newspaper.

"The council has also received final recommendations from the town planner and his staff. The council will make a final decision tonight. Our previous public surveys show much of the community agrees with the board's direction on this."

The mayor shuffled around his paperwork and, without looking up, said: "Mrs. McCoy?"

Dora stood. With her boot heel she pushed the sack further under her chair. It didn't take the mayor long to become visibly annoyed as Dora spent ten minutes recalling the history of the Gold Gulch project. She had apparently memorized every plat, every hydrology and soil study, every wildlife mitigation plan, including research that had revealed an estimate of how many elk droppings there were per acre of land on the resort's considerable holdings.

The mayor interrupted: "Yes, that's a lot of poop, Dora. We are well aware of the study."

"You might think this is awfully funny," Dora snapped. "But if you let them have extra land those animals have no place to go. Soon it's all golf carts and parking lots around here and more of those trinket stores we already got on Main Street. Why, the whole town is turning into a curio shop."

Dora turned to the audience. She was unsteady on her feet. The color had drained from her face. Her good hand was trembling at her side as she continued to plead her case. She wiped her forehead with her denim sleeve.

"Take my word," she said in a raspy voice. "Those jackasses are about to suck the life out of this town and when they're finished they'll go home and leave us with the garbage they made."

Dora McCoy coughed, a loud phlegmy rattle that startled everybody in the room. She brought her red bandanna to her mouth. She held onto her swollen left arm like she was afraid it might fall off. She spent a few more moments complaining about how the resort had encroached on the east fence line of her property with its snow making supply pipes.

"They ain't gettin' my water!" she shouted, waving her arm at the members of the town council. "And they ain't gonna kill those gophers and all the other poor critters on my property! They might be dumb rats to you, but they're smarter than all of you put together."

There was scattered applause and the mayor tapped the table with his gavel and looked at the wall clock.

"Mrs. McCoy," the mayor said. "Your water rights and any negotiations between you and the Gold Gulch company are not the business of this council tonight. Please stick to the agenda."

Dora had another vicious coughing fit as she stared unsteadily at the floor, the bandanna pressed to her mouth. Her long white hair had unraveled in uneven strands from beneath her hat and her shirt tail was undone. She wiped her face with her sleeve.

I'd heard all this before, of course. The part about how the Gold Gulch company had offered her a fortune for her water rights. The part about her homesteading grandfather and his sufferings and the days when the Ute Indians hunted in the valley. This one-woman show wasn't going to end anytime soon.

I couldn't watch the old lady embarrass herself again. So I stepped outside and waited for the board to make its predictable decision. I sat on the curb and looked at my own ten dollar watch, the one I'd been given by the Lions Club for publicizing its annual spaghetti dinner. I had only a few hours to write my front page story and lay out the newspaper and drive the flats to the printer in time for the press run at 5:30 the next morning.

It was cool outside, misty. The foggy glow of passing traffic lifted from the interstate highway. The new dim moon climbed above the highway and disappeared behind a cloud.

Dora's big blue roan stood on the sidewalk, its reins tied loosely around a lamp post. The horse looked at the interstate highway and aimed its ears toward the sound of a noisy semi as it passed the town off-ramp.

With its ancient tasseled saddle, the worn leather rifle pouch and saddlebags inscribed with the McCoy ranch brand, the horse was an artifact from another age.

A few people stepped from the cafe next door and crossed the street and turned and stared at the horse. They laughed and walked on.

It was the roan that first heard the screaming noises coming from inside the Town Hall, and it stomped its front hoof once on the sidewalk and then whinnied loudly.

The horse jerked back and reared, the reins snapping off the lamp post as the animal pranced sideways for a while and then galloped away, its hooves banging loudly on the empty asphalt on Main Street.

There came another loud crashing sound. I ran back inside. People were screaming and bumping into each other as they pushed and stumbled their way past me into the street.

I pushed my way through and saw the tipped chairs and tables. Spilled paper coffee cups scattered everywhere. Dora McCoy lay on her back on the floor, someone kneeling next to her.

The mayor stood cowering against the wall, a brown wet stain across the front of his shirt. He kept dabbing at the blotch like it was burning a hole into his chest.

An awful, rancid stink hung in the air.

The town attorney was wrapping something in a blanket. He held it at arm's length and carried it outside.

When he spotted me, the mayor pointed wildly over at Dora McCoy. The old lady lay blinking up at the ceiling, her abundant white hair fanned across the town hall's brown rug.

The mayor shook his tissue at Dora. "That insane coot belongs in crazy house. Maybe in jail. Threw a dead coyote at me! A damn putrid coyote! You every hear of such a thing?"

Dora was being helped to her feet. Her swollen arm had come undone from the sling and hung limply at her side. She smiled at me.

I looked around. You could tell how fast people had moved by the scatter pattern of the tipped chairs and dropped file folders and the way the big flip charts had been kicked away.

On the wall behind the raised dais on which the council members sat, a dripping piece of wet pelt hung by its own suction, gobs of gore radiating in every direction as a testimony to the velocity of Dora McCoy's airborne carrion.

I took pictures for the newspaper.

The mayor, still ranting, pinched the front of his white shirt with his fingertips and tugged the soaked fabric away from his chest.

"My god, please open a window!" he said, undoing his speckled yellow necktie. He unbuttoned his shirt and dropped it to the floor and pointed.

"I got varmint guts on my shirt. Come over here and take another picture! I'm covered in rotten varmint guts!"

He was, and I did.

The mayor started to swoon. Two pairs of arms reached out and guided him to a chair.

Dora brought up her good hand and smoothed back her hair and smiled at the two sheriff's deputies who came and took her into custody. One of the officers was about to cuff her but then looked at the sling and instead guided the old woman gently toward the door like somebody escorting their grandma from church.

One of the policemen spoke into his collar radio and called for an ambulance. The paramedics arrived and they put an oxygen cup to Dora's face and took her pulse. They wrapped Dora's bad arm in a gauze pressure sleeve and lifted her onto a gurney and wheeled her outside.

The mayor shouted: "Hey, what about me? I'm toxic over here!"

By this time almost everyone in the room had realized the absurdity of the event and a few nervous chuckles broke out. People walked up to the still-stuck coyote pelt as if they were forensic artillery investigators, pointing and making hand measurements to estimate the hide's speed and trajectory and angle of attack. They pointed to the empty bag on the floor near where Dora had been sitting.

The major couldn't catch his breath and started to hyperventilate and then staggered a few steps and sat down on the floor.

He kept repeating: "Why would a person do such a thing?"

He turned and wagged his finger at me. "I'm pressing charges, I don't care if she's a hundred years old. Did you hear what I said? I want you to quote me. Put every word in the newspaper. I want you to tell everybody exactly what happened tonight. And don't pull no punches."

I already had my headline written by the time I walked down the street to the posh international headquarters of the Bull River Falls *Beacon-News*.

Just as I was about to open the front door I heard a jingling sound and turned and saw Dora's big blue roan calmly grazing on the front lawn of the Bull River Falls pharmacy.

The horse lifted its head, chewed and stared at me, and then resumed its late dinner.

I heard a chattering sound and then something moved in the shadows. Lit by the murky glow of a street lamp, three heavily armed gophers were sitting on the curb. One of them casually gave me a salute and then lifted his black military beret and waved. It was too dark to see, but I knew who it was.

CHAPTER 40

At 2 a.m. nobody at the Bull River Valley Medical Center took notice when seventy-five heavily armed gophers dressed in matching black ninja outfits decided to rescue Dora McCoy, whom they believed had been the victim of a false arrest.

Chaz had been impressed with the old lady's defense of his clan's real estate rights. Dora's outrageous stunt at the town hall made her a heroine among the gophers of Bellyache Mountain, who considered a tossed putrid coyote corpse as the most romantic and touching expression of prairie dog advocacy they'd ever seen.

The Gopher King, however, didn't know I already had a fail-safe plan to persuade the mayor to drop the felony assault charges against the owner of the Last Chance Ranch. But by then the wheels of rodent justice were already in motion and it was too late to stop Chaz and his vengeful commandos.

As far as they were concerned there was a damsel in distress and, by god and against any odds, she needed immediate help.

And so a crew of Uzi-toting troopers was quickly dispatched to the hospital where Dora McCoy was being treated for her infected arm which, thankfully, wasn't a case of rabies after all.

The rodents were dressed in loose-fitting ninja garb, their oriental doo rag headbands emblazoned with the red star logo of the People's Gopher Army. Samurai-like swords, razor sharp Shogei knives and various poly fiber combat weapons were tucked into their black silk sashes, and they wore red Nike track shoes stolen from COSTCO. They wore spiked leather arm gauntlets.

Chaz himself, carrying monogrammed nunchucks, wore a tight black tutu, through which his neck fur stuck out explosively like a lion's mane. Twin Ruger 9mm pistols were strapped rakishly to his legs, cowboy gunslinger style. On his head sat an outlandish military parade hat festooned lavishly with gold braid. He had shiny epaulets on his shoulders.

He looked like a hairy, psychopathic Prussian field marshal on his way to a ballet lesson.

The squads of gophers rappelled from two miniature Chinook helicopters onto the roof of the hospital, entered the building through an AC intake duct, and dropped soundlessly on mountaineering ropes into a Department of Urology storage room, where Chaz instructed his troops to gather up packages of Depends incontinence pads; mens' size, extra large.

These they then soaked in clean warm tap water.

Next, they entered a Department of Anesthesiology patient recovery room, where Chaz's ninja rats quickly assembled simple catapults made from rubber medical tubing and the baby blue colored surgical breathing bags they found stacked on a gurney. Chaz had gotten this idea from watching a History Channel TV show on the siege of Carthage by the Romans in 149 BC.

Meanwhile, another squad of gophers downstairs fastened portable window alarms on every elevator door in the building and then sprayed hand sanitizer foam on the linoleum floor, transforming the hallway into a giant Slip 'n Slide yard toy.

They then marched into Room 104, where a heavily sedated and snoring Dora McCoy lay sleeping.

Upstairs, Chaz and two dozens gophers pushed a janitorial cart stacked with the wet Depends pads through the Psychiatry and Behavioral Sciences ward, where a patient sitting in bed calmly studied the strange sight for a moment and then resumed watching his TV show.

When everyone reached the downstairs lobby the gophers chained a 600-pound wheeled phlebotomy chair to the door of the hospital security office. They then synced the upstairs elevator door alarms to the hospital PA system, which had already been programmed by a team of prairie dog sound engineers to play a continuous loop of Jimi Hendrix's 1969 Woodstock rendition of the Star Spangled Banner.

Chaz made sure the volume was turned to 10.

Operation Gallant Fur Ball was about to commence.

On Chaz's signal, Jimi began his ear-shattering guitar solo. Then the rigged elevator alarms fired up, sending doctors and nurses and orderlies fleeing into the first floor lobby, where they were greeted with volley after volley of launched water-soaked incontinence pads. These screaming doctors and nurses and orderlies quickly slipped and fell, stood and fell again on the dangerously lubricated linoleum floor, and finally exited en masse through an open emergency fire door while more sopping wet pads were launched repeatedly from Chaz's Roman catapults.

Nothing runs faster than a professional and experienced healthcare provider chased by a dripping wet and airborne adult diaper.

In the confusion, Chaz's gopher commandos calmly wheeled a slumbering Dora McCoy through the front door of the hospital.

The bed mattress fit perfectly into the back of my pickup truck.

I drove off quickly, Jimi's patriotic guitar refrains drifting in the cool mountain night breeze, the tiny bright lights of Chaz's departing helicopters twinkling in the sky like stars.

Dora McCoy snored and wheezed like a locomotive all the way to her house on Bellyache Mountain.

I slept for about an hour at the newspaper office, and when I headed to the mayor's office in the morning to make sure he would dismiss the charges against Dora McCoy.

He studied me up and down and said I looked like hell. I sniffed and told the mayor he smelled like he'd been pickled in goat sweat.

"I hope you burned those clothes you wore last night," I said.

"I even burned the clothes I didn't wear last night," he said with a sigh.

I got right to the point. I reminded the mayor it was an election year and citizens might take exception to the calloused hand of government coming down on a frail and sick old woman who just wanted to protect her property.

"She's not frail," the mayor said. "She could beat the shit out of both of us."

"I'm sure she could" I said. "Point is, people won't see it your way. To them, she's a persecuted granny whose family has lived here for a hundred years."

I suggested that the image of a magnanimous, forgiving community leader would play better at the ballot box.

"It's your choice." I said. "You can either look like a wise, understanding Solomon, or a cranky red-nosed gasbag politician drunk with self-imagined power and importance. Your choice."

The mayor took a deep breath and looked out the window.

"Okay, but she'll pay a fine," he said. "And a hefty one, believe me."

"She's broke," I said. "She doesn't have a dime to her name. She can't even pay her real estate taxes."

The mayor now smiled. "I know," he said. "County tells me her ranch is about to go delinquent. If she doesn't pay up, then it's a Trustee sale and you know what that means. The ski resort people can't wait to get their hands on the Last Chance Ranch."

I started to say something but held my tongue. This wasn't the time or place to pick a fight.

CHAPTER 41

I'd promised Chaz many times that I would take him on a road trip and then hoped he would forget the conversation. But like a four-year-old child, his conniving memory is selective and very accurate.

And so he pestered me again to drive him to the thriving pioneer colony he'd founded up in Canada, but I refused. No international border crossings, I said. I'd ship all the free range rodent immigrants he wanted by UPS, but smuggling actual armed creatures through U.S. Customs by car was out of the question. Those tiny AK-47s would likely cause problems.

Then he begged me to take him to the U.S. Federal Correctional Institution in Jefferson County, south of Denver, where the government has a prairie dog habitat assessment study underway at a vacant 110-acre site across the street from a COSTCO. Gophers, natural hoarders, are also gifted shoplifters and they love to steal things from big box stores, and Chaz said he wanted to evangelize these captive guinea pig prairie dogs and train them in the finer arts of retail theft.

Again, he lied.

I knew the Gopher King's true motive: he wanted to sneak into the sprawling white collar jailhouse, voted as the "5th Best Place to Go to Prison" by *Forbes Magazine*, so he could get an autograph from it's most famous resident, a skilled hair stylist and the former governor of Illinois.

Chaz, who has this particular governor's picture hanging in his office, is fascinated by human politicians, but I still said no to his plan.

He asked me if our elected leaders, like Chaz himself and his Plutonium-239 riddled family of supernatural rodents, had magical powers.

I said human politicians often think they do, and that's when they usually end up in the Big Hoosegow.

"So they're not magical?" Chaz asked.

"They're magically full of shit, kind of like dangerous methane fumes rising invisibly from cows," I said. "Otherwise, no. They are not magical."

Then he wanted me to drive him to Ft. Meade, Maryland, the headquarters of the National Security Agency. A 1,700-mile trip by car with a chatty gopher? I don't think so.

"I've always wanted to visit the National Cryptologic Museum," Chaz said.

"I have a cousin in Baltimore. He's a pet being held captive against his wishes. I want to set him free."

"I must see Plymouth Rock. I have an ancestor who was a stowaway on the Mayflower. I want to visit his grave."

"There are no British prairie dogs," I said.

And so on. Again, all lies.

Chaz has lately been fascinated — transfixed would be a better word, with the case of a particular CIA spook and whistle blower who revealed that the U.S. government for years has routinely harvested our telephone calls, emails and mindlessly shallow online social media conversations.

I knew perfectly well that the Gopher King, no stranger to intrigue, wanted to get in on the action despite his general dislike of computers and the internet.

I explained how the United States government can't even make a simple website work, so how is it possible they can steal 70 million emails each day and make any sense of it?

I told his Furry Highness that such a long road trip was out of the question.

Meanwhile, Chaz's fears about online security prompted him to ask me to invest heavily on his behalf in companies that manufacture typewriters. He believes strongly that typewriters, along with No. 2 pencils, will re-emerge as the communication tools of the future.

"When you people ultimately destroy the world the person with a typewriter and a box of pencils will be very powerful," he said.

Chaz also recently purchased a homing pigeon farm in Texas. He is convinced that homing pigeons, tiny tubes of rolled paper fastened to their feet, will replace the internet as the next big thing in mass communications.

And so — as appeasement to his yearning for a road trip, I invited the Gopher King to another appointment at the VA clinic. I needed my prescription re-filled and I had another meeting with the nurse and her big words, who probably wanted to lay bare my brain on her TV screen again.

"What should I wear?" Chaz asked.

"Dress casual," I said.

Chaz showed up in a sleeveless denim jacket, *Da Nang 1970, 4th Infantry Div.* emblazoned in gothic lettering across his back. His hair was tucked into a man bun three quarters of the way up the back of his head, and he had a washable tattoo of a hand grenade exploding from within a scarlet valentine heart on his shaved forearm.

And so I put Chaz and a small bag of grassy snacks into a gym bag and told him not to wear any metal jewelry or carry a pocket knife because we would be passing through a metal detector.

The drive on I-70 from Bull River Falls through the mountains was uneventful until we reached the 12,000 ft. high Eisenhower Tunnel.

Chaz, who knows tunnel-making, was marveling at how somebody could dig such a perfectly positioned bore through solid rock beneath the Continental Divide, when he yelped and jumped off the dashboard and experienced what was apparently a catastrophic sphincter meltdown.

Maybe it was the altitude. I believe he was just excited about going to the big city. I can only describe it as rapid machine gun fire with disturbing olfactory consequences.

I drove with the windows open all the way to Denver.

Perhaps this was a mistake, unleashing a supernatural gopher in a major U.S. city.

Chaz mostly behaved himself when we got to the VA hospital, though he jumped out of the gym bag once and stole a bag of honey-roasted peanuts from the lunch tray of a guy wearing a World War Two Iwo Jima cap in the first floor cafeteria.

When I took a short cut through the Ear, Nose & Throat Department waiting room, Chaz asked if he could please sit and watch his favorite *Days of Our Lives* soap opera re run, the one in which Marlena is possessed by an evil demon who gives her super-human strength and the ability to levitate and shoot deadly laser beams from her eyeballs.

She is later seductively exorcised by a handsome priest on a church alter, thereby rescuing her tortured soul and thankfully allowing the plot to continue.

When I said we didn't have time to watch TV, the Gopher King threw a holy rodent fit and started screeching and kicking the inside of the gym bag. He threatened to use his spooky talents to shrink everybody in the hospital. But almost everybody in the ENT waiting room couldn't hear anyway, and the vets were too busy sneezing and coughing with allergies, so it worked out okay.

When I got to my appointment on the fifth floor — a place with a pale gray linoleum floor, Paris cafe scene photos on the wall, and a dozing security guard stationed at the elevator, I took a seat next to a nervous giant with a bushy beard and a shaved head who was wearing a sleeveless leather vest with "Binh Long, Vietnam" stitched in red, white and blue across his back.

"Easter offensive, huh?" I asked, staring at where brightly colored push pins on another map showed the location of every VA clinic in the land.

"Nineteen-seventy-two," the man said.

"I remember that one," I said.

He turned and shook my hand. He had a tattoo of a fanged serpent on his freakishly large forearm. The snake's tail graphically morphed into an American flag that seemed to explode into a shower of July 4th fireworks across his bare shoulder. He said his name was Butch or Bart, I forget, but his friends called him Bigfoot over at the VFW hall.

He had a very powerful grip and I didn't have to look down to know most of his fingers were gone, but I had the sense he couldn't care less if I noticed, anyway.

Hardly a visit goes by during trips to this place when I don't reminisce with a complete stranger about something we'd both observed when we were hopelessly stupid and young.

This time the guy with the disturbing snake tat launched into a monologue about tropical heat, the power of a Browning automatic rifle and the maddening design flaws of the M-16.

"Like the crazy retaining pin above the pistol grip," he said. "I gotta' ask, what fucking mechanical genius dreamed that up?"

Then we discussed the gastric side effects of Mefloquine malaria tablets when taken after a meal of canned MRE lasagna and Vienna sausage chased by Kool Aid made with warm rainwater.

We exchanged quips about the simple joy of taming a 104-degree malaria fever with an alcohol ice bath.

"The Army is never subtle," I said.

"Got that right, brother," Bigfoot said.

His face was horribly scarred beyond the edges of his beard and I recognized the poorly treated phosphorous burn. His creased cheek was thick and heavy below his good eye and where his jaw began the sagging skin hung in deeply wrinkled folds, like tilled earth, and was as white as wax. His milky and enlarged blind eye did not move when he smiled so that only half his damaged face seemed happy. Under the stark fluorescent lights of the hospital waiting room this dead half-mask seemed luminescent, as if the weapon responsible for the man's wound had left behind its vicious glow.

He pointed at the black and white photo on the wall, in which a beautiful woman sat under a cafe umbrella in the rain and gave us both a look of sexual eagerness from behind a raised coffee cup.

"Remember the old French church in Saigon?"

"By the old post office," I said. "The cathedral."

"Yeah," Bigfoot said, wistfully. "They'd put those yellow flowers in big pots outside during the New Year holiday. On the plaza. A busy goddamn place. I wonder if it's still that way."

"What is that?" The man looked at the floor by my feet.

I heard the sound of a zipper being opened. The Gopher King started loudly humming the melody to *I Got the Same Old Blues* by Lynyrd Skynyrd and so I pushed the gym bag under my chair and hoped for the best. Like I said, nobody could hear a damn thing in that waiting room.

I gave the bag a kick and prayed Chaz would shut up and take a nap, though I knew he was over-dosed on peanut candy. There's nothing more unpredictable than a prairie dog on a sugar high.

Bigfoot, whose massive leg had the same diameter as my torso, looked around and in a surprisingly soft and gentle voice — a good octave higher than what you'd expect from a man his size, turned to me and said:

"I love that song."

I sank into my chair and groaned. "One of my favorites."

The armed security guard who'd been napping in his chair near the elevator woke up and stared in my direction.

I looked down and Chaz was still squirming inside the gym bag. A furry little paw reached out and waved at me.

"I have to go to the bathroom," the Gopher King said. He whispered this, and his politeness impressed me.

I'd have some explaining to do if Chaz got loose. Bringing him here was a terrible idea. I remembered the sign above the hospital entrance: "No weapons. No Pets Allowed."

Meanwhile, my new large friend wouldn't shut up. He spoke loudly and happily, though nobody in the waiting room seemed to care.

I listened politely while Bigfoot recited a litany of prescribed pills he'd been given all these years

"Now they got me on a new pill," he said. "It's a pretty blue color."

From the gym bag, Chaz started singing *Take a Chance on Me*, by the weirdly tailored Swedish pop group ABBA.

Just then my name was called and I shuffled to my appointment with Nurse Ratchet.

When I returned to the waiting room there was Chaz, sitting on the open, unzipped gym bag. He and everyone else were intently watching an episode of the cable TV show *Monsters Inside Me* called "I'm Being Eaten by Maggots."

I quickly pushed the Gopher King back into the bag, zipped it and said: "Look, I can explain this."

Bigfoot smoothed his mangled two-fingered right hand over the top of his bald head and smiled. He looked at the gym bag, where Chaz was already starting to throw another fit.

"Don't worry. Nobody here gives a shit. But there is one thing," he said.

"What's that?" I asked, looking over where the security guard had once again fallen into a deep sleep.

"Your little buddy," Big foot said, pointing down at where Chaz's paw was beginning to appear from the flap of the gym bag.

"He's got it all wrong. It was the ninth infantry that was at Da Nang. The ninth. Not the fourth. He needs to get things right if he's gonna' wear that fucking jacket."

CHAPTER 42

As I drove home I listened to the war on the radio and daydreamed Chaz was dead asleep and passing Snickers farts on the back seat of my pickup truck.

I turned up the volume and heard the thumping sound of mortars and the scratchy background track of soldiers shouting. The sight of damaged men in their wheelchairs at the VA always makes me think too much about things.

The vines on the French plantation house so many years ago had reminded me of the ivy on the center field wall of Wrigley Field in Chicago.

"Hey, Sarge, did you hear me!" The PFC screamed that day after the ambush. "You gotta' cover me when I get that radio off Pappas. We have to call in our position!"

My mind was elsewhere. Hey, hey, another Ernie Banks homer.

While I lay in the grass, staring at where two of my boys floated face-down in the rice paddy, their green shirt backs puffed with air, I remembered thinking: Cubs, 1962. Banks, Altman, Billy Williams on the roster, Ashburn the lefty, Zimmerman, who could never run very well. The center field Wrigley Field vines shaking in the fishy summer breeze that came in warm gusts off Lake Michigan. Box seats at $2.50; free if you knew where the hole was in the chain link fence off Waveland Avenue. Front row center field bleacher seats were at the 400-foot mark, eleven feet above where the ivy started, for only seventy-five cents. But '59 was the big year when Banks made MVP for the second time in a row. The year the Cubs pitchers tossed eleven shutouts and the team hit 163 home runs. I remembered for no particular reason that Wrigley was named in 1926, the year Hack Wilson hit .321.

But now the PFC was staring at me, squinting: "The fuck were we doing on this road anyhow? Sarge, you listening to me? Why'd you tell us to take this road?"

I looked over at Pappas, the antenna swaying from the dead boy's twisted shoulder. I could have easily reached him and put on a tourniquet, or stabbed a morphine ampule into his ass to at least ease the pain before he died.

Mortar shells began dropping behind the plantation house, its rotted curtains blowing out from behind empty windows. The broken roof sliding away and crumbling within the rising smoke.

Curled up in the grass, again I remembered thinking: Top of the ninth, and Ritchie Ashburn took his swing and the white ball sailed and got caught in the thick green ivy of the center field wall at Wrigley.

The PFC screamed: "Hey, sarge! You listening?"

Hey, hey, said the WGN Radio announcer Jack Brickhaus, I'm in the shithouse, red brick shithouse...

"Listen to me!" the boy screamed again in my head.

The boy jumped up and down like an impatient child and stomped his foot. He pointed over at the radio.

"We need to see if that thing still works, Sarge. Cover me! We need to call in our position. Our guys are dropping shells too far down the trail. They're a thousand meters off target. If they don't shorten their drops we're dead meat. We're fuckin' meat! Now cover me. For Jesus fucking Christ, cover me."

"They'll figure it out," I said, rather calmly as if I were in a trance.

The PFC stared at me like I was crazy.

He said much more, but in the noise I could only see the boy's lips move, the chewing gum dancing behind his teeth. The 105mm artillery rounds were dropping closer.

"Cover me," the boy said again.

I said this into his ear: "We should stay where we are."

I remembered how meek I sounded, my voice tentative and child-like.

"You fucking crazy? You got the damn stripes! Tell me what to do."

The boy chewed his gum, Wrigley gum, Juicyfruit in the red brick shithouse.

Then he said, "Chickenshit. Sarge, you're a CHICKENSHIT!"

The boy turned and ran. His boots kicked up mud as he slid to a stop and crouched along the paddy dike, the dirt breaking away into the water as he tried to keep his balance, those jungle birds squawking and carrying on like they were now mad at only at me for ruining their beautiful day.

What happened next changed everything.

CHAPTER 43

Chaz was wearing Ray Ban Wayfarer sunglasses again, the fur at the back of his pointy head combed with a flourish into a 1950s-style ducktail. He had on a black leather jacket with silver chains dangling from one shoulder epaulet like he'd hopped out from some outlandish Marlon Brando biker nightmare.

Or James Dean returning from the hereafter as a rodent.

The Gopher King stood bobbing and jiving, a pair of enormous earphones clamped on his head.

I started to speak but he held up one claw.

"Wait. I love this song," he said, and he offered me the earphones.

It was Roy Orbison and he was singing *Only the Lonely,* his four-octave voice rising into a piercing falsetto. Chaz mouthed the words and closed his eyes and started swaying and bobbing again.

He sang, rather badly: "dum-dum-dum dumbdy-doo-wah, there goes my baby, there goes my heart." He sounded like a pair of rubber galoshes squeaking through a puddle.

Then he was somber and serious.

"I want you to do something for me," he said, deftly tapping his iPod with one claw. He slid the earphones down around his neckless shoulders and brought his paw over the top of his head and smoothed his fur. There was a hint of Brylcream or Vitalis, I don't know which, but Chaz had definitely had oiled his skull with too much of it. His fur glistened.

"What now?" I said impatiently. The trip to Denver had exhausted me and I'd been hoping for a few days of rest from my demanding little rodent. I was trying to catch up on work.

Chaz has no concept of distance or geography. China might be one mile away, for all he knows. So when he asked me to invest in a chain of bankrupt liquor stores somewhere on the east coast I told him he didn't realize how far away this was and that it might be a complicated financial transaction.

"Do it," he said and instructed me to tap his Bitcoin account in Tokyo and transfer funds to the PD Excavating & Landscaping Company, a Sub-chapter S Corporation I had created for him a while back. He had requested this after watching an episode of *The Sopranos* on TV.

I started to explain the intricacies of making such a purchase in another state, but he dismissed me with a wave of his paw.

"I've been thinking deep thoughts all morning so I've decided to be stupid the rest of the day," he said. "Just get it done. I'll make it worthwhile for you."

I told the Gopher King I was headed to Dora McCoy's ranch, where she was still recuperating after her rescue from the hospital by Chaz's commandos.

"She can't drive, so I'm taking her to Town Hall," I said. "She has to pay a fine for throwing the dead coyote at the mayor."

"Give her this," Chaz said. Two gopher soldiers carried out a cardboard box and placed it at my feet. The box was heavy and it smelled like peanut butter.

"It's a surprise," Chaz said. "Let her open it."

I figured Chaz's wife had cooked up a neighborly treat — could it be a gopher casserole whose ghastly ingredients I'd have to somehow explain to an old woman who didn't know gophers could talk and cook and fire weapons? Or rescue her from a hospital?

I drove to the Last Chance Ranch thinking of how Dora had told me she'd fired her husband's old Girand rifle at the Gold Gulch lodge building. I tried to visualize the direction of the shot and wondered if the round could have traveled, unimpeded by a quarter mile of trees, to the spot where they found Melinda Barstow.

Dora was waiting for me on her front porch. She still looked sick, but her putrid arm, now wrapped in a clean gauze sleeve, seemed better.

"I see they fixed you up," I said.

"It's all a blur," Dora said, wiggling her fingers. "I don't remember how I got to the damn hospital or how I got back."

She cussed most of the way to town, hollering about the mayor and the $300 fine she had to pay and how it was all the money she had left in the world.

"And I still owe those real estate taxes," she said as we pulled into the Town Hall parking lot. "I don't know where they think I can get thirty-thousand dollars!"

The mayor looked annoyed when he stepped from his office and snapped his suspenders and took the money from Dora's envelope. He stood behind the reception desk and counted the bills slowly like he had all the time in the world.

"I wouldn't cheat you," Dora said.

I stepped out of the way, figuring this conference might get nasty.

"If we didn't have all these fire problems I would have had you arrested," the mayor said without looking up. He put the money in a drawer. "But then the whole town would make me the bad man for jailing a frail old woman."

"I ain't frail. And you're no youngster yourself," Dora said, leaning over the counter top.

"And I don't act like one either," the mayor said. He handed over the receipt. He reached under the counter and brought out a sealed envelope.

"And here's the cleaning bill for my rug you dirtied up. And the wall that needs to get painted. So if you could take care of that as well, I'd appreciate it."

"I'd toss another dead thing your way if I had a chance," Dora said.

She stared at the envelope and let it lay on the counter.

Dora was chewing her Copenhagen. She looked for somewhere to spit. She stepped back and leaned out the door and delivered her load onto the sidewalk. She came back, took the envelope, and folded it into the front pocket of her denim jacket. She turned to the mayor and tapped the pocket with her good hand.

"Don't hold your breath."

"We'll take you to court."

"Judges around here don't scare me. I've known most of them since they was babies."

"You better damn well be afraid of jail, then."

"There's plenty of them TV folks in town who might love to hear my side of the story," Dora McCoy said. "I might just twist a fact or two. They don't seem care, long as they got a tale to tell."

The mayor spread his hands across the counter and glared, a terrible anger boiling up behind his red face.

"You best get out before I have you charged with a felonious public health crime."

"You big fat gas bag," Dora said. "And what make believe crime would that be?"

"I'll think of something. Just looking at you makes me mad all over again. Now get out. You never did act like much of a lady, so what did I expect?"

"My taxes paid for this building. I won't get out."

The mayor peered over his half moon reading glasses and pointed at the door. He jowls were shaking.

"I'm telling you to get."

He smiled: "County says you've not paid a dime in property taxes for years. So there goes your argument. I'll see you at the next Trustee sale. Be a pleasure to watch them kick you off your land."

"Just who did I hurt?" Dora McCoy said, and she too stiffened. She clenched her fist. The two leaned at each other across the counter, their faces only inches apart.

"The general public, not to mention myself, that's who you hurt," the mayor said.

"You're comparing a tossed varmint with what you and your bunch are letting happen?"

"There's one more dumb thing you've said," the mayor said. "What you did was wrong, not to mention a little insane. What we did was protect people's jobs and homes. This town needs that ski resort."

"You ain't protecting me."

"I say I am, even though you don't have anything that could be called a job at that miserable junkyard you call a ranch," the mayor said. "By the way, your hand looks something awful. You should go back to the hospital."

I was ready to take a swing at the mayor myself, but Dora brought up her fist and held it in front of his chubby face.

"Why, you're a stinker yourself," Dora McCoy seethed. "And I don't trust you like I don't trust them doctors."

The mayor took a deep breath and sighed. "You used to be civil, Dora. A little rough at the edges, but always polite in your younger days. Your husband Hector, may he rest in peace, would be ashamed of you."

Dora squinted and hissed. "Don't you dare mention my husband. I don't like his name coming off your lips, you sonofabitch."

The mayor leaned back like he was afraid the old woman might indeed take a swing. His red nose glowed. He puffed his cheeks and turned and stepped into his office and slammed the door behind him.

I guided Dora outside and let her calm down. She looked at the sky and breathed deeply.

"I don't know what I'm gonna' do, Stan," she sighed. "I'm busted now. Just a broke old lady."

"Wait," I said, trying to calm her down. "Just see what happens. Get your thoughts clear and then go to the county commissioners and talk to somebody. You know half the people at the county building. You could make payments."

When we got back into my truck I remembered Chaz's package. I opened the windows to let in some air.

"You got a peanut butter sandwich in here?" Dora asked.

I gave her the dented box, which had been sealed with packing tape. Something heavy inside rolled back and forth.

Dora peeled off the tape. "Whatever is this?" she said.

"An admirer asked me to give it to you," I said.

"I ain't got no admirers in this town," Dora said.

When she lifted out the heavy glass Jiffy peanut butter jar and studied what was inside Dora McCoy gave such a loud gasp, I thought she was about to have a cardiac event right there in my truck.

This thing wasn't your ordinary 8 oz. grocery store jar. It was the giant 64 oz. tub, the kind peanut butter freaks buy, and I knew right away Chaz the Gopher King had been robbing the COSTCO store again, a place where everyone seems to buy stuff as if preparing for the apocalypse.

The contents of the jar sparkled brightly.

Dora lowered the jar into her lap. She unscrewed the lid. "Looks like colored sand. Is this a joke?"

"It's no joke. And it's not sand," I said. I reached and stirred the sparkling gold dust with my finger.

"How much you suppose is in there?"

"More than enough to pay those taxes," I said. "And a little extra for a shopping spree or two."

"Who'd you say gave this to me?"

"I'd rather not say," I said, "He's kind of shy."

Dora smiled. "So, it's a gentleman?"

"Believe me, he's no gentleman," I said.

CHAPTER 44

I couldn't get much work done. My head was a mess and for a couple of days I'd locked up the office and taken naps behind my closed curtains just to get enough thoughts together to assemble the newspaper.

I sat there in my recliner in the dim afternoon half-light, the police scanner fuzzing away from behind my desk in the next room. I took a pill and had a drink and then, gratefully, dozed off.

At the familiar and unidentified barrier, on the other side of which I usually try to remain, I took my usual leap and landed with a rather youthful spring on both feet in the magical and pleasantly confusing land of the Gopher King.

And this is what I sorted out:

At some point and against my advice Chaz, unfortunately, and as a portent to the ultimate degradation of his species, learned how to use the internet.

I realized the limited space in his walnut-sized brain was about to be overwhelmed.

I explained how this unfortunate plunge into the World Wide Swimming Pool of Unencumbered Triviality would soon evolve into a spinning blob of sawdust between his ears and have his confused brain neurons firing like farts in a violent windstorm, but he just gnawed my ankle and told me to shut up and mind my own business.

And so I made him little rubber claw pads from pencil erasers (ironic, don't you think?), and with these he turned into a savvy two-fingered typist. For online purchases he uses a debit card registered to the P.D. Rodenthouse Benevolent Foundation, which is linked to a bottomless checking account funded by converted Japanese bit coins.

On his first drive along the dark and dangerously rutted gravel road that is the information highway, the Gopher King ordered a video called *Wild and Endless Love on the Prairie,* a plotless yet action-packed flick in which two female wildlife biology graduate students perform shockingly erotic and acrobatic feats while entwined in 180-thread count camo bedsheets, which is the only fabric that touches their skin during the 90-minute motel-to-motel romp across the alluvial plains of Nebraska and South Dakota.

"I thought it would be a nice movie about prairie dogs," Chaz told me.

Puzzled, the Gopher King said he watched the film twice, after which he asked me to explain a few things. I tried my best, but it did not work. He stared at me like a child who has just been asked to describe Einstein's quantum theory of light.

"But why would they waste those blueberry pies?" Chaz asked.

"And the trampoline. Why go through all the trouble?"

And then, obviously perplexed by what he had seen: "I just don't understand the bullwhip."

But it was the nude bungee jumping episode that had this rodent confused .

"I didn't sleep all night," Chaz said.

"Next time buy a video of *Lassie Come Home*," I said.

"What's that about?"

"A dog gets lost and then he comes home," I said.

"Sounds stupid," Chaz said.

This all happened before Chaz and I, after much pressure from the royal rodent, traveled to Alberta, Canada.

I drove, stopping along the way in Bozeman, Montana where I purchased a tee shirt that said: "The Green Coalition of Gay Loggers for Jesus."

From there I shipped Chaz by UPS to Edmonton, knowing I couldn't bear to spend fifteen more hours on the road with a chatty rodent who now owned a laptop computer.

The Gopher King booked me into a fleabag motel. It wasn't in the middle of nowhere. It was on the very edge of the middle of the farthest edge of the middle of nowhere — a vast prairie moonscape where I could see the curvature of the Earth from the parking lot.

My miserable room had an orange shag rug and a bright blue 1960s Zenith 12-inch TV, a broken hot plate and a leaking Bidet which the hotel owners, two expatriate socialist separatists from Quebec, had installed in hygienic homage to their French speaking homeland.

Chaz was very proud he'd mastered Travelocity and his heart was in the right place so I said the motel was wonderful and very adequate.

We were traveling to Alberta to inspect Chaz's outpost of pioneering gophers, which is apparently growing and now sports nearly a thousand colonists. It's like Jamestown, except it has refugee rodents. And the women don't wear bonnets.

So this is where I stayed for a while; once again neglecting the newspaper back in Bull River Falls, cooking Ramen noodles in a shabby motel on the windswept prairie in the middle of Alberta, a giant painting of Elvis in a Hawaiian shirt hanging over my bed. One night we watched the little vacuum tube Zenith TV and a documentary about the 19th Century vaporization of the American Bison by trigger-happy psychotic western hunters with bad teeth and mutton chop sideburns.

The film showed these grizzled cowboys loading train boxcars with Bison pelts bound for England so British dandies could wear soft leather boots. I could see Chaz was upset by the obvious parallels to the plight of his own kind. The Bison, at least, had been saved by thousands of happy burger eaters with a devotion to low fat meat. Prairie dogs, he knew, could hope for no such luck.

After blasting their way through billions of passenger pigeons, the riflemen of the 1890s promptly shot their way through several species of smaller birds, now also extinct.

In those few years England alone imported the furs of 50,000 wolves, 30,000 bears, 22,000 otters, 750,000 raccoons, 100,000 pine martens and a quarter million foxes. According to zoologist William Hornaday, one of the first advocates for saving bison from extinction, 40,000 buffalo hides were shipped east in one year from a single Kansas train depot. If not for the discovery of 200 of the animals loafing near a geyser pond in Yellowstone Park, nobody today would be able to order Bison meatloaf at a restaurant.

By any measure, Chaz's Canadian gopher colony was a success. Sixty-eight miles of burrow tunnels had already been dug. Schools were built. Wise-ass teenage boy gophers were pointlessly expending their energy at the new prairie dog paintball park.

Like the bad luck 17th century experiment at colonial Jamestown, in which 104 people unknowingly settled amidst 14,000 not-too-friendly Algonquin Indians, Chaz's utopian crap shoot in Canada is doomed.

The Gopher King's colony is located smack in the Athabascan oil sands reserve and only two miles from a proposed housing development. It also lay in the path of a new two-lane provincial highway.

Chaz's hope for a new beginning, the answer to the survival of his kind in a world free from manicured golf courses and real estate salespeople with nice hairdos, unfortunately sat atop 200 billion gallons of recoverable oil that has the strange consistency of cold molasses.

I agonized on how I should break this sad news to the Gopher King, who now seemed so happy and hopeful.

I decided I would not.

After all, he has an army of 20,000 cranky gopher commandos who do anything he asks.

CHAPTER 45

While Chaz was in Canada on a quick inspection of his experimental pioneer prairie dog settlement, sixteen gophers were killed by a backhoe digging an ornamental duck pond behind the new Gold Gulch Resort lodge.

I had to quickly arrange to ship the Gopher King home via FedEx.

The tragedy wiped out the entire membership of the Gopher Ladies Reading Circle book club while the group was at its weekly luncheon 15 feet below the fourth hole sand trap. They were discussing Ernest Hemingway's *Death in the Afternoon*, a famous testosterone-riddled tribute to bullfighting, swaggering Spanish matadors and disemboweled horses.

So I decided to pay my respects.

I had not been magically shrunk by the Gopher King for a while, but figured it was the least I could do in order to attend the funeral being held at the colony's extensive network of gold-rich caves on Bellyache Mountain.

And so I dressed in my one and only dorky dark suit, dug up a pair of decent shoes, and for the first time in many years appeared in public without wearing a baseball cap.

Chaz, for this somber gathering was dressed like General George Patton, in riding boots, a sheathed cavalry sword hanging from a black patent leather belt. Twin Ruger pistols hung at his side and his black beret was festooned with gold braid. He looked like a furry South American dictator.

"You're sure about this?" he said as he began to shrink me. "Just don't upchuck like last time."

I nodded and took a deep breath. The Gopher King touched my leg with one long glowing claw and closed his eyes and made a strange, melodic burping noise, like the under water song of a mating whale. His eyeballs rolled back into his head and his face fur bristled like he'd put his finger into an electrical wall socket.

I got that familiar vomity and feverish sensation, like I'd been hammered with a bad flu bug. My face got icy and numb, my scalp tingled and I blacked out. When

I awoke I was sitting at the entrance to a gopher burrow and Chaz was leaning against a dirt wall, an unlit cigar clenched between his teeth.

"How do you feel?" he said.

I squinted in the darkness and looked around. There was a dandelion growing next to the hole and it came up to my chest. I was not much bigger than a large hoagie bun, or a 12-inch tall Ken Doll dressed in a $35 suit.

"Not as bad as last time," I said, trying to touch where my ears might be.

Chaz bit down on his cigar, dropped to all fours and said: "Good, follow me."

It was a long and winding underground hike, mostly uphill through numerous side passages. At a point where three burrows intersected and formed a wide subterranean plaza, I stepped carefully over a resting spider as big as my foot. Dripping pale tree roots hung from the ceiling. An earthworm as thick as my arm swung its blind head back and forth from a hole in the wall and when I squeezed past it quickly sucked itself out of sight.

Two tattooed gopher street punks wearing camo doo-rags on their heads stood and glared at me and then saluted smartly as Chaz walked past. The Gopher King scolded them for smoking so close to the gold mine and the two tough guys sheepishly snubbed their cigarettes and walked off.

We climbed for a while up a widening tunnel, other gophers joining us in a long silent procession until the burrow opened into a massive stone cave, a long-collapsed gold mine, its far end cluttered with the rubble of boulders and broken timbers.

I shimmied over twisted iron rails and stepped past a tipped and rusted ore wagon. As we gathered for the funeral service, leathery bats almost as big as me hung upside down and blinked from behind cowled black wings that looked like damaged umbrellas.

I looked out and saw a thousand gopher mourners standing like an assembly of medieval monks, some wearing hoods, everyone dressed in black, most holding umbrellas against the constant stream of misty water that dripped from the mine's ceiling. Lit wall torches blazed and smoked, casting the shapes of all those sad rodents against the stone walls.

Many of the gophers wept, and it sounded like Tupperware lids being opened and closed. The sixteen coffins, each emblazoned with the People's Gopher Army logo, were lined up on a polished flat stone behind which a row of more lit torches made a light show of flickering shadows. A giant wall banner proclaimed: "Imperium Subterranius."

After all were assembled I stood aside as Chaz walked slowly to a podium bearing his royal seal and gave a short speech about the cruel vicissitudes of life and the immortality of honor and bravery and how often he believed his own gift of Plutonium-induced long life was indeed a curse he wished he could be rid of.

Choking back a sob, the Gopher King said he had now outlived 15 wives and one hundred sixty-seven children and his sweet memories of each of them only added to his sad and unavoidable burden. Mortality and its constraints were, he said, a blessing he would never know.

A platoon of heavily armed commandos then slowly raised their rifles and fired a thundering volley inside the mine, sending the bats flying in black sheets above my head. The soldiers presented arms and snapped to attention and saluted as Chaz walked and placed a wreath of some unknown tangle of grass and tiny flowers on each of the boxes of the dead.

He paused at one particular coffin and lay his arm across its lid and bowed his head and stood for a moment. His shoulders trembled.

The Gopher King wiped his eye and adjusted the tilt of his black beret and straightened himself and then he too saluted and stepped away as a lone gopher trumpeter standing on a rock ledge played a melancholy dirge for the departed.

And then the entire faceless gathering began to wail from beneath their umbrellas, as if this might be an ancient ritual among these strange rodent mourners.

They carried the coffins away and I was told each body would be customarily entombed like all the gopher dead — in the very burrows and tunnels where they themselves had lived, the places sealed away forever, it being forbidden at all to walk or visit there again.

As I expected, Chaz's revenge came swiftly the very next day.

CHAPTER 46

I imagined it might soon get much easier for Chaz to unshrink me so I would hardly experience the after effects, which sometimes included a short period of Tourette's-like madness and facial tics during which I'd cuss uncontrollably until the Gopher King's sorcery finally wore off.

I think this is what happened the day following the funeral:

And so...a squad of gopher commandos armed with chainsaws paid a visit to the giant lodge the Gold Gulch Resort Company was building south of town.

The rodents rappelled silently like Navy SEALS from a hovering Blackhawk at 2 a.m., entering the massive log structure through a second floor window which they removed using a kerfed diamond saw blade and a pair of rubber suction pads. It took only twenty minutes for the gophers to saw through eight critical floor joists that were perpendicular to the building's load bearing walls. They then removed a few i-beam bolts and quickly vanished into the night.

In the old days the gophers would have just bombed the place or slapped a few pounds of C-4 explosive randomly on the building's outside walls. But Chaz's version of revenge now demanded a more creative twist.

As I always feared, the Gopher King had now evolved into a dangerous rodent performance artist, determined to make a multi-layered artistic statement with each act of violence.

The next day, adhering to some mysterious corporate PR logic which I assume Chaz was aware of, the Gold Gulch company invited everyone in Bull River Falls to a free barbecue, where they presented a check for $25,000 to the fire department for its good work in defending the town from the blaze that had already burned nearly 25,000 acres on Bellyache Mountain.

The company created a scholarship fund at the high school, paid for an engraved brass plaque at Town Hall honoring the firefighting effort, sponsored a new men's softball league to the tune of a few thousand dollars, purchased tricked out Land Rovers for Bull River's three-person police department, and set aside another small fortune for a proposed new town exit off the interstate highway.

They also commissioned a sculpture, a frightening metallurgical nightmare depicting two twisted Mad Max-like skiers hurdling off a stylized cliff which would soon grace a grand plaza being built in the center of town — all on the company's dime, of course.

At the catered picnic a Gold Gulch executive made a speech from a bandstand in front of a giant white tent trimmed with red, white and blue bunting. The man identified himself as a senior vice president of corporate goulash & intrinsically meaningless affairs — nobody could remember his name — gestured grandly and spoke of how the "community spirit" of Bull River had overwhelmed him and forced him to rethink what was important in life.

The mayor and the town council sat on folding chairs in a row on the raised platform, along with a representative from the Governor's office, who looked miserably uncomfortable in his dark suit and tie and kept pulling up his argyle socks.

"I know we've had differences, and some of the criticism we do deserve," the Vice President of Stockholder Shenanigans & Memo-writing Virtuosity said.

"But today I want to publicly thank everyone who has supported this project and I wish to extend the hand of friendship and reconciliation to those who are still against it," he said, pompously lifting his arms as if to offer a Papal benediction. He then turned to point at the lodge building and I noticed he was the owner of a deeply embedded and probably painful wedgie. On such a hot day, poor man. Others noticed this too because I heard a fit of chuckling in the crowd.

At that moment a five-year-old girl with a cone of cotton candy in her hand pointed and asked her father why the lodge building seemed to be leaning to one side in the brisk wind that had begun to blow down from the mountain.

A loud murmur spread through the crowd. Dogs started barking. A bunch of birds squawked and lifted off the building and flapped wildly away.

There was a deeper groan when the roof suddenly shifted. A flag bearing the Gold Gulch logo on top of the roof flapped noisily before it snagged on its pole like a sailboat spinnaker. The flag then billowed violently. The building shook visibly and tossed off a corona of flying sawdust.

Unseen by everyone but me, a half dozen gopher-sized Chinook helicopters from Chaz's air force, each trailing a long cord tethered to the lodge, pulled with just enough force to make the structure's roof slide away.

With corncobs, barbecued baby back ribs and chili dogs in their hands, folks in the crowd started to point up at the swaying structure.

The thundering crash came just as the Gold Gulch Executive Minister of Ponderous and Unstoppable Verbal Wind was reminiscing how his company indeed had faith in the project decades ago, when they were first inspired to build a ski and golf resort "the whole world would come to."

The Executive Vice Admiral of Soaring Profit and Shareholder Benevolence spread his arms wide just as the main roof joist of the lodge shuddered and split in two. Sheets of loose cedar shake shingles fell away. The giant flapping flag then snapped off and fell with its thirty-foot pole like a spear, nearly impaling one of the county commissioner candidates who had taken advantage of the picnic crowd to hand out campaign flyers.

The mayor of Bull River Falls stood and screamed.

The massive Gold Gulch Resort Lodge, the largest building ever constructed in the county, collapsed within a towering plume of dust like a badly constructed child's Lego castle, the splinters flying everywhere.

The Gold Gulch executive hastily dropped the notes to his speech, leaped off the stage, and ran into the fleeing crowd.

CHAPTER 47

Chaz the multi-tasking Gopher King was humming the 1968 hit *Do You Know the Way to San Jose?* while he carefully studied an autographed photo of Dionne Warwick wrapped in a protective clear plastic sleeve.

This, while practicing his intarsia knitting skills on a pair of blue wool socks and once again listening on his iPod to Pavarotti while the singer hit his chilling tenor high note in Puccini's *Nessun Dorma* aria.

Chaz then turned and asked me to explain the stock market.

He was wearing his checkered Elmer Fudd winter hat. In this summer heat, for godsake.

"The whole market thing. I don't get it," he said.

With his padded claws Chaz typed something into his computer. I watched him order sixteen cases of paper towels and ten three-packs of giant 5 kg jars of Nutella from COSTCO and then ship everything FedEx to the experimental gopher colony in Alberta, Canada.

Chaz has been fascinated lately with his computer and told me he wanted to invest his Japanese bit coins in soft commodities.

"Perhaps wheat, sugar. Coffee futures," he said casually. I don't think he understood his own sentence.

I cautioned him about the Las Vegas-like temptations that playing the market might bring, but he shook his head beneath that stupid hat and told me to shut up and just give him my best opinion of Wall Street and capitalism and the alluring promise of everlasting wealth and happiness.

I suggested he think of the stock market as if it were a 15 year-old teenage boy walking into a room filled with naked women.

"I guarantee this person will have no judgment or exercise any caution whatsoever," I said. "That's what the stock market is. It's as wise and predictable as a mindless teenager boiling with hormones."

Chaz then logged onto the QVC Shopping Channel and ordered a dozen giant purple hoop ear rings and a lumbar pillow embroidered with a picture of Elvis. There's no telling how much money he would spend. When he gets like this you just have to walk away. And so I did.

Later that morning I had breakfast at the Grill & Griddle Cafe on Main Street, a place with great food and awful service, so I go there each Wednesday to fill up on grease and salt and all the nitrate infused morning meat I can find.

The place was packed and I nodded to everybody and they nodded back at me. There's a lot of nodding in a small town. It's annoying.

Over in the corner sat Dora McCoy and her son, who I heard had come down from Alaska to help his ailing mother while she recuperated at the Last Chance Ranch. Dora nodded to me and I nodded back and then a few more people joined in until there was a whole new round of senseless head wobbling.

I sat down and Dorothy the waitress nodded to me and took out her pencil and pad.

"Give me something to make my heart explode," I said.

"Okay," she said. "The usual then."

I nodded.

Two strangers then walk into the restaurant. They nod, but nobody nods back because they are, of course, complete strangers. Right away they make a loud ruckus, shoving chairs, pulling poor Dorothy the waitress by her apron and trying to give her an uninvited hug.

These men are giants, and their appropriately giant Harleys are parked outside. The biggest one wore a greasy Moses beard and was dressed in leather, head-to-feet. Chains hanging from every pocket. While he was insulting Dorothy he said something inappropriate, so one customer in the cafe he tried to stop it, but it took one slap to send him running out the door.

The biggest of them had a whole mural of tattoos, a fresco of ink twisting around his arms that told an unknowable story populated by serpents and fierce howling beasts silhouetted against a red moon and then German looking words tumbling up and down his biceps and into his cut-off denim sleeves.

You had to figure the rest of the tale got told on his chest, but I didn't want to know the whole story. Another burst of ink ran up his neck and into his whiskers.

Those two boys got bigger the more you looked at them, and then they started banging their knives and forks, asking for a menu. Cussing. The big guy grabbed Dorothy again and tried to smooch her but she twisted away and ran back into the kitchen.

Dora McCoy leaned over and spoke to her son, who calmly mopped his breakfast eggs with a muffin, chewed carefully, and then looked over at the two troublemakers.

Nobody ever saw him walk across the room. Dora's son just appeared in front of those two men twenty feet away like he'd drifted there on air. I never saw such a thing. All the sound left the room.

The two big guys stood and crouched, moving at Dora's son like somebody had banged the bell in a boxing ring. They brought up their fists and grinned like they'd been waiting for just such a thing all day. The smaller man took a roundhouse swing and Dora's son waved off the blow like he was being bothered by a fly.

Then Dora's son brought his hand flat against the side of the man's thick neck, like he was taking his pulse or checking for a fever. Just held his hand to the spot like there were suckers on his fingers. The troublemaker gave a goofy soprano squeak and just crumpled up. When he hit the floor it was like somebody had dropped a piano. The whole restaurant shook. My fork and spoon skittered off the table.

Dora's son then jerked the man's arm in a funny pretzel wrestling hold I'd never seen before and took him by the collar and dragged him away. The man weighed God-knows-what, but Dora's son just dragged him away like he was a piece of luggage.

The bigger of the two, who had his hair trussed up into a pile of Jamaican rasta knots, pulled from his back pocket a bandanna tied to a heavy padlock. He took a swing with it, but Dora's son danced away.

Yes, I said he DANCED away. I thought I was watching Mikhail Baryshnikov do a leaping ballet pirouette in *The Nutcracker*.

The giant biker tried to make a tackle but Dora's son reached out and gave him what looked like a lazy poke under the jaw, his three fingers together, straight and stiff like you see when a Boy Scout swears his oath. And then he stroked the biker behind the ear with his palm, his touch quick, the fingers aflutter and rubbing back and forth, and all of a sudden he gives a hard yank. I don't know what happened, but the big biker started choking and gasping like he was drowning. He gurgled and bubbled, his eyes bulging. Started rolling across the floor, kicking aside chairs with his legs.

Dora's son carefully lifted the biker from behind by the armpits and dragged him out the door, where he sat him down and tapped him on the shoulder as if he were saying goodbye to an old buddy.

Dora's son helped the other man to his feet and began to escort him outside. The man tried another dizzy swing but Dora's son caught his wrist, put his other hand into that woolly beard, and slammed the man into the wall like he was a doll. He too was taken outside.

Everybody in the cafe was standing back against the walls and they watched while Dora's son stood outside talking to both men for a while, pointing at their parked Harleys as they sat on the curb like obedient children listening to a lecture about motorcycle safety.

When he was finished Dora's son tucked in his shirt and calmly walked back to his table. He took a few bills from his pocket and left an extra tip for Dorothy. He steadied his mother gently by the arm and escorted the old woman slowly out the door.

It was very quiet in the cafe except for the loud hissing sound of the cappuccino machine in the kitchen, which sounded like a cheering crowd at a sports stadium.

CHAPTER 48

"Melinda Barstow of Bull River Falls died July 24 of multiple gunshot wounds, according to police, who are investigating the incident as a homicide. Her body was discovered on the south bank of the Bull River, near the controversial and so-called Ute Indian burial site south of town. She was employed by the University of Colorado as an archaeology field assistant working under contract with the Bureau of Land Management. She was 22 years old.

"Melinda was born July 27, 1994 in Bull River Falls and graduated from Castle Peak High School with honors. She was a senior at the University of Colorado in Boulder at the time of her death. She had returned for summer break to work on a project through the high school's science intern program in which she was also employed as a student teacher and faculty assistant. She planned to pursue a career in forensic archaeology, according to her field advisor, county coroner Carmen Ruiz.

"Melinda enjoyed reading, skiing and hiking. She planned to pursue graduate studies at the University of Wyoming after completing her Bachelor of Science program.

"In high school she was actively involved in sports, including stints as team captain for the basketball team, for which she played center. She was also in the marching band and a member of the debate team and was a four-year participant in the 4-H Club, where she was awarded a first place ribbon for her champion rabbit. She was one of only a dozen Colorado high school seniors chosen for a foreign exchange program in Bath, England where she was part of a team restoring artifacts at the city's famous Roman ruins.

"Survivors include her father Robert, of Bull River Falls; her mother, Mary Bannon of Henderson, Nevada; grandfather James Arthur Barstow of Glenwood Springs, Colorado; grandparents Mona and Sean Bannon of Falmouth, Mass., and numerous aunts, uncles and nieces and nephews.

"Rev. Jimmy Ogden of the First Baptist Church officiated. A memorial observance attended by an estimated 300 was held at the high school. Burial will be at Sunset Ridge Cemetery. The date has not been announced. In lieu of flowers, contributions may be sent to the Castle Peak High School Youth Achievement Fund c/o Castle Peak Bank."

***

I always disliked writing obits, but I knew I needed to ask Bob Barstow to look at this one to make sure I didn't make any mistakes.

At the jail, I sat on a metal bench next to a steel sink and a lidless prison toilet. The fiberglass bed was bolted to the cement wall.

Bob Barstow's left eye was swollen. Across his face lay an oblong bruise. He kept putting his hands in and out of his pockets. When he spoke the welt on his cheek turned darker.

"They took away my suspenders" he said. "That would be a trick, hanging myself with suspenders."

Barstow was still wearing his dirty firefighting clothes, the yellow field shirt torn, most of the buttons missing. The scratches ran across his throat.

"Suppose I could swallow these shoes and kill myself," he said.

"Rules." I said.

"Do you think he did it?"

"Jergen? Can't say."

"I guess I'll make the TV tonight," Barstow said. "They're letting me go in a few hours. They booked me like I was a crook. I don't know what came over me."

"You don't have to talk to anybody if you don't want to, Bob. Me included," I said.

"I don't want rumors around saying she was a home breaker. The guy is married. I don't want people talking trash. They'd been seeing each other for a while."

Barstow rubbed his hands together like he was keeping himself warm as he stared at the painted gray concrete floor.

"I saw a TV thing once," he said. "Guy's wife was murdered. He waited at the airport because he'd found out they were transferring him out of state to another jail, and when the police were walking through the terminal with the killer in handcuffs he jumped up and shot the bastard in the head. It seemed fair, I thought."

Barstow turned. "Do you think he did it?"

"The cops might be too eager on this one," I said. "From what I hear he was working at the lodge and just happened to be near where they found Melinda."

"She liked him," Barstow said. "She told me he was moving to Wyoming so he could be with her when she headed to graduate school. She told me about his wife. The marriage wasn't working. You just don't want your kid getting into something so complicated. Life is messy enough. I guess I snapped. I don't even remember hitting him."

"You missed," I said. "You both got lucky. You might be getting an invoice for a windshield."

Barstow turned to the window. The back of his neck was bandaged. The seat of his pants were split. "Could have taken his head off."

"The boys at the firehouse raised bail," I said.

"I didn't know. Shit."

Barstow pointed at the window and started putting his hands in and out of the pockets, like he was digging for loose change.

"She'd play out there when she was little," he said, still facing the window. "In that meadow by the old state patrol building. I'd watch her feed grass to the horses. She'd sit under a tree pretending she was a pioneer girl. She'd bring pots and pans like she was making supper. She'd carry on whole conversations with herself. It sure is shitty to have memories come back when they hurt the most. I don't know why it works that way."

"Things heal, Bob," I said, knowing they didn't.

"Everything's gone to hell."

I handed over my draft of Melinda's obituary and he looked it over and nodded and put it down on the bed.

"They won't let me bury her until they finish the investigation," he said.

I then said, "Bob, what did the police tell you?"

"Asked cop questions, you know. My head wasn't clear at the time, but I told them what I knew. The two of them together. How we'd argued. How I'd been trying to talk her out of seeing him."

"Tom Cherry is out of his league on this one." I said.

"There is something," Barstow said. "Her voicemail messages. Police wanted them, but I had already deleted a call from a man who was inviting Melinda to meet him. It wasn't the boyfriend's voice, I'm sure of it. I'd have recognized it. I remember how Melinda was upset when I told her. She left the house in a hurry."

"They said she was working at the quarry," I said.

"Yeah, on the Indian thing. She was there a lot that week. Said it was important."

"She ever say what it was?"

"By that time we'd already argued too much. I was the last person she wanted to talk to. Her work and those bones at the resort was the last thing I was interested in."

We talked for a while about the fire. He said I looked like shit and I agreed. I reached and embraced him. The heavy metal cell door banged loudly when I swung it shut.

Barstow called out to me, his face pressed between the upright bars, "Where's it heading now? The fire."

"Toward the town," I said. "They know who did it. Guy was a known troublemaker. Moved to town last year and seems to have a hair up is ass about the resort. They found weapons at his house, kerosene fuses, crazy fire drawings on the wall. Enough to make it a no brainer. Now it's just a matter of finding out where the sonofabitch is."

At the memorial service they sat a framed photo on Melinda's closed coffin. Her cheerleader jacket was draped next to it on an empty chair. They played rock music I didn't recognize.

Barstow stood at the front of the church and tried to say a few words. He seemed diminished in his loose-fitting suit. He managed to get out a few thoughts but his voice cracked and he apologized and walked back to his seat. Barstow and his ex wife sat together in the pew, both of them careful not to touch each other. The wife looked lost, but she never wept. She was heavier than when I'd had seen her last, and she held a tissue in her lap and kept tearing it into pieces that she dropped one-by-one to the floor between her shoes. The two never spoke, never looked at each other. They left the church in separate cars.

CHAPTER 49

When my wife was gone there was no bottom to how I felt.

The night she died I held her hand and listened to the nurses walk past the room at the hospice, the improbable sound of marching band music faintly drifting from the ceiling speakers. The plush rug in the hallway and the way the rooms were lined up made the place look like a quiet hotel. On the wall were hung pictures of boats and tropical beaches and lonely white wooden piers.

A hand touched my shoulder and I was asked if I could please step outside. I sat on the hallway sofa and heard sobbing in another room. From the cafeteria came the sound of clanking dishes.

When I returned to the room they had her arms folded on her chest and an open Bible lay on the nightstand. She was propped against a fresh white pillow and there were new sheets on the bed. They had taken the medicine bottles and the extra chairs and the medical machines out of the room. Gone were the cotton balls in the big jar on the shelf, along with the pink sponges on sticks I'd used to wet her lips. They'd emptied the waste basket where I'd seen her blood on a square gauze bandage.

A blue candle burned next to the Bible and it smelled like flowers. Her hair was combed but it was so thin I could see her scalp. Her hair was combed all wrong. She never slept on her back with her hands folded that way. Now there was churchy music playing on the hospice intercom; monks singing, the voices echoing.

I kissed her and she tasted salty. It wasn't her fault she was so salty.

I paced back and forth in the room, though I wasn't thinking of anything at all, and each time I passed the foot of the bed the guttering candle beside the Bible leaned and flickered. I touched her cold toes once beneath the clean and starched sheets and they were not stiff at all. I told her I did not want to leave. I told her I could not leave.

Maybe it was the yellow candle flame and the way the room was softly lit but she looked more alive than when she was sick.

They expected me to pray, but I did not. The Bible lay open to the Psalms, but I could not go near it. She never combed her hair that way.

I walked out the back door so the nurses would not see me go, and I stood in the empty parking lot in the dark and it was a long time before I went back to the truck, where I sat even longer.

On the way home the whole world looked different.

I had just worn her out.

CHAPTER 50

On the way home I watched a TV truck cranking up its satellite dish across the street from the Town Hall. Carpenters were building a platform so reporters could do their stand-ups with a properly dramatic view of the mountains in the background — in this case a setting sun, the fire smoke refracting the solar light into balls of gold.

The mayor stood in front of a camera, thumbs hooked into his suspenders, and talked to a news lady who glanced suspiciously at where a whole section of Bellyache Mountain was glowing red. She wore a black skirt and high heels. The mayor's shirt tail hung free from beneath his paunch as he motioned expansively in the direction of the golf course, where the gophers had done new damage. Bystanders on the sidewalk pointed and smiled and took selfies with the TV news truck.

At home in bed in the half dark I touched together my fingers and tallied those I'd killed.

I knew for every one of them there were a pairs of others who had suffered because of me: daughters, sons, broken-hearted fathers and mothers. I'd murdered them as well. In my dreams they stood assembled before me and looked up and pointed as I flapped my arms and flew away, afraid to land for fear they would tear me to pieces.

There was a commotion of vehicle noise on Main Street as I drifted into a familiar half-sleep that felt like I was hovering inches above the bed.

The soldier, the PFC, was soon standing next to the bed. All these years and the sonofabitch hadn't aged a day.

The boy's face was speckled with dirt, his lank dark hair pasted flat. He wore a shit-eating grin. Water dripped from the rifle. He was wounded beneath the torn green poplin shirt, dried blood a dark blotch across his chest. A flap of skin hung from his forehead and the PFC pushed it back like you'd smooth a hank of unruly hair.

"Sarge," he said, his voice scratchy as if he'd been screaming. "You fucked up and killed us. Pappas and everybody. How's that feel?"

He pinched up his face like he'd swallowed a lemon.

"Chickenshit," he said.

I woke, huffing as if my heart had stopped.

The pool of dusky light on the floor made me believe there was a wet spot where the soldier had stood. There was the loamy stink of wet dirt. I reached and touched the floor to make sure it was dry. I knew it would be dry but I had to touch it.

And then my sweet wife's hand lightly touched my shoulder.

"I'm sorry," she said. "I thought you knew I was here."

She pressed against me beneath the bedsheets.

"You had another one, didn't you? Did you see doctor whatshisname this week?"

There had been so many visits to so many doctors during all those years that she always said the same thing — *doctor whatshisname.*

"He keeps giving me pills."

She turned onto her back. She pulled up the sheets. I could tell she was fussing with her hair ends in the dark. She leaned and kissed my neck.

"I miss you so much," I said.

"I know."

I took her hand, as if thanking her for something. She was cool and soft and I could smell her soapy skin like she'd stepped from the shower.

I explained what the boy looked like; the wet rifle, the sound as it dripped, the way his hair lay on his scalp as if he'd just pulled off his cap. His unlaced boots.

"I never remembered my dreams," she said.

"When you only have them once, it's easy to forget."

"You never told me that. All those years and you said nothing."

I feathered my hand along her shape as if to reassure myself she was there. For all I knew, it might be a dream within a dream, like Dr. Nguyen had once suggested. Her foot scraped hopefully against my leg.

I listened to the coyotes outside. Others joined in. I could hear the pack moving, chasing something through the grass.

"Sure you want to hear this?" I said.

I got up and walked to the window.

"I should shoot those little shits. They shouldn't be in the middle of town."

"Come back, Stan."

"Should I shoot one?"

"Of course not," she said. "Forget the poor little coyotes. They have to make a living."

"It was a dark and stormy night..." I began.

She slapped my shoulder. "Be serious. We've done this before. Many times. Now tell me everything."

"I was nineteen years old. I'm old enough now to be his father."

"This soldier in the dream?"

"Of course," I said.

"I'm just trying to help," she said.

"It's my oldest relationship," I said, surprised at this discovery. She stroked my face.

"You're not stopping, are you?"

"I was just thinking," I said. But now I didn't want to continue. It was as if I'd started a speech in front of a crowd of strangers.

The coyotes carried on outside and I heard a squeal and then it was quiet.

"Let me just shoot those little shits," I said.

"Forget about the poor coyotes," she said. "Look, you're shaking." She put her arms around me.

The coyotes caught what they were hunting and again I heard it scream.

CHAPTER 51

I heard the familiar sound of a claw tapping on the front window of the trailer.

I was casting headline text for the newspaper on my 1922 Model 5 Linotype. I adore the stink of boiling lead.

Chaz's furry skull, on this day encased in a backwards facing Chicago Cubs baseball cap, was backlit outside by the broken blinking neon sign from the Tumbleweed Motel across the street that said: "R__ms Av__able."

I'd just opened an envelope from Madeline Schlumberg, whose gossip column in the newspaper chronicles all matters of immediate importance in a town of 875 people; such as the annual St. Ignacius Altar Society Spaghetti & Chili Dog Dinner, a list of notable local pregnancies, hay prices, and mentions of who had out-of-town guests at whose house during the past seven days.

Madeline is also my best obit writer and knows by name and ancestry every person who has died hereabouts in the past fifty years.

Her column, as always, came hand-written in pencil on yellow legal paper, every paragraph indented and aligned like perfect calligraphy, each word's swirly serif rendered so carefully that I hated to throw the paper away once it had been typeset.

This week Madeline submitted a photo of what looked like a dirty walnut. Or a small deformed moon rock. Or a dusty prune. You get the idea.

And she wrote this note: "Will you put this on the front page? On Sunday at the hospital Orel Mondragon of Derbytop Mesa was relieved of a kidney stone measuring 4.75 inches, which is just shy of the world record of 5.11 inches. It's true. I looked it up. Orel says he's fine and plans to display the stone at the County Fair Pavilion. There will be a barbecue in his honor Saturday night at the Bull River Falls town park."

Of course I would.

I suppose I'll take a picture, too. I imagine they'll fasten Orel's rock to a walnut plaque and present it to him like a bowling trophy.

The claws kept tapping.

And so I hid my cup of coffee because Chaz likes to wash his feet in the stuff.

The Gopher King stepped inside and gave me a thumbs up sign and motioned for his two body guards to stay in the Hummer parked beneath the dead potentilla bush by the front door.

He took a shit on the floor, so I knew he was excited.

Besides the Cubs cap, Chaz was dressed in a camo hunting vest and beneath that he wore a bright pink tee shirt illustrated with the grinning face of a Christmas snowman. He jumped on my desk, took off his flip flops, and looked around and started humming a Burl Ives holiday song.

"We found him," he said. "The one who burns things."

I stepped to the window and pulled down the shades. I'm careful about people seeing me talk to a rodent.

"What?"

"The big fires. The man who starts the big fires."

"You know where the pyro is?"

Chaz picked up a paper clip and started picking at his toes. I looked over where a few dozen milk duds were scattered across my linoleum floor.

The Gopher King looked at me smugly and said: "You owe me big time for this one."

And indeed I did because he began to explain how his scouts had tracked the arsonist who had been starting fires all summer up in the mountains surrounding town. The blaze had been under control for weeks now, but unexplained flares were still appearing.

The police knew the pyro was holed up in the hills.

"He's at the old gold mine," Chaz said. "He's sleeping in one of the cabins."

I picked up the phone to call the sheriff.

Chaz smiled and raised his paw. "Oh, there's no hurry," he said. "He's not going anywhere. I think he's waiting for you."

CHAPTER 52

The Executive Vice President of Something at the Gold Gulch Resort lives in a sprawling 6,000 sq. ft. craftsman bungalow situated in picturesque and taxable splendor along the golf course. It's by far the biggest house in Bull River Falls.

Each Sunday morning, weather permitting, after finishing his breakfast coffee and reading the newspaper on his spacious redwood deck overlooking the 9th Hole, he enjoys shooting prairie dogs with his CO2 powered 10-shot repeater air rifle.

On a good day he'll get two or three. On this morning, however, he could swear he'd made a half dozen clean kills and the little buggers just wouldn't go down.

He'd see fur fly, the hollow point .777 caliber lead pellet would toss up dirt behind the apparently assassinated creature, and the gopher would just scratch its head with one paw, lean back, and then pop back up again like a carnival target.

Frustrated, he brought out his hunting scope and took a closer look, but the little rats would only come out when he raised his rifle.

He poured another cup of coffee, sat on the top step of the deck, and studied the long meadow that ran parallel to his half-acre backyard.

Months earlier a group of prairie dogs had been stranded there after his company poured asphalt to complete a hiking path that encircled the golf course. Despite exploding fumigant canisters, baiting the gopher burrows with grain laced with aluminum phosphide poison, and serious digging with a road grader, the rats refused to leave.

He lifted the rifle. On cue, a furry head appeared and the Executive of Undoubtedly Important Matters squeezed off two perfect skull shots. The animal spread its arms, swayed backwards like a posturing acolyte praying to the sky, and immediately popped back up unharmed.

The sharpshooter, on this morning garbed in pale blue sweat pants and matching shirt monogrammed with the interlaced wedding font logo of his employer, carefully sighted and took aim once more. He fired. The gopher came back up.

He only had time to say, "You sonofabitch..." when he heard the low humming noise directly above his head.

It sounded like a flying food processor.

The three dark blurs raced past and then circled to hover directly above the roof of his house. The strange shapes then skittered back and forth like crazed dragonflies.

The kids down the street were playing with their toy drones again, he thought. But this time they wouldn't get away with it.

The man was calling the Bull River Falls police on his cell phone when he heard the sharp popping sounds. A loud explosion came from the direction of his barbecue grill.

Accompanied by a hot wind, a tumbling teak lawn chair missed his face by inches.

A potted palm, two German garden gnomes his wife had named Heidi and Fritz, and a pair of bush pruners catapulted through the air like warfare shrapnel and impaled themselves 100 yards away into the windshield of his neighbor's brand new black Lexus sedan.

The miniature 70mm rocket rounds from Chaz's trio of Apache attack helicopters scored two more direct hits on the large $1,500 stainless steel barbecue grill, severing the gas supply line. A plume of blue flame shot violently into the sky like a giant laboratory Bunsen burner.

The blast sent chunks of metal sailing through the second story bedroom window of the home, where the executive's wife was jogging in sweaty bliss on a treadmill, listing to *Cher's Greatest Hits* on her iPod. The machine tipped and tossed the woman into a 200-gallon fish aquarium. In mid-flight, her yoga pants were torn off.

When the man raced up the stairs, he found his screaming wife sitting cross-legged on the floor next to the shattered tank, a pair of giant Gourami fish and a small octopus squirming in her naked lap.

The fish tank water cascaded downstairs, flooded the kitchen with chunks of fake coral and kelp, gushed out the door and extinguished the burning patio furniture like somebody had practiced this maneuver at the fire department as part of a training exercise.

From his seat in the Apache, the Gopher King wiggled the toggle switch in his lap to make sure the toy spring-loaded stuffed prairie dog on the ground was still operating properly. Up it popped. And down it fell.

With his upright claw tracing a circle in the air, Chaz signaled the other gopher helicopter pilots to head home. The Gopher King briefly hovered above the house, from which he heard much shrieking.

A single brightly colored tropical fish flopped briefly off the edge of the wet patio deck and disappeared into the grass.

Chaz was sure the sharpshooter would be using his rifle again very soon.

This time, the Gopher King would have a much bigger surprise waiting.

CHAPTER 53

The prairie dog family in the framed photograph on Chaz's fireplace mantel stood arranged in a long row, like descending bottles on a shelf.

The Gopher King, the tallest, dressed formally in a 70s style tux with black velour lapels, had one paw resting on his wife's shoulder. The children, 14 of them, cascaded in height down to the smallest, a runt named Bloom.

I once gave Chaz an audio tape of James Joyce's *Ulysses* and he'd named this youngest child after a character in this famously dense novel written many years ago by a half-blind Irishman with bad teeth.

My rodent friend had shrunk me, but re-entry as a full-sized human being was taking longer than expected. Seems the Plutonium-235 charge in Chaz's magical paw had given me a radioactive overdose.

It would be another twenty-four hours before I could go home as jumbo me.

On that day the Gopher King scanned me with a Geiger counter that looked like a TV remote control.

"We can't do this again," Chaz said, showing me the alarmingly high four-digit number.

"It's like getting ten barium enemas."

"Will I die?"

"Not for a while," he said, smiling. "But don't let anyone see you in the dark."

And so to pass the time I spent the day at Chaz's sprawling underground lair, where we mindlessly watched Christmas classics and sports on the Gopher King's array of six wall-mounted 72-inch TV screens, which he'd stolen from COSTCO.

We ate Fritos, clogged our arteries with bean dip, napped in matching leather recliners, and enjoyed a pleasant daytime buzz thanks to the beer served by Chaz's disapproving wife, who more than once called us lazy, unproductive, no-good slugs.

Chaz popped another can of stout and studied his wiggling toes. He reached and pinched his wife's butt. This was a mistake. She angrily gave the Gopher King

213

the same left jab that drove Joe Frazier nuts when he fought Muhammad Ali in Manila in 1975.

Chaz raised his paws in apologetic surrender and rubbed his chin.

Like a TV-addicted psychopath, I pointed the remote and madly changed channels on the wall-mounted screens:

To the video of an old Broncos-Chargers game. To *It's a Wonderful Life*, and a *Sons of Anarchy* re run. To a reality show called *Dude, You're Screwed*. To a documentary on corrupt Brazilian drug lords. To a shirtless guy in Louisiana wrestling a large alligator into a very small aluminum boat.

Chaz looked at the German Black Forest cuckoo clock on the wall and grabbed the channel device from my hand and switched TV No. 6 to the start of a 15-hour PBS marathon of British cooking shows.

"Oh, no!" Chaz screamed.

"Yeah, what a stinkin' pass," I said, referring to the Broncos' quarterback's interception on TV No. 1.

The Gopher King pointed to TV No. 2, where Jimmy Stewart had just dived into the icy river in Bedford Falls to save Clarence the Angel.

"He'll kill himself!" Chaz said.

"It's just a game," I said, my eyes still on TV No. 1.

After more frantic channel changing, Chaz announced that we were headed topside.

"I need you to see this," he said.

The golf course executive whose home Chaz had recently bombed was exacting his own revenge and the half drunk gopher king wanted me to witness what such things looked like while I was still twelve inches tall.

"It will give you perspective," he said.

The dark tunnel leading from the house was cold and wet. It was crowded with happy gophers carrying gift-wrapped boxes. Holiday carolers dressed like Charles Dickens characters nodded to us.

"Why are they doing that?" I said. "It's the middle of summer."

"We don't care," Chaz said. "We have Christmas three times a year."

Two of Chaz's body guards came along, each armed to the teeth with the usual weaponry — AK-47s, Glock pistols, grenades dangling from black velcroed SWAT vests.

Our Hummer sped through the mud. I got smacked senseless through the open rear window by a dangling cottonwood tree root. Chaz loudly munched his Fritos.

We emerged in bright sunlight onto the Gold Gulch Golf Course. In the distance, carpenters clambered up the side of a half burned house. A worker with a wheel barrow was hauling away the mangled remains of a destroyed barbecue grill. Charred timbers were piled where a redwood deck once stood.

Chaz pointed to a row of construction backhoes positioned in the distance like yellow tanks on a battlefield. A man standing out in a meadow took off his hard hat and waved it like a field general directing a military attack.

"This is nothing new for us," he said. "But I want you to see it in person."

It only took a few minutes.

One by one the backhoes growled to life and started to approach what remained of the prairie dog town that once covered this entire valley. The place was soon a broken wasteland of dirt and rising diesel smoke. From the raised bucket of one machine great clods of clinging gophers dropped and scampered away as the backhoes continued to gouge out the meadow. I heard plaintive cries from those who were now buried. Other wounded rodents limped and crawled from their ruined burrows. Women screamed and baby prairie dogs wailed as the giant vehicles rumbled on.

Our two gopher commandos raised their rifles and took aim.

Shaking his head, Chaz said to put down the weapons. We took our seats in the Hummer.

I asked the driver to pull the vehicle into the driveway of the house.

"What are you doing?" Chaz said.

"Trust me."

We parked. I stepped out of the vehicle. Up on a ladder a woman dressed in a hoodie and black leotards stood pruning the limbs of a backyard spruce tree. She waved to the man out in the meadow, who lifted his hard hat and waved back.

I reached into the Hummer and honked the horn.

The woman turned. I honked the horn again. I jumped up and down. She stared down at me from the ladder and I raised my arms and started waving.

"Yeah, I'm one foot tall! You'll have a whopper nightmare tonight! Go ahead, look at me. Look at meeee!

The woman dropped the pruning shears and stumbled backwards down the ladder, all while looking at me as I tossed clods of dirt at her and screamed in my teeny Alvin and the Chipmunks voice:

"Look at meeee! Go ahead, look at meeee! You're gonna' have nightmares tonight!"

I tried to follow her as she flailed her arms and ran up the front steps of the house, but those steps were just too damn high for me to climb.

CHAPTER 54

In the heat of the bedroom I woke and touched her cool skin and it was as real as anything.

"You fell asleep," she said. "Now tell me what happened. Try to stay awake."

I explained to her how the lieutenant was killed.

"He screamed. He had a deep voice but when he got shot he screamed in this high pitched voice just like a little kid. Second lieutenants never lasted very long out there."

I told her about Pappas. How everybody fell in the grass one by one.

"Somebody came from behind and pulled me down," I said. "I was just standing there like an idiot."

Her hand stroked my shoulder.

"The boy who I dream about?"

"Yes?"

"This is where he comes in," I said, as if describing a theatrical character's stage entrance.

He said: "Go! Go! Go!"

"That was him?"

"Yes."

Now I couldn't shut up. I sat up and leaned against the headboard of the bed. I felt vomity. The room was so warm but the heat made me colder. I wanted to go outside and shoot the coyotes, who were chasing something again.

The PFC shouted and pointed: "Go! Go!"

I explained how the boy was chewing, the wad of gum bouncing inside his mouth. Then he hollered: "Sarge, cover me!" The PFC pointed toward Pappas, the Greek boy who had read the works of Euripides.

"Hey...hey Sarge, did you hear me! You gotta' cover me when I get the radio"

The PFC gave me a pleading look. In the terrible noise and unaccountable violence, with the smoke and overwhelming clatter, I could only see the soldier's lips move.

"Cover me," he said again.

Someone tossed another smoke grenade. Two soldiers were shouting at each other from opposite sides of the clearing. I saw the shape of an abandoned M-60 tripod sitting there in the grass.

"Maybe," I said to the boy in a voice I did not recognize. "We should stay where we are."

Now he pleaded: "Aw, sweet Jesus, please, please cover me."

The boy ran off, his boots kicking up clods of mud.

I saw the khaki uniforms and pith helmets of the North Vietnamese regulars as they walked in a line through the trees.

"You see..." I said, and touched the memory of her face.

"I killed him. It wouldn't have been hard to cover him. He could have made a call on the radio. But I froze up. I killed them all by using that trail. And then I just froze."

I explained how on that day in the jungle so long ago a tiny metal speck struck my left eye. The pain came like the touch of a sharp piece of ice.

"My boys get killed and I get a few scratches. Can you believe such a thing?"

Night came the way it gets dark in the tropics; an opaque curtain falling quickly behind the silhouetted trees. There was a pile of fallen debris in a pond and I crawled into the stinking mess of branches and uprooted trees, the water covered with bugs and clumps of floating manure. I leaned onto my elbows, stooping in the water, and waited.

The NVA soldiers walked out quietly like they'd been part of the darkness all along, apiece with the trees and shadows like wholly formed forest creatures, mute in their sandals as they moved in ranks along the edge of the rice paddy. I looked through the wicker tangle of branches and watched the soldier bend and take the weapons off my dead boys. They took web gear. They took shoes and belts. They searched the ground for every available piece of scrap they could find. Someone picked up the M-60 tripod. Pistols flared as they shot the wounded. They walked up to a kid named Tommy Swain from Adel, Iowa, yanked him by the hair, and fired. Once they seemed to understand everybody was dead the Vietnamese spoke among themselves in trilly voices, squatting to inspect and share their booty. A shout came from the trees and they stood and immediately were gone.

I stayed in the pond for a long time, not wanting to decide what I should do. I studied a spot where the moon hung from the branch of a tree beyond the place where the ambush had happened, the rice paddy water still and shiny in its yellow light.

I crawled away and found Pappas and took the radio.

I told her: "I should have done like the kid asked in the first place. Covered him, you know. Let him save poor Pappas. I should have at least tried. The not trying is the worst part."

I had been thinking this for so many years that I said it flatly and without emotion.

"I murdered them."

"You can't blame yourself," she said.

"I was in charge. They trusted me."

I explained how I crawled over to the dead PFC. The boy's mouth was open, the chewing gum stuck there with tooth marks on it. His teeth white against what remained of his face. His forehead was moist, his nose snotty.

The body seemed much too light as I carried him. The legs were gone. Only a head and shoulders and arms remained. A torso and nothing below. Where the legs once were it was caked dirt and sticky grass.

I took Pappas' leg and placed it next to the PFC. I dragged the other bodies one by one, as well as the parts I could find and I sat beside all the wrongly matched pieces. I rocked on my knees and apologized. I tried to rub my hands clean on the grass, but the stickiness would not go away. Everyone lay dead in the bright moonlight.

The NVA regulars returned and sat in a circle in the meadow, talking as they ate cold rice from their palms like it was a picnic.

The moon grew brighter. You could see their faces plainly as they lifted their hands to eat, nodding and laughing.

I had retrieved our M-60 from the bushes. I shouldered two ammunition belts and squatted and cleared the chamber and smacked the butt of the weapon on the ground and reloaded, not caring if they heard me. I started firing.

I turned and she was gone. The bed smelled like lavender. I drifted to sleep.

CHAPTER 55

There was the usual public funeral. The windy speeches. The F-22 Raptor jet flyover.

Peter, Paul & Mary impersonators sang *Puff the Magic Dragon* while gopher sky divers dressed in Red Baron styled World War One uniforms joined hands, tossed bright red smoke grenades and plummeted from a circling Chinook helicopter.

The Gopher King, his face fur combed into a pair of Kaiser Wilhelm whiskers, was dressed in his Prussian field marshal uniform. He wore skate board sneakers and Louis Vuitton sunglasses that he'd stolen from the cockpit of a parked private jet at the county airport.

Chaz's hairy face glistened with tears as he gave his eulogy about steadfastness and the heavy burden of grief and how revenge and anger must be transmuted.

For the first time in weeks, it drizzled. Several thousand assembled gophers wept from beneath their black umbrellas.

"The dopamine reward pathways in my brain are all worn out," the Gopher King cryptically told me afterwards. "I don't know how much longer I can tell lies to these people. It's hard to be optimistic anymore."

I shrugged. Even Chaz is often disheartened and I only hoped this latest sad event wouldn't unveil his darker, more violent side, which I knew lurked behind those beady rodent eyes.

At the burial, beneath a long row of fluttering People's Gopher Army banners, the coffins were carried by white-gloved pallbearers wearing moderately expensive aviator sunglasses. The departed were arranged in a row at the edge of a cliff on Bellyache Mountain.

Chaz explained to the assembled mourners what he planned to do next. Violence, he said, often requires more of the same.

The salty tears of the multitudes turned to cheers.

I never like it when Chaz uses his talents like this. It is best to distrust him when he shows his charisma. We should all be suspicious of charisma.

It has been in the Gopher King's nature to practice subterfuge and guile and to elevate trickery to poetry of a sort.

In this case, it was a Shakespearian sonnet of epic nastiness.

Three days following what was being called the Massacre in the Meadow, the Gopher King's commandos re-routed the sewer system at the County Fairgrounds, including twenty-six bathroom stalls beneath the rodeo arena (it was Beer and Chili Dog Night), into a narrow six-inch PVC pipe which served as the main water supply at the Gold Gulch Golf Course clubhouse.

The resulting, highly pressurized plume of raw sewage backflow erupted with the force of a Class III river rapid and burst through the ceiling of the clubhouse kitchen like a geyser, sending with it a $16,000 eight-burner gas range that landed a thousand feet away in a sand trap at the 18th hole.

The gurgling lake of toxic waste then quickly overflowed onto US Highway 6. The soupy tsunami created a three-foot effluent tidal wave, on which you could have surfed. It smashed through the walls of the golf course Special Events Pavilion, where a wedding was taking place.

Chaz later came to my office and lectured me about putting his picture in this week's newspaper. He was not happy.

I told him I had no choice. And so he gnawed my ankle and said he wanted to have a meeting at his place and make plans for the future.

"I can't get small and crawl around in those crummy tunnels anymore," I said. "And you don't listen to my advice, anyway."

"Okay, your office," Chaz said and started to make a move for the coffee cup on my desk. I pushed him away and told him that wasn't the way gentlemen washed their feet.

"I have to see my shrink next week at the VA," I said.

"Take me with you," the Gopher King said. "I promise this time I'll leave my weapons at home."

"I'll think about it," I lied.

CHAPTER 56

Ancient nautical maps often warned sailors of danger with labels that marked where hideous beasts and untold catastrophe surely dwelled.

In an age when only the world's fringes had been explored, these crude marine safety bulletins would proclaim in a flourish of exaggerated script: "THERE BE MONSTERS HERE," followed by frightening drawings of all manner of colossal demons who might devour a careless traveler.

I wanted to give my shrink at the VA the same message, explaining how certain parts of anyone's head shouldn't be explored too closely, lest angry dragons and serpents be awakened.

The wildfire forced me to re-schedule my appointment in Denver with my brain doctor, who wears tweed jackets and starts each of our sessions by puffing once on his Meerschaum pipe before he says, "So how are you, my good man?"

Dr. Nguyen has liver spots on his wrinkled bald head and a wispy white chin beard that makes him look like a cross between a billygoat and Ho Chi Minh.

The rodent, always prepared to complicate my day, appeared with his wife at the newspaper office early one morning and announced he and his commandos had hijacked a load of clothing from a Macy's semi trailer parked for the night at the town visitor center off the interstate highway.

"We want to model fashions for you," he said.

Two gopher commandos walked through the front door and started assembling an impromptu Haute Couture runway, complete with boom lights, a ceiling glitterball, heavy drapery and a sound system that started playing *Who D'King?* by *Cheap Trick*.

Boxes were wheeled in. I locked the office door and pulled down the window shades. Nobody in town needed to see this.

Chaz's wife appeared and blushed shyly as she shuffled past in a pink chintz bath robe. When gophers blush the very tops of their ears turn scarlet, like the ends of habanero peppers.

At Chaz's signal the stage lights were dimmed. More music blared, this time an obscene rap song of which I was not familiar. A bright spotlight came on. The Gopher King introduced his wife with a gallant bow and a graceful sideways wave of his arm — like a matador with a cape performing a perfect veronica in a Pamplona bull ring.

She walked with mincing steps down the runway, confident and haughty on her stiletto heels. She struggled for a moment as she adjusted the lace Bustier she'd put on backwards. She stumbled and regained her stiff-legged gait, which must be difficult when your legs are five inches long.

Chaz grinned proudly and clapped like a crazy man.

She twirled daintily in her A-line skirt with the accordion pleat, then stepped behind a dressing curtain from which she emerged moments later wearing a black cocktail dress with a nightmarish argyle scarf that clung halfway up the side of her face like a twisted wool hospital bandage.

Her bangle bracelets — too many of them on one arm, rattled as she stumbled on her platform heels while trying to pull out a pair of giant 1960s Jackie-O sunglasses from her Michael Kors leather shoulder tote.

Next, she modeled a pair of wrinkled gaucho pants and a tiny Bolero jacket, which accentuated the tufts of brown fur bristling beneath her chin.

Twisted tightly around her head was a transparent pink organza veil, like she was the drunken bride of an Argentine cattle baron. Chaz's wife then cussed loudly as she tripped and wobbled off to change into another outfit.

Polka dot leggings. Fluorescent garters. Tiaras. Tunics and turbans. Blue makeup smeared thickly on her face like salve. Even a Polynesian sarong with Espadrille sandals and pinstriped leggings. In the next hour she made more costume changes than Cher on her sixth farewell tour.

Meanwhile, Chaz the Gopher King beamed and clapped his paws and whistled as his wife emerged wearing her final outfit: a red corset worn over black chiffon lingerie, accompanied by enormous d'Orsay heel shoes and a jaunty cap with Breton stripes.

She turned to me, did a little curtsy, and said:"How do I look?"

She looked like a small hairy werewolf hooker just released from a 19th century French prison.

"You look marvelous," I said and blew her a kiss.

Then Chaz, God help me, announced it was now his turn.

Accompanied by *A Sharp Dressed Man*, by *ZZ Top*, the Gopher King emerged from behind a curtain dressed in a black tux and cummerbund. He wore odd Dave Clark Five boots and a white fedora. His pink shirt had an English tab collar and beneath the tux he wore a double-breasted striped vest.

He smiled from behind aviator sunglasses, pulled aside the satin lapel of his jacket and revealed a Glock G41 tactical pistol tucked into a leather shoulder holster.

"How do I look?" he said, taking off his hat to reveal a pile of gelled hair gobbed up into a cowlick.

He looked like a mansome metro-sexual hipster gangster dude at a Las Vegas roulette table that had, thanks to a botanic miracle, mated with a Chia plant.

"You look marvelous," I said and gave him a thumbs up and wished I had not canceled the appointment with my shrink, though this encounter with the Gopher King might take a lot of therapy to fix.

CHAPTER 57

He came to me again later in the day while I sat at my desk, staring at the wall and taking deep breaths like the nurse had taught me at the hospital.

Chaz was alone and wearing a pink Bob Marley tee shirt.

His hair was twisted into short and frizzy plaits. He jumped on my desk, loosened his tiny Ruger SR9 shoulder holster, and eyed my steaming cup of coffee, which I lifted out of his reach.

The Gopher King likes to bathe his toes in hot java.

He stared at me and pointed at his head.

"How do I look?"

He looked like a crazed, earless Rastafarian Easter Bunny.

"Marvelous," I said. "You look marvelous. How many times do I have to tell you that today?"

The Gopher King took out the Ruger and idly flipped its ambidextrous safety switch on and off. This switch is located at the backside of the weapon, just below the slide lock, so you'd think a rodent with no thumbs would have trouble. He did not.

He took out one of the 17-round magazines and wiped it off on Bob Marley's silkscreened forehead, then replaced it with a quick slap of his paw. He sighted the pistol up toward my broken ceiling fan and then holstered the weapon again. He looked at where the broken piece of rope was still tied to the fixture.

"Why is the rope still there?"

"I was doing repairs," I said.

"You're a liar."

He changed the subject and said: "Sometimes I don't understand what I understand. Why do they do things like that?"

I knew Chaz was aware of the latest round of construction at the new outlet mall.

"The new mall," I said.

Chaz looked around for my coffee cup, then glanced up at the ceiling again and studied the frayed piece of rope.

"Of course, the mall," he said.

He frowned and shook his head. "They're killing more of us over there."

Chaz has lately asked me explain human beings. As much as I'd like to give him a Cliff's Notes on how we operate, I told him I can just barely explain myself to me.

But in this case I thought I'd try. I took a sip of coffee and, out of sympathy, put the cup back on my desk. Chaz took off his 82nd Airborne-styled paratrooper boots, rolled up his camo pants and started drowning his feet.

I told the Gopher King that killing animals for the sake of shopping has nothing at all to do with prairie dogs. If Mother Teresa lived in a hole in the ground, they'd kill her, too. It's about our own incapacity to choose propriety over the juicy temptations of greed. And it's as much about lazy thinking as it is about convenient money and easy commerce. People usually avoid breaking a sweat to get at the truth.

Chaz stared at me. "I don't know what you just said."

I excused myself and let the Gopher King soak his feet. I had a repair to do on a stuck piston in the mold disk of my old Linotype typesetting machine. I stepped into the back room and worked for a while. When I came back and checked on the Gopher King, who was watching a show on TV called *My Baby's Got an Extra Head.* He changed channels and settled on another program called, *I Was on Vacation and Maggots Ate My Feet.*

Chaz turned and again shook his head: "And here I thought *my* civilization was coming to an end."

I returned to the Linotype machine. It was 1:30 a.m. I had to get things working in time to deliver the newspaper to the printer by 9 a.m.

When I returned, Chaz was digging into a bag of peanuts at my desk. He was watching the *Weather Channel.*

Chewing, he turned: "Why do you people get so excited about the weather?"

"We like to scare ourselves" I said. "It's why we tell ghost stories."

"What's a ghost story?" Chaz said.

"It's like a weather forecast."

I continued my repair job. I was exhausted. I was thinking I'd take Chaz to the VA with me on my next trip to Denver. He would enjoy it.

I should have kept my mind on the task at hand, because while I was messing with the Linotype a dose of molten lead spilled from the machine and onto my hand. I dropped my tools and danced around the room and issued forth every profanity I ever knew.

I bounded into the room where Chaz was crouched in the corner, watching an *Animal Planet* documentary on poisonous tropical snakes.

The Gopher King saw me and he too started chattering and running in circles. I stepped to the sink and ran water over my wound, which looked like a red fried egg had attached itself to my hand.

Chaz was beside himself. He shit on the floor and skittered half way up one wall. He shit again and somersaulted over the kitchen table, ran a figure-eight, then stood screaming and watched while I wrapped a towel around my hand and tried to find my truck keys so I could drive the twenty miles to the hospital.

Chaz's spontaneous defecation continued. He took out his pistol and began to shoot wildly at the ceiling, shitting the whole time like a mad and possessed Pez dispenser loaded with explosive Milk Duds — pardon the mixed candy metaphors.

Chaz calmed down as if a blanket of peaceful Zen munificence had enveloped him.

"Let me see that," he said.

I showed him my grotesque hand, which had swollen into a glistening five-digit bratwurst.

The Gopher King placed his open paw directly onto the wound, not the most sanitary thing to do, I thought. His black eyes fluttered and rolled back into his head and those ridiculous Rasta hair knots stood on end and quivered as if Chaz had just stuck his finger into a live wall socket.

His mouth opened and he clicked his yellow buck teeth together; one, two, three times.

My hand turned icy and numb and a quivering sensation shot up along my shoulder. The Gopher King took away his paw and stepped away, out of breath and trembling. He pointed at where the wound had been and in its place there was now a neatly healed scar, like a small pucker in a bed pillow.

I made a fist. "How did you do that?

Chaz, breathing heavily, turned and picked up the remote and started surfing through the TV channels, at last settling on a show called: *Sex Sent Me to the Emergency Room.*

I asked him again: "How did you do that?"

Without turning around, the Gopher King said: "Where have you been?"

CHAPTER 58

Her pale shape sat upright in the bed and she leaned to gently kiss my cheek, and in the quiet room the only other sound was the sheets hissing as I turned and embraced her.

"Oh, you shouldn't be here again with me," I said. "I was nothing but trouble for you."

"I wondered where you were," she said.

"I tried the sofa. I couldn't sleep. This whole week is screwed up. I've been nodding off at my desk, just dreaming about the weirdest things. Even when I'm awake my head runs away with itself. I don't know what's real anymore. I don't know if I can keep going like this."

She touched the scar on my neck and traced it with one finger as if studying a map. I lifted her beneath the smallest part of her back and pulled her close. I combed my fingers through her long hair and in the moonlight it was shiny against my hand.

"Just lay here for a while. Let's not do anything," I said.

"I'm a patient girl."

"I'm trying to be better. You were always so patient with me. All those years when I was crazy, I'm sorry."

"You're okay now. You can talk more if you want."

"Those soldiers just stared at me." I told her about the night after the ambush.

"They never reached for their weapons. One of them sat behind a recoilless rifle. The weapon was 12-feet long. He could have cut me in half, along with the trees behind me. They thought I was a ghost. I was covered with blood, just soaked with it. I looked like shit. Blood and grass sticking to my face. I walked up to the first one and took his head off. I emptied half the ammo belt into that bunch. Didn't lift the muzzle to aim, just kept firing from my hip, like I was pissing in the snow. And they never once moved while I reloaded. Never lifted one of their own weapons. They just watched me while they died. I was an avenging round eyed ghost. I must have looked spooky.

I sat up and brought my head down into my hands and said nothing. She didn't speak, but I knew she was still there.

"The last one kept shouting and holding his hands in front of his face. I chased him around a tree like we were kids playing a game. He was a runt, just the smallest man I ever saw. His hair was sticking up. He pulled out an envelope from his pocket and inside was a little photo and he showed that to me. Maybe it was his wife; she was holding a baby. I could see it very plain in the moonlight; a girl, skinny and small just like him, a sad look to her. Dark skinned. She had this shiny front tooth. He kept showing it to me, wagging the picture back and forth, smiling and then looking discouraged like he couldn't decide how he was going to bullshit me out of killing him. He rocked his folded arms back and forth like he was holding a baby. He held up the picture again, this wrinkled snapshot that looked like he'd been carrying it in his pocket for months. He had snot in his nose, a little snot plug that kept going in and out when he took a breath. I wanted to give him a tissue to blow his nose. It bothered me. He pissed me off with that thing in his nose. Like nothing ever had made me so angry. It just drove me crazy."

I stopped talking. I didn't want to have a crying jag in front of her. She'd seen enough of those.

"I put the barrel against his forehead. The metal was so hot it burned him. Like you'd brand a cow, it left a mark. He closed his eyes and relaxed and stood with his arms at his side and he looked at the tops of his feet like he knew it was the end.

I fired until most of the bottom half of him was gone. He held onto the picture the whole time. It never left his hand, can you believe it? He was just mush and he was still holding the goddamn picture. I don't know why, but I took the picture and the envelope, looked at the writing on the back of it — an address, and put it all in my pocket. What crazy sonofabitch does that?

"They said later in the after-action report that I killed about twenty of them. I sure wasn't counting, and I don't know how they ever found that out. And I don't know why I remember every stinking minute of it."

I explained how I stayed on the radio all night, calling in my position as I walked ahead on the trail in the direction from which the last group of NVA had come. I didn't care what might happen and I wasn't hurt bad. I didn't know what else I could do.

I walked for a long time. I wish I could walk that long uphill today with these knees. When I got to the top of a ridge above a gully that stretched into a small valley hidden between overhanging cliffs, there was a whole company of them.

The perimeter glowed with small cookfires. I could hear heavy equipment being moved through the trees. I saw freight wagons with big wooden wheels being pulled by teams of men in rope harnesses. Other soldiers were transporting boxes piled in crooked heaps on a jerry rigged bicycle. They were winching artillery pieces up the side of a steep ridge I don't think a goat could climb, hauling dismantled old Howitzers I didn't recognize. Scouts on platforms high in trees stood guard above the single trail that led through the center of the valley.

The trail followed a stream that was fed by a waterfall flowing down from the jungle. A yellow glow came from where each of their tunnel openings were. I'd come upon a supply terminus. There had been no reports of anything this big anywhere near where we'd patrolled all week. The lieutenant had shown me the aerial photos. Not even the low flying scout aircraft with their starlight scopes had seen a thing.

I crawled to where a cliff overhang gave me a complete view of what lay below, and from which I thought a radio signal might possibly carry. I took out the map I'd taken from Pappas' pocket. With the edge of my field knife I measured and scored off one kilometer and notched another three equally spaced marks into the thick waterproof paper.

When I reached someone on the radio I identified myself. There was a long silence. I could hear laughing, like I'd interrupted a conversation. Like these guys had been hanging around all night with nothing to do.

A voice said, "You're kidding."

"No, I'm not," I said.

The scratchy voice on the radio said: "Say those coordinates again."

I looked at the map and tried to read the numbers.

"What's your unit?"

"I'm my unit."

"Is this a joke?"

I named my battalion and my company and my platoon and then my brigade commander at the base camp. I described the sand bagged quonset hut that served as my unit's mess hall. I gave details about the division insignia formed by the round river rocks that decorated the camp's badly landscaped entry gate.

"You want me to tell you who won the World Series last year?"

The voice on the radio said: "You're supposed to be three klicks south."

"Well, now I'm not."

I described what I saw. I estimated the number of soldiers and said what I could about how they were dressed. I explained if the valley was approached by air from the west nobody would be spotted until it was too late because of the cliff I now lay on.

"What's your rank, soldier?"

"Sergeant, sir. I'm a buck sergeant E-Five."

"And what's your name, sergeant?"

I told him.

"That's an interesting name," the voice on the radio said. "I won't try to spell it."

There was a long silence of hissing static and the whispery pieces of intercepted random conversations from another frequency. A pilot somewhere miles away. Artillery numbers from a frantic voice out in the field. Chinese music from a stray channel that brought with it drumming and the sound of two people having a casual chat in a language I couldn't recognize, their voices echoing deeply like they were talking inside an empty corn silo.

"Okay," the voice said. "You know what you're in for, don't you?"

"Yes, sir. I do."

"Okay, then."

"What do you want to know?"

"Tell me what you're seeing," the voice said.

"It's like a base camp. Just like one of our base camps. Buildings and stuff, except, you know, like with those huts they build. Just wooden shit made from sticks, except bigger. Everything is made from wood." I said. "There's a little water tower with a ladder and they got guards up there. They've been here for a while, I think."

"You know you can't be there when the shit starts to fly," the voice said.

"Negative, sir," I said. "I have to stay. You can't calibrate if I'm not here. If you come in short they'll be gone. Or into these caves they have. And then I'm fucked, anyway, because they'll move in my direction and then I'm surrounded. And I sure as shit don't have anywhere to go right now. There's plenty room for them to move away, sir. They got those Chinese trucks and they tied tree limbs over the road so you can't see them from the air. Christ, they're using LANTERNS strapped to the sides of their trucks. I never saw that before."

"Once we start we can't stop, you know that."

"I've never seen a place like this, sir," I said.

"You can stop calling me that."

"Okay," I said. "They've got artillery on the side of the mountain. It looks like big guns backed into caves they dug out themselves. I can see a dozen places with more lanterns burning, so there's a shit load of them. They tied the tree tops together over the road so nobody can see them. Did I tell you that?"

"Forget the trees, sergeant," the voice on the radio said. "The one-hundred-first has four artillery batteries. You're within their range.

"I know," I said. "My lieutenant told me yesterday."

"Is he anyplace, your lieutenant?"

"He's dead," I said. "Everybody is dead."

There was a long silence and I could hear the man breathing into the radio mic like he was thinking of what to say.

"Well," the voice then said. "It's mostly one-fifty-fives. Two twin dusters, too. Can you give us grids after they register?"

"They have caves cut into the rock. And there's artillery backed into the caves, did I tell you that?"

"What?"

"Caves. They're lit up with those lanterns."

There was another long silence and then again with the breathing.

"Sir, I'm not stoned," I said very calmly and slowly. "It's the truth. I'm not playing any game here."

"I didn't say you were high, sergeant. It's just that none of the reports show any of this. Nothing you're describing is supposed to be where you say it is. I have to be careful. We've had people flying over that area for two days. I just have to be careful. I'm in a difficult situation here. We've been trying to reach your unit for hours."

"I already explained," I said.

"I'm in a difficult situation."

"I'm not doing too good myself," I said.

"Of course," the radio voice said.

"So we're good?"

"We're good."

There was another long break during which the radio fizzed out and then came alive in a burst of loud static. I could hear whoever was on the radio pressing and releasing the tap button. There was a conversation going on between the taps, but I couldn't make out what they were saying.

"Begging your pardon," I said. "I think you're wasting time, if you don't mind me saying so, sir. These questions and all. I'm telling the truth. You should start calling that arty."

"That's not a good way to talk to an officer."

"I know."

"You can get into trouble if this turns out to be bullshit."

"I'm already in trouble, sir. I'm sitting on a rock in the middle of a whole shit load of regulars. They're in front of me now, but in a half hour they'll be behind me, too. And then I'm fucked, anyway. You know what I'm saying, sir?"

"Stand by," the voice said. I heard someone chatter up artillery coordinates.

"Yes, sir," I said.

I'd never figured out artillery scales and tables. It was confusing stuff. It was like high school Trig. It gave me a headache, so I'd always faked it. I could read a map, though. I could read the map Pappas died with.

"Yes, sir," I said again.

Down below, men carried sacks of rice and lugged ammo buckets on shoulder poles. A whole new group of them appeared from the trees as they hauled fully assembled and wheeled artillery pieces out of the jungle with bamboo rope. They probably didn't expect anybody to be alive from my squad after the ambush, and the group I'd killed earlier had likely been a mop up crew, sent to stand as forward security scouts for the night.

Five minutes later everything rumbled beneath me, and as I lay on my stomach I could sense the percussions coming up through the rock, a deep and thunderous kicking. The sky pulsed red, the thin high clouds turning into streaks of pink beneath the shining full moon. There was a long, shearing white light as the tops of the trees swayed with each impact. Below me I saw a group of them kneel and look up, covering their heads. They stayed that way, crouched like illuminated penitents praying in a vast forest church.

I looked up from between my folded arms and saw two AC-47 ground attack ships appear from behind me, the slow-moving aircraft circling the area with suppressing fire from their three mini guns. One round every two meters in three-second bursts, each volley tossing spurts of flying dirt that traveled up the length of the small valley.

I shouted into the radio for the next two hours. I heard the calm and detached voices of the pilots, each taking turns as they confirmed their coordinates. They told me to move back a half kilometer. I walked crouched as fast as I could, hardly able to carry the heavy radio pack and M-60 on my shoulder, and when I met two NVA who were running behind push carts piled high with rice bags I dropped the radio and killed them both. I could hear more aircraft circling unseen above the trees.

And then the whole world exploded, every tree I could see swaying behind me as if a giant invisible hand from the sky had reached down and pushed aside the entire jungle. I kept moving back toward the ambush site.

The dust-off Hueys landed at daybreak.

The medics found where I had carefully placed the bodies. I'd arranged those I could find in a straight row, the loose parts matched to each corpse. I'd covered their faces with palm branches. If they still had their hands and arms I folded those across their chests. I wanted everything to be neat, because their disorderly deaths required it.

Before the choppers landed I'd already taken Pappas' machete and walked over and stabbed what was left of each of the dead Vietnamese regulars where they lay. I returned the machete to Pappas and tucked it into his pack.

The two medics lifted me onto a stretcher, thinking I was wounded. They dropped the stretcher, and they picked me up again. They pushed a needle into my arm. Foggy morning air rushed through the open doors as the helicopter lifted. Somebody pressed a wet cloth against my bleeding eye and out of the other eye I watched one soldier take out a morphine ampule, pull open my belt, and stab my groin. I felt myself float away deliciously and then watched as Ernie Banks pulled a hanging curve ball into the left field seats. The crowd stood and roared, their shirts white above the green ivy wall at Wrigley Field. The sweetest swing in baseball. Hey, hey. I saw juicy fruit gum bouncing in the PFC's mouth. Hey, hey.

"He's bleeding bad," the medic said, his echoing voice sounding like it was fifty feet away.

I wanted to tell them it wasn't my blood. All I had was that scratch on my eye and a few lousy cuts on my face. I tried to speak and tell them I wasn't hurt but the lovely morphine would not allow it.

The medic brought his face close: "Sarge, can you hear me?"

I lifted my hand and tried to nod my fifty-pound head.

"Man, everybody was listening to you," the medic said, stroking my forehead. Another hand came with the wet towel and wiped my face.

"Heard the whole fuckin' show on the radio. How'd you find that place? How'd you do it? Guys back at base, they recorded everything. You really did it, sarge. They had you on the speakers. That was one party. One bad ass party. Brass at Brigade is shitting their pants over it. Just shittin' up a storm about what you did. What's your name, anyway? Sarge, what's your name?"

After the story was finished we lay in bed, not touching. I brought the sheets to my chin, hoping it would cover the welt on my neck, which she'd already seen many times.

"They wrote me up for the medal the next week," I said. "You could tell it was for politics. Things had been going bad over there for a while. Medals like that are good PR.

"You want me to stop?"

"No," she said.

"I can stop if you want me to."

"What happened then?" she said.

"A major who looked like Beaver Cleaver's TV dad pinned something on my pajamas at the evacuation hospital. The pajamas were blue. My slippers matched.

233

The hospital floor was cement and it was gray and from my window I could watch the sea and it was blue. Like the pajamas."

"You remember that?"

"I remember stupid shit; you know I always have."

I explained how the next week they read a letter to me that said I was being recommended for a bigger medal.

"There were doctors and nurses standing next to my bed and they all clapped their hands. I don't know why they kept me in the hospital that long. I wasn't hurt. It was all bullshit. I tried to explain you can't win that medal unless there were witnesses. Well, there weren't any goddamn witnesses. It was just me. My whole squad was dead. Nobody saw anything. I didn't do anything so special. It was my fault it happened in the first place."

"You don't have to say anything more," she said. "If you want to stop now you can stop."

But I just couldn't stop. I had never said anything to her all those years and now that it was too late I wanted to talk about everything.

"Whatever I said, they just looked at me like I was crazy and took my picture with the Beaver's dad. They said my radio transmission was all the witness I would need. They had recorded everything. Said I saved my brigade. If that NVA outfit had gotten their shit together they would have attacked the next day. Nobody knew they were there. It was a feeder terminus for the Ho Chi Minh Trail, for godsake. They'd cut the road in less than forty-eight hours. Right under our noses. Nobody knew it. It was a complete accident that I saw it. Nothing but a lucky accident. Just like it was a lucky accident that I was alive.

"They just wouldn't shut up about it. Nurses came and hugged me. I was on the front page of *Pacific Stars & Stripes*. They sent a copy to my parents. The papers at home ran the same fucked up story. I was on the same page as MacNamara and a story about John Lennon still explaining about the Beatles being more popular than Jesus. Guys at camp shook my hand. They gave me another stripe. I was never so ashamed."

"Did they send you home after that?" she asked.

"I stayed at a hospital in Busan, Korea for a while after my eye infected. They quarantined me. Then they flew me to Koyota in Japan. They sort of reassigned me."

"With that eye?"

"The eye was fine for a while. It got worse a little at a time and then just stopped working. Woke up one morning and it was like looking at the world through a peephole. But it fixed itself. I got sent back for eight more months. Got hurt again, this and that, but it was no big deal."

"Why on earth wouldn't they send you home?"

"I'm tired," I said, changing the subject.

"I want to know why they kept you there," she said. "Why didn't you ever tell me this? You could have told me all this before. I always wanted you to tell me about everything."

I pretended to fall asleep. I didn't want to talk anymore.

"I never wanted to freak you out, you know," I said.

She tried asking more questions, but I pretended to snore. She held me and then her arms loosened and fell away. Briefly, there in the peace of the night with her shape beside me, it seemed like I could hold fear at bay. Like I'd escaped from something. I lay and stared at the broken moonlight on the bedroom ceiling. I should tell her the rest. Just let it spill until there was nothing left to say. But I could not. And she wasn't there, anyway. It was too late for talking. I'd had my chance, and now it was too late.

I turned and painted her shoulder with one finger, hoping she wouldn't wake. But she was never going to wake up ever again.

The coyotes rustled through the grass behind the house, playing, celebrating their kill.

When I turned she was gone, the pillow undisturbed.

I took my hunting rifle from the closet and walked outside. I walked from the house and stood in my bare feet and underwear and fired at the first thing that moved.

Somebody is always firing a gun around this town.

CHAPTER 59

Chaz accompanied me again to the VA hospital in Denver where I met with my shrink, the impassive and tweedy Dr. Nguyen, to whom I described a repeating nightmare in which I stand in a rice paddy at night wearing only polka-dotted boxer shorts while I trade vintage baseball cards with a man dressed in rope sandals who is pointing a rifle at me.

I didn't bother to tell the doctor that he himself was also starting to appear in my dreams, competing with my wife and Chaz and all those crazy rats.

Behind this tropical sports fan walk soldiers in pith helmets carrying sacks of rice and wooden ammo buckets. Another group, dressed like shabby rustics from an obscure and unremembered war long ago, pull ancient artillery out of the jungle with bamboo rope. There's the funky bouquet of shit and cabbage and that fishy fermented sauce everybody cooked with, which is the dominant odor I remember from Vietnam.

The man's breath reminds me of stinky feet as he argues loudly that one Ernie Banks, a Curt Flood and two badly laminated Carl Yastremskis are easily worth my pristine 1952 Mickey Mantel rookie card, the one where the Yankees slugger looks like a teenage Oklahoma farm boy in a badly fitted Little League uniform.

"I want you to toss in Lou Brock, Reggie and Willie Stargell or I walk," I demand as I listen to the rubbery *thwump!* as an unseen mortar sails over my head and explodes in a muddy cloud in the rice paddy. There's small rifle fire nearby but neither of us gives a shit. These are baseball cards we're talking about.

"No way," says this runty guy in colonial pidgin French, his hair sticking up wildly like he's just been pulled backwards through a pipe.

"I'll give you Johnny Bench and Don Zimmer."

He lifts his rifle and aims at me.

"A stinkin' Zimmer?" I say. "A Zimmer for Micky? I'm outta here."

In this dream I speak French, yes.

He starts shooting as I walk away, the AK-47 rounds bouncing harmlessly off the back of my shirt. I flutter my hands and began to fly, rising above the tree tops.

Then a whole squadron of tiny helicopters filled with uniformed prairie dogs comes to my defense, the sky covered by a curtain of fiery rockets and M-50 tracer rounds as I flutter into one of the rescuing gopher aircraft like a sparrow returning to its nest.

Chaz the Gopher King is wearing an ascot and World War One aviator goggles and he hands me a beer as the Huey lifts and banks sharply away from the fiery chaos below.

At the VA, Dr. Nguyen scratched something in his notepad and sucked on his meerschaum pipe. He blew a smoke ring in the shape of two fighting cats who floated away and vanished into the ceiling tiles of the doctor's office.

"Eat more prunes," he said, handing me a prescription refill for my pretty blue pills. "I'll see you next month."

I had locked the Gopher King away in my backpack along with a Reese's Peanut Butter Cup and trail mix. Out in the hospital hallway, I looked inside and Chaz, now in a deep fructose coma, was curled up like a fur glove, snoring and twitching like he too might have nightmare problems to sort out.

I dropped the backpack on a chair and got my pills from the pharmacy.

Chaz behaved himself all day. He politely informed me — seven times during the two-hour drive to Denver — each time he required a roadside potty break.

Only once did he lose his sphincter cool, but that was because I played his favorite Jimi Hendrix song, *Castles Made of Sand*, and so he understandably and with much joy started shooting milk duds all over the front seat.

Before we walked through the security gate at the VA, I frisked Chaz to make sure he wasn't packing any heat. I found a .22 Magnum mini-revolver strapped to his ankle, two M-7 smoke grenades under his camo shirt and an M-7 army bayonet tucked against the small of his furry back.

"Nice try," I said. I motioned for the royal rodent to withdraw to a secret compartment I had created inside the backpack.

The security guard groped the bag, unzipped it, and looked inside.

"That's a lot of candy," he said.

"It's a long drive."

"Kind of funky in there."

"It's a hospital. Everybody here has a problem."

"In understand. So sorry," he said and waved me through the screening arch with a metal-detector wand that I believe also featured a lint roller attachment.

When I came out of the pharmacy Chaz was standing on a metal folding chair, raising his paws and gesticulating like he was making a political speech. Like Lenin

237

in Red Square in 1917. Like Teddy Roosevelt making a stump speech from a caboose in Peoria, Illinois.

The giant man listening to Chaz was dressed in a sleeveless denim jacket with "Chu Lai, 1968" emblazoned across his back. He had chains coming out of his back pocket, another chain around his neck, a chain bracelet, and a single silver chain link hanging from his left earlobe. He had a neck tattoo. His forehead was oddly dented. When I approached them both, the human shook my hand and complimented me on my "pet."

"He sure talks nice," he said.

Chaz got angry when he heard this and started screeching, and so I grabbed him by the legs and stuffed him into the backpack.

"You take the blue one I see," the giant man said, pointing at the bottle of prescription pills in my hand.

"Yeah. The blue ones," I said.

"They're pretty," he said. "I love the pretty blue ones."

He took my hand and shook it.

"You and your little buddy take care," he said and limped away on his cane.

We got to Bull River Falls in time for me to take the Gopher King to the FedEx office. He had a business trip to Alberta, Canada, where the Bellyache Mountain coterie has a thriving pioneer settlement — a diaspora enclave of sorts, refugees who've fled Colorado for a new life atop the Athabaskan tar oil sand fields.

I packed Chaz into a wax-impregnated, 275-lb bursting strength rated, ISTA certified live animal container of my own design, handed him a dozen Snickers bars and an iPod loaded with *Procol Harum's Greatest Hits*, and sent him on his way, overnight delivery guaranteed by 10 a.m.

CHAPTER 60

That week the old Voorhorst general store burned down.

Abandoned since the 1960s, the shop once sold food, medicine and gasoline and also served as a U.S. Post Office for ranchers on the mesa north of Bull River Falls. To get there you drive on a crooked washboard road along the Colorado River. It is empty country with an excess of nothingness.

When I got there the property owner was standing next to a pile of smoking junk and twisted metal, dusting off an old Sinclair gasoline pump, one of those with the glass overflow bulb. The fuel price meter was stuck at .19 cents a gallon.

I took my pictures for the newspaper and wandered around. There were paper scraps everywhere. Bound ledgers and burned three ring binders lay in a pile at the side of the road. I found burned sales receipt pads dating back to the 1930s. I picked through a stack of broken apothecary bottles and tried to read the ingredients to Dr. Hamlin's Wizard Oil, a "…healing antiseptic ointment." The label proclaimed in big red letters: KEEP AWAY FROM FIRE!

Inside a warped cardboard box were a dozen assorted other elixirs, such as: "Pure Rattlesnake Oil for Persons Afflicted with Deafness." And there was "Dr. Kilmer's Female Remedy — A System Regulator." And something with the cryptic name of "4-11-44," which was for treating "Gonorrhoea, Kidney & Bladder Affections."

Another bottle, this one rather elegantly shaped and colored a deep brown as if to hide its mysterious contents, proclaimed in simple understated script: "Menlo's Manly Powder." The Voorhorst place had once been a one stop shopping mecca.

The owner, who seemed bored and oddly casual about the destruction of this piece of local history, pointed through the trees to where he'd sold land to somebody who was building a giant log vacation home with a four car garage and a flagstone patio as big as a parking lot. A gazebo stood in a garden that was being landscaped and construction guys were lifting a propane tank onto its struts. The house overlooked the river, which from where I stood made an ox bow loop through a deep canyon that glowed red in its shadows.

"You want that old thing?" he said and pointed to the antique gas pump.

"Go ahead and sell it, you'll make money," I said. "But I'll take this old bottle, if it's okay."

I sat on a rock where I could watch the river and ate lunch from a plastic grocery store bag. Tourists in a red rubber raft floated through the rapids below, and from this height it looked like a small shoe bobbing in the water. It was hot and quiet, the unblemished sky cloudless and perfectly blue, and I could hardly hear the water rushing below. A pair of wild doves cried to each other from within a grove of aspen trees.

On a rock ledge far below me teetered the wreck of an old Model A Ford that had slid off the gravel road ages ago, its rumble seat crushed, the black paint bleached dull gray. The window glass busted out. Bumpers missing. The front seat yanked halfway through the skeleton door like somebody had tried to retrieve it and then given up.

I took my time getting home and when I got back to the newspaper office I saw two gophers on ATVs dressed in full medieval plate armor, carrying long jousting lances as they raced toward each other at full speed.

An audience of gophers were chattering wildly from bleacher seats erected in my backyard. Heraldic banners were waving from the tops of little white circus tents. Two female gophers dressed like tavern wenches were fighting in a mud pit and tearing at each other's hair.

A squeaky voice called my name. I looked over and Chaz the Gopher King was waving at me with a battle axe, his furry neck draped with all manner of gemstone necklaces and decorative gold chain jewelry, like a furry little Lord Mayor of London.

He wore leather hip boots and a pointy tasseled silver cap that sparkled in the late afternoon sun. A broadsword was strapped to his hip. A small cutlass sheathed in a prissy pink scabbard hung from one shoulder. His chest fur sprouted from behind the ruffles of a strange orchid-colored shirt that a looked like underwear torn from a sleeping wild west saloon chorus girl.

He looked like a deranged and drunken costume thief and fly fisherman who'd been wrapped in velcro and then dragged through the HBO wardrobe room on the movie set of one of those mythical cape and sword extravaganzas.

If Liberace was a violent man, he would have looked like this, except without the piano.

Chaz had asked me that morning if he could use the newspaper office for a family event and I agreed, assuming it was for a wedding or an official clan gathering. He doesn't have room for that sort of thing in his underground burrow on Bellyache Mountain so I gave him the keys to the storage shed behind my building and told him to keep away from the windows so nobody walking down Main Street would see him.

"And no guns, understand?"

"Of course," Chaz said.

"And the helicopters, I don't want those here. The neighbors think they're drones, and around here people shoot drones, got it?"

"I promise there will be no modern weaponry of any kind," Chaz said.

Six hours later, back from the peace and tranquility of the mountains, I watched while rodents carrying cross bows lined up atop the parapets of a fake styrofoam castle wall and fired down on a horde of other gophers lobbing rocks with wooden catapults.

There were food stands and gopher jugglers and fire-eating rodents with shaved heads, and from a small theater stage draped in red, white & blue political bunting puppets performed for clapping prairie dog children. A prairie dog wearing a court jester costume handed me a three-inch-long roasted turkey leg.

The Gopher King ran to me and tugged at my pants and screamed: "I can explain! I can explain everything!"

The little rat jumped on my leg and started biting me as I tried to walk away.

He screamed: "Wait! I have to explain!"

That's when the little bottle of Menlo's Manly Powder fell from my pocket.

Chaz took off his little silver cap, pushed those goofy shirt ruffles away from his chin and started reading the label. His lips moved.

"Can I have this?"

"What for?"

"Never mind," Chaz said. "Can I have this?"

"Yea, now get outta' here," I said. "And take your army in tight pants with you."

CHAPTER 61

The basement office of part-time coroner Carmen Ruiz was close enough to the County Building's furnace blower so when the AC fired up, the vibration knocked evidence boxes off the plywood shelves that ran the length of the autopsy room. Ruiz, a hospital pediatric nurse, was dressed in her green medical scrubs.

We hugged.

"Delivered a lot of babies this week," she said. "I'm guessing it was the snow storm last fall. I got your message. Weren't you supposed to come here two days ago?"

"I had a doctor's appointment," I said. "You're probably busy enough without me bothering you."

"The TV people won't leave me alone. Excuse the boxes," she said and pulled out a bulging envelope tied with twine. The room reeked from disinfectant.

She started reading: "One wound. Forehead. Thirty-degree trajectory from the vertical center of the cap of the skull. Force of it knocked her backwards against a tree hard enough to dislocate her shoulder. What prints we could see says she was facing the shooter. Blood spray indicates the shooter was on the hill ahead of her, a little left of her center."

"East?" I said.

Carmen nodded. "She was stationary at the time. We could have gotten more, except the scene was very ratty. Appears she'd been down on the grass earlier, from what I could see of the final body position. But I think I can explain that in a minute."

"What about any shell casings?"

"No ID from the wound or the missed round that hit the tree," Ruiz said. "Excuse me."

She walked to a metal wall locker.

"I've been in these things for fourteen hours."

She peeled off her hospital scrubs behind the open locker door. Beneath it she wore a tee shirt. She took out a comb in front of a mirror hung from a clothes hanger and flipped back her short dark hair. She snatched a clean blouse off a hook and turned and buttoned up.

She pointed at the stack of files on a wooden table. "All this came yesterday. A boy on the fire crew got killed. How do they expect me to handle it all? I'm a staff of one.

"Anyway, they found the slug hole you called me about. It was stuck in a two-by-four at the lodge, a long way up the hill from the scene. Same trajectory, almost from the same angle as the shot that killed her."

"Almost?"

"Ten degrees, give or take a gnat's fanny," Carmen said. "But another round that could have ricocheted, according to marks on rocks directly behind the body, would have been fired from even further up the hill. Afraid we don't have any answers for that one, except it likely came from the direction of private property somewhere near the subdivision and the McCoy ranch. Might never know. FBI sent a box of things to Quantico. We'll have to wait a few weeks."

"Melinda was dressed for work," Carmen said. "Her pack had rock samples, a bag lunch, pens and a calculator. Her BLM contractor identification. A rock pick. Not the stuff you'd take on a fun hike. We didn't find her cell."

Carmen flipped through more papers.

"One day I might just get a computer made in this decade," she said.

"Let's see...she was down for about six hours. Normally the animal bite on her leg would have been unusual, but with this fire that whole river area has a lot of wildlife activity these days."

"Police say the fella they arrested admitted he was with her," I said.

"Ah, Mr. Jergen. Had sex with the victim, consensual I'd say, within two hours before her death, if that's what you mean. Like I said, she was prone on the grass for a while before she was shot. I haven't seen the results of the residue test, but even in that hard soil he left boot prints all over the scene.

"No sign of a struggle. I don't know if she saw the shooter, but she was looking in that direction. There were tracks uphill from where she fell, but that could have been from a resort employee, anybody. Firefighters have been walking through here all week. There's the new subdivision uphill from the river, so people are in and out of those woods all the time. The company locked off old logging road, but people don't pay attention to that stuff. There was a report of shots fired from the ranch."

"And Jergen?"

"Oh, he had blood on him. Plenty of it. Her hair was all over him, too. No scratches, though. Nothing on Melinda's hands, under her nails, the routine stuff. I don't believe there was any struggle. No defense marks of any kind."

She pulled out an envelope from under her pile.

"Sorry," she said. "It doesn't look like much of a system, but I manage to find things, eventually."

I tried to stifle a yawn, and when I apologized Carmen leaned forward and tapped me gently on the knee.

"Stan, more than a few folks have told me they think you look miserable," she said. "You still working both sides of the clock?"

I yawned again.

Now Carmen put both of her hands around mine and squeezed.

After an awkward silence I asked her about the bones they'd found at Gold Gulch.

"I hear you're involved in that burial site?"

She pointed across the room. "I volunteered to help the feds catalog artifacts. They're busy with the fire and the state archaeologist has his whole staff downstate at a big highway project."

The steel lab table was draped with a white sheet, which Carmen pulled away to reveal a row of human bones that looked like they'd been cooked in a sauce.

She picked one up. She arranged a few more. "Have to give an inventory to the feds by next week," she said.

The room smelled like cleaning solvent. The walls were lined with shelves stacked with plastic storage crates. Two rows of school desks sat in the middle of the room, facing another long metal lab table. Rolled up maps and blueprints lay on one of the desks. She picked up a bone.

"Tibia," she said and pointed toward her shin. "It's from Melinda's work site. She was hired to retrieve the artifacts because she had experience from when she worked with the Ute tribe during a CU project. It was a good summer gig. The scrape you see is where Melinda took her sample."

She held up a glass vial filled with powder.

"So?"

"Traces of arsenic and mercury."

"You're losing me," I said.

"The police found a notebook in her backpack. Melinda had determined the residue on the bones were not native to the valley. This sample could not have been contaminated this badly while the person was alive. There's no trace of those substances at Gold Gulch. It's wetland there, which is an impossible spot for a grave site. Nobody would have camped there and certainly not an Indian hunting party. There's peat bogs thousands of years old and these bones are only about three centuries old. There's been no discovery of remains this large, except at the old gold mine."

From a wooden sieving box Carmen took a round stone.

"There was rock, the kind of scree you'd find at a much higher elevation, in this batch."

She rubbed the rocks into her palm. Dust fell, and she swiped her gloved finger through it.

"Mercury, zinc, arsenic. A cocktail of nasty stuff. It's all from the tailings pile at the mine, as far as I can tell. Melinda made the connection right away. Those bones were transported from somewhere else."

Carmen covered the bones with the sheet.

"Look, me and a lot of people in this town wish Gold Gulch would just go away. I don't like the resort at all or the people who own it, but this was a set-up. Maybe a prank. It doesn't matter now. But Melinda knew it was fake and now she's dead."

Carmen unrolled the map on her desk and smoothed her palm across where Bellyache Mountain formed a long ridge that pointed to the ghost town.

"The area around the mine was a favorite elk hunting area for years. Miners used to talk about the herds getting in their way. Place is full of old hunter's fences and ambush traps, mostly pre-Columbian. Anybody who grew up around here knows where they are. When I have the time — just as a side job, I've been cataloging things there for about a year for the BLM. Taking GPS readings, taking pics. If you remember, the fires started not to far from there, which is why I want to go this week and take archive photos before it all goes to hell."

I stepped over to a metal sink. There were more bones.

"Looks like a game of pick-up-sticks, doesn't it?" Carmen said. "I've been washing them."

She held up what looked like a knobby brown hammer handle.

"Male, about 25 years old, very good teeth — they all had good teeth — but this fella had a severe limp. There were only three skulls in the batch. Most of the rest is from the same individual. The limp made him compensate, so one of his leg muscles got bigger. This spur here on the upper part of the bone shows us that. You know how people talk about the good old days? Well, in the good old days he would have been a middle aged man. In a few years he would have been an elder of his group. I'm surprised he lived this long with this damage. He was in pain his entire adult life." She held the bone under a lamp.

"He also didn't have much status. See those round marks?" The welts looked like oblong coins.

"This spur shows he had to carry heavy things and he did it often. Today you'd see that in a man twice his age who worked in a heavy labor job."

"Then how did he die?" I asked.

"Blows to the head. All of them."

"Cowboys and Indians?"

"No cowboys at that time. At first I thought it was a war party. There are no other marks, and I thought the reason the bones were so scattered was just natural shifting at the original death site. No defensive marks on the arms or digits. If they had time to fight you would have seen marks on different parts of their bodies, forearms, missing finger joints. But they all got whacked in the same way."

"What changed your mind?"

"It's so simple I missed it. Most of the mine is at the bottom of an avalanche chute. Loose scree everywhere. The Indians just had the bad luck to be caught in a rock slide. There's absolutely no place for a rock slide in the middle of that valley by the Gold Gulch resort, just loose gyp."

She stuck her finger through a hole in the skull. "At first, this looks as if a dull weapon caused the trauma. But the opening is too new. These people had nothing made from any metal, but the opening in the bone was caused by a metal object. Stan, the whole thing was the work of a sloppy joker. "

"So they closed off a multi-million dollar construction project because of a joke?"

"Whoever did it had unexpected help."

She rolled open another topo map showing roughly where the bones were discovered.

"Notice how they were scattered over such a wide area? Such an event would never happen naturally, not in this terrain."

"Rain storm? Gyp soil can get oozy in the spring," I said.

"None of that checks. Any rock is too far above the peat bog and the wetlands are very stable. Only a glacier would have moved these bones this far apart. And no glacier ever came this far south."

"Looks like a bomb exploded," I said.

The round colored stickers marking where bones had been found were scattered over several acres of Gold Gulch property and far beyond the small area already marked off by the police.

"A head here. An arm there. We found a shin from the same man over 400 meters apart."

"So, somebody threw the stuff everywhere."

"Nobody could have spread it all by themselves in such a short time period without being seen. That's what made it look so natural at first."

Carmen smiled. "This whole property supports one enormous prairie dog colony, probably several thousand animals. My guess is the colony just didn't take kindly to somebody dumping this mess in their backyard. They're fussy homemakers, so they did what came natural. They moved everything away."

I said: "So, after a while those bones would have been spread all over the resort property and not just at the dig site?"

"In another month, these bones would have been moved up and down the valley. Construction at the whole resort, even the new subdivision they're building at the far end of the valley, would have come to a screeching halt.

"Before nursing school I was an archaeology major. That's why I still do this stuff for the BLM whenever I can. My professor told us a story. Down in the Four Corners near Mesa Verde one gopher colony moved about a ton of pottery, tools, and valuable Anasazi items a mile from the original dig. It only took them a few days. Nobody could plot anything after that happened. Couldn't make reliable GPS readings. The whole project was compromised. Those little stinkers ruined the entire dig site and blew a hole through the school's budget.

"Melinda Barstow knew what was going on. She knew exactly what she had found. Why she didn't say right away we'll never know. She might have been trying to decide what she should do since there's a lot of politics involved with the resort. But I think somebody knew she was going to tattle."

Carmen handed me a copy of the autopsy report and as I was about to leave, she said: "I heard you had trouble at your place."

"No big deal. Just a burglary," I said and then changed the subject.

"You think it's smart to go up to that Indian fence? It's right at the edge of the fire line. Not too safe, if you ask me."

"No choice," Carmen said. "I told the tribal people I'd do it. It would be a shame if those things get burned and forgotten."

"Carmen, the guy who started the fire is up in those mountains."

"I'll be okay," Carmen said. "He's doesn't have a beef with me."

"That sonofabitch has a beef with anybody who gets in his way."

I walked her to her car.

"The rope you gave me the other day?" she said. "I haven't had the time to look at it, sorry."

"Whenever you can. It's for a story," I lied.

CHAPTER 62

"It was a dark and stormy night..." is the way Chaz the Gopher King introduces himself in the first draft of his autobiography *Chaz: My Life Underground*, which I am now reluctantly editing. As if I didn't gave better things to do.

At first I refused this daunting task, claiming I was too busy, but Chaz handed me an empty Ragu Marinara Sauce jar filled with pure gold dust and this quickly changed my mind.

"You should write something less gloomy," I gently suggested after skimming the first few dozen pages.

Chaz said: "How about: it was a bright and stormless night when I proposed marriage to my wife by swearing everlasting love and fealty and promising we would dig holes together and eat zinnia seeds until death do us part."

"Better," I said. "Very romantic."

Chaz's manuscript right now sits at 1,200-plus single-spaced typed pages, much too long for the fickle publishing market he wants to crack. These days only books about love-struck teenage vampires and/or dystopian revolutionaries with orthodontically perfect teeth carrying bows and arrows who rebel against grownups get published.

Most of Chaz's book is over-written and poorly paced, and because he's convinced abundant sex will make his effort climb the best seller charts, it is riddled with scenes in which he says stuff like:

"...and her rubbery lips quivered like a pair of animated Gummy Worms as she clutched my sweat-moistened fur with her long sensuous claws and howled piercingly in the night while doing backflips in our subterranean burrow of Rocky Mountain lust."

Or there's this one, where he gleefully relates in painstaking detail the upside of being married to his favorite spouse, Tinka:

"Of my five lovely wives she alone is familiar with the ticklish dent on my forehead where long ago I was clobbered with a nine-iron at the fourth tee of the

Gold Gulch Golf Course, and which has since become a freakishly sensitive love button that only she has learned to activate, thereby making me explode with an intense animal passion I can only describe as celebratory and life-changing."

The book is violent to the extreme, and I have counseled Chaz that though publishers are not reluctant to selling blood and guts and carefully selected carnage, there are indeed literary limits one must respect.

Hence, I suggested he delete the following scene from a chapter whose name and prose style might be uncomfortably familiar to anyone who flunked American Literature 101:

The chapter is titled: *A Farewell to Arms and Legs:*

It reads: "In the late summer of that year I lived in a deep hole in the ground that looked across the river and the plain to the mountains.

"In the bed of the river there were pebbles and boulders and both the pebbles and the boulders were very round and onto them were snagged plastic Walmart bags and the desiccated wet parts of Burger King Whopper onions and soggy Papa John's pizza cartons whose remaining pepperoni and petrified mushroom ingredients shone brightly in the sun.

"Though the fishes in the river were dead there were more pebbles and boulders, dry and white in the sun, and also very round because of constant hydraulic abrasion, and the water was clear and swiftly moving and blue in the channels where men in expensive rubber hip waders and fashionable water proof sports vests cast fake insects at the pale and poisoned trout, none of whom seemed to be hungry.

"My soldiers carried their AK-47s as they marched down the road and past my burrow and the dust they raised powdered the leaves of the trees. The trunks of the trees too were dusty and the leaves fell early that year because of the troops marching along the road and the dust rising, the leaves stirred by the hot breeze and falling and the soldiers marching and afterward the road was bare and white except for the leaves and the dead fish and the very flimsy plastic Walmart bags fluttering in the wind like a happy Buddhist birthday party for old Minnesota Lutherans, at which they might serve giant vats of green bean casserole and drink Schlitz beer like starved and drunken Vikings who had lost their favorite swords."

This goes on for fifty-two pages as the violence progresses until there are enough body parts flying through the air to fill a fleet of medieval corpse wagons during the Black Death of 1346.

Then Chaz confusingly flashes back to the year 1512, when the Gopher King's ancestors followed the Spanish explorer Francisco Coronado from Old Mexico into what is now New Mexico and the town of Alamogordo, where, as you know,

Chaz was born and where he was exposed in 1944 to the Plutonium-240 isotope, thereby gaining him his magical powers.

You can see, I have work to do.

It's been two weeks now and I'm still on Chapter 1, which Chaz is convinced represents his strongest writing.

God only knows what the other 1,146 pages will be like.

But money talks and for the sake of art I will march on.

CHAPTER 63

The soldier had lately transformed himself into a winged apparition, his detached scalp flapping, arms spread as he descended en crucifixio from the ceiling to hover above my bed.

Red water dripped from his rifle. When the boy opened his mouth the chewing gum was there, impressed with teeth marks and dirt.

And then he said, "Fuckwad, you killed everybody."

He hung within his tattered and filthy clothes, tubes of blue gut swinging. The flesh gray and speckled with dirt.

I tried to speak, the dark room swirling, the PFC windmilling his arms slowly.

He smirked: "Where you go, I go."

On this night I told him: "You made that voodoo doll. Now I remember."

The PFC stopped moving and hung suspended like he was on a wire.

"What?"

"Your girl," I said. "Monica. Mona, Monique..."

"Marsha," the boy said.

"Yes. She broke up with you and you made a voodoo doll," I said. "Out of sticks, and you poked it with your knife. Made dolls out of grass. You carved her shape out of bamboo. Made dolls out of mud. You'd hum her name. Fuckin' humming drove me crazy. You'd sing it. Chant it. Drove us all nuts."

"I wrote her name on my entrenching tool," the boy said, smiling proudly, the giant corpse teeth white within his butchered face. He wrapped his arms around himself as if he were cold.

"Made a doll with C-4 explosive. Marsha, Marsha..."

I shook my finger at the ceiling.

"You hung her picture on a tree and shot it," I said.

"Don't forget the letter she sent me," he said. "Shot that, too."

He grabbed his straying rope of wobbling intestine and gathered everything under his shirt carefully, an annoyed look on his face like he'd had to do this bothersome task before. He looked at the space above his groin for a while to make sure the mess would stay.

He looked down at me. "So you remember the Marsha thing," he said tenderly, as if he were touched that I'd recall such a thing.

"I do," I said. "Immortal and everlasting Marsha, alive and well with her name written on the best latrine walls in Vietnam."

"I said her name a dozen times a day. It was the only way to forget her."

"Did you?"

"Look."

The boy pulled open his shirt and on what was left of his chest, tilted between the severed rib bones that poked from his skin like broken splinters, was the fractured tattoo of her name in crude upper case letters.

And then the boy was gone, replaced by Dr. Nguyen, who was taking notes, scribbling furiously. He was dressed in black vietcong pajamas and tire rubber sandals. His goatee had turned white.

I awoke with my legs blanket-twisted on the sofa, my hands choking the pillow.

In my quest for sleep I'd tried taking naps to break slumber into safe daytime shifts, but someone was always there, waiting behind my eyelids. The PFC. Chaz. My shrink. My wife.

That night I turned on every downstairs light, switched them off, put them on again, as if testing my bravery. I put my head under the kitchen sink faucet and let the cold water drill my neck, cooling the red and swollen welt.

Whenever I bothered to twist myself in the mirror for a look I saw the thick wrinkle that raced across my back. I'd never seen where the scar ended, only felt its path, a crazy trail of bumps and interrupted dents of hardened tissue that ended near my ass. I remembered the man, his small dirty feet, and how soft his throat was. The Laotian was strong and muscled and a good fighter, but his throat was soft.

After the ambush they'd allowed me to heal up in the hospital, making a great fuss about the medal. They sent me to a camp five miles from the Laos border, where I trained Hmong tribesmen. I was the only American, and me and a squad of the Yellow Tiger Brigade would cross the frontier each week with only pistols and our knives, our rations limited to what we foraged at villages.

They gave me another award. They could not stop giving me medals.

"You know we'll say we don't know you," the officer said when they assigned me to a brigade populated by dour looking Green Berets and dipshit South Vietnamese regulars, whose officers wore tailored shirts and ascots. The regulars and the greenies never mixed. At the time we were at Dak To, ready to cross into Laos.

"This is strictly..." the officer searched carefully for a word.

I remembered the ceiling fan in his office. The cane chairs. The odor of liquor coming from the open bottle on the officer's empty desk. Two tumblers, upside down on a clean white towel. A can of Brasso sat alone on a shelf.

"Clandestine," he said, releasing the word as if he'd been holding his breath.

"Officially, you've been transferred. But the paperwork is classified. The oak leaf cluster for the commendation medal we just gave you is fiction. The paperwork in your file says you got it for work in Saigon, clerical shit at MACV. We saw you had some army journalism training from the army school in Indianapolis, so we made you an assistant to the PIO. You now exist where the paperwork is. Wherever we want the paperwork to be."

He tapped the manila folder on the desk with his finger.

"Nobody will give you orders where you're headed. I assume you know what your duties are. Is this all clear? You asked for this, remember? Why you volunteered for it, I don't know. Crazy revenge shit, I'm guessing."

He looked at the folder. "You were at the A Shau Valley?"

"You know I was," I said.

I didn't like this man who had no name tag, only the silver insignia of a lieutenant colonel. Shiny silver on a brand new jungle poplin shirt. He should have been wearing black insignia. It was all wrong, the way he was dressed: the too-new stitching of the infantryman badge, the gold Bulova on his wrist, him wearing polished parade boots like they'd just been issued at basic training, the sideburns creeping non reg past his earlobes. No light colonel would wear improper field rank badges. He had long carefully tended fingers and wore a wedding ring. His hands were clean, soft. Pruned fingernails. His neck hadn't seen a sunburn in years.

"Why me?" I said.

"You asked to be reassigned, I just told you. You're apparently motivated to remain in combat, so it's our job to be creative with your talents. This is the kind of re-assignment people like you get. I also know you have incentive. You lost your squad and, for whatever reason, you perhaps want to make amends. It's not like you didn't expect this."

"That's not what I asked."

The colonel smiled. "It's what you told the medical staff in Japan."

"I thought that stuff is private."

I had gotten very cocky lately. My brief celebrity had given me an unspoken edge. People who outranked me seemed to invite familiarity, and there was none of the arms-length coolness and tentative friendliness that officers usually practiced with enlisted men. My salutes got sloppy. Officers stopped me to chat about baseball. They asked about the now famous ambush. I seemed to be rankless and could go as I pleased. I was starting to act like a civilian.

"There's not much about you that's private anymore. I know your file up and down," the colonel continued, opening the folder. "I know about the English lit major in college. Then you enlisted for a three-year hitch in your junior year. You enlisted and they sent you to Fort Ben Harrison in Indiana and they said you'd be trained as an information specialist, but Uncle Sam made you an infantry grunt instead. Sent you off to AIT, despite your objections. You tried to write your congressman, but that shit never works. In fact, it made things worse. I know everything."

The officer poured himself a drink. He held up the other empty glass and I waved it away.

"Chevas," he said. "Came in this morning with the mail from Tokyo."

"No thanks," I said. "Your all-seeing magic mind should know I caught hepatitis at the evac hospital after my eye infected. Doc said I can't even look at booze for another year because of my liver."

"Look," the officer said, annoyed. "You play it right and you've got it made in the shade back home. Not everybody gets that goddamn medal. Pick your career, buddy boy — they'll all want you working for their company. Hell, I wouldn't rule out politics. A good looking boy like you? Just you play the rest of the way with us. Understood? You look like a smart kid, so I know you understand."

"Who's the we that's sending me home? You're not sending me home."

"Not right away. On your last mission you showed a certain aptitude we must take advantage of, given the present political situation."

The colonel leaned back and squinted at the ceiling. He folded his manicured fingers behind his head. His uniform had starch. Starched jungle fatigues. In this humidity, for chissake. The colonel took delicate sips of his drink and then a longer, thoughtful swig and then he swallowed and wiped his lip with the heel of his thumb.

"What the fuck is your problem?" he said.

He pointed downward through the top of the desk with both hands.

"I'd cut these off to have what you got," he said. "That's a ticket for a lifetime, if you play your cards straight. All I know is you requested this mission, and now you're in too deep to bail out. I don't know why the hell you did, but you did. Myself, I'd have gone home. I'd have taken the glory, all those stories in *Stars and Stripes*. Said goodby to this heat and the ridiculous food and got back home and let them take my picture for the hometown newspaper. All the pictures they wanted. Don't give me this rebel shit, sergeant. It's too late."

He flipped through my file, still holding the empty glass in one hand. He shoved a sealed envelope toward me.

"There's two battalions of regulars, all of them operating from behind the border, where it is strictly verboten to be if you're an American," he said. "We want you to find as many of the enemy as you can. We're sending those Hmong fellows you trained with you. What you do with them is your business. It's no longer the business of the United States Army. You'll have other people to help you with supply runs; maybe arrange political interference in Saigon. As far as we're concerned it's a free fire zone up and down the border. Get all the air support you need. Cash if you need it. You'll get additional orders as required. There will be pick-up LZs five klicks apart located as far in-country we can go without an undue political risk. The map is in the envelope. That's all I'm authorized to say right now. There's a 2nd Cav ship waiting outside. The crew have been instructed not to communicate with you. No small talk, nothing. They don't even know who you are. Their flight is off the log book. You won't see anybody wearing rank insignia. The aircraft has no tail numbers. If it looks well cleaned and brand new, that's because it just came off a Navy vessel just to take your ungrateful ass to your next assignment. The type of assignment, I remind you again, that you specifically requested."

"What if I change my mind?" I said.

"They'll put you in the brig. Even celebrities like you can get an Article 15."

"That would be bad publicity."

The colonel smiled.

The colonel who wasn't a colonel then leaned forward and shoved closer the paperwork in the envelope fastened with a metal clasp and I dropped the envelope on the floor as I walked out the door, lifting my middle finger over my shoulder that would soon have another scar on it.

"That's off the record," I said on my way out. I headed to the waiting helicopter.

CHAPTER 64

It was important to keep my head busy.

And so I traveled twice to Alberta to deliver gold to the new refugee colony, where the cost of setting up Chaz's new settlement has been more expensive than anyone expected. At one point I was transferring so much cash to Canada from the G. K. Rodenthouse Foundation's money market account that the bank here in Bull River Falls called and asked if I could come in for a meeting. I try to do the exact opposite of what a bank tells me to do, so I'm ignoring their request.

I saw Chaz at the Athabasca oil sands field, after I'd shipped him there in a UPS crate so he could rally his dejected settlers, who were finding it difficult to create a utopian paradise in such desolate landscape. While waiting for an audience with the Gopher King at my favorite shabby motel near the North Saskatchewan River I had nothing to do except watch Stanley Cup hockey re runs on a black and white 12-inch Zenith TV, eat Hostess Hickory Sticks (Juliennes a L'Hickory) and read books from the motel's eclectic library, which included titles like, *The Medical Histories of Roman Emperors*.

I was drinking a bottle of Brewsters Blue Monk Barley Wine when I learned that Claudius Galenus, a second century Greek and personal physician to Roman emperors, had strong opinions about our preeminence among all living critters on earth.

"Voracious animals," he said, paraphrasing Plato "...feed continuously and incessantly eliminate, leading a life truly inimical to philosophy and music, whereas nobler and more perfect animals neither eat or eliminate continually."

Galenus, viewed through the fog of antiquity, can be forgiven for his ignorance since he practiced medicine long before the invention of Fritos, bean dip and hot wings binge-eating during long NFL football games.

He also never met the Gopher King, who — though he eliminates profusely with the frenzy of a supercharged Pez candy dispenser and never seems to stop eating, has also has read Kierkégaard and Socrates and can name all five band members in *Earth, Wind & Fire*. He also recently started playing classical guitar. Quite the accomplishment for a rodent with no thumbs.

Chaz's artistic interests are dynamic. I once saw him weep when he first listened to the famous soprano aria that opens Act II of Madame Butterfly — which is preceded by two tragic-sounding flutes playing in unison, in which a particular Japanese geisha girl hopes for the return of the American guy she loves, whatever his name is.

On a whim, the Gopher King asked me a few months ago to drive him almost 1,000 miles from Bull River Falls to Clear Lake, Iowa so he could visit the cornfield where Buddy Holly and Ritchie Valens perished in a plane crash in 1959. When I refused, he had a fit and locked himself in his Hummer and played *La Bamba* non stop and full blast for three hours.

Chaz's relentless quest for musical inspiration is twisted. After reading Saint Augustine's "City of God," he excitedly quoted a passage in which the 4th century theologian mentions certain performers of his day who had "…such command of their bowels, that they can break wind continuously at will, so as to produce the effect of singing."

Wind instruments now have a brand new meaning for me and I'll never listen to another Benny Goodman clarinet solo in the quite the same way.

Now close your eyes and imagine a whole troupe of these performing flatulists, "*fartistes*," as the French would call them, marching backwards down the street during a boisterous New Orleans Mardi Gras parade. What a joyful sound they would make.

Chaz the Gopher King told me that in the 1200s in England, one "Roland the Farter" was the entertainment headliner at the court of King Henry II each year at Christmas. Those Brits: always on the cutting edge of music.

If only Dr. Galenus, M.D. could have known how wrong he was about the difference between his fellow human beings and animals, who know more than we think they know.

When I met with Chaz in Alberta he was sitting alone on a small wooden bench beneath a tree on the road to town where the bus shuttle stopped each evening to take workers to the oil fields.

It was the only tree for miles and miles and I don't know which looked more lonely…Chaz or the tree.

We sat and talked for a while. The wind blew. The kind of blustery and unrelenting weather that made pioneers go crazy in Willa Cather's novels. It was like Nebraska, except much colder, the icy gusts blowing swirls of gritty dirt that made us both squint as we spoke there on the bench in the middle of god damn nowhere.

Chaz looked depressed, and for the first time I noticed a slight streak of gray fur on the back of his head. When he pointed over at a field of parked construction vehicles his paw trembled and he quickly dropped his arm into his lap.

"What's wrong?" I asked. "You don't look right."

Chaz stared out across the Canadian prairie moonscape and gave a long sigh.

He said he'd done everything he could to sabotage the oil fields in order to establish his new colony. He put Nutella and oatmeal into the gas tanks of every truck he could find. He scattered nails onto the highway, smeared Brylcream hair oil on the access ladders of cell phone towers, hacked into a PA system so it played an endless refrain from Puff the Magic Dragon and packed cow manure into fracking hoses on a submersible pumping rig so the poop heated to 400-degrees and exploded.

He shredded the tires on tailings dozers and he and his commandos once loosened the bucket bolts on a giant hydraulic rope shovel vehicle, sending tons of toxic overburden onto the main highway that supplied the mining operation. He cut power to cafeteria freezers and attacked the local office of the Royal Mounted Police one night and packed their tall black boots with Cool Whip.

But nothing was working.

Chaz adjusted his iPhone ear buds and I asked him what he was listening to.

"John Coltrane," he said. "The *Giant Steps* album, nineteen-fifty-nine, I think. How's my book going, by the way?"

Chaz was referring to his autobiography, *My Life Underground*, a ridiculous 875-page effort of aimless meandering which I am now reluctantly editing.

"I think the entire chapter on Francisco Coronado and your ancestors following him from Mexico has to go. And the thing about making bombs from corn syrup, that too. And the sex scenes…it's just too much. Nobody's going to believe anything with the trampoline and the petroleum jelly."

Chaz gave me a lame smile, the only sign of life I'd seen in him all day. "That's what you think."

Still, I sensed there was something seriously wrong with Chaz. I asked him about the money I'd sent to the Gopher King's second-in-command, the wise old prairie dog named Jools, who served as the coterie's comptroller and financial boss.

Chaz coughed and spit and picked at one of his big yellow front teeth with one claw. He poked my arm as we both watched a dust devil spin across the empty black asphalt highway.

"Jools dropped dead yesterday," he said. "And I need to tell you something."

CHAPTER 65

Jools was one of Chaz's equally ancient cousins, and though not gifted with the Gopher King's powers he also was exposed in the 1940s to Plutonium-239 at Alamogordo, New Mexico while the government was secretly making the first atom bomb.

Like Chaz, he seemed immune to whatever usually kills wild prairie dogs before they are five years old. Jools was 74.

Chaz's second-in-command was in charge of the colony's increasingly complex finances, including the G.K. Rodenthouse Foundation, which he helped me devise in order to account for the Bellyache Mountain coterie's vast storehouse of gold. He introduced me to Japanese bitcoins, with which I make the Gopher King's bigger purchases: Harley-Davidson motorcycles, grotesquely large TVs, professional grade cappuccino machines, other showy and unnecessary kitchen appliances…that sort of thing.

Jools had an odd, left-swooping part in his hair and walked with a tilting limp, thanks to his encounter with the Honda lawn aerator at the Gold Gulch Golf Course. I liked him. He didn't care for me.

The gopher bean counter's sudden death put Chaz into a dark and depressed funk, and he was doubly upset when he realized the accommodations at the Alberta, Canada prairie dog colony were inadequate for a proper funeral. He wanted Jools to have the usual jet fly over, the uniformed honor guard of Uzi-toting commandos and the ritual paid mourners dressed like drunken barmaids who perform Serbian folk dances around the coffin while gulping shots of 110-proof slivovitz plum brandy. Tradition is very important to the Gopher King.

So I shipped Jools' corpse home by UPS in a corrugated plastic box with instructions to keep him on ice for a while.

I didn't want to leave the Gopher King alone after such a tragic event, so I had an idea.

"Let's take a trip," I told Chaz. "You always wanted to see the ocean, right?"

He looked at me and blinked.

"Malibu," I said. "We'll rent a place for a couple days. You can listen to Beach Boys songs and that Linda Ronstadt CD you've been raving about. Wiggle your toes in the sand. Sort things out. You need a rest. We both do."

Money wasn't a problem, of course. I'd brought along the Foundation's debit card and explained we could probably gift money to a worthy California charity and call it a business trip.

Chaz blinked again and grinned faintly. "Can I dig holes in the sand?"

I patted Chaz's walnut-shaped little head. "Of course. All the holes and tunnels you want."

So I rented an enormous beach house on Airbnb, booked a non stop first class red eye flight and arranged for the most expensive rental car I could find at LAX. On the way to the airport in Edmonton I bought a $1,250 leather Louis Vuitton pet carryall ("…with cocoa-brown fabric interior and leather trim") and instructed Chaz to keep his mouth shut when the TSA asked what breed of creature I was hauling on board.

He blinked at me from behind the heavily monogrammed canvas bag's mesh window.

"Just don't say I'm your pet," he said.

On the plane I leaned the Vuitton bag against the window so Chaz could watch the clouds float by. The Gopher King couldn't control his bowels during the trip, of course, and I guess it was because he was so excited about seeing the ocean and going on a bus tour of movie star homes in Beverly Hills.

The one hour drive along the Pacific Coast Highway fascinated him. He didn't make a sound, and he pooped only once. I looked inside the bag as we passed the Venice Beach turn-off and he had on his ear buds and was mouthing the breezy lyrics to *Ventura Highway*, swaying contentedly on his hind paws, squinting at the blue Pacific swells and beachy scenery like a rodent Buddhist who has just been admitted through nirvana's golden gates.

It was blazing hot outside when we arrived at the beach house, where a hipster surfer snark wearing giant Maui Jim designer sun glasses and a white linen suit jacket met me at the front steps and handed over the key. He looked at the Vuitton bag and fanned his face with one hand and asked what I had in there.

"A pet," I said and heard a howling screech from inside the bag.

"Dude, that thing stinks."

The house was enormous. Like living in the lobby of the Ritz-Carlton. The zillion-thread-count bedsheets were embroidered with Egyptian tomb script, and where most people would sit and eat breakfast stood a giant lacquered white table with 16 chairs, more suited for a United Nations conference room than toast and a bowl of Cheerios. The expansive window facing the beach was the size of a Macy's store window, and outside on the massive teak patio deck sat a stainless steel 10-burner grill and two lounge chairs, one of which called to me by name…and so I plopped myself down.

It had been an exhausting trip and the abrupt change from blustery and cold Alberta to palm trees made my head spin. By now Chaz was squeak-barking and clawing loudly inside the bag and so I let him loose. He spent a few minutes sniffing around and then hopped in my lap and we both stared contentedly out at the ocean, where a guy and his dog were bobbing on a surfboard like a cork, waiting for another wave to come in. The Gopher King soon fell asleep there on the sunny deck and so did I. It was dusk when I woke with my face on fire, and when I screamed Chaz jumped up and screamed too and then fell twenty feet off the deck and onto the sand, where he ran in circles like a crazed rat, crapping like a fool until he tipped up his rear end and started digging madly.

I found a tube of 100+ SPF sun tan lotion, strong enough for summer on Mars, and smeared my face. Greased up, I must have looked like an escapee from a hospital burn ward because when Chaz emerged from his sandy Malibu beach burrow he took one look at me and yelped and disappeared back underground.

Inside, I checked out the fully stocked double door fridge. Again, it was industrial sized and packed with every variety of sushi this side of Tokyo, along with a whole rack of imported beers and funny looking plastic tubs of gluten free veggie dips and exotic sauces and God knows what else those people eat out there. I shoved aside labeled containers of stuffed clams in lemon foam, seared Wagyu tenderloin, razor clams in daikon sauce and a baggie filled with octopus parts arranged on lollypop sticks. I looked under a tray of Maldavian long line caught yellow fin tuna. Next to a hunk of Turkish hazelnut crumble cake sat a fat tomato impaled on a toothpick carrying a sign that said, "These are Heritage!"

I looked for the Slim Jims and Fritos and bean dip and beef jerky and something truly carbonated and sugary but sadly there was none. Not a drip of ketchup or hot sauce. Not a potato chip.

It was like the satanic beach barbarians of the apocalypse had stormed a dystopian Food Network TV studio to stock their waterfront zombie fort and culinary torture chamber with the last of the world's expensive and pretentious inedibles.

I stood there and reluctantly ate what I found and drank beer and belched and soothed my blistered face in the cold air of the open fridge door like a starving midnight insomniac.

I walked back outside carrying an armload of crab and cucumber rolls and tiny kelp sandwiches, one of which I handed to Chaz, whereupon he barfed explosively and started clawing at his mouth with one paw.

The Gopher King stared out at the beach, now draped in a honey sunset light. The guy and his dog were still out there, two silhouettes bobbing in the ocean.

"There's no grass here," Chaz said and pointed at the sky. "And there's too many birds. I don't like big birds."

"It's a beach," I said. "And those are seagulls."

"I don't like this place."

"Suit yourself," I said and stepped inside and watched old Dragnet re runs on the 110-inch TV for a while. Later I heard a commotion outside. Chaz was jumping up at a dive-bombing seagull who was feasting on the sushi leftovers.

The Gopher King never set foot inside the house, but instead spent three days underground in a beach burrow that kept caving in on his head. We never toured Beverly Hills. We never saw Universal City. I never showed Chaz the Roxie on Hollywood Boulevard, where I paid only $3.50 to see Bob Marley sing in 1976. He would have liked that.

And so we departed Malibu in our rented Mercedes E-Class sedan, Chaz still the moody rodent as when we left the cold Canadian prairie. No amount of dreamy California sun and surf was going to cure this sad gopher.

On the way to the airport I decided I wanted real food, so I took a detour in Los Angeles and stopped at Pink's hot dog stand off La Brea Avenue to get a chili cheese dog. I asked if they could wrap the thing in bacon but they refused.

Chaz was sleeping soundly in his posh portable leather castle in the back seat when I took a wrong turn off the freeway and ended up lost in a neighborhood where most of the cars were parked at odd angles on the front lawn. Creeping along in the rented black Mercedes so I could read the street signs, I found myself in a dead end alley where two large human beings in hoodies suddenly appeared in my headlights.

When I tried to turn the car around, one of the men hitched up his sagging sweat pants and revealed the shiny barrel of a pistol stuck in the waist band.

The two men then began walking toward the car.

"This isn't good," I said out loud. "This is not good at all."

CHAPTER 66

I was enjoying my dripping chili cheese dog when I took that wrong turn off the freeway into a neighborhood that reminded me of a dystopian novel. It was a scene from a dark, abandoned world: a convenience store with tree saplings growing from an asphalt parking lot, where a half-crushed Dodge Dart sat nosed against where they'd covered the front door and windows with plywood. A skinny half naked man in flip flops sat drinking from a paper sack and he raised his desiccated arm to wish me well as I drove slowly past, searching for a street sign that might point me back to the southbound 405. Cars sat parked on weedy front lawns. Newspapers and filthy paper cups blew down the dimly lit street. Cats howled from behind dead bushes draped with torn plastic Dollar Store bags that fluttered in a hot breeze.

Chaz kept up his gurgling sleep apnea song from the back seat, stirring once in a while in his little bed within the confines of the $1,250 leather Louis Vuitton pet carryall, which I'd also charged to the Foundation's debit card. The fat tab for this trip — the fancy rental car, the fully-stocked beach house, the last-minute first class flight tickets, had cost thousands, give or take a few extravagant curios Chaz wanted me to purchase at the Universal Studios gift shop.

When I tried to turn the car around, one of the large men in hoodies reached for the shiny pistol stuck into the waist band of his sagging sweatpants and ran toward me. The other man, the largest, sprinted ahead and slammed both hands on the car hood and then made a twirling motion with his hand, indicating I should roll down the window.

I stupidly did.

I tried to ask for directions.

"What's in the trunk?" the man said. "Open up the trunk."

I figured I'd smile at him for a while so he would go away, but that never works.

"Open the trunk."

Meanwhile, the other guy walked a long, slow circle around the car. He studied the license plate. He stooped and noticed the pet carryall in the back seat.

"Luggage," he told his friend, who reached inside the unlocked back door and took out the Louis Vuitton bag.

"Nice," he said. "What else is in the trunk? Open the trunk."

You'd think a pricey black Mercedes sedan would have a convenient interior button with which to pop the trunk. I pressed a button at random and my seat violently jacked my head into the roof. Another button and the side windows mysteriously darkened. I looked around and pushed another button and the gas tank door swung open. The wipers turned on.

I gave a lame grin. "It's a rental car."

"Tourist," the biggest guy said.

"I took a wrong turn and…"

"Open up the trunk. Let me see what you got in the trunk."

He was covered in tattoos. Starbursts and crimson hearts, lightening bolts and cubes filled with slogans written in unreadable gothic letters. Triangles and circles and snarling dogs with flashing canines and serpents slithering alongside his muscular neck where another whole paragraph of cryptic script raced south across his bare chest like the text of a riddle written by drunken Masonic wizards that explained the world's coming doom and destruction.

The other man examined the pet carryall where Chaz the Gopher king still lay curled up and sleeping. I heard faint muttering from inside the bag. The man began to carefully unzip the bag.

"Whew!" he said, fanning his face with a hand crowded with gemstone rings connected to each digit by a gleaming silver chain. "You got something dead in there?"

"Laundry and stuff," I said.

The other man, apparently familiar with the trunk button on an over-priced German luxury automobile, reached inside and pushed away my leg and pulled a tiny lever next to the rug mat.

He rifled through my duffel bag and pulled out the giant Godzilla movie poster and the plastic souvenir Oscar statues. He examined the commemorative Hollywood snow globes and pitched one down the street, where it skittered and exploded against the curb. Dogs started barking.

He took out the Marilyn Monroe salt & pepper shaker set and put it into the pocket of his hoodie.

"Gimme your wallet," he said. "And your phone."

I sputtered: "Look, this is…"

"Gimme the damn motherfuckin' phone," he said and pulled out the pistol.

I gave him my temporary burner 2002 Samsung flip phone and the man examined it closely as if I'd handed him an antique 1903 Thomas Edison phonograph.

"You kidding me?"

"It's a political statement," I said and pointed at the weapon in the man's hand.

Now I started babbling: "Ah…a Glock G-17," I said. "You know, I don't like the trigger, but it's better than most striker-fired pistols. I don't like the grip handle, either, and the trigger safety…wow, it makes me nervous."

"Shut up."

He hit me with a left uppercut and then slapped my face with a sideways swipe of the pistol barrel, and I collapsed cross-eyed into a strange yoga sitting position there in the street, legs folded under me like an old disheveled, bleeding hippie acolyte who'd smoked too much happy gas at the Ashram. My Chicago Cubs hat slid off my head and fell into my lap.

And then Chaz woke up.

"Stop," said the squeaky helium party balloon voice from inside the Louis Vuitton bag. And then the Gopher King's furry head appeared, the red star on his black military beret catching the soft glow of the Mercedes' headlamp.

The guy with the pistol had already cocked his arm to give me another wallop when Chaz sleepily crawled out of the bag and stood there scratching his crotch — all eight inches of him, dressed in camo fatigues, the silk neck scarf, his shined paratrooper boots bloused mid-calf like he'd just graduated from 82nd Airborne school at Ft. Benning.

Chaz spoke calmly: "Put down the gun, Mister Saggypants."

The man with the Glock pistol turned to his partner and smiled. "He got a hamster," he said. "He got a tame pet hamster."

The other guy disagreed: "That's no hamster. That's a damn gerbil."

"Maybe he got him a chipmunk," the guy with the pistol said. "And he's wearing clothes."

Both men stared at me.

I tried to speak and explain why he shouldn't use the word "pet," but my lips were already swollen together.

"How come your pet be dressed in people clothes?"

The two men started to laugh.

Chaz ran to the first man and gnawed his ankle, then did a smooth Olympic backflip and landed on the hood of the Mercedes, from which he vaulted onto Mr. Saggypants' shoulder. The guy started screaming and twisting back and forth and when the pistol dropped to the street I reached out with one rubbery leg and kicked the weapon into the gutter. More dogs started barking and then a few neighborhood porch lights turned on. Cats yowled.

Chaz jumped from one man to the other, gnawing at their faces, clawing his way up and down their backs. When the guy who'd pistol whipped me took a swing at the Gopher King his over-sized sweat pants fell down and pooled around his ankles. He tried to tug them up, and that's when it happened.

I'd seen it so many times before. Once, Chaz shrunk an Angus bull to the size of a poodle. Another time he'd miniaturized a pallet of Cheezos at COSTCO to the size of a lunch box. When he needed a new Chinook helicopter he and his commandos just headed to the Colorado Air National Guard hangar at the airport. It was his greatest and most magical gift and Chaz was usually careful with this power to shrink any living or inanimate object. But he was angry now and I could see there was no stopping him.

Both men took out their knives and started swinging them back and forth in wide arcs as they chased Chaz, who was still leaping and biting and doing gymnastic backflips like a hairy little Errol Flynn on a pirate ship.

The Gopher King stood his ground and when the first man approached, Chaz reached out with a single claw and touched the man's shoe. There was the familiar glow, then the throbbing corona of pale blue vapor encircling the man's face. I heard a muffled groan that grew higher and higher in pitch as the man began to get smaller, his pants already at his ankles. There came a final windmilling of the arms and then the formerly six-foot-five tattooed big shot with the Glock G-17 was the size of a Ken Doll. Except for the badly fitted bright red Converse Chuck Taylor sneakers, he was now dressed only in those blue boxer shorts. And when he started cussing and jumped up and down you couldn't understand a word he said because it sounded like the fast-forward lyrics of an Alvin and the Chipmunks song.

The other man was already running away down the street, one hand clutching the back of his sagging pants as he shouted terrified blood oaths over his shoulder. Two growling pit bulls began to chase him down a dark alley.

Chaz calmly walked over to his tiny victim, with whom he now stood eye-to-eye, and gave him a flat-handed slap to the side of the face.

"You better go hide," he said to the man. "Before a cat eats you."

On the way to LAX we stopped at a convenience store and I bought a package of frozen peas for my swollen face. We didn't say a word until I suggested to Chaz that he hop back into the pet carryall before we dropped off the car and walked through the airport.

"Don't make any weird noises," I said.

"So you keep telling me," Chaz said.

"I just don't want any trouble."

"We've already had trouble."

"That guy," I said. "He'll be full sized in a few hours, like usual?"

"Most of him," Chaz said.

"What's that mean?"

Chaz smiled at me from inside the plush Vuitton pet carryall bag with the cocoa brown fabric interior and imported leather trim.

"Like I said. He'll be okay, but certain parts just won't be right. They'll stay small."

"Nice touch," I said.

"I want to go home now," the Gopher King said as we stepped onto the crowded escalator that was headed toward the security gate, where the TSA guy was already staring at my busted purple face.

"What's in the bag?" he said. "Open the bag."

CHAPTER 67

The mayor of Bull River Falls embarked on a violent binge of annihilation, mindlessly destroying prairie dog towns with the fierceness of King Henry VIII's dissolution of English monasteries in the 16th Century.

They back-hoed. They detonated and burned. They poisoned and flooded with such blind determination that when Chaz and I returned from our beach nightmare in Malibu the Bellyache Mountain coterie of revolutionary gophers had been reduced by half.

Those who remained — haggard and starving, most living in desperate squalor at the abandoned gold mine south of town, their COSTCO supplies of stolen food reduced to a few bags of Fritos and a single giant three-jar pack of Extra Creamy Jiffy peanut butter — were however still heavily armed.

When I arrived at the Gopher King's subterranean war bunker, an impenetrable chunk of reinforced concrete any Egyptian pharaoh would envy, Chaz was sitting in his leather recliner watching a TV infomercial called, "The Best Steam Mop Ever!" He was simultaneously reading a political blog on his laptop and typing comments using the fingertip claw pads I had designed for him so he could communicate with the digital world.

The article, written by a guy who likely spoke with a long-voweled and plummy New England accent, was 3.6 paragraphs long and Chaz asked me to read it.

"You want my opinion?" I asked.

"You're the only human being I know."

I explained that I thought the article was a crudely and self-righteous series of purposely obscure cosmic statements assembled into a pretentious galaxy of gassy word farts designed to be inhaled by people who are unable to read anything longer than a Tweet or Facebook post.

"This is garbage," I said.

"I thought so," the Gopher King said, and he showed me the comments he wanted to submit to the blog author, a rambling mishmash of hate-fueled vulgarities and psychotic insults, none of which made much sense.

"Who is Ziggy Monkeyface?" I asked.

"That's me," Chaz said. "It's my screen name."

"If you're going to call somebody a sonofabitch, at least use proper punctuation," I said. "That's my only suggestion. Otherwise it's a very fine letter."

Chaz tapped the return button with one claw, closed the laptop and looked at the TV, where a lady in a sparkly cocktail dress was swabbing the inside of a filthy cat litter box with a steaming mop that looked like an upside down one-legged Raggedy Anne doll.

"I have to get one of those," he said.

Then a heavily armed gopher commando wearing a Duck Dynasty do rag came rushing in, saluted crisply, and handed Chaz a message.

Apparently there was a stand-off over at the Gold Gulch Golf Course. A group of town road and bridge department employees were being held at bay, surrounded by a battalion of angry rats who were armed with shoulder-mounted missiles, M-60s, and the usual assortment of mortar and grenade launchers and a seemingly limitless supply of ammunition that had survived destruction.

Chaz strapped on his twin Rugers. Someone handed him a new black beret. He stooped to blouse his paratrooper pants and then turned to me and asked: "Would you like to be a soldier again?"

"Does duck snot taste awful?"

"What does that mean?" Chaz said.

"It's like saying, 'do bears crap in the woods'?"

"Of course they do," Chaz said.

"Exactly," I said.

Chaz twisted his face and scratched his head. "Where else would a bear take a dump?"

"Ask me again," I said.

Chaz thought a moment, then said: "Do you want to join our band of revolutionary brethren and abandon your hopeless and piteously mundane and pointless existence in favor of a life filled with honor, glory and the pursuit of truth and …"

I immediately said: "Is the atomic weight of Cobalt 58.9?"

"Ghost Busters. The line from Ghost Busters!"

"Exactly," I said.

Chaz aimed his Uzi and sprayed a semi-circle of 9mm bullet holes in front of my feet.

And then, using the same magical powers he employs to miniaturize an M4 Sherman tank, he shrunk me to the size of a cereal box.

We stepped into a waiting Blackhawk attack helicopter, the rotor wash blowing off my Chicago Cubs cap as I strapped myself into the canvas bench seat next to the Gopher King, who was frantically issuing orders into his helmet mouthpiece. I watched my cap blow sideways off a cliff as we lifted off, the aircraft banking left to assume its position at the head of a squadron of a dozen other choppers. Four cargo Chinooks joined us in flanking pairs, each filled with helmeted gophers dressed in full assault gear. Far off above the horizon two A-10 Warthog attack aircraft were heading this way to join us.

Chaz handed me a chest pack, its pouches filled with M-16 NATO rounds stolen from the Air National Guard station. A holstered .45 pistol hung from a hook on the wall and I strapped that on, along with two extra ammo belts I looped over one shoulder. I looked like an army surplus store thief, but I didn't care. Sound doesn't travel well at altitude and though I was surrounded by all that flying hardware everything seemed surprisingly muffled and silent as we headed south toward the golf course.

Below lay the town; the darkly coursing river, the gray gypsum hills. The Blackhawk approached a sheer rock wall as we banked over Dora McCoy's ranch. I saw her truck parked next to the barn, white laundry fluttering from a rope that ran between the house and the tool shed where the old lady kept her riding tack. The lake appeared, and next to it the smoking ruins of the prairie dog town. The earth everywhere was scarred and tilled. They had scooped up a pile of the dead and the tiny brown bodies lay next to a dump truck overflowing with gopher corpses.

Chaz tapped my helmet and signaled that I should turn on my radio.

"They're burning them over at the county dump," he said, pointing down where I could see the tiny shadows of our aircraft as the squadron circled and headed for where the surviving gophers were making their stand on a mesa north of town.

Chaz lifted the camo-patterned 8x30 military binoculars to his face. These things cost $300, but they're free if you know where the UPS trucks park overnight at the Bull River Falls interstate rest stop every Wednesday evening. The Gopher King's furry hands trembled in anger as he studied the devastating scene below.

"Boss, you okay?" I said.

"Nope. I'm not."

CHAPTER 68

Glass melts at 900-degrees, aluminum at 1,000. Copper at 2,000, while a hot wildfire burns at a toasty 1,100-degrees. This was a hot fire.

At the Incident Commander's office I was handed a scrap of campfire junk they'd found near a trailhead.

"You should see this," one of Gus Curry's men said, pointing at the dented top of a metal screw cap.

He fished out something else from a folded rag.

"And this," he said, handing me the clump of melted metal. "Takes a lot of hot sauce to do this to copper."

I drove up a bulldozed road and fishtailed through a patch of spilled slurry. Vehicles were parked ahead: school buses, the big airport fire truck, flatbed trailers and tenders and pea-green U.S. Forest Service SUVs.

I thought of Carmen's planned trip to her beloved Indian fence. She'd promised to check with one of the trailhead crews before going far into the active fire zone. She needed permission to enter the National Forest but her county credentials might be enough to get her past the check-point.

"Don't worry. I'll call when I get there," she said while loading her Jeep in the county building parking lot. "Stan, you said yourself the fire line was a mile away from that spot. Don't be such a worry wort."

"Nobody knows where that thing is moving," I said. "Could have traveled twice that much since last night. In any direction. I'm just concerned."

"If it did, I'm sure I'll be told," she said. "This is important to me."

She waved and drove away. I had a bad feeling.

At the command post I changed into my gear inside a borrowed Gold Gulch construction trailer. Smoke rose behind the camp like a hanging black bed sheet. Two slurry bombers flew a tandem approach and banked away in opposite directions, followed by a formation of National Guard Black Hawks.

I grabbed coffee from the trailer and tried to remember if I'd taken my pill. I checked to make sure the bottle was in my shirt pocket.

With the crew I marched to where the backhoes were digging a trench. Higher up the hill the sawyers were clearing trees, their whining chainsaws louder than anything else on the mountain.

I squatted and studied a topo map and followed my group past a four-foot-high suppressing berm. My knees were throbbing. I hailed Gus Curry on my walkie.

Curry said: "Tankers are supposed to come over in twenty minutes, then we'll head due south of you."

"Did Carmen ever show?"

"I didn't see her," Curry said. "Left word with the boys, though. She was spotted driving up the lower access road. She shouldn't be here."

"Seems the BLM gave her the okay yesterday, but I wish they would have checked with you first."

"Feds. You know how that tune goes," Curry said.

The radio faded out. I lifted my arm and waited for the man at the far end of the fire line to raise his pulaski, the signal that the crew was properly lined up.

And then everything began to happen quickly.

I thought the blaze might follow the drift of the wind to the tree line where it would starve itself of fuel on the bare rocks of a long cliff that poked from the ridge. But it wasn't happening. The fire continued to burn in the most unexpected places and in unlikely patches that seemed to be driven not by wind but by the convenient availability of overgrown tinder that hadn't been thinned in decades. I remembered how a few years ago the county had pushed for a controlled burn in this same area, but the feds said they were busy elsewhere. A few townies protested that the burn would destroy old growth timber and scar the mountainside, and I always thought they were the ones who killed the idea.

I'd heard the spotter report that morning. The blaze had broken into pieces that seemed to be burning free-form in all directions. I hoped it hadn't turned toward the wrong side of the Last Chance Ranch, where Carmen's Indian fence was located.

I unclipped my walkie and hailed anyone on the open channel: "This one is all over the map," I said. "There's no leading edge at all. Any good news up there?"

Curry's voice replied faintly through static:

"That you?" he said. "The powers that be want the jumpers on the hill. We need ground pounders in the valley. That's where you should be headed. They want to keep the fire from getting at the lodge. Orders."

"Whose orders?"

"Doesn't matter," Curry said. "This isn't a democracy, you know that."

"Seems it would be smarter to backfire further up the hill," I insisted.

"Just keep it away from the lodge. You sure you're okay tagging along with those kids? I know I asked you to help but I didn't mean for you to be a grunt."

"If my knees give out I'll head back," I said. "So who gave those orders? You never answered me."

"Look, a county commissioner called a congressman who called the Secretary of the Interior and he called the governor and he called the county manager and he called the district manager — my boss. The turds rolled downhill from there, right into my lap. I'm not sure you'll see a pumper for the rest of the day. But I told those boys with you to keep the fire from crowning in the valley trees. With all that equipment parked next to the friggin' lodge and the fuel stored down there, I think it'll blow awfully bad."

I screamed into the walkie.

"Those pricks at Gold Gulch were told to move their diesel tanks last week!"

"I'm just the miserable messenger, Stan."

"Three thousand gallons of accelerant sitting there and..."

"I know, I know," Curry said. "Sorry. I'm cutting out..."

I kicked up dirt and looked to make sure I could still see the crew. The trail was a tunnel of smoke, the sky black, the tops of trees vanishing. The pines were burning like lit wicks and the needle-packed forest floor was a carpet of hot coals, glowing in the murky ash. The fire had feasted on peripheral fuel and doubled back on itself and then somehow continued to burn. I had never seen anything like it.

The fire was headed toward the valley, pushed by a wind that had broken away from an unexpected cold front. Heat thermals had sliced the wind in half like you would change the flow of air in a room with a hair dryer. The freak breeze had kicked the fire back on itself, and the men now worked with the twisting blaze sneakily chasing them, threatening to crown in the trees alongside the trail.

The resort's storage yard was only a quarter mile away, where those thousands of gallons of diesel sat in wheeled tanks like three portable bombs just waiting to ignite.

The fire didn't even have to reach the yard; the peripheral heat alone could blow up everything.

The wall of fire was a hundred feet high and two miles wide, a wedge of flames traveling like a glowing plow blade. The blaze had likely encircled the Last Chance Ranch and was being sucked directly into the grassy valley that sloped toward the town.

The crew moved at a half trot keep their ten-meter intervals. The very edge of Bull River Falls appeared behind the smoke. Two helicopters dipped their bags into the river, one aircraft rising to return to the fire while the other waited to refill its canvas bucket. I heard the growl of a pumper truck and the low rumble of a crushing tanker plane. The falling slurry rattled in the trees like sand.

The blaze defied customary physics, thanks to the lay of the valley and its quirky winds. The fire was bouncing, lifting and crowning in the pinetops before dropping to lick up fuel only to rise into the trees again, gaining speed as it grew.

This kind of fire was hardest to kill because it traveled along no predictable fuel path. You could only guess where to dig or where the flames would jump to next. It was as if a torch wielded by a giant was blowing wildly down from the sky.

I heard men yelling, and when I turned I saw one of the crew step into a stump hole and hop out and slap away the coals that clung to the back of his leg. He danced a jig and returned to the hole and raked it with the pulaski.

"Cover that thing good!" I screamed at the man, a rookie who'd been inspecting smoke alarms in town just a week before and had never been in a wildfire. They'd shown him a training video, given him a shake-and-bake course at the airport and then issued him his yellows.

We reached a campground, where the soil was packed hardscrabble. This is where everyone decided to take a rest.

A burned RV sat on charred wheel rims in the middle of a black field. The top of one of the resort's water hookups had been busted off and the broken pipe was spouting feebly. The men filled their canteens from it.

I thought if they could perhaps trench a perimeter and try to slow the fire and turn it from the cedars that grew at the edge of the campground, it might slow things down. But if the fire had enough strength it could surely take another leap, and from there it would be a clear shot to the resort's storage yard.

If those diesel tanks ignited, the super-heated air would lift the explosive mist above the trees, the wind spreading the flames like an enormous aerosol blowtorch toward the town.

I had no sympathy for the lodge. I did not care if the multi-million dollar building burned down. But there were homes nearby, the new subdivision that began a few hundred yards from the resort's front gate. Once the blaze took hold in the bunch grass flats and fallow meadow hay left from when the property was ranch land, the town itself would be an easy target.

I walked the trail, my knees throbbing as I tried to keep up with the younger men. I called out and waved everybody into a circle. I kneeled and stabbed the rocky soil with my pulaski.

"This is it right here," I said, marking where the fire was. "I think it's wise to make sure your safety tents are ready. If you see the sonofabitch skip into the trees I want you to run down-wind and down-hill. Don't stay grouped together. Keep those separations. We have a chance to dig around this thing, but not a good chance. I just want you to know. Just give me a straight trench across the road you came down, just beyond the cedars. We know what kind of fuel is down there and this thing needs to be starved. If it all turns to shit, then just run your ass off. Downhill, remember. You won't be able to see anything, so let your feet do the thinking. Just follow the ground. Questions?"

The circle of sooty yellow helmets nodded.

From the river, red embers lifted from trees that seemed to hang suspended in the smoke. I watched my feet and tried to walk on the slippery riverbank stones, the cobbles covered with wet ash. A dirty spray lifted in the wind.

Carmen would be somewhere below here, on the south slope, past the Gold Gulch equipment yard and beyond yesterday's trench line.

That morning I'd had seen the spotter report that showed the fire moving wildly in no known direction, so Carmen wouldn't have a clue she was in danger.

The blaze seemed different today. It was vibrant, almost buoyant. I knew the fire had long ago consumed the oxygen at its center. The vacuum that now remained was desperate for any air it could get, for the fire at that spot was starving. The smoke above the fire's red heart had appeared to us all on the trail like shreds of black wool hanging from the sky, churning in tall spinning columns of thermal wind that rose hundreds of feet above the mountainside. Everybody in the rookie crew had stopped and stared at it. None of them had ever seen such a thing in any training video.

By now I was certain everybody in town could see it, too.

The feds closed off fifty square miles of air space to commercial traffic. They'd locked down the interstate for a dozen miles east and west of the town, causing stalled traffic in both directions that reached to the county's borders.

The air above the forest was heated past the point where ignition could occur, so when the grateful blaze found any oxygen at all it would instantly became hot enough to melt metal. Wood, even untouched green trees within fifty yards of the fire's licking tongue, was no match for such heat. The fire, igniting at will and without any recognizable pattern, now burst into an explosion of ash so quickly that it speared upward into the rising smoke it had itself created.

From a distance the fire was a chemistry spectrum chart; dazzling white and hot yellow at ground-level, above that a cooler orange, then red in a curtained layer below the fresh black carbon smoke.

I understood why the fire now appeared in reverse, a mirror image; the blaze itself rising while the lazy, cooler smoke remained below like the top of an upside down barstool. Few in this young crew, I knew, had seen anything like it except during training class slide shows or in the three-ring government binders the Forest Service issued at its spring certification class.

The fire was inventing itself over and over again, rolling greedily as the conflagration followed a natural vacuum across the mountain to search for more things to eat. Tendrils swung from the tops of trees like yellow rope. Like smoke from a giant chimney, the afterburst of bloated clouds boiled still higher and followed the contours of its own thermal column as it searched for richer air. Whenever the fire managed to find its food the smoke appeared tellingly as if it had been pierced with holes that were as bright as red paint.

That stark cherry color is what 1,000-degrees looks like.

A fire that has begun such a new life creates its own wind, and so the blaze began to manufacture a square mile of custom weather in the middle of a calm, windless day.

In the valley behind me things remained deceptively ordinary, with light breezes from the south, while on the trail where the crew now walked it was as gusty as an ocean gale.

I hoped the weather might change, but where the flames were making their own wind I knew such a wish had terrible odds.

The crew was behind me, and when we joined up at the river I took a few of them back up the hill. Carmen had been seen driving along one of the service roads that had been declared safe behind yesterday's perimeter. I shouldn't have trusted the earlier report.

The fire began to work its way to where it had already burned, leaping across two hundred yards of black grass that had taken a slurry drop. A sheet of Halloween-colored flames bowed twenty feet over my head and as I crouched and flattened myself, I felt the heat swipe along the length of my body like the caress of a giant hot hand. The flame then aimed itself into a patch of beetle-killed lodgepole pines that had been standing dead and dry for years. Within seconds the entire grove crowned and exploded. I felt the percussion in my feet.

That afternoon the fire doubled in size.

You could hear the deep explosions thundering. Like an artillery onslaught of Howitzers pounding a distant enemy position.

Flames washed toward the crew, forcing the men to leap unwisely into the few trees that had not yet burned. Most of the men — all in their twenties, all part-time volunteers and not eager to be left standing in the middle of all that fuel, were enveloped in superheated wind and ash, surrounded by trees that could spark at any moment. I knew they would not escape if the fire changed direction again.

There was nowhere else to run. We had used up our luck.

The two joined blazes continued to march toward Gold Gulch. The fuel tanks stood parked against a high rock wall that would force any blast directly toward where we were trapped in the pines.

Red spikes of fire formed on both sides of the trail as the cold air sank and pushed down the rising heat. A convecting wind, the kind you make when you open two windows at opposite ends of a house, flattened the fire for a while, compressing its heat. The fire then forced itself into the prevailing wind of the valley.

I waved my arms. The noise, a falsetto howl, made it impossible for the crew to hear anything. I motioned for everyone to take out their safety covers. The men gathered up, their yellow helmets touching like players in a crooked football huddle. A few of them fumbled with their foil covers, shrouding their heads while I made more crazy arm signals.

Behind us the fire lifted burning branches and broken chunks of tree bark and tossed the debris ahead of itself as if someone was angrily throwing lit torches from behind a moving barricade.

I counted heads, shouted instructions, and motioned for the crew to begin digging.

The men staggered away, their silver safety shelters bungied within reach outside their packs, and they began to spade the heated ground. The crowning fire, excited by the sudden abundance of trees, happily carried on as if it wasn't sure of which direction it should turn.

A helicopter passed loudly overhead, rotors thudding in a steady baritone. The air was moist, but I knew it was now too hot for the water falling from the chopper to reach the ground. It was also too late for the slurry tanker, which would not make a drop until it knew where the crew was located.

I heard strange voices shouting, though I knew all this noise from the fire made such a thing impossible. I felt the familiar weight filling my head, the voices louder. It was chattering nonsense; vaguely recognizable words, occasional whole phrases, like snips of disconnected conversation bouncing inside my skull. Like a madman with an audio tape playing things backwards. Slamming doors. Footsteps stomping up a staircase and then more indignant shouting. The rustle of fabric, gunfire, people arguing. A woman's scream. The crackle of underbrush beneath someone's booted feet. A shower of sparks fell on the trail and I cringed, thinking it was a mortar.

Pappas the radio man hollered my name. I saw the muzzle flashes of AK-47s firing at us.

One of the crew, only a few meters away, stumbled and fell while he was digging his line. A gust of wind blew his helmet off. At first he looked as if he was wearing unusually tight clothes and I wondered why he had taken off his yellow safety shirt. But then I saw that the man was naked except for the cuffs of his pants and his boots. The blowing fabric was his peeling skin. The heated wind was so strong, the flesh on his arm flapped like black linen and I saw white fat appear and then darken as ash blew onto the wound. The firefighter fell, his legs curling like he was preparing for sleep. Somebody came and dragged him away, and the two phantom shapes vanished into the smoke.

The fire rose above the forest in jubilation as it found more glorious air to eat.

I shouted for anyone within hearing distance.

I ran ahead and pulled a half dozen men together into another huddle.

"I'm heading for those fuel tanks!" I shouted, pointing toward where I vaguely knew the ski lodge might be. The closest man cupped his ear and shook his head. I pointed up the trail.

"Stay here!" I screamed into the side of the man's face and then flattened my hands and made a motion toward my feet. I dropped to one knee. The others did the same.

"I'm backfiring those tanks," I said.

One of the men silently mouthed the words: *fucking crazy.*

"You're right. Only something half crazy might fix this," I said as the others shuffled closer.

I kicked the duffy soil at my feet until I struck the hardpan mineral caliche. I smoothed this with my gloved hand. With a charred stick I scratched out the shape of two intersecting ovals. The men each wrapped themselves in their shelters and drew the safety foil close, cape-like, over their heads. Together they made a bumpy silver tent in which it seemed easier to hear and breath. Somebody took out a flashlight. I squatted and with the stick scraped a straight line through the center of the cartoon drawing.

"This is our trail," I said. "A hundred meters more and it hits the Last Chance Ranch property. You'll see the split-rail fence with all those No Trespassing signs, if it's not burned down. Over here, past the cattle guard, that's the Gold Gulch storage yard."

I made sure all of the men could see, pulling them by their shirts closer into the huddle. Embers and blowing dirt rattled against the foil tents and a hot gust of wind nearly blew us sideways.

"The water pipes are right next to the fence. They've been dead-headed. Just PVC. I saw it the other day. Knock off those caps and they'll twist right into the yard. Hopefully there's enough juice to piss on those trucks long enough for you boys to dig a line on the lee side just above it. Nothing fancy, just scratch away what you can and hope it holds for a while."

One of the men said, "Yeah, then what?"

Six filthy faces glared at me. The flashlight lit our heads like goblin masks.

"Me," I said. "I'm gonna' knock the shit out of those pipes and pray for water. Lots of it. My guess is they're pressurized to the max."

The men looked at each other. More shaking of heads.

Somebody shouted that there was two hundred meters of burning scrub oak between where we now were and the water pipes. Not much more than a narrow alley of flames to run through, if you could run at all. If you could move without falling head-first into a burning stump hole.

"Look, you boys need to cut a trench or the backfire won't work," I said, deepening the scratches into the dirt.

"There's no choice. I'm the only fucker who knows where the pipes are. If I have to show each of you and then we all take the time to get back and trench, then we're toast. It's the only way. We've got about a half hour before this place crowns and then this all has a clear path towards the town. Does everybody understand?"

Silence. There came the sound of another Black Hawk trying to make a water drop from above. The huddle of joined shelter tops heaved and rustled in the wind. A fine mist fell, settling onto the foil covers like a gentle drizzle. The men studied my dirt drawing, which now began to blow away. Somebody passed a canteen around.

"What about the tanks?" one of the men asked. "So you get them wet and then lay a backfire. Then what?"

"Is Ruxton here?" I said, looking around. A shape squeezed forward. A filthy young face pressed closer.

"Teddy, that you?" I said, grabbing the man's sleeve and pulling him closer. "You remember why I put your name in the newspaper back in high school? You were what? Seventeen?"

The man nodded. "I sort of..."

"You sort of hotwired a county Road and Bridge Department backhoe and drove it over to the baseball field and dug up home plate. You remember that stunt? Something about the coach kicking your ass off the team for smoking weed in the locker room."

"I guess, yeah." There was muffled laughter.

"Well, there's a Mini-Cat parked down there with an open switch ignition. Think you can remember those juvenile delinquent skills and fire up that baby and haul those tanks up the road? Just hitch them up. They all have tow cables. Not far, just a quarter mile or so upwind. Take somebody with you."

I looked around. "Any more questions?"

"Take two of us with you," one of the men said.

"There's two dozen water heads, and there's six of us. You do the math. It takes only one man with a pot to light that backfire, but I need the water to buy me time. You boys will be plenty busy digging the line."

They all gave a reluctant nod. I pulled down my goggles and stepped away. I was swallowed immediately by the smoke.

As I walked and tried to follow my feet I could hear my walkie chattering on my chest. I fumbled with it, and then the palm-sized radio dropped away into the dark. I ran.

The men in the crew cut their way through the timber and hiked to where they could see the storage yard below. They dug their line. They waited until they saw me standing a few hundred yards below them. I moved away behind the stands of burning trees and walked back and forth and kept the backfire burning. The wind flattened the fire and turned it toward where I had burned my line at the edge of the yard.

When the two fires — my artificial one and the flames of the larger blaze finally met, the joined wall of fire twisted and wobbled until it had nowhere to go. And so it turned backwards on itself, more powerful at first, but then it weakened and flattened. The men in the crew used this opportunity to move onto the charred meadow which minutes before had been covered with red flames. They managed to move through the tangle of smoking brush and found their trail again, and they headed toward the storage yard where I had already dropped my fire pot and had begun circling toward the Gold Gulch water supply pipes. The men could do nothing but watch.

At first I stood motionless, the pulaski in my hand as if I'd come to my senses and was reconsidering my risky decision. I raised the tool and pointed, counting the pipes. I waited for the wind to turn and when it did I walked from pipe to pipe, smacking each head with the hoe-end of the pulaski. One by one the white plastic heads broke open and burst or turned on their threads, some spraying fine plumes, other exploding into powerful, shapeless gushers. When each head was fully open I twisted and aimed them toward the yard. Most of the sprays were strong enough to reach where the fuel tanks stood near the leading edge of the fire, which was now growing and threatening to breech my temporary backfire. A pond of flooding muddy water pooled and began to form a barrier at the base of the hill.

The crew made its way downhill and grouped behind the broken pipes, while Teddy Ruxton and another man headed in a dead run toward the parked Mini Cat. I watched Ruxton jump into the cab. His legs hung free from the door while he twisted around beneath the dashboard. The vehicle shook, stalled, then kicked to life. Teddy climbed in and took his seat and backed the vehicle to the first fuel tank, jumped out and coupled the hitch, and with a lurch slowly tugged it away.

The slanted wall of fire was moving closer, burning a few dozen meters above the remaining fuel tanks.

Teddy returned and hooked up the remaining tanks. When they were chained and pulled safely away Ruxton jumped out of the Cat and yanked his silver shelter over his head like a hoodie and ran back toward the crew, zig-zagging through a field of glowing stump holes.

The Gold Gulch storage yard was quickly swallowed in a rolling cloud of smoke, and then the trees above it crowned.

The explosion of orange flames towered over my head.

CHAPTER 69

Upwind of the spraying water pipes, you could see the fuel tanks parked safely away from the fire. The crew continued to dig along the ridge. I waited until the flames lifted and walked toward them.

A branch snagged my leg. I fell. The shouting voices were in my head again.

"Hey, chickenshit..."

Tree sap exploded and I moved away from the noise that sounded like a bursting mortar. The trees appeared as men standing motionless, their branchy arms drooping silhouettes against the red flames. From above came the rumble of another chopper. I reached for my pistol. But there was no pistol and there were no men and the trees were just trees. I heard the PFC's raspy voice whispering in my ear, and then the avalanche of strangers' voices, the boy cussing at me in the background.

"Hey...Stan, you fuckin' CHICKENSHIT!"

I swung my arm through the hanging smoke.

And then the two shapes appeared.

At first they seemed like phantom trees trying once again to impersonate my long-dead squad. The ghostly strangers walked hip to hip, their synced footsteps measured like lovers on a stroll. I recognized Carmen's walk, her hair lifting with each short stride.

When the smoke cleared, Carmen was limping ahead of the man, who was pushing her down the trail with his hand on her back. The man was not wearing his yellow gear. A fireman would not be carrying a weapon. He would not be wearing military fatigues or a bandoleer of rifle shells across his chest.

The mumbling voices grew louder, as if people were now trying to get my attention.

"Hey, chickenshit!" the boy said, his mutilated body floating down from the dark trees.

"Got any smart ideas now, sarge?"

Carmen stumbled and fell and the man took her by the hair. He turned to face me, feet spread like a cowboy in a showdown. I recognized the AK-47.

A slurry bomber passed overhead and released its load, the misting chemical painting the trail red.

I called her name.

The first shot nicked my shin. The blood ran into the top of my boot and pooled inside my sock. Another round thumped into the dirt at my feet.

Now the voices in my head were silent, except for that of the PFC.

"Sarge? Got any bright fuckin' ideas?"

Birds lifted from the plantation house, their squawks swallowed by small arms fire that sounded like popcorn crackling in a foil pan. The heat turned humid and heavy, and when I straightened myself the man on the trail was firing the weapon again. I felt a painless hot pressure against my leg and my foot went numb.

I tore the cuff of my pants and knotted the ends around my leg. I pinched the long raw wound with two fingers until the bleeding slowed. I pushed aside a piece of sharp bone that poked from the bulging muscle tissue and took dirt and ash and smeared that into the cut. There was no pain, but a dull heat throbbed in my hip and when I turned to see where Carmen was I nearly blacked out.

Around me, I imagined my men being ambushed, their shapes falling. I heard their cries. I heard a metallic thunk and the mortars fell randomly, dropping between the blackened trees. The evac chopper was trying to land for a dust off. The shouting voices returned, the crowd of rude people in my head awakened. My men moaned as they lay in the grass. Their beckoning arms lifted and fell. A rockfall of boulders ahead turned into the broken shape of the old plantation house. A row of burned lodgepole pines were transformed into a company of NVA regulars, their shapes visible in the smoke as they walked toward me in ranks.

Get a grip, Stan. Don't let your brain run away.

The man ahead stood and aimed the AK-47.

I circled, the pulaski in my hand. Something wobbled loose inside my leg. Stumbling, I touched my pack, but the radio was gone. A grove of scrub oak burst into flames and I shouldered through it, slapping the burning coals off my shirt, swiping back and forth with the pulaski as I charged the place where I'd last seen the man with the rifle. My bad leg snagged on a branch and I felt the wound open.

I shouted Carmen's name. The voices in my head were now a chorus, urging me on. The PFC chanting: "Chickenshit, chickenshit...chickenshit."

A shaft of fire corkscrewed up from the dirt.

The PFC in my nightmare was floating above me, his shirt empty below his waist like the ends of a torn flag. He was legless, a head and a chest and only those waving arms gesturing, a wise-ass smile on his face.

"Chickenshit," he shouted. "You're nothing but a chickenshit!"

I stepped over a glowing hole and felt the heat rise into my crotch.

The man on the trail fired three short bursts. I circled closer, thankful that my leg was now completely numb.

CHAPTER 70

Another shape appeared. The horse lifted one hoof, then another as it stepped carefully through the trees.

A tree burst into flames behind Dora McCoy's old blue roan, which now backstepped and bowed into a turn as if it had deciphered what its rider did not yet know. The old woman leaned and held her hat over the roan's eyes and sawed the animal around and heeled it up the trail. In mid-gallop, the reins tucked beneath her good arm, the horse hopped over a fallen tree as she pulled her rifle from the saddle scabbard and lay it crosswise over the bouncing saddle. Dora's hair came undone and blew freely.

The man was dressed in camo hunting clothes and he appeared again like an apparition. He wore black boots and bloused trousers like he was ready for improbable combat. He fired, the muffled shot sounding like a foot kicking a cardboard box. Two louder, piercing rifle shots came after that, the sound amplified as the smoke drifted away.

Dora raised her dead husband's Springfield Garand .30-06 rifle and took aim, her arm wobbling under the weapon's weight.

The man in the boots moved away behind another wall of smoke.

Dora dallied her reins on the saddle as the horse sidestepped, turning on one hind leg in a cantering spin through the burned jackpines. She ducked beneath a cowl of rocks, the horse growing more excited, its hooves slipping in the mud, the roan's legs splayed apart dangerously. A few feet away the ground slanted into a deep gully and the horse began to slide sideways toward it.

Dora hooked her leg and dismounted, the rifle on her arm. She tried to tie the horse with her bandaged arm, but the animal jerked its head and broke free, giving one last whinny as it galloped away, the fully-packed saddle bags bouncing against its rump.

More smoke came erased everything. The man fired, though you couldn't tell from which direction. Then he was standing ten meters away and he fired again and I rushed ahead and knocked him off his feet. How I didn't catch a bullet, I don't know. The rifle dropped from his hand, but he immediately pulled out a knife and jumped at me, swiping the blade back and forth, his bent arms spread apart, one shoulder held low as if a weight had settled there. His green military camo shirt had come undone, the collar yanked free through the looped ammunition belt on his chest. He was filthy. He swung the knife, the blade snagging my shirt. I stumbled away as he brought up the knife once more. With his free hand he lifted the rifle and managed to squeeze off a wobbly shot. He missed.

I limped toward him and took the Kalashnikov by the barrel. He fired again. The kick pulled my hands forward. He stumbled and fell to his knees and now brought up his pistol with a crazy theatrical flourish, as if he'd practiced such a move many times before, his mouth lifting into a wild grin as he pushed the weapon against my jaw.

I swung my closed fist sideways into the man's ribs and the weapon discharged and burned a powder stripe up my shoulder. Something moved and popped inside my leg again and when I looked down at my stomach I saw that the yellow shirt fabric was black with blood.

From the forest came a sound like someone changing stations on a TV, a racket of disconnected clicks and poorly modulated conversation and the familiar chatter of a walkie talkie.

I thought it was only the sound of fire crackling, and then someone shouted the familiar call sign from the BLM base camp. Gus Curry's voice grew louder, his approaching shape assembling itself in the smoke. I saw a head, then shoulders, then striding feet as Curry walked toward me holding the walkie to his face. His shape appeared in silhouette as if shoved on mechanical rollers onto a theater stage.

Curry abruptly stopped. He looked around, fiddling with the walkie dial and talking the entire time as he carried on his conversation with the incident commander's office.

The pyro kept his pistol pointed at me as he rose to his feet. Unseen, Gus Curry stepped forward with one long stride. His gear rigging, loose pack flaps and rope fasteners, the ends of bungee cords swaying, all of it blown sideways by the hot wind. A goggled Nordic warrior in boots dropped from the fiery heavens.

Curry lifted the pulaski high with both hands.

The pyro kept the pistol pointed at me. Curry stepped closer and swung the heavy tool with a careful, lazy motion, like they taught you to do to conserve energy when you were hacking a fire line. He buried the blade in the pyro's shoulder.

The man spun away and looked back at Curry as he tried to keep his balance, the metal point of the tool protruding next to his ear like an upturned raptor claw. His tongue pushed from his mouth, as if he'd eaten unpleasant food. He tried to speak but could not. He stared at me. He seemed to be pondering a question. He swallowed. I stepped away and picked up the dropped AK-47.

When Curry yanked away the pulaski the man spun around. He wore a confounded expression, as if contemplating the revelation of a great and sudden truth.

He fell and lay on his back and brought his arm up slowly. He placed his hand on the wound and troweled it back and forth, blood flowing between his fingers, as if careful smoothing might make the ugly hole disappear. He never made a sound. He looked at both of us. He groaned and wobbled to his feet and stumbled away into the dark.

Curry looked at me and then in the direction where the man had run.

"Mind telling me what the hell just happened?" Curry said.

"I appreciate your timing," I said. "I'll explain later."

"Whoever that was, he won't last long out there."

"Spooky sonofabitch is far from dead, believe me."

"You sure you don't want to tell me who he was?" Curry said.

"Does this look like a good place to talk?"

Curry held up the bloody pulaski. We both studied the tool as if it might explain things.

"I saw your shirt," I said.

"I thought you were one of my own boys, too," Curry said. "Couldn't tell with the smoke. Am I right, was he getting set to shoot you? I saw him aim and I just reacted."

I winced and leaned onto the rifle. "I'm happy you did."

"And you still don't want to explain?" Curry said.

"There's no time."

Curry told me about Carmen's cell phone call. Nobody knew who it was, he said, and when they tried to call again the signal went dead. Twice more the phone rang. Carmen's voice was pleading. She was in trouble. On the next try she just had enough time to explain where she was.

"She had her GPS, thank God," Curry said. "She kept apologizing and said you'd warned her about coming up here. It took a while to get our bearings in this smoke, but I found what was left of her tent. She must be up the trail not far from here. I guess I got lost, too. My crew is up the trail. They're still digging line. Fire is moving this way fast, so we better get going."

I studied the swaying treetops. I picked up the pulaski.

"You sure you don't want to explain who that dipshit was? I just saw him aiming the gun at you and I swung."

"Not now," I said.

"Your boys told me about the stunt you pulled back by the storage yard," Curry said. "Very foolish, if you ask me. But it worked. They joined up with my crew and everybody's trying to head down the logging road together. We're hoping a chopper can get a clear shot and rope us up. They're boxed in."

I walked away.

Curry hollered, "Hey, how'd you know about those water heads down by the yard?"

I kept walking.

Curry followed me to where Carmen lay twisted against a tree, her legs pulled up, one arm around her knees. Her other hand was bowed, the broken wrist swiveled backwards and her fingers splayed apart as if she were trying on a pair of gloves. A terrible gash raced up her forearm and ended where her shirt was bloody at her shoulder. She was shivering. One of her eyes was swollen shut.

"Jesus," Curry said. When he tried to give her water I took the canteen away.

"I'll do that."

"Christ, where did you find her?"

She took baby gulps and moaned when I tried to lift her.

"Look, I still don't know what this is all about, but you should follow me to the trailhead while we have time," Curry said. He looked at Carmen. "All I know is we found her and we found you and there's still a chance we can get back. That guy, whoever the hell he was, is on his own. Let the cops take care of it."

I ignored him and attended to Carmen.

"Don't do that," I said when she tried to move her arm. I fussed with the sling I'd made from the sleeve of my shirt and lifted her to my shoulder.

Curry said I was bleeding and pointed at the tourniquet on my leg.

"I know," I said.

"This is nuts," Curry said. "You need more than that sorry-ass rag. You're bleeding bad. My God. Look at your stomach."

I pointed at the burning forest.

"I'll call artillery. They've got one-oh-fives a kilometer from here. So you make sure you stay within the perimeter. Take three men and scout one click up the trail. Then pop me a flare. Understand?"

A streak of blowing embers, like red tracer rounds, flew past.

Carmen was breathing heavily as I tried to gently balance her weight on my shoulder.

Curry gave me a look. The voices started chattering in my head again.

"She'll be okay," Curry said, holding up his hand as if he thought I might take a swing at him. "Now, I don't understand what the hell you just said, but if you can get back to the truck we'll get a stretcher and make her comfortable. But I'm afraid all we can do is treat her and then wait until this fire figures out where it's going. We might have to spend the night if the chopper can't land."

There was no sky, only sheets of rolling gray smoke twisting through the tree tops.

"She won't last that long."

"We have medical gear at the truck."

I said. "Your damn truck. Where is that?"

"Five miles up the trail."

"And it's three miles to the valley. If your gear isn't what she needs, she'll die. There won't be time to head back. She's not going to die."

"Stan, the fire is right in your path. You'll be walking through it. Shit, you can hardly stand on that leg. Stay with me and the crew. I'm asking you."

But I was hearing the voices and they were telling me what to do.

"I won't let her die here," I said.

Again Curry insisted: "That's pure crazy. We can bandage her. We've got splints and...."

Curry shouted angrily: "Your leg won't hold. Your knees are fucked. You'll die yourself and that won't save her."

But I had already limped away.

I carried the rifle for a while and tried to keep Carmen steady on my shoulder. After a while I used the AK-47, barrel down, as a cane and walked ahead into the timber. Curry tried to catch up, but he probably knew he would get lost too if he followed. He turned, kicked angrily at the dirt, and headed back toward his crew.

I walked.

After a time I found a spring that probably fed the creek that might point the way to the river. I cleaned my leg and tightened the tourniquet, though I knew the wound was too deep. The shot had nicked a vein. I was dizzy when I put weight on the leg.

I strained dirty water through the cleanest part of my shirt and let it drip into Carmen's mouth. She licked gratefully. I filled Curry's canteen with ashy water and splashed my face. I touched the back of my head and with my thumb pushed back a plug of scalp that was hanging over my ear. I pressed it until I thought the bleeding might have stopped.

For the first hour I tried not to bump Carmen around too much. It was getting darker, the hot wind gusting at my back. When I eased her to the ground she was wheezing in quick breaths, her eyes opening and closing like she was trying to see.

She kept mumbling. Once, she pushed me away and cursed. She spoke crazy mixed up Spanish and English and then pidgin nonsense that ended when I gave her more water. She slept. I lifted her again and walked on.

I made my way toward a patch of light gray sky and thought I might try walking to the lowest leading edge of the fire. I knew the Last Chance Ranch was somewhere uphill from the trail, though I had no idea of where I was. I knew I would not be able to walk directly to the valley. If I could only manage a glimpse of the resort, I might get my bearings.

The voices came back. *Chickenshit,* the PFC said.

I limped through a grove of burned cedars, their low sharp branches like nails on my bleeding leg. I carried Carmen on my shoulder. There were stump holes glowing in the forest like buried lanterns. The cookfires of my enemies, I thought. Fiery holes into the underworld. I sensed the burning earth hinted of what would certainly come from the ruins of its ashes.

Carmen was breathing badly and I found a patch of unburned soil and put her down. I tightened the sling. I could not stop the bleeding on her arm. I brushed back her hair. I tried to wash her face with the filthy canteen water. I fussed with the buttons on her shirt. I smoothed her hair again. She seemed broken and so small.

I walked ahead to scout what I thought might be a trail. I saw bare hills rising and thought it could possibly be the ranch pasture next to the lake, where the old woman had talked on and on about the gopher colony. The valley and the town lay below. I knew the fire was following me. I didn't have much time. Then the wind died and everything lay silent, the falling soot settling into the bare branches of the burned trees.

I heard the pyro long before I saw him.

He took one quick step out from the smoke, as if playing a hide-and-seek game. He pressed the pistol against the side of my head.

"Any more bright ideas, fuckhead?" he said.

His shoulder was broken beneath his shirt. He held his head at an angle, as if the weight of his skull pained him.

I jerked away and the dropped weapon discharged as I swung the AK-47 like a baseball bat and clipped him squarely in the back. He fell and tried to reach for the fallen pistol.

Dora McCoy must have been standing off in the distance for a while, watching us fight.

When he saw the old woman the pyro turned and squeezed off two missed shots.

The old woman fired back and her rifle shot was high.

The man dropped to one knee and aimed with the .45. He missed and Dora looked away as if watching where the bullet had gone.

The next shot struck the old woman squarely and she folded up and fell.

Dora rolled over one of the burning stump holes, which flared briefly. She tried to stand but the man pivoted on his knee and fired again. The old woman lay still.

I swung the rifle again and knocked the .45 from the man's hand.

He jumped toward me and made a grab for the AK-47 and as he did he stepped directly into the stump hole like he was aiming for it.

He stood still, as if contemplating his terrible mistake. He looked at his feet, then at me. He continued to stare at his feet as he slowly sank into the ashes. The yellow flames, awakened by the rush of oxygen, licked up his legs. He sank further. He got shorter. The pyro, for whom fire had once been so magically appealing, looked very surprised. He glanced at me as if he might get advice for his sudden problem. The fiery rope turned red as it coiled around the man's hips.

When he sank as far as he could go he let out a howl. He tipped his head and screamed as the hole took advantage of the fresh fuel and suddenly exploded. The flames torched past his hips, funneling into a spinning yellow ball around the man's bearded face. He waved his arms as the fire swallowed him. And then he stiffened like he'd been turned into a puppet, his head jerking within the contained windstorm, his arms animated as if they were being pulled by strings. It was like looking at the flickering image of a vintage kinescope, the man's stiff cartoon arms waving left and right as if trying to master an exotic and difficult dance step.

"Asshole," I said.

I looked around to see where the old woman had fallen.

The bandoleer of bullets on the man's chest began exploding. His blistered face and his clothes dissolved away, skin sloughing off in fatty strips. He opened his mouth wider than a mouth should open, and I looked back and saw the man's white teeth inside a red halo as if he had turned suddenly into a grimacing church saint, his face melting into the flames.

The hole then gulped him up, sparks lifting, the heated wind tossing out burned flakes of what remained of the man's clothes.

"Hey, chickenshit!" I shouted over the noise of the exploding rounds. "Got any more bright fucking ideas?"

When it was finished I went over to Dora and carefully lifted her head.

I told her: "I'm so Goddamn sorry. I don't think I can't help you very much, Dora."

The old woman forced a nod. She swallowed. "Follow the spring next to the trail. It looks like it's heading into the fire, but it ain't. It gets you below the ranch. You'll be okay then."

She gasped: "Is that sorry bastard dead?"

"Worse."

"Good," Dora McCoy said. "I heard the shots. My horse bolted, the old nag. I tried my best, Stan."

"You did right."

"I hope the poor thing finds its way."

"Don't worry about the horse."

"I got lost on my own damn ranch," she said. "I got that nag loaded with blasting caps and powder charges. She's a walking bomb with all that gear in the saddle bags. Goddamn horse is going to explode. I was headed up to blow away a ditch when the fire caught me."

"Don't talk so much, Dora."

"I guess I won't," she said, now barely whispering. "You'll remember what I said about the spring?"

Dora tried to catch her breath. Her eyes opened wide then closed, then opened again. She took the front of my shirt and pulled me close.

"I believe I killed that poor girl that night," she said. "I was so damn mad, I fired the rifle at the resort. Dear lord, it was an awful accident. I didn't think anybody was down by the river."

"You didn't shoot anyone," I said.

"Didn't mean to."

"You didn't, believe me."

From behind us, the stump hole that had swallowed the man hissed out sparks as if it were belching after a good meal.

"Fire cleans everything," Dora McCoy whispered, her face so close I knew she'd been chewing her tobacco.

"If you follow the spring to the creek you're safe."

"I think I saw it," I said.

"Go back and follow the water home."

"You didn't hurt anybody," I said again, but the old woman was already staring off at something, studying it. She took a long deep breath and held it. She tried to breath again but she could not. And she closed her eyes.

All that night I walked. Carmen seemed weightless on my shoulder. There was no pain. I struggled up the rising trail and when there was no discernible path I pushed through more burning shrubs and trees that were still shedding heat.

I found Dora McCoy's hidden stream ebbing from a gravel fan hidden behind the rocks. I followed the vague rivulet as it disappeared and surfaced again and to reveal the slope of a hill I thought might lead to the valley. It was much too far to walk. I would never make it.

I lay Carmen down and sat against a tree and slept effortlessly for the first time in weeks, a total deep slumber, dreamless and complete. In the cold dark I woke and didn't know where I was.

In a strangely dim and gray dawn I had never seen before, I walked. The stream bowed and vanished, and each time it surfaced its course changed once more, unaffected by any slope or tilt of the land. I shuffled downhill and kept the fire behind me.

I rested beside where the stream widened into a broad and shallow pool, where I wet my hand and pressed it to Carmen's cheek. The wound on her arm was caked and black, a knob of broken bone showing beneath the bruised skin.

I put my leg into the icy water and peeled away the torn trouser. The burned fabric stuck to my skin and flaked away. Blood lifted in wisps from my submerged shin. The dirt I had packed into the wound dissolved away. The bullet had formed an oblong furrow, the white bone in which it had lodged canted through the skin like broken pottery.

The wounds from the tree branches looked like awl holes. I lifted my shirt. Another of the shots had cut a crease across my stomach, next to where the knife had gone in. When I breathed, gray gut bulged out like the tip of a balloon. I pushed it back with my finger, surprised it was painless, and it popped back into my palm larger than before. I pushed it back again and held it and pulled out my belt and strapped it tight across the wound. It hurt to breath. In the clear water the blood twisted away from the leg.

We would burn and vanish together, our nameless remains turned to useless duff on the forest floor. We would become powdered soil for trees that would rise from our ashes.

I bound the leg and stood. I lifted Carmen, and I walked.

The voices came again as a chorus of screams and mindless howls.

My brain unspooled and as I walked I became a young man, that hopeless pilgrim in Paris. I walked along a dark alley in Saigon where window whores in pajama robes leaned and called down to me. Hey, yankee boy. Disheveled in loose bedclothes, their black hair gathered up, the women fanned the humid heat with their hands and called out as they lifted their morning tea cups and toyed with their hair curlers. Hey, yankee boy. Hey yankee boy you come here. Hey GI boy you got money for me?

I clearly saw the photograph I had taken from the hand of the man I had killed after the ambush.

I tried to imagine what justice had brought me to this place, but I could not. I always thought I might one day figure things out, but it was impossible. All my plans and guesses had been wrong.

I walked.

The PFC from my dream was the first to appear.

For a time the legless half-body followed alongside like an orphaned puppet. It floated as if a butchered version of my own slanted shadow had taken shape beside the smoking trail. The silent corpse touched my shoulder. And then he became transformed and appeared again, as young and alive as I remembered him on the day we walked patrol. He once more had legs and the shrapnel wounds had healed nicely and his shirt was neatly buttoned, his M-16 rifle strapped smartly on his shoulder.

I closed my eyes and tried to trick my head. Tried to keep it busy, Dr. Nguyen always told me. I checked my shirt pocket but the bottle of pills were gone.

Now, make sure the weapon is unloaded and cleared. Press the magazine release and watch the magazine fall clear of the magazine well. Hold the charging handle at the rear of the receiver and draw it back. Look at the chamber to make sure it's clear so you don't fucking kill somebody. You can smell the oil when you get this close. Now find the retaining pin...

Your glucocorticoid receptors are going crazy...

Pappas appeared, talking trash with the PFC. The dead radioman walked jauntily, and then he too was changed into something alive. His uniform brand new. His field hat cocked. Both young soldiers shook hands. The PFC touched Carmen's shoulder as if dispensing holy benediction, his hand glowing.

I tried to think of something else.

The rifle.

Now take off the and bolt-carrier, I thought. Push the forward retaining pin free. Another damn pin. Lay the top and lower receivers and the charging handle aside. Take out the bolt cotter pin which secures the square-headed asshole tucked in the dent below the gas tube vent. Take out the bolt and firing pin.

The nurse at the VA said: *And your hippocampus is too small...*

I looked for my pills again but the shirt pocket had been torn away.

"She's sure a looker, sarge," the PFC said. "Oh, you got a real looker."

"It's not like that at all," I said. "She's just a friend."

I leaned on the AK-47. I could no longer sense where my legs began or ended.

"Oh, I got no ideas about that stuff at all," the PFC said. "Isn't that right, Pappas?"

"Nada," Pappas said. "Dead or not, you have not had a decent idea in years. Not one shred. You are an idea vacuum."

"Not too lively yourself, dickwad."

"Am so," Pappas said. "Look."

And then Pappas performed a perfect cartwheel, bounding down the trail like a rubberized cartoon acrobat. The radioman returned and both soldiers laughed and slapped one another's shoulder.

"You clowns finished? I'm in serious shit here."

They nodded and walked on, stifling laughter. The PFC had that same shit-eating grin that he had in the photo album I'd found in my closet. His expression was reckless, the startled fake-smile of a hopeless delinquent.

"Good, then I want to know if you're with me," I said. "Are you real?"

Both boys gave the thumbs-up sign and shouldered their weapons and marched on.

"All the way," the PFC said, marching. "Hup-two, hup-two."

"Follow you any fuckingwhere, sarge," Pappas said.

The three of us walked. For a mile more we followed the riddle of Dora McCoy's disappearing stream until it bubbled up within a cairn of rocks in a meadow where columns of smoke rose above the crowning trees. It looked like the birth of a new and virgin world erupting from its forgotten creases. The wind roared and lifted heavy broken branches, each tree for as far as I could see torching into the red sky. I leaned into the heat and the two boys walked alongside and together we pushed further until we came to a quiet clearing where nothing had yet burned. Green trees swayed in a breeze, a pond shimmering in the sun. There was fresh grass and I saw the wetlands beyond and for the first time I heard birds singing.

A house stood beside the pond, its newly painted balustrade winding around the structure like a vine. All from an age long past. Rice shoots grew in the shallow paddy where we'd been ambushed and where everyone but me had died so long ago. The sunwashed soldier boys, now fresh and clean in their uniforms, stood alongside the trail and watched. The voices in my head were now laughing as if they had realized a common joke.

Pappas said, "Almost there, sarge. "We are with you."

We walked unafraid into the burning trees.

I thought it might be morning. Pappas spoke. He carried on about our patrols and nights spent in our sandbag fortress in the jungle. He spoke of drunken card games. He spoke of beautiful girls half-dressed in their ao dais and how sweet they smelled with their PX perfumes and the murky colored lights of the tiny shacks shining on the slippery alley stones of Saigon.

"You shouldn't have done the re-enlisting thing," the PFC said. "What did it prove? We didn't ask for any revenge."

"But I thought..." .

"No, you didn't think at all, you dummy. Killing those poor people like that. It wasn't their fault and even if it was, none of it was your business. It wasn't anybody's business. That whole hot fucking place was nobody's business."

"I thought it would help."

"You helped yourself but not us," the PFC said. "Isn't that right, Pappy?"

"That's the truth." Pappas said.

"I rest my fucking case," the PFC said. "Carry on."

We walked. Then Dr. Nguyen himself appeared and bowed slightly, as if introducing himself for the first time at a heavenly dinner party. The three of us stared at the old man.

"If it isn't the sonofabitch commie bullshitter himself," Pappas said.

The old man was dressed in his black baggy shirt and pants. Those narrow bony shoulders and the feathery white chin beard. The red embroidered star on his cap. He bowed again and as we passed by he too touched my shoulder and suddenly there was no more pain. The leg was fine. I was sleepy. I wanted the fire to come and take me away forever. I wanted to turn off the lights.

"Hey, look at that," the PFC said.

Nguyen was pointing down the trail. I saw an enormous stand of burning lodgepoles that had just crowned, their torched foliage falling away as the blaze encircled the meadow. The old man motioned for us to keep walking.

"I don't know if that's a good idea," I said to the boys.

The PFC smiled. "Go on, sarge."

"You sure?" I said. I looked around for Nguyen.

The PFC spoke: "Just forget about that old Viet Cong fart, sarge. Look ahead. Do you see it?"

"Shit," Pappas said. "I see it." The two boys high-fived each other.

"Shit," the PFC said. "Will you look at that."

"Now I see it," I said.

"You going, sarge?" the PFC said.

"Yeah," Pappas said, making as if he were holding a bullfighter's cape in his hand. He tipped himself sideways and pointed the way. "You can go. We have to stay here. It sucks, but we have to stay here."

"You do?" I said.

"You know we do," the PFC said, and he and Pappas stepped back and the two boys lifted their hands and they waved. They stood at attention. Saluted. They were both sobbing.

"Shit, look at me," the PFC said. "Blubbering like a candy ass."

Behind me, beyond the miles of burning forest, lay the headwaters of my entire life. The grand sweep and riddle of everything. The world with its red mouth open, my life now contained within this one fleeting moment.

"You boys come on with me," I said, frightened now to go alone.

"You know it's okay," the PFC said.

"I'm scared shitless," I said.

The PFC laughed. "Don't be a chickenshit."

Then the two soldiers were gone. The smoking world lay quiet.

I lifted Carmen to my shoulder and looked back once more and I walked. I passed what remained of Dora McCoy's saddlebag, once filled with the ditch-clearing explosives that had scattered along the trail. The pack lay shredded and smoking, an open track of cinders spreading ahead of me along the trail, the small accidental backfire keeping the flames at bay for a while.

I walked to the horse and extended my hand and spoke. The roan lifted its wet muzzle from the creek and looked at me and then calmly resumed drinking.

CHAPTER 71

The Everly Brothers were singing *Cathy's Clown* on the hospital intercom and the hallway was filled with TV and newspaper reporters. I had asked Tom Cherry to put a cop outside Carmen's door. It would take time before she got better.

After a week of interviews, not too many reporters were interested in what I had to say anymore, which was fine with me. They'd talked to my boys at the fire line, who'd told them what happened. Teddy Ruxton, the firefighter who had hot wired the backhoe and then hauled off the Gold Gulch fuel tanks, was flown to New York to appear on a national morning TV talk show. I put his picture on the front page of the *Beacon-News*.

Tuesday brought the Underwood typewriter and my mail to the hospital and I wrote my column for the newspaper with the machine sitting on a plastic food tray. I spilled coffee on the keyboard, but nothing can damage that thing. My arm was still bandaged, one leg trussed into an orthopedic sling that made it impossible to type anything.

I was sifting through the mail and setting aside the past due bills when I came across the letter, which had been part of a neglected pile of mail that had been sitting on my desk since I got back from my stupid trip to Vietnam.

By the look of the international cancellation stamps and the scrawled *Return to Sender* notations, you could tell one particular envelope had been a long time getting here.

I propped the thing up on the Underwood keyboard and studied the Vietnamese postage stamps before I took a plastic knife from my breakfast tray and opened the envelope.

The photo, a less worn version of the one I'd left on the shelf at the house on So Loi Street in Saigon, fell into my lap. The image of the woman and the baby was without creases or scratches and you could tell it had been cared for.

Dearest Sir:

I discovered your name in the internet telephone directory of your city, a fact revealed after extensive research which made me fear always that the result of my curiosity might be embarrassing or cause your anger at my knowledge of the source of the funds that my mother has received from you for so many years.

I have no idea why you would provide us with these monies, though they were, I hastily point out, put to honorable use. For many years my dear mother explained to me that they were a type of reparation payment she assumed came from your government, since the checks had on them an American eagle and such official looking writing she feared to question their origin or to mentioned them to all but our closest family for fear that this would cause jealousy among our neighbors. Or a recrimination from our own government, which was common in those days.

And so each month we would wait at the old French post office, where my mother would receive the funds from a postal worker who was a family friend. There was fear in years past, you see, that there would be trouble if such a thing were delivered directly to our home.

This money, I further wish to say, and proudly so, was used by my mother for my own education. She never traveled far from her home after the American war and indeed spent none of the funds, save for the worst of emergencies, which included helping family members escape from their bad circumstances. I was her only child, my father having died during the war. I was told he was killed under honorable circumstances. His body was never returned to us and sadly I never knew him. I attended university in Hanoi and then in Australia and for a short time in your state of Louisiana, in which I further studied medicine.

My mother — she was named Anya, recently died and it was then that I received, by way of our courts, your most recent check in the amount of $3,475.78. The times are more liberal now and the source of this money was not questioned as much as I had expected.

I enclose a copy of a photo, the only such image of my mother and myself that survived the war years, taken while I was an infant. It dates from the winter before my father was sent to An Loc Province, during the celebration of Tet, the New Year, and was taken at the historic wharf in Ho Chi Minh City. You should know my father's name was Ngu Tol Pak and he was a lieutenant and he died in the A Shau Valley, Thua Thien Province. I assumed such a history might interest you. If not, I apologize for my presumptions. I am sentimental, a trait which my mother reminded me of many times. She said my father was so inclined as well and always feared that his sensitivity would be a handicap for a soldier. She herself seemed always to lack any sentimentality, as did many who survived the terrible wartime years and its many horrors.

I suppose, my dear sir, you might be wondering now if I am about to appear unannounced at your door in America, perhaps with my hand extended with a request for more funds. I assure you I have no such impolite plans!

My intent is simply to give you my belated thanks on behalf of my family. Perhaps it is best I not know why you sent us money for so many years. Perhaps you are wealthy, and as the publisher of an American newspaper (yes, I discovered this), you may have simply found my family as a convenient and fortunate recipient of your sincere charity. I have been told of such things and it is in my nature to hope this might indeed be true. Nevertheless, I can only express my emotions to you now in the only manner I know.

I have struggled about whether or not I should make this gesture or simply allow the envelopes to be returned. To remain anonymous, I decided, would be rude and ungrateful. I understand nothing of you: whether you have a wife and children. How you happened to know of my mother in particular, or how you chose her among so many others. Was it pure luck our paths crossed? Perhaps I was one of many to whom you sent funds. It is not important.

Lastly, please respect my wish that you discontinue sending your kind monies. It is a small matter of pride, I confess, as well as a practical concern. You see, I am to be married within the year and will have, by the time this letter reaches you, moved north to my husband's city, where I expect to continue my service as a physician. My husband has no knowledge of these funds or their source, and I choose not to inform him of such, since it might complicate matters.

Please indulge me, sir, and forgive me for what might be perceived as ungratefulness — is this a proper English word? — on my part. I wish you the very best in your life and ask that you honor my simple request. I hope you are not offended. I expected you might be, and with great agony I still question whether I should have written this letter at all.

I will imagine you as my mother did for so many years — as our kind and mysterious American patron.

If my father were alive, perhaps he would thank you as well. We shall never know.

On behalf of my honorable parents and in their memory, I am grateful.

Sincerely,

N. Trinh Ho, M.D.

Socialist Republic of Vietnam

**

During my trip down the burning mountain, I had tied Carmen behind me with the saddle bag straps. How I got on Dora's horse I don't know, but I remember it started to walk toward town right away like it knew where it was going. Like I'd pushed a button. I can still hear the hooves clomping on the trail and how they sounded when we got out of the burning woods and onto the hard asphalt of the old county highway. That's when I must have blacked out.

The first good snow arrived in late November, which seemed disappointing, although I don't know why. Not everybody likes it when the temperature is 75-degrees on Thanksgiving, but that's what happened until one night the cold finally came in a sudden blast from the north like somebody had opened a refrigerator door. Some people believed the late appearance of winter to be a portent of climate-addled polar bears moving to Miami, though wearing shorts in autumn is always okay by me.

With the snow the new ski area opened one of its intermediate runs on a Saturday, just to get the PR machine rolling. Dora McCoy's son announced to me in a phone call that he'd sold the family ranch to the Gold Gulch Company.

They refurbished the old lady's ranch house and barn and moved it to the historical society frontier museum over near the county fairgrounds, where tourists now pay five dollars to see it. It was a big event in town and everybody stood along the state highway when they rolled the log cabin and four clapboard outbuildings buildings down the road on top of flat bed trucks decorated with corporate Gold Gulch promotional banners.

It took half the day, the vehicles creeping with their load like parade floats. But nobody cared. People brought their barbecue grills and the Lions Club sold bowls of chili and the mayor served hot dogs from a converted Airstream travel trailer. They'd left the white plaited curtains on the window of Dora's homestead cabin and the flimsy muslin fabric fluttered as the building rolled past where I sat on the front steps of the *Beacon-News* office. I had to turn away.

What remained of the colony of prairie dogs on Bellyache Mountain was bulldozed and turned into a maintenance supply depot and parking lot for the Gold Gulch Resort and Golf Club.

I figured I would never see or think of Chaz again.

I decided to write one more newspaper column about the magical gophers of Bellyache Mountain and figured that would be the end of it.

After she was released from the hospital, Carmen phoned me one day to report that she'd received the test results from the kitchen rope I'd given her months before. The Colorado Criminal Investigation Bureau, backlogged with work on the arson forensics for the wildfire, concluded in a brief two-paragraph report that the rope had been severed by "non-mechanical or inanimate means" but there wasn't enough organic matter remaining on the fibers "to determine an animal or human cause."

I'm sure I didn't chew that rope.

I stopped seeing Dr. Nguyen. The VA hospital helped me get off the blue pills, as well as shake a few other habits that weren't doing me any good. I stayed cranky for a long time and people generally avoided me, though I got more work done at the newspaper than I had in years.

I saw the tracks in the snow one day when I visited my wife at the cemetery.

It was cold and sunny and windless. I'd brought along a folding chair and was sitting beside her stone, looking at the blue winter sky and watching snow blow in thin sheets off Bellyache Mountain. The far off cackling of ravens was the only sound. I reached and pulled the brown dried stalks of dead summer flowers from the foot of the gravestone and smoothed out the snow with my gloved hand.

And then I saw the tracks, five-toed and wiggling away from behind the grave toward the frozen river. I followed them across the ice and through the bare willow trees to where the pines started at the base of a hill. I walked on until the running paw marks stopped abruptly in the deep snow. Here there were rough patches, a dozen or so disturbances where it looked like many more prints had converged. Like a crowd had jointly decided to run around and play an impromptu game of winter tag. I believe I saw the imprint of a little snow angel.

I wasn't in the mood to let my head play games with me anymore, and I wasn't taking any pills, so I hurried back to the truck and just sat there, staring out across the meadow and up where Dora McCoy's old ranch property came to the very edge of the valley at an overlook where I imagined Chaz and I could have once stood.

I thought I saw something flying around up there in a wide and lazy circle, a scouting hawk maybe. But then a whole flock of objects appeared and seemed to purposely hover in the air before they began to move slowly toward me.

Birds don't do that.

EPILOGUE

The Bull River Falls Beacon-News
Headline: Insane Gophers Destroy Town Internet Service
By Stan Przewalski, Editor

I should have been suspicious when the Gopher King asked if I knew the diameter of RG-60 and RG-11 underground telephonic cable, and whether our television service provider in Bull River Falls had problems with something called "electrical impedance" when running either cable at less than 50 ohms.

I absolutely didn't understand any of that.

Then this pot-bellied, 12-inch tall rodent who likes to wear Bob Marley tee shirts asked if I knew if cell phone tower engineers, as a general rule, use WiMax or CDMA transmission technology.

"And spectrum frequency," Chaz said, taking off his iPod earbuds. "That's very important. How much MgH do they need?"

I told Chaz I didn't know what an ohm was. "It might be a Buddhist thing," I said. "And I think MgH is what they put in Chinese food."

When asked what music he was listening to, Chaz said it was *A Whiter Shade of Pale* by *Procol Harum*.

I knew something big was up. The only time the Gopher King listens to this 1967 song is on the eve of a commando operation. The Bach-like organ riff, those meaningless yet profoundly unfathomable lyrics...it inspires him. Myself, I like to read undecipherable poetry because it makes me believe that I understand the meaning of life.

I should have been suspicious of Chaz's scientific concern for our local communications grid. Twenty-four hours later, the 875 residents of Bull River Falls were suddenly without phone or internet service, the community's main antenna tower array vaporized by M-129 grenades fired from a squadron of Black Hawk helicopters the size of kitchen ovens.

Three miles of phone company optic cable within the town limits of our little village was transformed into an underground junkyard of chewed plastic and conduit.

I was grateful for the digital lull, but it brought out the worst in people. Others, faced with Tweetless oblivion and unable to access their social media accounts, suffered spontaneous nervous breakdowns. Many businesses had to close down.

One teenage boy, unable to locate a capacitive phone screen to scroll with his electrically charged fingertip and confused by those mysterious chrome analog buttons on the pay phone booth outside the Grill & Griddle Cafe, smacked the strange contraption with a baseball bat and ran screaming down Main Street.

Marjorie Pfaff, age 88, and the owner of a bright pink rotary dial Princess telephone her husband gave her during the 1962 Cuban Missile Crisis, was, by some lucky technological quirk, among the only two civilians in town with access to the outside world.

She made a fortune selling $5-per-minute phone calls to her desperate neighbors.

Pale people stumbled around town like zombies, holding their useless phones high in the air as they searched for a cell signal. Many climbed trees.

Over at the high school, mute teenagers who long ago had forgotten how to decipher facial expressions or the subtle intonations of the human voice, silently swiped each other's actual foreheads with their fingertips as they tried to communicate.

It was pointless, of course. With their now purposeless thumbs, they could neither text or Tweet or post. They could only mumble and sputter and clutch their deceased phones to their pounding hearts.

Many anxious local citizens sat alone with their laptops on park benches and street curbs, shivering in their underwear, rocking back and forth like mentally ill zoo elephants, squinting at the sky, wishing for one of those WiFi ohms to magically drop from the sterile heavens like fairy dust.

A network TV news crew that had arrived in town to cover the wildfire clean-up encircled their satellite truck (and the satellite phone which it contained) with military-grade concertina wire in order to keep the feverish phone freaks at bay.

While the smart phones, laptops and 70-inch COSTCO TVs of Bull River Falls were turned into paperweights and sleekly designed boat anchors, Chaz the

Gopher King and his amused rodent army took advantage of the confusion by flattening every tire on every phone and cable service company repair truck parked in six locations within a 55-mile radius of town.

When the tires were repaired they poured pickle brine and Nutella into every gas tank of said vehicles.

Mrs. Pfaff, her monthly Social Security check seriously supplemented, silently thanked her late husband Angus for giving her the Princess phone so she would be safe from Fidel Castro.

Marjorie made $6,473.29 in her first week of helping Bull River Falls citizens stay in touch with the outside world.

Days later, when cell service had returned to our town, and when I came home to my lavishly furnished double-wide trailer, there was a group of teenagers skate boarding on the sidewalk.

Three of them sat on my front steps, taking selfies and texting wildly on their phones and looking deliriously happy and content.

They ignored me as I unlocked the front door.

"Excuse me," I said. "Are you gentlemen re-purposing social media data into an acceptable and non-alienating infomorphic aesthetic?"

They looked at me and nodded.

I smiled. "I thought so. Carry on."

What could possibly go wrong?

-END-

ABOUT THE AUTHOR

Gojan Nikolich is a former Chicago newspaper reporter, editor and public relations agency executive. He graduated with B.A. and M.A. degrees in English Literature from DePaul University, served as a decorated Army sergeant with both the 2nd and 4th Infantry divisions and worked as a journalist in Korea and Japan. He lives with his family in Colorado, where he and his wife once owned a weekly newspaper.

NOTE FROM THE AUTHOR

Word-of-mouth is crucial for any author to succeed. If you enjoyed *The Gopher King*, please leave a review online—anywhere you are able. Even if it's just a sentence or two. It would make all the difference and would be very much appreciated.

Thanks!
Gojan

Thank you so much for reading one of our **Humor** novels.

If you enjoyed our book, please check out our recommendation for your next great read!

Parrot Talk by David B. Seaburn

"...a story of abandonment, addiction, finding oneself—all mixed in with tear-jerking chapters next to laugh-out-loud chapters."

– Tiff & Rich